Nicola Gill lives in London with her husband and two sons. At the age of five, when all of the other little girls wanted to be ballet dancers, she decided she wanted to be an author. Her ballet teacher was very relieved.

By the same author:

The Neighbours

We Are Family

NICOLA GILL

avon.

Published by AVON
A division of HarperCollins*Publishers* Ltd
1 London Bridge Street
London SE1 9GF

www.harpercollins.co.uk

A Paperback Original 2020

A catalogue copy of this book is available from the British Library.

ISBN: 978-0-00-835542-5

This novel is entirely a work of fiction. The names, characters and
incidents portrayed in it are the work of the author's imagination.
Any resemblance to actual persons, living or dead, events or localities
is entirely coincidental.

Typeset in Bembo Std by Palimpsest Book Production Limited, Falkirk, Stirlingshire

Printed and bound in UK by CPI Group (UK) Ltd, Croydon CR0 4YY

MIX
Paper from
responsible sources
FSC
www.fsc.org **FSC® C007454**

This book is produced from independently certified FSC™ paper
to ensure responsible forest management.

For more information visit: www.harpercollins.co.uk/green

*For Dad. I know this would have made you nearly
as happy as Manchester United winning the Champions League.
Miss you always.*

Chapter One

'Whatever have you done to your hair?'

Those were Laura's mother's last words to her.

Neither of them had known it at the time, of course. Although Laura couldn't shake off the feeling that if her mother had known, she wouldn't have changed a thing.

'If you could get here as quickly as you can,' the nurse from the hospice had said.

But Laura couldn't get there very quickly at all. Jon was missing in action with his mobile going to voicemail which meant that, at the time Laura was supposed to be clutching her mother's tiny, emaciated hand and righting thirty-seven years of wrongs, she was actually trying to persuade Billy that he did like fish fingers and he wasn't going to watch *Trolls* unless he had at least three mouthfuls of peas.

Laura sat in the back of the cab pulling at a particularly rambunctious curl. You might have thought that a woman high on a cocktail of opioids and staring down the barrel of death wouldn't have noticed that you'd had a disastrous haircut but her mother wasn't one to miss something like that. 'I went to a new hairdresser,' Laura had explained, remembering how, when she'd first sat in the chair, Mario had stood behind her clutching random handfuls of her hair with a pained expression on his face before saying, 'What are we going to do with *this*?'

'Whatever you think best,' Laura had said, flushing with shame. Which were pretty much the only words she'd said until she told him the final result was 'wonderful' before tipping him extravagantly and then leaving the salon to cry even more extravagantly.

The traffic on the South Circular was horrendous and despite the fact that it was a freezing January night, Laura could feel the sweat start to bead under her armpits. Although she had no idea why she was stressed about the time now; it was like killing yourself to get to the theatre when you knew you'd already missed the start of the play.

She fished a bottle of Gaviscon out of her handbag and took a swig.

'They make tablets, you know,' her mother had said to her reprovingly.

'The liquid works quicker,' Laura had replied. And yet the next time she was in Boots, she'd found herself picking up a packet of the tablets.

The driver scowled in the rearview mirror. He was obviously disgusted by her swigging too. She shrank back in her seat. Perhaps she should tell him? He wouldn't be scowling then. But then she would be faced with unadulterated stranger sympathy, which would surely be even worse.

Jess had arrived at the hospice within twenty minutes of getting the call from the nurse, of course. No question that her perfect elder sister would be there on time.

Her mum's death shouldn't have come as a shock, really. They had known this was coming. But it was still weird to think that three hours ago Laura had been at work talking to her editor about whether she should pursue a story about a woman addicted to eating washing-up sponges (sometimes it occurred to Laura that her journalism wasn't quite of the 'Changing the World' variety she'd once imagined). 'I've got to shoot,' Dani had said. 'Let's pick this up again tomorrow.'

Little did either of them know that Laura wouldn't be in tomorrow. Because presumably you didn't go into work the day after your mother had died? Even if the two of you hadn't been that close.

Tears bubbled in Laura's throat. Now there would never be a chance to be like other mothers and daughters. She'd tried so hard since her mother's diagnosis. But somehow, however well-intentioned you were on the journey there, however much you thought you'd be the kind and solicitous daughter, my God, the reality was hard. Was Laura trying to choke her, holding the beaker like that? No, not that blanket! Why had she brought Billy with her? Did Laura really think she wanted a five-year-old behaving like a *wild animal*?

'It's the drugs making her cranky,' Aileen, the kind red-headed nurse had said, putting her hand on Laura's arm.

No, it isn't.

It had taken five missed calls and two voicemail messages before Jon had finally called her back this evening, and even then, she could barely hear him over the sounds of a noisy pub. 'What's up?'

'It's my mum,' Laura had said, choking on the words and staring at last night's Chinese takeaway containers, which were still littered across the kitchen worktops. Splatters of Kung Po sauce looked like blood.

Jon had been home less than twenty minutes later, smelling of beer and an outside world that didn't know or care that Laura was running out of time. He'd pulled her into a hug and told her to get a cab. Billy, naked apart from his Spider-Man socks, was jumping up and down on the sofa. 'Does he know anything?' Jon asked. Laura had shook her head and said there was nothing to know yet.

And right on cue, her sister rang. 'We've lost her.'

Lost her. Like they'd all been ambling around M&S and their mother had last been seen by the frozen foods.

3

The cab had arrived minutes later. Jon told Billy to wait inside while he put Mummy in the car. He did up her seatbelt for her, squeezed her hand. 'I'm sorry, babe.'

Laura was an orphan now. She felt faintly ridiculous at the thought. After all she didn't have a flat cap or a grubby face or go around begging for more. Plus, she was thirty-seven years old. Two dead parents still made you an orphan though.

The cab pulled up outside the hospice.

Laura took a deep breath. *Here I am, Mum. Better late than never.*

Chapter Two

Laura raced down the road, sweaty and agitated.

She could not believe she was late for the appointment at the funeral director's. And, if being late to the hospice hadn't been her fault, well, this time it was definitely on her. It was just . . . nothing had gone right this morning. Billy couldn't find Captain America, she couldn't find that pile of clean T shirts she'd folded the other day – she *really* had to tidy up this flat. Then Billy had knocked over a whole bottle of milk just as she was trying to get some breakfast into him. She must have shouted 'Billy!' much louder than she meant to because Jon appeared in the kitchen doorway, rubbing his eyes.

'I knocked over the milk,' Billy said. 'And Mummy shouted at me.' His lower lip wobbled.

Jon kissed the top of his head. 'Mummy didn't really shout. Now eat your Cheerios while I clear up the mess.'

'I don't like Cheerios!'

'They're a superhero's favourite cereal.'

Billy looked unconvinced but started eating.

Laura had stood at the kitchen sink with her back to them, taking a long, deep breath as tears welled in her eyes. Jon stepped over the river of milk and put his arms around her. 'Sssh, no use crying over spilt milk.'

Twenty minutes later, Laura was shivering and pulling her

coat tighter as she stepped out of the house. It was one of those grim January days where it seemed as if it would never be warm again, that maybe the sun had just forgotten how to shine. She glanced at her watch, noting that she just might still make it to the funeral director's in time if everything went like clockwork. And as luck would have it, she could see her bus arriving as she got near to the bus stop. She broke into a run.

A large man going in the opposite direction barrelled into her, elbowing her hard in the chest just as the bus pulled away.

Great! She bet Jess was there already. I'm quite early, she'd be saying. I'll just sit here and catch up on a few things. Like she had anything to catch up on. She'd have been up since 5.30 a.m. micro-scheduling the day ahead. She'd once told Laura that if she didn't make herself get up at 5.30, the day 'just ran away from her'. Laura, who routinely hit the snooze button until about seven and a half minutes before she had to get Billy to school and herself to work, had been utterly appalled. What normal person routinely gets up at that hour? In her book, it wasn't even morning.

Six minutes until the next bus. Six minutes! Laura took a discreet swig of Gaviscon and hoped she wouldn't spontaneously combust.

By the time she had got to the hospice the other day, Jess had already spoken to the funeral director. *We're meeting Robert the day after tomorrow at 11 a.m.* Robert? Christ, how had the two of them become bessies so quickly?

When Laura got off the bus she immediately started running again. Was it normal to be so out of breath so quickly? She needed to lose some weight and get fit. Jess ran four times a week (of course she did). Thinking about her sister made Laura speed up a little, despite the wheezing. It was nearly twenty past eleven and she knew Jess would have started the meeting without her. In fact, she may well have their mother buried by now. Time is money.

Finally, the funeral parlour loomed into view. Robert Butler & Sons, a family firm (was this supposed to make death feel cosy and unthreatening?). It was sandwiched between a shoe shop and a convenience store. And Laura couldn't help but notice that there was a huge poster for *The Walking Dead* just around the corner.

'Robert Butler,' a rotund man said, proffering a bear-like and slightly sweaty hand. 'I'm so sorry for your loss.'

Was he sorry? This was his business, for goodness' sake. If people didn't die, he didn't eat. No, she was being unfair. He could be sorry and not sorry in different ways. Besides, someone had to do this job. She must stop being so weird.

'Did you have far to come?' Robert said.

Laura shook her head. 'Dulwich.' Robert gave a purr of approval. It was strange that despite having rented a flat on Croxted Road for years, Laura had never really thought of herself as a Dulwich person. She didn't know the Farrow & Ball paint chart off by heart, had never thrown a dinner party and happily ate non-organic carrots. Jon's ambivalence about the area was even more pronounced and he'd been known to tell strangers he lived 'near Brixton', presumably because Dulwich just didn't seem like an edgy enough hood for a white public schoolboy who grew up in Surrey.

Robert ushered Laura into a small, murkily lit room where her immaculate-looking sister was already arranged elegantly on a sofa. Jess – who *hated* people being late – glanced at her watch in a move so classically passive-aggressive that Laura had to resist the urge to chuck the half-drunk green tea her sister was holding all over her.

And was that Mum's necklace Jess was wearing – the one Dad had bought her? Blimey, she hadn't wasted much time getting her hands on that.

Laura was determined she was not going to apologize for being late. Or chuck green tea at anyone. Or wrench necklaces from their throats. 'There's a poster for *The Walking Dead* right outside!'

Both Jess and Robert stared at her.

'Unfortunate media placement, don't you think?'

'Umm . . . May I get you some tea or coffee?' Robert said.

Well, so much for lightening the mood. 'Yes, coffee please.'

'How do you take it?' Robert asked.

'Milk and two sugars please.'

'I've given up sugar,' Jess said. 'And I feel like a different person.'

Try giving up being smug, Laura thought irritably.

A few minutes later Robert reappeared with a rather muddy-looking cup of coffee and picked up his notebook. 'Now, where were we?'

And suddenly, there were so many decisions to be made. Where did they want the service? What time? Cremation or burial? Pine or oak? Chrome handles or gold? Live music or a playlist?

Laura's head pounded. She didn't know the answers to any of this stuff. She had tried to talk to her mum about some of it but now, sitting here in this unfeasibly hot little room, she could hardly remember what she'd said. She knew her mother wanted to be cremated but that was about it.

Jess, of course, was absolutely the opposite and fired back answers as quickly as a quiz show contestant. St Anthony's. Next Friday. Cremation. Oak. Fastest fingers on the buzzers!

Laura almost wanted to disagree with some of the decisions, just on principle. Had Jess really ascertained that live music was critically important to their mother? Or was that just something Jess wanted? Laura wouldn't put it past her sister to be considering the reaction of her Instagram followers. Jess Tomlinson, Mistress of the Tasteful Funeral.

'We'll have more choice if we have a playlist,' Laura found herself blurting out.

Robert stopped scribbling in his notebook and scratched his head with a sweaty paw.

'We can have Mum's favourite songs,' Laura continued. Don't ask me what, don't ask me what!

'Like what?' Jess said, straight-backed, discouraging and palpably amazed to have her decisions questioned.

Laura's head spun. She could barely think of a single song, let alone one her mother had loved. What the bloody hell was she going to suggest? 'Another One Bites the Dust'? 'Err . . .'

'It's just she did say she wanted live music.'

Laura sighed. 'Fine.'

'But if you're not hap—'

'*Fine.*'

Robert scribbled in his notepad. Did they know how many readings they were having and who would be doing them?

Laura sat back in her seat and stared out of the window. Let Jess sort everything out. She'd probably have made a spreadsheet by now. She was, after all, The Big Sister, Chief of Chivvying, Queen of the Family WhatsApp.

Laura let her mind drift to the night before. Her friend Amy had popped over with a huge bunch of flowers. Amy and Laura worked together at *Natter* magazine and, coincidentally, lived a few roads apart.

'I'm so, so sorry,' Amy had said to Laura, her eyes filling with tears, at which point her toddler Josh, who was balanced on her hip, started to cry too and Laura had been the one dry-eyed person in the awkward three-person hug. Laura felt like a bit of a fraud. She had had a very complicated relationship with her mum. Yes, she was sad. But also a bit relieved. And she knew that made her a terrible person, but it also happened to be true.

She tuned back into the conversation in the funeral director's just as it turned to flowers. Jess – of course – had very strong feelings about them. There were to be *no* chrysanthemums and *no* lilies, she said, shuddering at the very thought. They also didn't want red and they didn't want pink.

Even Robert looked a bit bemused. There were two florists he normally recommended, both local. Now, he said, that just about concluded things for the day but there was just one other matter. Would the deceased want make-up?

Laura and Jess didn't miss a beat. Yes, the deceased absolutely would.

On that much, at least, the two of them could agree.

Chapter Three

Laura wasn't quite sure why she'd agreed to have lunch with her sister. Because it seemed too churlish to say no when Jess suggested it? Because by that point Laura's stomach was growling so loudly she assumed people in France might be able to hear it? Or because she couldn't face being alone with her contradictory and scary mass of emotions?

She and Jess sat across the table from each other in awkward silence.

'So, how's Jon?' Jess said.

Christ, her sister was annoying. The seemingly innocent question with its oh-so-glaring subtext: *How's that loser you live with? Is he managing to be supportive? He didn't exactly get off to the best start by being in the pub when Mum was dying.*

Laura was still smarting about a conversation she'd had with her mother a couple of months earlier. 'Jess and I both think you're an idiot when it comes to that man.' The words had stung, of course, but what was even worse was the idea of the two of them talking about her behind her back – a witches' coven.

'Jon's fine. He's been fantastic.'

'Good,' Jess said.

Laura stared wistfully at a group of women a few tables away who were laughing loudly at something.

'It's weird to think Mum and Dad are both gone, isn't it?' Jess said.

'Very.' Laura's mind flashed back to *that* day when she was twelve. Coming home from school, seeing Uncle James at the door and thinking it was nice that he'd come over – and on a weekday, too – but then looking at his face and knowing something was terribly wrong. Her mother on the couch. There had been an accident, their father was dead. The world tunnelling around Laura. Not being able to understand. An accident was when their little cousin peed his pants or someone broke a vase.

'I guess we should decide what we want to eat,' Jess said.

Laura picked up her menu. 'I'm supposed to be on a diet,' she said, more to herself than anyone else.

'The grilled salmon is nice here,' Jess said.

The waitress came over to take their order. She was wearing a lipstick that was almost black and said 'perfect' like a verbal tic. One Diet Coke and one sparkling water? Perfect. Some mixed olives? Perfect.

'I'll have the fishcakes, please,' Laura said. Jess' face dropped for a fraction of a second. She had ordered the grilled salmon and was no doubt perplexed by Laura not doing the same despite being *told* to. Laura could practically see a flashing neon thought bubble above her sister's head: *Thought you were supposed to be on a diet.* 'And chips,' Laura added.

'Perfect,' the waitress said.

Laura glanced across at the table of laughing women. Maybe they wouldn't think it was too weird if she joined them?

'So I guess we'll have the wake at my house?' Jess said.

Laura felt her shoulders go rigid. Jess' huge house in Clapham looked like houses do in magazine spreads, right down to the large bowl of lemons on the island unit that always made Laura wonder where all the normal fruit was kept and why there wasn't a lone banana that was too ripe for anyone to eat but not yet overripe enough to be consigned to the compost bin. To say that Laura and Jess' homes were different would have been to employ a powerful use of understatement. 'We could have the wake in a pub or a restaurant?' Neutral territory.

'If you prefer. It's just an additional expense though.'

'Who's having the fishcakes?' the waitress asked, arriving with their food.

'Me,' Laura said.

'Perfect.'

'It probably wouldn't cost much,' Laura said.

'Probably not,' Jess said, taking a mouthful of salmon. 'But, if we have it at my house, it won't cost us anything.'

'Fine.'

'Look, if you really feel strongly about it . . .'

Jess always did this: bullied you into doing what she wanted and then suddenly came over all reasonable when it was too late. 'I said it's fine.'

The waitress reappeared. Was everything okay over here? They told her it was. Perfect. She beamed.

'We need to sort through Mum's things,' Jess said.

Laura nodded. It was typical of her sister to be in a rush about something like this but, for once it suited her too. Since Jon had scaled back his shifts at the restaurant, they'd got into a bit of debt. 'Yeah, we'll want to get the flat sold as soon as possible.'

Jess speared a piece of broccoli. 'Well, actually I've been thinking about that. The market isn't great at the moment so I think it would make more sense to rent it out for a while.'

What? No! Not everyone had the big, fat financial cushion behind them that her sister did. 'I don't want to do that.'

Jess' brow scrunched. 'It makes *much* more sense financially.' Her tone was so imperious and emphatic Laura wanted to slap her. 'I don't think we're going to get loads for the flat at the best of times,' Jess continued. 'I know Mum had already borrowed a bit against the value: an equity release scheme.'

'How much?'

Jess chewed thoughtfully. 'No idea. The power of attorney still hadn't been registered by the time Mum died so I never did get to help her sort out her finances.'

Laura was ashamed to find she took a small amount of pleasure from this. For all her brisk efficiency, Jess hadn't managed to hurry along the Office of the Public Guardian.

Laura had been hurt when her mum announced that she wanted Jess to be her power of attorney. 'Oh, for goodness' sake, Laura!' Evie had said, noticing her starting to cry. 'Don't be so over-emotional. It's just Jess is so much more financially savvy than you. Or me, for that matter.'

Laura knew she shouldn't let it upset her. Or, indeed, surprise her. Her mother was always going to pick Jess. She was better with money (notwithstanding her husband's big, fat salary). Also, Laura had spent her life on the bench. She took a mouthful of her fishcakes. They were cold in the middle and she knew she ought to send them back but she couldn't face the conversation with the waitress: *not* perfect. 'I want to sell the flat straight away.'

Jess put her head to one side. 'Let's decide once we've gone through all the financial stuff.'

She *always* had to be in charge. As though because she'd been born two years and a month earlier than Laura, it was her God-given right. 'Fine,' Laura said wearily.

A message flashed up on Jess' phone screen and reflexively Laura glanced across.

'Stop reading my messages,' Jess snapped, snatching the phone off the table.

'I'm not reading your stupid messages!' Laura said. She was taken aback actually. Jess wasn't normally like this. Bossy and controlling, yes, but short-fused not so much. What did she

14

have to hide, anyway? Probably a series of lovey-dovey messages from Ben (they were the type for nauseating pet names).

There was an uncomfortable silence, which Jess broke. 'Going back to the subject of the wake, I don't think we need to go crazy in terms of food. But we do need to offer something because some people will have come a long way.'

Laura put a chip in her mouth. Her diet could start tomorrow. Well, not tomorrow; when the funeral was out of the way. No one should have to be thinking about calories and coffins at the same time.

'Maybe just some sandwiches and a couple of cakes. I wondered if you'd do the cakes. You know how much better you are at baking than me.'

Laura nodded, wishing she didn't feel like the child who'd been given the fairy cakes to make so she wouldn't cause any trouble.

Chapter Four

Then

Laura could still smell her mother in the air. Years later, she would recognize the scent as Shalimar and the merest waft of it could cause the breath to catch in her throat. But, at five years old, it was just the smell of her mother.

She clutched her monkey tighter and squeezed her eyes shut to hold in the tears. They had started when Daddy had been reading her a bedtime story, but then he did all the funny voices of the characters in the book and gave Laura such a big cuddle she forgot to be sad. But when Mum had leaned over to kiss her goodnight, Laura felt the tears coming again and she was furious with herself for being such a stupid baby. Jess wasn't crying. She was lying on her tummy on the other bed with her feet in the air, flicking through her book.

Mum was cross too. 'Oh, Laura,' she said, using *that* voice. 'Don't spoil Mummy's evening!'

A siren wailed in the background.

Laura had somehow swallowed down the tears, told her mum she looked beautiful and been rewarded with a smile. Her mum held open her arms and Laura snuggled in, enjoying the sensation of the slippery satin dress under her fingertips. Her mum was wearing the new necklace that Dad had bought for her birthday and Laura felt relieved that she really liked it (the shoes he had got her last year not having been a success). The necklace was heart-shaped and apparently you could put teeny-weeny photos inside it. Laura was a bit worried there was only room for two photos though. If Mum put Dad on one side, would she have to share the other side with Jess? Or would it just be a picture of Jess?

Laura hugged too hard and too long. 'You're ruining my hair,' her mother had said, pulling away from Laura and surveying her gravely. Laura pulled at her hot, itchy nightie. 'Come on now, be a big brave girl like your sister.'

Laura nodded. Last time Mummy and Daddy had gone out, Mummy had been cross with her for making 'such a fuss'. So tonight, she had tried extra hard to be good. She hadn't looked sulky when Jess showed off yet another sticker from school, she'd eaten all her yucky supper, she'd gone up to the bath the second her mother told her to even though *Blue Peter* wasn't finished.

But now she'd spoiled it.

Chapter Five

- *Order of Service*
- *Phone funeral director*
- *Book Calvin the Clown*
- *Tidy flat*

Laura looked at her notepad and sighed. This was the first time in her life she'd made a to-do list. She was turning into her sister. Only she wasn't, because none of the things on Laura's list were getting 'to done'. (The clown wasn't for the funeral – that really would be weird – he was for Billy's birthday party, which was three days afterwards.)

Today was Blue Monday, which meant it was officially the most depressing day of the whole year. A day when the 'stay in PJs all day and eat brie for breakfast' joy felt as if it was a lifetime ago and not just weeks earlier. And surely there must be extra misery points for the bereaved? Laura wasn't sure she was extra miserable though; in fact, she would have been hard-pressed to say exactly how she did feel since it seemed to change dramatically from one second to the next. Although if she'd had to settle on one constant, guilt would have been a strong contender. She felt guilty for not getting to her mother's bedside in time, guilty for mindlessly surfing the internet when she was supposed to be making funeral arrangements and guilty that she still seemed to be able to both sleep and eat (*really* eat – perhaps it could be deemed 'comfort eating'? Except, it was how she ate all the time . . .).

The trouble was there was no manual for how to behave. At one time, when someone died, you drew the curtains, donned a wardrobe of black (which was pretty much Laura's normal wardrobe) and went into a period of almost hiding. Now the bereaved were expected to carry on with their day-to-day lives, but this presented so many challenges. Laura felt weird chatting to a mum acquaintance in the school play-ground and not mentioning her mother's death – it was like it was of no consequence – but she felt uncomfortable at the thought of bringing it up too – *I don't deserve your sympathy.* And what about laughter? Jon had been telling her a funny story the other day about a couple of women who were in front of him in the queue in one of the delis in Dulwich Village. One of the women was lamenting her child's 'laziness' because he had said he was too tired to do his homework after being at school all day, then swimming fifty lengths at Tiger Sharks and going to his piano lesson. 'How old would you guess the poor kid was?' Jon said. Laura said she didn't know. 'Younger than Billy. Four – tops!' And they'd both laughed and laughed, but then Laura heard herself and thought: *your mother died three days ago.*

Laura pulled up the draft of the Order of Service she'd started work on earlier. She'd do some more – even if she couldn't control her inappropriate laughter or moods, she could at least make sure she did the things on her list. Jess would have done everything on hers by now and would be busily making new lists.

One person who didn't seem particularly blue this Blue Monday was Jon, who had gone out drinking again with his mate Jimmy the Guitar. 'Just a quick one after leaving the office.' Jon and Jimmy loved that gag – neither of them had ever worked in an office in their lives. 'Are you sure you don't mind?' Jon had said to her tonight. 'Of course not,' she'd replied, because she didn't really feel right playing the grief card and because they both prided themselves on her being a cool chick who didn't nag about stuff like that. She would kind of like him back now though. And preferably not completely hammered.

Laura's eyes landed on the book she had found herself buying on impulse the other day: *Good Grief.* She had no idea what had made her get it. She'd only read the 'Stages of Grief' chapter so far and it had got on her nerves by implying that bereavement was simply a tick list. Also her grief wasn't like other people's grief, so the book would almost certainly be utterly useless to her. Terrible jaunty title too, now she came to think of it.

She didn't suppose *Good Grief* would make any mention of sometimes feeling almost happy about your mother's death. That wouldn't be in there because other people – normal people – wouldn't suddenly be hit by this strange feeling of lightness; a feeling that they'd been released from a stronghold and could finally be who they wanted to be. That was the feeling that made Laura feel like a *very* bad person.

Laura felt like she ought to be doing better with grief – not to mention life in general – since she was the agony aunt for *Natter* magazine and, as such, the purveyor of knowledge and wisdom. When the trained counsellor who used to write the column had become the victim of budget cuts, Laura's editor had 'asked' her to take on the role. Laura was horrified. 'I'm not qualified,' she'd stuttered.

'School of life,' her editor had shot back without looking up from the pages she was checking.

Despite Laura's reservations about her ability to dispense sage advice, being an agony aunt had quickly become her favourite part of her job. She spent way longer than she should reading the emails and letters that came in and carefully crafting her replies. She'd even insisted on doing this week's column despite being on compassionate leave. (The rest of her work they could split between the team. She wasn't going to fight anyone for the chance to interview the woman who was in love with her father-in-law.)

'Mummy,' Billy said, appearing in the doorway. 'I can't sleep.'

Every now and again Billy had a certain expression, a sort of hesitant half-smile that reminded Laura very much of her dad. Once, when Billy was about three, Laura had made the mistake of pointing this out to her mother and been amazed by her mother not only disagreeing but disagreeing in a way that suggested the comparison irked her. 'Oh, I don't see that *at all*.' Laura hadn't said anything but she was hurt by the realization that Evie wouldn't cherish the likeness.

Laura got up from the table and picked Billy up, burying her face in his warm, yeasty-smelling neck. 'How about Mummy lies down with you? Just for five minutes though.'

Billy nodded approvingly.

She tucked him under his dinosaur duvet and lay down next to him.

'Grandma is dead!' Billy trilled.

Laura held her breath. Objectively she knew that when you're not even five yet, you have no frame of reference for death. That Billy might well be expecting her mother to pop back up like one of his cartoon characters, but his sing-songy tone was still a little disconcerting.

'Dead, dead, dead,' Billy continued.

'Yes, sweetheart. And we are *very sad* about it. But Grandma is in heaven.' Probably.

'With Roger?' Billy asked.

'Roger?'

'Dorothy's goldfish,' Billy said, as if he couldn't believe Laura didn't know that.

'Yes, with Roger.'

'Can you read me a story?'

'Sweetheart, it's really late already. You ought to be asleep.'

'Pleeeeeeeeeease. Just a little story.'

Laura sighed. 'Just one.'

Chapter Six

The to-do list was going to have to be put off a bit longer because Laura had to pull together this week's *Dear Laura* column (suddenly her insistence that she wouldn't hand it over to a colleague despite being on compassionate leave didn't seem quite so smart after all).

She leaned back in her chair. As she'd walked Billy to school this morning, he'd been hopping up and down and talking animatedly about what Grandma and Roger the goldfish might be doing together in heaven. He thought they might be eating ice cream, only goldfish weren't allowed ice cream. But maybe they were when they were dead? Laura knew he was only little but still wondered if his unbridled enthusiasm about his grandma's death was a little odd. Not for the first time it crossed her mind that she ought to be writing in to *Dear Laura* instead of being the person dishing out the 'wisdom'. She'd certainly have lots to ask: Dear Laura, Is my four-year-old normal? Dear Laura, Am I sad enough about my mother's death? Dear Laura, My bossy sister drives me bananas.

She turned to her real letters and emails. When she'd first taken on the role, Laura had expected that hardly anyone would write to her. In the internet age, the idea of an agony aunt felt anachronistic. And, even if you were going to pour your heart out to one, well, why make it Laura, whose bio at the top of the page made her sound extremely hokey? *Laura got her agony aunt qualifications at the School of Life* (if that was how her editor justified it to her, that was how she'd justify it to the world). *She's here to answer all your personal, sexual and emotional problems. Sorry, but she can't reply personally.* Laura had been amazed by just how many letters and emails she did get, and it was always really tough to whittle them down to the three a week she could fit on the page.

Dear Laura, one email read, *I am married with a beautiful two-month-old baby boy. My problem is my mother-in-law who is always telling me what to do. Why don't I give my son formula top-ups, then he wouldn't be so hungry all the time. Why do I rock him to sleep . . .*

Laura decided that this problem was definitely one for this week's page. Interfering mothers-in-law were a perennial hot topic. She popped the email into the appropriate folder on her computer, her mind already fizzing with things she would put in her reply.

She glanced down at her food-stained pyjama bottoms. It was a good thing she didn't often work from home because honestly, if she did, she wasn't sure she'd ever wear proper clothes again. Even bothering with a bra felt like Making An Effort. In the school playground this morning, she'd been pretty sure that people had noticed she was still in pyjamas underneath her coat and she knew they'd have been quietly horrified. Dulwich mums did *not* wear their nightwear to school drop off. Even the women in gym gear wore full make-up.

She scrolled through a few more emails. A woman who wanted to know whether to stay in a loveless marriage, someone who wasn't sure what to do when her friend made racist remarks, three people in love with a colleague (not the same colleague, although how intriguing that would have been).

There was a heartbreaking letter from a nineteen-year-old who said she felt desperately lonely and desperately ashamed of admitting that. Laura decided that not only would she make sure an answer was included in this week's column, but also that she'd call a trained therapist to ask for their take on this. She often did this if she felt a problem was serious and beyond her (let's face it, limited) skill set, and even though her editor Dani had challenged her on why she was wasting time, she allowed Laura to do it as long as she didn't pay the therapists. Which meant Laura was left feeling bad about not paying the therapists but less bad than she would have done if she hadn't got their steer. She just hoped the namechecks the therapists got helped them sell their books or promote their private practices.

Right, so she had the woman with the interfering mother-in-law and the woman who was lonely. What would balance those nicely on the page? One of the people who'd fallen for a colleague, perhaps? Yes, that would work.

She set about drafting her answers.

Maybe you could get your husband to have a gentle word with his mum . . .

I am so sorry to hear you feel lonely . . .

An office romance creates all kinds of issues . . .

When she finished, Laura read back her replies. She still wanted a therapist's input into 'lonely' but, that aside, she was pretty pleased with what she'd written. Other people's problems are always so much easier than your own.

Chapter Seven

'Grandma's dead!' Billy said, opening the door to Laura's sister and her two daughters, much like one would say, 'Happy Christmas!'

To Jess' credit she managed to mask any shock, unlike Lola and Hannah, who were staring at Billy with the cold condescension that eight- and ten-year-old girls are so good at.

'We were just passing,' Jess said to Laura. 'So I thought as we had so much to discuss, we may as well pop in.'

So much to discuss? That was code for: I'm checking up on you.

Laura had had to fight Jess for a share of the to-do list and now she was going to have to prove she was actually doing it (tricky when, for the most part, she wasn't). 'Come in,' she said, trying not to mind that the flat was even messier than usual. The coat stand had collapsed again, which meant there were coats and hats and umbrellas all over the hall floor, along with the ever-growing mass of footwear. And she was pretty sure last night's pizza boxes were still out on the kitchen counters.

'Shall we play hide and seek?' Billy said to Lola and Hannah.

The girls exchanged a look of amazement at being asked to take part in such a childish pursuit but then said yes, that would be lovely.

26

In the kitchen, Laura cleared a pile of washing off the chair so Jess could sit down. 'I've been working today,' Laura said, hating herself for feeling the need to apologize. 'I had to do my *Dear Laura* column.'

Jess nodded. As usual, she looked immaculate in a hot-pink satin slip skirt with a red slogan T shirt, freshly blow-dried hair and the type of no-make-up make-up that takes forever. Laura supposed she had to make an effort since it was part of her job – and it still seemed weird to call it that – as a fashion blogger. She remembered her mum telling her Jess was going to give up her job as a management consultant to make StyleMaven a full-time pursuit. Laura's first thought had been: Why writing? Writing is *my* thing. It reminded her of a summer when she was nine years old and obsessed with making papier mâché animals. Then Jess had breezed in and made a perfect pig and Laura never picked up the PVA glue again. Over the years, her antipathy towards Jess' new career had grown. Everyone knew that the rise in popularity of digital influencers had been a huge factor in the demise of women's magazines, so it was difficult for Laura not to feel like a vegan whose sibling had suddenly decided to open a slaughterhouse.

'So which of the world's problems was *Dear Laura* solving today?' Jess asked.

Laura's shoulders tensed. Was Jess being snarky, or was she just making conversation? So much distance had built up between them over the years that Laura often found her sister hard to read. She decided to take the question at face value. 'Oh, interfering mothers-in-law, loneliness, office romances – the usual sort of stuff. Luckily, I didn't have any adulterers to deal with today. I often do, and I find it a bit hard to dish out sympathy.'

'Maybe you shouldn't be an agony aunt if you can't be sympathetic,' Jess snapped.

Laura spun around. 'Excuse me?'

Jess shrugged. 'Sorry,' she said, sounding anything but. 'I was just trying to make the point that nothing in life is black and white. That, of course, affairs are terrible – everyone knows that – but it doesn't mean that everyone who has one is beyond the pale.'

Laura's brow scrunched. This was the second time Jess had snapped at her in a matter of days (maybe this was the new her? Bossy, controlling *and* short tempered.)

Also, it seemed extremely odd for her sister, Little Miss Perfect, to be putting up a defence for adulterers. Jess was no doubt just mouthing words she thought sounded 'woke' and Instagram-worthy. It made Laura sick. She'd had two boyfriends who were cheats and she could still remember how it had destroyed her. In a matter of seconds, all trust had evaporated, years of good memories had been rendered fake and she'd had to live with the stark realization that she wasn't enough. One of the many reasons she loved Jon was because, despite his laid-back take on life, he'd told her very early on that he believed unequivocally in monogamy (her mother and her sister might be quick to brand her an 'idiot' when it came to Jon, but they just didn't know him like she did).

Laura looked at her sister, oblivious and smug, and was so tempted to tell her that she had *no* idea what it felt like to be cheated on, that not everyone had a perfect marriage like hers, and not to gob-off about things she knew nothing about. But today she simply couldn't face the fight. 'Would you like a cup of tea?'

'That would be nice,' Jess said. 'Have you got any green?'

Laura made a face.

'Builders' will be fine.' Like she was doing Laura some kind of massive favour.

Laura filled the kettle, Jess' words still reverberating around her head: *Maybe you shouldn't be an agony aunt.* Laura threw a

28

couple of teabags into some mugs and poked at them angrily with a teaspoon before sloshing in some milk.

She was just wondering if maybe she should have said something after all when she turned back round to discover that her sister had started to cry.

'Hey,' Laura said, setting the tea down. She knew she probably ought to give Jess a hug, but as they didn't really have a 'huggy' type of relationship, settled for roughly patting her on the arm as if she was trying to keep to some sort of unheard beat.

'I'm being silly,' Jess said, pulling a tissue out of her handbag. 'We knew this was coming. Also, she was kind of a nightmare.'

Laura made a face. 'Yes, but she was *our* nightmare. And you only get one mum.'

This set Jess off on a fresh wave of crying. 'Sorry,' she said eventually.

Laura squeezed Jess' arm, feeling guilty about her own lack of tears. Earlier she had helped Billy with his homework, which was to fill in his family tree, and she had got a teeny bit tearful as she dug out photos of her mum and dad and was struck by the realization that she was no longer anyone's child – but only a *teeny* bit tearful.

What was wrong with her?

Jess was crying and she was normally relentlessly positive – the type of person who posted endless 'inspirational' quotes on Instagram. (Laura's idea of an inspirational quote was the one she had as her screensaver at work: *Don't talk to me until I've had coffee. And you've developed a personality.*)

'I wish I didn't remember Mum like she was at the end,' Jess said. 'I hate thinking about how she was in the last couple of months. I want to remember her as strong and vital. I want to think of her racing around at a thousand miles an hour and making me laugh. I even want to think of her being bloody infuriating.'

Laura nodded; she knew what Jess was talking about.

Recently it had been the husk of her mother lying in that bed, albeit one who could occasionally still make a joke that was just the right side of dark ('This cancer will be the death of me'). But Laura also knew she hadn't experienced their mother's demise as intimately as Jess had. One day she'd arrived at the hospice and asked Jess why her clothes were damp. Jess explained she'd had to get in the shower with Evie to help her. Laura had felt a rush of sympathy and guilt. No one should have to wash their mother's bottom. But there was also a touch of envy. Maybe the hard bits were a price worth paying for a lifetime of being the chosen one.

Once, one of her mother's doctors had expressed surprise upon meeting Laura: 'I didn't know your mum had two daughters.'

I've tried to get more involved, Laura wanted to shout (had she? How hard?) but my sister always muscles in telling me I'm doing it all wrong. Mum doesn't like that dressing gown because it's itchy, we've already tried audiobooks, don't try to move her like *that*.

It was exhausting. Especially when Laura knew it was Jess that Mum had wanted anyway.

Eventually, Jess stopped crying and blew her nose.

'Okay?' Laura said. Jess nodded. 'Right, let's cheer you up with some to-do lists.'

Billy burst into the kitchen. The girls followed in his wake, looking solemn. 'Grandma's dead!' Billy sing-songed. 'She's in heaven with Roger!'

Was this normal four-year-old behaviour? Or was Laura's sweet, mussy-haired baby actually a psychopath?

Billy scratched his head. 'We need biscuits!'

'Do you mind?' Laura said to Jess, wondering if Jess' whole family had given up sugar with her. If she tried to make Billy give up sugar it would immediately eliminate eight foods from the list of ten he deemed acceptable.

Jess said it was fine and Laura handed out the biscuits.

When the kids disappeared Laura made a face. 'Do you think that "Grandma's dead" thing is normal?'

Jess laughed. 'Yes! He's a baby. He doesn't understand what death means.'

Laura suddenly loved her sister so fiercely it was as if all those years of petty fights were wiped out in an instant. Hell, at this moment she could almost forgive her stealing her platform sandals, even if it was the day of the sixth-form prom and even if Laura had planned her whole outfit around them.

'How are you getting on with the Order of Service?'

Laura was pleased to be asked this. Despite the fact she'd ended up reading Billy not one, not two but three extra stories last night when he couldn't sleep, she'd still worked on the Order of Service late into the night. It was the one thing on her list she'd actually made good progress with. 'Pretty good. Do you want to have a look?' She opened the file and pushed her laptop in Jess' direction.

There was the world's longest pause before Jess said, 'I think it's a great start.'

Laura dug her nails into her palms. 'But?'

'Is that typeface very "Mum"? And don't you think we should include a couple of photos?'

Laura pulled the laptop out of Jess' hands and snapped it shut. She was a writer, for goodness sake. She could knock up an Order of Service without being micromanaged. And even if Jess had strong opinions on EVERYTHING from the flowers to the food, Laura would be The Boss of the Order of Service.

'I think it looks great,' Jess said.

Laura snorted. Never trust a woman who steals your new shoes.

Chapter Eight

Laura had one tab open on party-bag gifts and one on flowers for the coffin.

Flowers for the coffin weren't actually on her list because Jess had appointed herself High Priestess of Tasteful Flowers, but she was getting on Laura's nerves so much, Laura was tempted to order something super-tacky just to spite her. She'd sent Laura fourteen messages since she'd visited yesterday – fourteen! *Just checking you've done this, just checking you've done that.* Like Laura couldn't be trusted (she couldn't, in point of fact, but Jess didn't know that).

Laura scrutinized a heart-shaped pink and white chrysanthemum spray – that would infuriate Jess. Then she stumbled across an arrangement spelling 'Mum' in carnations – better still!

'What are you up to?' Jon said, appearing behind her.

'Trying to find flowers Jess will really hate for Mum's coffin.'

'Mature!'

They both laughed.

'Oh, my goodness, look at these!' She pointed to a floral arrangement that had been crafted into a giant mobile phone. 'Can you imagine Jess' face?' Jon grinned. One of the lovely things about having been with Jon for over a decade was that they hardly ever had to explain anything to each other. Let's face it, if you told someone you'd recently started dating you were thinking of ordering hideous funeral flowers just to annoy your sibling, they'd think you were more than a little unhinged.

Laura glanced at the time. 'Shouldn't you have left for work by now?'

Jon shrugged. 'Yeah, I'm running a little late. I was really getting somewhere with the writing this morning so I didn't want to stop.'

Laura knew full well he'd only got up half an hour ago but she said nothing.

'Anyway,' Jon said. 'What's the worst they can do? Fire me?'

'Well, that would be quite bad.'

'Would it? I'm a manager in a crappy pizza place. It's not like it's my dream job. I'm at a stage in my life where I'd really like to be able to concentrate on my writing.'

There were so many things Laura wanted to say. Did he think every minute of her working life was a breeze? Did he realize that while he may find his boss Greg annoying, her editor wasn't exactly a delight? Also, if Jon cared so much about his novel, why didn't he spend more time writing the bloody thing? After all, the muse was unlikely to pitch up in the Hope & Anchor. 'It's a job though, isn't it? And we need the money.'

Jon shrugged as if she'd mentioned something incredibly trivial.

Laura swallowed down a football-sized lump of irritation. She'd told Jon over and over again that *Natter* magazine was in trouble. That the team had been cut not just to the bone but to the marrow. That the subs desk was now just one lonely – albeit scary – sub/proofreader and Laura now did the work that three people used to do (without any increase in pay, naturally). She'd told him that all around her, titles had closed and no one would be surprised to see *Natter* go the same way. 'I just wouldn't take my job for granted.'

Jon brushed the comment aside. 'We'll be fine.'

Would they? If Laura did find herself out of work, she wasn't entirely sure how easy she would find it to get another job or to find freelance work. There were a lot of unemployed journalists out there, most of whom probably had CVs way more impressive than hers. She would never forget her mother's face when she'd told her she'd been promoted to Real Life Features Editor at *Natter.* Underwhelmed doesn't really cover it.

'It would be good if you didn't get yourself fired,' Laura said.

'Yeah, yeah,' Jon replied, grinning. 'Shall I avoid calling Greg a knob to his face then?'

Despite herself, Laura laughed. 'If you could.' She mustn't wind herself up about nothing. Jon might not be Mr Nine-to-Five but he wasn't completely reckless. Plus, it wasn't beyond the realms of possibility that *Natter* would survive the inexorable 'pivot to digital' she was sick to bloody death of hearing about.

'By the way,' Jon said. 'I might need to borrow a bit of cash, just to get me through until the end of the month.'

Just like last month, Laura thought, and then she checked herself because surely she hadn't become *that* person? She and Jon were a team; what was hers was his and (theoretically) vice versa. 'Of course.'

'Thanks,' Jon said. 'Hey, talking of money, you'll be coming into some, won't you?'

'I wouldn't count on it,' Laura said, taking a swig of Gaviscon and clicking back to party-bag gifts. 'Mum probably left everything to Jess.' She scrolled down the page. 'Are whistles a bad idea for the party bags? Probably.'

'Definitely. Anyway, do we even have to do party bags?'

'Yes. Everyone does them.' She knew Jon thought she was making too much fuss about this party. *They're five,* he'd said to her the other day, *how complicated can it be?* But she wanted to give Billy a proper party. 'Do you think we ought to invite Angus Murray?'

'Angus Murray?'

'The kid who hits everyone.'

'No!'

'It's just I feel a bit sorry for him. And his mum is so nice.'

Jon shrugged. 'You ought to make sure you get half.'

'Half what?' Laura said, hastily scribbling an extra invitation for Angus.

'Your mum's money.'

'I guess,' Laura said, putting the invitation into an envelope and sealing it.

'It's only fair,' Jon said. He sat beside her on the sofa and slid his arm around her. She leant her head against his shoulder. 'I love you,' he said.

'I love you too.' They sat there for a minute in utterly comfortable silence, Jon gently stroking her hair. 'You really do have to get to work,' she said finally.

He laughed. 'I do. Don't suppose you happen to know where my work jacket is?'

'Yes, I hid it along with your keys and wallet. You know, just for fun.'

'All right, sarky-pants.' He started rooting through a pile of clothes on the floor.

'We really have to tidy this place up a bit.'

'It's fine.'

'Oooh, I think this would go down well. Rainbow slime.'

'For the funeral or the party bags?'

Laura laughed.

Jon kissed the top of her head. 'Bloody hell, the slime is nearly two quid a pop. How many kids did you say you're inviting?'

'Twenty-five. No, twenty-six now we're including Angus.'

Jon laughed and rolled his eyes theatrically. 'Twenty-six kids coming here? Are you completely mad?'

'Probably,' Laura said, laughing.

He kissed her goodbye. 'I might go for a quick one with Jimmy after we leave the office. That okay?'

Laura knew the subtext here: *Your mother died a week ago so you get to make unreasonable demands.* But, again, who wanted to be *that* person? 'Of course.'

'Love you, babe. Don't let your sister grind you down.'

Laura felt a stab of irritation. She could slag off Jess but she didn't want anyone else joining in.

Chapter Nine

Laura's mum might be resting in peace but Laura felt anything but peaceful. When she'd joked about her mum leaving every-thing to Jess, she hadn't imagined that Jon would take her seriously. Or that the idea would begin to worm its way into her consciousness. Because, now she came to think of it, leaving everything to Jess was *just* the kind of thing that her mother would do. A slap from beyond the grave.

Stop worrying about something that hasn't even happened yet, Laura told herself (goodness knows there was already enough to deal with in the realms of reality). But her mind refused her attempts to quieten it. The more she tried to push away any thoughts of an unfair split, the more they forced their way into her mind. She even found herself waking up in the night (finally the insomnia of the *properly* bereaved, even if hers wasn't for the right reason).

Which is why Laura had to have this conversation. She dispensed with the elegant run up; there was no easy way to say this. 'Look, I wanted to talk to you about Mum's will. If, when we come to look at it, we find out she hasn't split things equally between the two of us . . . well . . .' Laura's mouth was dry and she couldn't look up. 'I want you to know I don't think that's fair. You may have been her favourite but I was her daughter too and we ought to split everything down the middle.'

The night before, Jon had told her that even that was crazy. 'Jess doesn't need the money.'

'That's not the point,' Laura had told him. Anyway, she was happy with half. She just wanted things to be fair (for once).

She rooted herself back in the present. 'I would rather not fall out about this.'

Silence.

She paced around the room, took a swig of Gaviscon. Jon had kept telling her she had to fight this for Billy's sake. She took a deep breath. 'I hope we can sort this out amicably but if we can't, I want you to know I'm going to take legal advice.'

Silence.

Laura's head pounded and she clenched her fists. She wasn't a greedy person. In fact, she'd always prided herself on not being materialistic. (Mind you, so had Jon and to hear him spending this inheritance in his head before she'd even got it was quite something. They could pay off all their debts. Put a deposit down on a flat. He'd love somewhere with a home office so he could really concentrate on his writing. He'd even talked about scaling back his shifts at the restaurant. Scaling them back *more?* Laura felt like saying.)

'I know you don't believe me but I promise you I mean it. I'll take you to court if it comes to that.'

Silence.

The thought of going to court made Laura feel sick. The whole orphan label felt Dickensian enough but now she and Jess were going to turn into those characters who lost their entire inheritance in legal fees: Jarndyce and Jarndyce. Laura did not want to be them. 'Splitting everything down the middle is the fair thing to do.' She looked up. Still no response.

But then, what did she expect from one of Billy's teddy bears? Now she just had to hope the real conversation went better than the rehearsal.

Chapter Ten

Laura should not have opened that bottle of wine and should not have been sitting there winding herself up into a frenzy.

She was angry with *everybody*.

Jon for being out with Jimmy again.

Billy for refusing to eat his tomatoes or do his reading properly.

Her mother for dying.

Jess for bossing her about. (And saying she was an 'idiot' when it came to Jon. And taking the locket without so much as asking. And . . . well, the list went on.)

Laura poured herself another glass of wine (sod Dry sodding January!), a little sloshing over the edge of the glass. She was supposed to be finishing the Order of Service, addressing Jess' unwelcome feedback (jeez, it was just like work), but instead she was going from Facebook to Twitter on her laptop. Every now and again a pop-up ad for the mobile-phone-shaped floral display appeared and Laura would smile. Jess would be *so* mad.

Earlier, Laura had been to the beauty counter of a big department store having decided that, overdraft notwithstanding, she was going to treat herself to some proper, grown-up make-up; Jess-type make-up. She'd had quite enough of just making do with what was left in the beauty drawer at work because, although Natasha the beauty editor always made a huge thing of how she shared out all the freebies, everyone knew she kept the best stuff for herself and what was left was slim pickings. When Laura had walked into the store, she'd felt giddy with the excitement of it all and suddenly remembered her mother sitting at restaurant tables and fishing a rose-gold compact out of her handbag in order to touch up her lipstick while Laura looked on, knowing she could never be so impossibly glamorous. A woman approached and asked if she could help. Laura explained that yes, she was looking for some new ideas, that she was a bit rubbish with this sort of thing.

'Take a seat,' the woman had said, half smiling. She'd examined Laura under the spotlight, her perfect brows furrowing. 'Oh dear,' she'd said. 'Oh dear, dear.'

Laura felt hot with shame. Whatever was the matter? Did she have chronic halitosis?

'Your skin,' the woman said, poking at her. 'It is so dehydrated. So prematurely aged. So *damaged*.'

The memory made Laura feel horrible all over again. She poured herself more wine and was surprised to see she had finished the bottle. Never mind – tonight she needed it.

She had left the store £148 lighter, and it wasn't just the price that had made her eyes water. Her hair was something of a disaster zone but she hadn't actually thought her skin was that bad. Granted, her *regimen*, as the woman had insisted on calling it (it was all Laura could do not to shout: we call it *regime* in England), was somewhat of the quick cleansing-wipe sort but it seemed to do the job.

She bet Jess had a really full-on regime/regimen. She probably blogged about it. Without thinking, Laura found herself typing in 'StyleMaven'. And there was Jess looking radiant and talking about all manner of things from how she'd renovated her living room (err, paid someone a bloody fortune to do it) to her high-street cashmere edit. *There's something so glorious about cashmere,* Jess trilled, *it just adds a touch of luxury to everyday life.*

Pah! As if everyone could afford bloody cashmere every day. Honestly it made Laura so furious. Jon was right when he said Jess had no idea how real people lived. Someone ought to put her straight; remind her that not everyone had a hundred quid to blow on a jumper. Laura couldn't say it, of course, but she wished *someone* would.

She took a swig of her wine, noting that she really did feel quite drunk and perhaps it would have been sensible to have more than a chocolate HobNob for dinner. The pop-up of the mobile-phone-shaped floral display appeared again and, purely for her own entertainment, she added it to her basket and filled out the order details.

She still had her order for the party-bag presents open too. She couldn't decide whether to go for the rainbow slime or the football erasers and pencils. Either way, she mustn't forget to complete the order once she'd made up her mind.

Perhaps she would get her hair cut before the funeral? There must be a hairdresser out there somewhere that could tame her unruly locks? If her hair looked better it might distract from her terrible skin. She Googled good haircuts for bad hair. She quite fancied a swishy bob . . . could her hair ever be swishy?

Maybe she could tell Jess that cashmere wasn't an everyday choice for most people? Not in person, of course – where it would go down about as well as the proverbial cup of cold sick – and not even online as herself, but she could say it anonymously. She'd be doing Jess a favour, really. No good leaving her to say things that would garner lots of hate.

Laura quickly created a new account. Now what could she call herself? ILoveDoughnuts? No, Jess would know that was her. Truthteller? No, too portentous. MsRealityCheck? Perfect.

She started typing. *Perhaps don't talk about cashmere as an everyday choice? I'm pretty sure if you're a teaching assistant or a nurse you don't think like that.*

She posted it and felt an immediate rush of shame. She had always thought of herself as a reasonably decent person – she bought the *Big Issue*, considered the interests of people less fortunate than her when she voted, avoided trolling her own sister.

On the other hand, she hadn't said anything really horrible. And it would do Jess good to think more about some of the things she said. She needed a reality check.

Laura finished the last of her wine. She wondered what time Jon would roll in. At least if she'd gone to bed before he got in, she wouldn't have to listen to him going on about her mother's will again. She was tired of having to remind him that she hadn't actually seen the thing yet; that it wasn't entirely impossible that her mother had split everything straight down the line. Tired of him looking dubious and saying he hoped so but that it didn't hurt to be prepared. I've been having practice conversations with Billy's teddy bear, Laura would think irritably – what more do you want?

Laura stretched and decided that there was no way she could face the Order of Service tonight. It would have to get done along with everything else on the long list of things she was hoping to squish into tomorrow.

She could at least order those party-bag presents before she went to bed though. The rainbow slime was perfect and there was absolutely no need to overthink it. She clicked on the order and paid before she could change her mind.

42

Chapter Eleven

Then

Laura's chest hurt and her legs screamed but she didn't stop running. She was catching up with Charlotte Davies. She was overtaking her!

Laura so wanted to do well in this race. The day had not got off to a good start. First of all, there had been a scene because Mum had forgotten to wash her red T shirt and Laura had been all 'bratty' about it. Mum had said she should have reminded her and although Laura was pretty sure she had, and more than once, she didn't argue. Her mum told her she'd just have to wear another T shirt and Laura had started to cry because she was on the *red* team. In the end she wore an orangey-red polo shirt of Dad's that came down almost to her knees.

Dad was at the side of the running track cheering her name and Laura went faster and faster. She overtook Ruth Morris. She was near the front. She could hardly believe this was happening. Jess was the one who was good at running. (Jess was the one who was good at everything.)

After the upset about the T shirt, there had been another row at breakfast when Mum took Jess' side in a dispute about the last of the cornflakes (even though Laura ought to get priority, of course, since she had her race that morning whereas Jess was just going to sit in a classroom). Then they were late leaving the house because Mum was hunting around trying to find some flat shoes to wear for the mothers' race. Laura stood in the hallway feeling panicky and her dad told her not to worry because he'd get her there on time even if that meant he had to drive like Stirling Moss. Laura had no idea who Stirling Moss was but she smiled anyway.

Laura could see the finish line, but her heart felt like it was going to burst out of her chest. She felt a bit sick too and wished she hadn't eaten so many cornflakes. The trouble was, she'd felt she had to after making such a big fuss about getting them.

'Come on, Laura!' her dad shouted.

She kept going, squeezing her eyes shut as she burst through the finish line.

She was third! She was going to get an actual trophy!

Her dad was suddenly there, high-fiving her and wrapping her in a huge hug. The lemony smell of his aftershave mingled with the smell of freshly-cut grass. He told Laura he was so proud of her, his little superstar!

Laura leaned over and put her hands on her thighs while she got her breath back. Even though it wasn't quite ten in the morning, it was already baking hot. Laura had commented on how warm it was when they'd first arrived and her mum had laughed and rolled her eyes. 'It's a beautiful day. Honestly, there's no pleasing some people!'

Mrs Harris was using a loud hailer to announce the next race even though Mrs Harris was the last person in the world to need a loud hailer as she had a built-in one.

'Where's Mum?' Laura said, thinking she must still be somewhere near the start of the track.

Dad pointed in the direction of the gates and Laura saw her mother, resplendent in hot pink, surrounded by a clump of people, all of whom seemed to be roaring with laughter.

'She got chatting,' Dad said, shrugging ruefully.

'She didn't see me run?' Laura said.

Dad shook his head. 'No, but we're going to tell her all about it and she's going to be so super-proud of you!'

Laura nodded and swallowed down the lump in her throat.

Chapter Twelve

Laura cut a rectangle of baking parchment and used it to line the base of the traybake tin. 'What are you going to wear for the funeral? And what's Billy going to wear?'

Jon didn't look away from the football on the TV. 'I dunno. Trousers, a shirt?'

'Don't you have a suit?'

'What am I, an accountant?'

'What's an accountant?' Billy said, looking up from the dinosaurs that he was lining up across the floor.

'Someone who is clever with money,' Laura said vaguely as she got out butter, caster sugar and flour. She started to zest a lemon. *I thought I'd do one lemon drizzle and one chocolate cake*, she'd said to Jess. *Perfect*, her sister had said. She wasn't always difficult. Perhaps she'd be similarly easy-going if Laura had to talk to her about splitting their mum's money straight down the middle? (Yeah, because the decision over what cakes to have was just like the divvying up of thousands of pounds.) God, Laura hoped she would never have to have that chat with her sister. Apart from anything else, what really mattered to Laura wasn't the money itself but whether her mother had treated her and Jess equally. If Evie hadn't done that, then no amount of cash could make Laura feel okay.

'I is going to eat you all up,' Billy's T-rex said to his diplo-docus.

Laura measured out her ingredients. She could hardly believe she was making the cakes five whole days before the funeral just so they could sit smugly in the freezer. That was the sort of thing Jess would do. In actual fact, Laura had intended to get even further ahead by making the cakes yesterday but then she had been unravelled by the sight of her mum's favourite teabags on the supermarket shelf and suddenly found herself in floods of tears. It was quite embarrassing really, especially when an assistant who looked young enough for her to have given birth to him tried to comfort her. She could see his thin, white neck developing big red splotches as he asked if she wanted to sit in the staffroom for a minute. His badge said: *Happy to help!* but Laura was sure he was anything but happy to have to help with *this*.

'RRRR, RRRR!' went Billy's T-Rex.

'For Christ's sake, Arsenal!' Jon shouted.

The doorbell rang.

'Could you get that?' Laura said to Jon.

'I will, I will,' Billy said, jumping up. 'Grandma's dead!' he announced to whoever was at the door.

Was this normal? Really? Laura wiped her hands on a tea towel and went to the door to see Amy with Josh balanced on her hip.

'Hey,' Amy said. 'How are you doing? I've been thinking of you so much. Such a terrible time. I just wondered if there was any chance you could have Joshy for an hour? This friend of mine from LA just texted and she's in London for a couple of days so I said I'd go and have one drink with her.'

'Yay!' Billy said. 'Josh can play dinosaurs with me!'

Billy loved younger kids (surely that meant he couldn't actually be a psychopath?) and was particularly keen on Josh. As was Laura, for that matter. She was just slightly more realistic about the fact that no eighteen-month-old just happily plays dinosaurs unattended for an hour. And the fact that

Amy's 'hour' was always about three hours long. 'Umm, I'm actually making a cake for the funeral.'

Amy's face fell. 'Oh, I guess I'll have to take Joshy with me then.'

'Well, if it's only an hour.'

'You're the best!' Amy said, shoving Josh into Laura's arms.

'Hey, Joshy!' Jon said. He also liked little people so perhaps Laura would be able to carry on making the cake after all.

Laura put Josh down on the floor, where he sat and earnestly chewed an ankylosaur while Billy told him what all the other dinosaurs were. Laura felt as if her heart might burst.

She put her cake ingredients into a bowl. She felt bad now about suggesting she wouldn't take Josh. Not only did Amy keep her sane at work, but the pair of them shared the special bond of feeling like the world's worst Dulwich mums (neither of their offspring had been exposed to a single flashcard and both were more likely to be found eating a chicken nugget than an olive).

Now where on earth was the electric whisk?

As she pulled her head out of the recesses of the cupboards she saw Josh had pulled a chair over to the kitchen counter and was now attempting to scale it. 'Jon!' she said, scooping Josh up.

'What? That's more like it, Arsenal!'

She plonked Josh into Jon's arms.

'I don't think he wants to be held,' Jon said.

'Maybe not but I want to make the cake.'

'Joshy wants to play dinosaurs,' Billy said.

'Give him one to play with on the sofa then,' Laura said, starting to whisk the cake ingredients. She couldn't believe the funeral was a matter of days away. She hoped it would all go okay.

Her mind flashed back to her father's funeral. Her and Jess sitting side by side on the hard pews, their legs almost touching. She was twelve, Jess fourteen. She'd been so ashamed of herself for falling apart. Jess had kept it together. Comforted her and their mother. Thanked people for coming. Read from the Corinthians in a calm, clear voice: 'You have not gone away . . .'

'I think he's done a poo,' Jon said.

'Eww, eww!' Billy shouted.

'Could you change him?' Laura said, pouring cake batter into the tin.

Jon opened his mouth to protest but thought better of it. 'Where's the nappy bag?'

Laura had no doubt that Jess would be just as together on Thursday. She wondered what she would wear. As StyleMaven, she tended to go for an explosion of animal print and brights, but that was hardly suitable for the day you buried your mum. One thing was for sure though: whatever Jess wore, she'd look perfect. As would her husband and the girls. Lola and Hannah were the very model of solemn, grief-stricken granddaughters the other day. Not like Billy. Laura glanced up at him and felt a wave of guilt.

'Oooh, that was a bad one,' Jon said, returning with Josh and a nappy bag.

'I think you do need a suit for the funeral.'

'I'm not a suit kind of guy.'

Laura sighed. 'You're not a funeral kind of guy either. Some things are out of the ordinary.'

'I don't want to blow loads of dosh on a suit.'

Laura rescued Josh just before he stuck his finger in the plug socket. 'I'll pay for it.'

'Bloody hell, ref, that was miles offside!' He reached down his tracksuit bottoms and adjusted himself. 'Well, if it's important to you.'

'It's important to me.' Laura may not be in control about anything to do with this funeral – from the typeface for the Order of Service to her own swirling mass of emotions – but she could control how her family looked.

Chapter Thirteen

It was 11 p.m. the night before her mother's funeral and Laura was making the icing for the chocolate cake and wondering where on earth the day had gone.

At least she had finally managed to put on the face mask that bitchy beauty counter lady had sold her, which meant her skin was being sorted out at the same time as the cake.

She broke up the dark chocolate and put it in a bowl over a pan of simmering water. She had already ruined one lot of chocolate, which had turned into a lumpy and unusable mess because she'd let it get too hot. Luckily, Jon had picked up his mobile for once so he'd grabbed her some more chocolate from the corner shop on his way home from the pub. She wished she hadn't had to have the conversation with him about how he much preferred milk chocolate but what can you do.

The face mask was making her skin tingle a bit which she assumed was a good sign. According to bitchy beauty counter lady it contained high levels of retinol which was a 'must' for people with skin that was 'so badly damaged'. Anyway, the packet promised youthful suppleness and radiance would be dramatically improved with a single application, so Laura was hopeful.

Laura took the melted chocolate off the heat, grateful that it looked smooth and glossy and she wasn't going to have to go to Spar in her pyjamas. She set it aside to cool down a little.

She could do with cooling down herself and felt like she'd spent the whole day being either angry or weepy.

First, she'd been angry because – despite her thinking she'd got ahead on the cake-making front – she'd ended up having to make another chocolate cake this morning (having burnt the one she made on Saturday because Josh had somehow managed to switch off the oven timer).

Then Laura had turned her somewhat sour attentions to today's batch of condolence letters. One woman had just put 'Thinking of you. Bella.' What good was *that* to anyone? Laura supposed it was better than the long-winded flowery numbers though. Heaven has got another angel . . . *eeeeurgh!* The absolute worst, though, were people who said, *Let me know if there is anything I can do.* Don't ask, just do something!

Laura beat the butter with the icing sugar. She knew she should have sifted the icing sugar first, but frankly it was too late, and she was too tired.

When Laura had got to the undertakers, there were a whole host of new people to be annoyed with, from the woman with the irritating high-pitched laugh in the next room, to her bossy sister (wearing the locket again!), to Robert, who had done her mother's hair all wrong.

Laura folded the melted chocolate into the butter and sugar mixture.

From the undertakers, she had gone to the printers to pick up the Order of Service (Jess having visibly paled when Laura told her they were still not in her possession). She sat in the bright orange-and-white reception doing a quick proofread and was horrified to see that the eulogy was to be delivered by 'Little Miss Bossy', which didn't seem quite such a funny thing to call Jess now as when Laura had originally put it on the draft, just for her own entertainment. Now she felt furious with herself for being so childish and for leaving everything to the last minute. Luckily the printers had said that, if she could give them a couple of hours, they could sort it out and do another run. Which was great even if it did mean that Laura lost a big chunk of her day.

The face mask really did feel quite stingy now. Laura guessed it was just doing its work.

When she'd got back from the printers, Jon was still in bed and she bit back a wave of annoyance. It was normal to sleep later when you worked nights (although Jon only did three shifts a week and they finished at midnight; he wasn't exactly a junior doctor). 'Are you going to do any writing?' she'd asked him. 'In a bit,' he'd replied, not looking up from his phone. As if starting your day before lunchtime was a ridiculous ask. They'd probably have ended up having a row if Laura hadn't opened her laptop right at that very moment to find Jon had hidden a Post-it note inside, telling her he knew things were tough right now but he loved her and they were going to get through it together.

Laura spread the icing over the cake, making sure she put a particularly generous amount over the cracks and trying not to think of that as a metaphor for her life. She really ought to get the face mask off now; it had been on considerably longer than instructed.

By mid-afternoon, Laura had ditched angry in favour of weepy. Why had she left it until now to get shoes for tomorrow? Why hadn't she resolved things better with her mother before she died? (Like resolving things was the work of moments.) Why was she throwing a children's birthday party *three days* after her mother's funeral?

By the evening she was both weepy and angry (yay, full house!). She'd snapped at Billy for not wanting to eat his tomatoes and then burst into tears when he'd said she was mean. The note by then a distant memory, she found herself saying 'really' in a sarcastic voice when Jon had asked her if he could wear his trainers with his funeral suit, and then sobbing after he left for the pub even though he'd told her several times he didn't have to go.

She stepped back to look at the cake. It wasn't perfect but it would have to do. Now all that stood between her and her bed was getting this face mask off.

She really hoped she would manage to sleep tonight (hard to believe only days ago she was feeling guilty because she had been sleeping fine – perhaps she'd jinxed herself?). She had meant to get to the GP to ask for some sleeping tablets but it had somehow slipped off the list, along with getting her hair cut, losing half a stone, and sorting out some storage solutions for this flat (boy, did it need storage solutions).

Laura was determined that she wasn't going to completely lose it at the funeral tomorrow. Or, for that matter, stay totally dry-eyed. She needed to be the *right* amount of sad.

Still, if she couldn't seem to control what was happening on the inside, at least by using this super-expensive face mask she was making sure she looked slightly more polished on the outside.

She washed it off and looked in the mirror to see if she'd been transformed into a clear-skinned beauty of twenty-one. But instead what stared back at her was a puffy, red face.

It looked angry and sad. Which Laura supposed was pretty appropriate, really.

Chapter Fourteen

Laura was lying on the bed with a cold flannel over her face, trying not to think about the job ad she'd seen on a journalist Facebook group this morning. What kind of a person thinks about new career opportunities the day of their mother's funeral? (Particularly when they're not especially career-focussed to start with. Laura was more 'lie back' than 'lean in'.)

Her skin was glowing – and not the good kind of glowing that Natasha the beauty editor was always banging on about.

How could she have done this to her face, today of all days?

Her mother would have something to say about it.

Her mother would have *had* something to say about it.

Despite herself, Laura started thinking about the job ad again. It was for a health and wellbeing editor at *Inlustris* magazine. She could remember the job description pretty much word for word. *Applicants will be passionate about wellbeing and mental health, proactive at chasing a story, and brimming with ideas for creative, original and engaging content. You'll also be responsible for our advice column.*

Laura pressed the flannel into her forehead. It sounded like pretty much her dream job. Not only would she be able to keep up the agony aunt work she'd come to love, but she'd also get to write articles that were genuinely useful to people.

No more stupid 'Shock Confessions', no more manipulating people into telling you things they'd later regret.

Also, *Inlustris*! One of the big monthly glossies. Even her mother would have been impressed by her getting a job at *Inlustris*. Well, no, probably not, but any normal person . . .

She pressed the flannel into her cheeks, wondering if there was any way in hell her face was going to calm down in the three hours and forty minutes before the funeral. She could hear Jon telling Billy that they were both going to wear 'big-boy suits' today.

Could she get this job and make up for all the lost time in her twenties when she was just pissing about? Could she reclaim those 'lost years'?

No, of course she couldn't.

And anyway, she shouldn't be thinking about it today.

Chapter Fifteen

'What the hell were you thinking?' Jess said, before Laura had even got through the door of the undertakers.

'What?' Laura said.

Jess pointed behind her to where their mother's coffin was sitting waiting to be loaded into the hearse. On top of it was a huge orange and red floral display that was fashioned in to the shape of a mobile phone. It was about three feet long and covered most of the top of the coffin.

'I . . . I . . .' Laura suddenly remembered putting it in her basket just for fun. She must have ordered it by mistake instead of the party bag presents that night she'd inhaled a bottle of wine. Which meant she'd spent goodness knows how much on that monstrosity and she hadn't ordered the party bag presents. 'I must order rainbow slime.'

Jess' brow scrunched. 'I'm sorry?'

'Nothing,' Laura said.

'I suppose you think this is funny?' Jess said.

Laura had been on the point of apologizing and saying that of course the flowers were a mistake, but there was something so imperious in her sister's tone, she wanted to hit her. 'She was my mum too, you know. I get a say about what flowers go on her coffin.'

Jess shook her head. 'You do NOT actually like those, Laura. You were just trying to wind me up.'

'They're very . . . colourful. Also, Mum loved her mobile phone.'

Jess rolled her eyes. 'You are too much. I can't believe you'd let Mum's coffin look like that just to spite me.'

'I like them.'

'Liar! Also, what on earth have you done to your face? You can't be sunburnt – there hasn't been any sun.'

Laura's hands fluttered to her cheeks. 'I'm just a bit hot is all.' She headed towards the toilets to put on another layer of foundation. 'Do not touch those flowers,' she shouted back over her shoulder.

Chapter Sixteen

What kind of person struggles not to put someone straight about what their mother was *really* like when they're standing five feet away from her coffin?

'Your mother had a big heart,' the woman said.

Laura bristled. Did Evie have a big heart? Was that why she'd phoned Laura in the hospital, on the day of Billy's operation, and banged on for forty minutes about a row she'd had with her current boyfriend? Was it because of their mother's kindness that Laura and Jess had spent huge swathes of their childhood at the receiving end of her froideur because of the most minor transgressions? Was it Evie's huge heart that had made her think of her – and *only* her – when Dad had died?

Laura shook herself. She was a monster thinking like this. She smiled at the woman, said thank you and, yes, her mother really did have a big heart.

Rule number one: You do not speak ill of the dead. You do not even *think* ill of the dead.

The woman tottered away, her feet spilling over the edges of her court shoes. Laura wasn't sure who she was. Someone from her mother's pottery class, perhaps? The church was filled with people she didn't recognize. Her mother had always thought long-standing friendships to be rather a pedestrian thing. Whenever Laura mentioned Clare, her friend since primary school, her mother's perfectly-groomed eyebrows would shoot up into her hair line. 'Are you *still* friends with her?' In her mind, friendships should be like butterflies: beautiful, bright and short-lived.

Laura glanced at the floral mobile phone sitting on top of the coffin next to Jess' hand-tied bouquet of white roses. She was actually pretty surprised Jess hadn't made her take her display off. Now she had to go through the whole day insisting she loved it and smiling when people said it was so 'unusual' or 'interesting'.

Laura shivered. It was cold inside the church, the sort of damp chill that spreads through your bones. 'It's been a miserable January,' a woman had said to Laura earlier, seemingly unaware of the layers of meaning.

Jon and Billy were both in their new suits. Billy was driving one of his small toy cars along a pew. 'You okay?' Jon mouthed at her.

She nodded. He'd been great today. Been up before her, told her her skin just looked a little 'sun-kissed' and managed to brush Billy's hair without him noticing. And now, in this seemingly endless wait before the service began, he was keeping Billy happy while simultaneously greeting people and chatting to Jess' husband.

'I'm so sorry for your loss,' a pale, elderly man said, placing a liver-spotted claw on Laura's shoulder.

Laura felt a rush of shame. She didn't deserve people's sympathy. She was a fraud. Well, not a fraud, because she *was* upset. But, oh . . . it was so complicated. When Dad had died it hadn't been easy but it had been simple.

The service was about to start. Laura could do with some Gaviscon but she didn't think sipping it in church was a good look really. She took her place at the front, Billy to her left and Jess to her right. Jess smiled at her and Laura smiled back.

The vicar was a tiny but robust-looking woman who had

told Laura and Jess that in some countries in the world sixty-one was a very good age. Laura hadn't been sure what they were supposed to do with that. Feel guilty? Grateful?

Now the vicar was talking about how she hadn't had the pleasure of meeting Evie herself but had learned a lot about her from her two daughters. Evie was strong and funny and even in her last days she could still make a joke.

They stood for a hymn: 'Immortal, Invisible'. Laura felt as if her voice wasn't coming from her.

Lola was going up to do the first reading. 'Is she old enough to do that?' Laura had said when Jess first suggested it. 'She wants to,' Jess had replied. And, of course, here she was now, as composed and calm as someone who had spent a lifetime public speaking. Jess' mini-me.

'Is my party this Sunday?' Billy said in the world's loudest whisper.

Jon nodded and put a finger to his lips.

Another hymn, a reading from their mum's self-proclaimed 'best friend', a title she no doubt felt she richly deserved having been in Evie's life for a whole ten years. And more or less without breaks, too, except for that time after they went to Ibiza together and stopped speaking for three months.

Now Jess was going up to the pulpit to do the eulogy. *Do you want to do it together?* she'd asked Laura. Laura had shaken her head, said Jess was better at stuff like that. Which was true, but not the whole reason. Seeing her sister up there all alone now, with her voice trying not to shake, made Laura feel incredibly guilty. Jess kept fiddling with the button on her white jacket (of course she hadn't worn black), as if twisting it would release some kind of superpower.

'You were great,' she whispered to Jess when she came back to her seat. And she had been great. She had dished out the praise and honour a eulogy demanded, yet still not been dishonest in any way. It was no mean feat.

They bowed their heads for a moment's silent reflection. Laura started thinking about how much she missed her dad, how people were talking shit when they told you that time healed everything because, yes, things were less raw now and she could talk about her dad without bursting into tears, but that didn't mean she didn't miss him every single day. It didn't mean that the sight of his favourite chocolate bar or a Manchester United shirt couldn't make her feel as if she'd been winded. Her dad had died twenty-five years ago and, ever since, all the nice things that had happened to Laura had been less nice, and all the bad things worse.

The sound of someone crying snapped Laura into the present and she felt a sharp stab of guilt: today was supposed to be about grieving for her *mother*. Her mother who had only been dead for two weeks. Laura was a bad person.

'Is Angus Murray coming to my party?' Billy said.

Laura nodded and told him to shush.

'I hope he doesn't hit me!'

'Sssh!' Laura said, glancing across at Lola and Hannah, their small heads bowed and still. They were older than Billy, a lot older.

'Am I getting a Nintendo Switch for my birthday?' Billy whispered.

'Sssh,' Laura and Jon said.

They stood for the Lord's Prayer. Jon put his arm around her, as if he somehow knew she suddenly felt unsteady on her feet. Laura said the words, almost surprised she remembered them. She felt a pang of envy towards people who had genuine faith. Death must be an altogether different prospect if you didn't believe it was the end.

The vicar was doing the wrap-up. Laura felt a surge of relief. The funeral was over and, in so far as these things can, it had gone well. All the bickering she and Jess had done in the lead-up to this had been set aside, and Jess hadn't killed her over the phone flowers. It wasn't just Laura and Jess who had been on their best behaviour either – Jon had been sober, suited and supportive, and Billy had refrained from shouting, 'Grandma's dead!'

They were the perfect family.

Chapter Seventeen

Then

They had to sit in this big black car, just Laura, Jess and Mum. In front of them was another big black car, which was carrying Dad's coffin. They were driving very slowly but Laura's stomach lurched and plummeted.

She couldn't believe Dad was in there. The coffin didn't look big enough. She would have liked to have seen him but Mum had said it wasn't a good idea, that he 'looked a mess.' Laura didn't care how he looked, she just wanted to hold his hand. She knew better than to argue though.

Mum was sitting between her and Jess, her huge black hat pushing the girls to the edges of their seats. She had been worrying she was going to have 'hat hair' later. She didn't want to face all those people 'looking a sight'.

She turned her head towards Laura and made a face. 'For goodness' sake, Laura, you look so pale. Jess, have you got any blusher in your bag we can put on your sister?'

Jess said she hadn't and their mum sighed. She reached over and pinched Laura's cheeks. 'That'll stop you looking quite so washed out.'

Laura knew her mum was trying to be nice but the pinching hurt.

'Now,' Mum said, 'what have I told you both about today?'

Laura and Jess exchanged a glance. Laura let Jess speak because she was better at stuff like this.

'We need to be brave. There will be a lot of people there watching us today and we need to show them that the three of us are a united front and that we're fine.'

Laura nodded even though she felt anything but fine. She could scarcely believe that Dad was gone. That he'd never tease her again about being a Dolly Daydream, that next time they ordered a Chinese takeaway no one else would want the lemon chicken (Jess and Mum both hated it), that he'd never give her one of his great big hugs that made her feel safe.

Yesterday, she'd taken one of his jumpers to bed with her. It still smelled of him. Her mother had seen it when she'd come in to wake Laura up and her lips had pursed. She brought the subject up over breakfast. 'You're a bit old for a comfort blanket, aren't you?'

Jess had said that she couldn't see the harm and Mum, who wasn't used to Jess siding against her, had been frosty with her for the rest of the day.

Eventually, Mum had forgiven them both; hugged them and said this was so difficult for her. She'd lost her soulmate in that car crash. She might not ever meet someone else now she was so old.

Jess told Mum that that was crazy talk. She wasn't that old and she was so pretty.

Her mother hugged her tight and told her she was her 'best girl'.

Someone else? Laura thought. Why did Mum want someone else? You couldn't replace Dad.

Chapter Eighteen

'Oh my God, you are not taking selfies at your mother's wake?' Laura said to Jess.

Jess shrugged her shoulders. 'I'm very honest in my blog. I write about all aspects of my life.'

Laura snorted. Jess was not very bloody honest in her blog. She looked perfect in every photo. Her husband and kids looked perfect in every photo. Her idea of being 'very honest' was saying that the weather hadn't been great for their picnic but they'd still had an amazing time. Or saying that something was part of a paid partnership but she would have wanted to talk about this awesome collection anyway. (Laura was sick to bloody death of the word 'awesome', which people seemed to use *all* the time. It means inspiring awe, people. Does it really inspire awe that we've got a date in the diary for that meeting?)

Auntie Shelia and Uncle James came to say their goodbyes. They wanted to get on the motorway before it got dark. They used to drive at night no problem but, well, they weren't getting any younger. Had Laura been away on holiday? Auntie Sheila said she looked a little sunburnt. Laura said she hadn't been anywhere and there was a slightly awkward silence before Uncle James said what a lovely service it had been. 'Beautiful,' Auntie Sheila said. 'And I must say your home is absolutely gorgeous, Jess.'

After they'd gone, Jess turned back to Laura. 'I'm obviously going to do a post about Mum passing away.'

'I thought it was a fashion blog? Also, I really hate the term "passed away".'

'Fashion and lifestyle. What's wrong with "passed away"?'

Laura made a face. 'I dunno. It's just so . . . eeurgh. So what the hell are you going to write about? Grief hacks? Five fun ways to bury your mother?'

Laura looked across the room at Billy, who was ensconced on the chaise longue chatting to an old lady with hair that looked like peach-coloured candy floss. 'Grandma's dead!' Billy told her. The woman looked so utterly charmed that Laura could only surmise she must either be deaf or have dementia.

Lola and Hannah were handing around plates of sandwiches. They really were preternaturally well-behaved.

'You can be as snide as you like,' Jess said. 'But I think it would be odd if I didn't mention that Mum pass— died.'

Laura shook her head. 'Yup. Look, I didn't mean to be snide.' Which wasn't entirely true because she had very much meant to be snide, only now she felt guilty about it.

They were interrupted by Corinne, a 'friend' of their mother's who had repeatedly told her she could beat cancer if only she would think positively (yup, it's that simple). 'What a shame Evie lost her battle,' she said.

Laura had to zone out as Corinne carried on talking, lest she tell her how unwittingly but unspeakably cruel she thought she had been. *Are you really stupid enough to think a mindset could have done what chemotherapy and modern medicine couldn't? Do you really think my mother – who was actually very positive by nature – somehow failed?*

'My God,' Laura said to Jess as Corinne finally drifted away. 'Don't you just hate her?'

'Well, I try not to hate anyone,' Jess said.

66

Laura, who could find at least three people she hated on a single tube journey, was just about to tell her sister not to be quite so insufferably sanctimonious when they were approached by a woman with big, red glasses and teeth that looked like they were trying to climb out of her mouth. She had worked with their mother back in the day, she told them. She complimented Jess on her 'gorgeous home' and told them both she was so sorry for their loss.

Laura and Jess made murmurs of thanks but the woman was keen to get back to the subject of Jess' house. Where had she got those cushions? How clever to use green as an accent colour. Was that table an antique?

Laura made her excuses and went to find Jon. She walked past Billy, who was telling his peach-haired admirer that he was having a birthday party this Sunday. 'I'm going to be five!' he told her, showing her all five fingers of one hand. 'How old are you?'

The woman lifted up both her papery hands and stared at them for a very long time. She was going to need *a lot* of fingers.

Jon was talking to Jess' husband, Ben. Laura suddenly heard her mother's voice in her head: *Jon and Ben are* so *different*. The comment had irritated Laura, somewhat irrationally, really, because the two men were indisputably different, but Laura had known what her mother was really saying was that she deemed Jon the lesser.

'Hey, babe,' Jon said, snaking his arm around her waist. 'How are you?'

'Fine,' Laura said. Her mother had rarely said 'fine' when people asked her how she was. To her, such a question wasn't just a conversational nicety but something that deserved a full and frank answer. And if that meant hearing about her piles, well then so be it.

'I was just asking Jon how the novel is going,' Ben said.

'Slowly,' Jon said. 'But then no one said to Michelangelo, "Look, mate, you're taking quite a long time on one ceiling," did they?'

Ben laughed and Laura did too, even though she'd heard this joke – A LOT – and frankly she *was* a bit worried about the progress – or rather, lack of progress – on this novel. Last time she had sneaked a peek it was three pages long. Given that Jon had been working on it for ten years, she could only assume he was meticulously crafting each word syllable by syllable. Also, and she felt so disloyal even thinking this but she couldn't help herself, when Jon had described the idea to her, it hadn't sounded that great. It was about a tortured spirit-guide, apparently. Once she'd said to Jon that she hoped his humour would really come across on the page. It was meant to be a compliment but he'd been furious with her. He didn't want to write funny books, for Christ's sake. He wanted to write important books.

'I don't know how you do it,' Ben said. 'I know they say everyone has a book in them but I don't think I could write one if my life depended on it. Well, not unless it was some boring textbook about corporate law.'

At least corporate lawyers earn a decent salary though, Laura thought. A salary that lets them buy a much-admired five-bedroom house. A salary that means their wife's only 'job' is uploading photos of herself in her new jumpsuit. Whoa! What the hell was she thinking? Surely, she wasn't turning into one of those bourgeois women she'd always hated. 'Excuse me, I'm just going to grab another drink.'

Laura stood alone in the kitchen suddenly feeling really strange. She had this pain in her chest and her heart was racing. She felt weak and a little faint too. Christ, she was having a heart attack! Surely not; thirty-seven-year-old women don't just keel over from a heart attack. She clutched the worktop and took a few deep breaths and gradually she started to feel okay again. She must start looking after herself better though. She owed it to Billy.

'Hello,' a woman with dreadlocks said, coming into the kitchen. 'I'm Joanna. I knew your mum from Zumba.' She touched Laura on the arm. 'It was a lovely send-off.'

'Thanks,' Laura said, grateful that no one needed to be planning her send-off right now. She was definitely getting a gym membership though.

'Your mum had such a great sense of humour,' Joanna said.

'Yes,' Laura said, grateful for a compliment about her mother she could unequivocally agree with.

'And isn't your sister's house lovely?'

'Perfect.'

Laura and Joanna walked back into the living room together. Billy's peach-haired friend was now absentmindedly dripping coffee over the cream chaise longue. Laura knew she should make a move to repair the damage or at least prevent more but she stayed rooted to the spot. Jess could write a 'very honest' post about stain removal.

'Your mother would have been so proud of you today,' Joanna said.

Laura looked at her, smiled. She obviously didn't know Evie very well at all.

Chapter Nineteen

Then

'Oh, do stop upsetting everyone all the time,' Mum said.

Laura felt like she'd been slapped. All she'd said was that she couldn't face a Chinese takeaway because if they got food from Imperial Treasure and didn't order a lemon chicken it would seem wrong.

The pipes clanked and hissed. The house had felt noisier in the last few weeks: hostile. Laura stared through the open door into the hallway where boxes and boxes of Dad's belongings were piled up, ready to be taken to various charity shops or the rubbish dump. Mum had been ruthlessly efficient about getting rid of nearly everything and Laura had had to force herself not to cling on to each shirt and jacket and sweater. If it had been up to her, they would have kept everything of Dad's, right down to his socks and underpants, which would have remained in the big oak chest of drawers all neatly rolled, just how he liked them. She'd been almost hysterical when she noticed there were only three toothbrushes left in the mug by the washbasin.

'We've all got to be brave,' Mum said firmly.

Laura nodded. She ached with trying to be brave and sometimes she just couldn't. Like the other day when she'd been sitting in double maths and she had suddenly realized that she couldn't remember the sound of Dad's laugh. She knew it had been a brilliant laugh, but she couldn't hear it in her head.

Now her mum put her arm around Laura and she was hit by a wave of Shalimar. 'Come on, buck up.'

Laura tried to smile. She'd got herself in such a state earlier because Mum had been half an hour later than she said she'd be getting back from work. Laura had started to picture terrible things in her head. Her mother walking across the road without looking properly, a lorry not being able to stop – *bam!* Her mother walking past a building site and a piece of loose scaffolding falling from a great height and landing on her head. Laura knew she was being stupid thinking like that and that the odds of something happening weren't high. But then what had been the odds that Dad – a good driver – would wrap his car around a tree? By the time her mother got home, Laura was in a terrible state, just like she had been when Jess had been late home from netball the other night. Just remembering those feelings of sicky panic made Laura start to cry.

Her mother rolled her eyes. 'Don't, Laura. You'll upset your sister.'

Laura looked at Jess, who was sitting at the table quietly getting on with her homework and didn't look the least bit upset. Laura noted, not for the first time, how much better her mother and sister seemed to be at this grief business. Although she did often hear Jess sobbing in the middle of the night when she thought everybody else was asleep. The sound leached through the wall and made Laura wish she and Jess still shared a bedroom because then she would just get out of her bed and creep into Jess' like she used to when she was little (somehow having to open two doors and go into a completely separate room made this seem impossible, so Laura settled for just putting her hand on the wall and hoping that Jess would somehow be able to sense her presence). Even her mother, who normally played the plucky widow to perfection, had her moments. The other day she had lost the locket that Dad had bought her and she'd been inconsolable until it had been found.

'I'm sorry,' Laura said, staring at the saggy, dark green armchair that Dad always used to sit in. She could picture him there now, his head buried in the newspaper or shouting at Manchester United on the telly.

Mum raked her hands through her hair and shook her head. 'It's hard enough trying to cope with everything without you turning something straightforward into an emotional minefield. I was suggesting a takeaway because I've had a long day at work and because I thought it would be a treat for everyone.'

Laura nodded. She had registered the warning shot in the words 'long day at work'. After years of being a stay-at-home mum (though very much not of the cake baking, gingham apron variety) Evie had been forced by Dad's death to go back to work. Given the fact that she'd been out of the workplace for fourteen years and had a rather sketchy employment record before that (she'd been a singer on the working man's club circuit and had a part-time job in a high-end bra shop), Evie had made little fuss about going back to work. In fact, she was often highly entertaining when she talked about her day working in an upmarket department store looking after what she affectionately termed as her 'fat ladies' (rejecting the store's preferred moniker of 'plus size'). However, if she was feeling aggrieved with the girls in any way – and she was frequently aggrieved – she was quick to point out that she was 'killing myself to put a roof over their heads' and that 'a little gratitude wouldn't go amiss'.

'It's a shame people aren't bringing us food now,' Mum said, rifling through the dresser drawer for the takeaway menus.

Laura knew exactly what she meant. In the beginning they had been deluged with lasagnes and roast chicken and cakes.

Like the food could somehow fill the cavernous holes in their hearts. Shamefully, a great deal of that food had ended up going bad and being scraped into the bin because none of them could face eating it (not even Laura, who ate through most crises), or even had the wherewithal to put it in the freezer. And now no one came with casseroles anymore.

'Right,' Mum said, 'what do the two of you want – Chinese or Indian?'

Laura shrugged. She just didn't feel very hungry.

Chapter Twenty

Laura certainly hadn't imagined that she would be spending the morning of Billy's birthday at the hospice but, as she'd watched Billy rip open his presents and tuck into his birthday breakfast of pancakes (having scrupulously removed every single blueberry), she'd known it was exactly what she had to do.

She had waited until Billy was completely absorbed in playing with the Lego ship they had bought him and asked Jon if he'd mind if she popped out for a couple of hours. He looked confused when she said she was going to the hospice. Had she forgotten to collect something of her mother's? She'd said yes because it was a lot easier than trying to explain the real reason.

She walked up to the main entrance, her heart thudding unpleasantly and a feeling of nausea rising. *The last time she'd been here . . .*

She propelled herself through the double doors. The woman on reception recognized her and gave her a confused smile.

'Is Aileen working today?' Laura said, suddenly realizing how epically stupid she'd been to get on two buses and travel nearly an hour without checking that first. Especially on her son's birthday and with a kids party tomorrow, for which there still seemed to be so much to organize.

'She is,' the receptionist said.

'May I have a quick word with her?'

The receptionist said she'd see what she could do.

Laura sat in the waiting area staring at a poster for the Samaritans. When she was at uni she'd thought seriously about volunteering for them. A girl in her year had died by suicide and – although Laura hadn't been close to her – it had just struck her as so awful that someone had felt that alone. When she'd mentioned the idea to her mother, Evie had been appalled. 'You'd be *terrible* as a Samaritan, darling – you know how over-emotional you get.'

The waiting room looked out on a small garden. It was a tiny space but the hospice had gone out of their way to make it pretty and, even though it was only the beginning of February, there were already a few flowers bringing splashes of colour. A woman in a wheelchair with an oxygen tank next to her was sitting out there laughing and chatting with a boy who looked like her teenage son. Despite the fact they were both wearing thick coats and the woman was also cloaked in a blanket, it was really too cold to sit outside. But Laura knew the woman probably didn't have the luxury of waiting until the weather got warmer.

Looking at them made Laura feel sad (or over-emotional, as Evie would have said) so she started scrolling through Facebook. Before she knew it, she was staring at the ad for the job at *Inlustris*. It really did look pretty much like her dream job (once you'd removed ice cream taster from the equation). A proper 'bossing it' type of job; a Jess-type job. Also, unlike *Natter*, *Inlustris* was not teetering on the verge of collapse. Laura would never get the job there though. She'd be punching way above her weight.

'Laura,' Aileen said, appearing in reception. 'Did we forget to give you something of your mum's?'

'No,' Laura said. 'I just wanted a quick word with you.'

'With me?' Aileen said in her soft Irish lilt. She brushed

away a hair that had sprung free from her bun. 'We'll go into the office, sure we will.'

Laura stood up to follow Aileen. She knew just how hard the nurses worked here. How there was always someone who needed their pain meds or to be fed and that the nurses rarely, if ever, took their breaks. She made a mental note that, while she may need to have this conversation, she also ought to make sure she had it quickly.

The office was a small, cluttered room with shelves that were groaning under the weight of folders and big, fat medical books. Aileen smoothed the sleeve of her uniform and looked at Laura expectantly.

'I wanted to thank you for the kindness and care you gave my mum.' Aileen smiled but they both knew Laura hadn't come all the way here to say that. 'And also, the weekend before my mum died you were on duty on the Saturday—' Laura had started to cry now and, although *Good Grief* was fantastically enthusiastic about the healing power of tears, they weren't helping Laura get the words out. Aileen reached across and gently squeezed her arm and eventually Laura managed to gather herself. 'That Saturday when you were on duty, you came into the room just as I was snapping at my mum about refusing to take haloperidol—'

'Laura,' Aileen said, interrupting. 'We don't judge.'

'I judge myself,' Laura said quietly. She bit the inside of her cheek and took a deep breath. 'And the thing I wanted you to know is that I never felt that loved by my mother. She always preferred my sister and I never felt good enough. So that's why—' She interrupted herself. 'No, it's not *why*. I mustn't make excuses for myself. I should have been kinder and more patient. It's not *why*. But it is context.'

Aileen was looking at Laura, her expression gentle. If she was thinking she didn't have time for all this, she was much too kind to show it.

But Laura suddenly knew that Aileen wasn't the person she really wanted to be having this conversation with. And that, unfortunately, that person was someone she would never be able to talk to again.

Chapter Twenty-One

As she stood at the kitchen sink trying to work her way through several days' worth of washing up, Laura kept going over the visit to the hospice in her mind. Why hadn't she tried to have a similar conversation with her mother before she died? Unlike her dad's death, her mother's hadn't come as a shock (well, it had, but she'd still known it was coming). She scrubbed at a greasy pan.

Laura heard Jon coming in from the mystery errand he'd had to run and then a few seconds later heard Billy squealing with delight. She peeled off her rubber gloves and went into the hallway to see Billy raining kisses all over Jon's face and telling him he was the best daddy in the whole world. 'Someone's excited!' she said.

'Daddy got me an extra birthday present!'

Laura smiled. It was nice to see Billy so happy. She really wanted him to have a lovely birthday but, despite her best efforts, it had been a kind of low-energy day and she was finding it hard to drag her mind away from the words she'd voiced earlier: *I never felt that loved by my mother . . . I never felt good enough.*

Plus, when Billy had opened his presents that morning, Laura had seen in his face that he was a bit disappointed not to get the Nintendo Switch he'd been banging on about. And although she knew they just didn't have that kind of money and that anyway it wasn't good for children to get everything they asked for, well, everyone wants to see their kid's eyes light up, don't they?

She bent down and peered into the cardboard box that was sitting on the floor. 'You bought him a hamster?'

'Guinea pig actually,' Jon said.

Laura puffed out her cheeks. 'Without talking to me?'

Jon stared at her, his face a mask of confusion.

Billy's small hands were reaching for the little ginger and white bundle that was cowering in the corner of the cardboard box. 'I love him! I love him!'

'Could you come into the kitchen for a minute?' Laura said to Jon.

Jon continued to look confused. 'Don't take him out of the box yet,' he said to Billy. He followed her into the kitchen. Laura was standing at the sink with her back to him, her shoulders rigid. She turned and walked across the room to shut the door before she started to speak. 'Why did you go out and buy Billy a pet without so much as a word to me about it?'

Jon blew out his cheeks. 'Because it was a surprise and I thought you'd be pleased. I mean, you have to admit today has felt a little flat.'

'Oh, yes my mother's death was very badly timed.'

Jon rolled his eyes. 'That's not what I meant and you know it. Anyway, Billy's been going on about wanting a pet for ages.'

Laura bit the inside of her cheek. 'You could have asked me.'

Jon shook his head. 'I don't see what the big deal is. It's not like I bought him a puppy.'

Laura laughed bitterly. 'Oh, I'm supposed to be grateful for that, am I? You go out and buy a pet that I'll have to take care of without even consulting me but, hey, at least it's not a puppy.'

'You're being completely unreasonable. What taking care of does it need? It's only a guinea pig. You know what? If you're going to be like this, I'll take it back.'

Laura spoke in a low hiss. 'What? Now Billy's seen it? You're going to completely break his heart because of Big Bad Mummy? I don't think so, Jon.' She opened the kitchen door and went back into the hall where Billy was introducing the guinea pig to some of his toys. 'This is Marvin Monkey,' he was saying in a low voice, 'this is Mr Ted and these are some of my dinosaurs. They look scary but they're not really.' Billy's eyes fixed on Laura's. 'He is a beautiful guinea pig, isn't he, Mummy?'

Laura knelt down next to Billy. She nodded.

'I'm going to call him Buzz,' Billy said. Then he shot off towards his bedroom saying he had to get someone else for the guinea pig to meet.

'I really don't think there's much you have to do for them,' Jon said.

Laura looked at him.

Billy came back with a small pile of plastic action figures which he plonked inside the box with the guinea pig. The guinea pig tried to shove itself even further into the corner.

Laura stood up. 'Where is its cage?'

'Oh, I didn't buy one,' Jon said. 'They were stupidly expensive, and I thought it seemed ridiculous when he'll be quite happy to live in his box. I bought lots of hay and food.'

Laura bit the inside of her cheek. 'Isn't a cage quite essential?'

Jon shrugged. 'The guy in the pet shop said it was, but then he would, wouldn't he? I reckon it's baloney. I mean, Buzz doesn't care what his house looks like, does he?'

'No, but surely the box is too small? Also, he can't see out. And it'll rot when he wees in it.'

'Then I'll get him a new cardboard box. He can have a

new one every week if you want. That'll save us the job of cleaning the cage too!'

Laura gave him a look.

'Okay, okay,' Jon said. 'I'll get him a cage.'

'Can I pick him up?' Billy asked.

Jon shook his head. 'Actually, the guy in the pet shop did say it was best not to for twenty-four hours. Buzz is probably a bit scared right now, and he needs a bit of time to get used to his new surroundings.' Billy looked crestfallen. 'Oh, you know what?' Jon said, 'The guy was probably just being precious. I reckon giving him a little cuddle couldn't hurt.'

'No,' Laura said in a low voice. 'No. If the man in the pet shop said we need to give him twenty-four hours, that's what we're going to do. Let's start doing this right.'

Chapter Twenty-Two

Then

Laura hadn't wanted to see the therapist. When her mother had first said that Laura 'wasn't coping well' with her dad's death, it felt like a rebuke. *Jess and I are managing to be brave but you're not.*

Despite this, Laura had grown to really like coming to see Helen. Helen didn't seem to mind what her mother referred to as her 'constant blubbing'. In fact, she always had a huge box of tissues on the pine coffee table that made crying seem not just okay but the 'done thing'.

Today Laura was telling Helen all about her dad redecorating her doll's house for her when she was little. How he painted the rooms in the doll's house exactly the same colours as the rooms in their house and put working lights in it.

Helen listened to everything Laura said as if it was completely fascinating. Laura hadn't thought Helen was very pretty when she'd first met her. She had small, round glasses and pale, limp hair that stuck to her head like clingfilm. But now Laura thought she was rather beautiful, in a quiet sort of a way.

'It seems to me that you have a lot of happy memories of your dad,' Helen said.

Laura nodded. She loved the funny, gentle way that Helen spoke. 'It seems to me' was one of her favourite phrases. She also liked 'I'm wondering if . . .' and 'what I'm hearing is . . .'

Before Laura had come to the first session, she'd been worried she wouldn't have anything to say and that she and the then unknown therapist would just sit and stare at each other in silence for a whole awkward hour. But actually, Laura found the words came tumbling out, often almost tripping over each other in the process. 'Helen is just so easy to talk to,' she'd gushed to her mother one day as they were driving home from an appointment.

'Well, of course, she is,' her mother said, snorting. 'That's what she is paid to do.'

That had made Laura feel a bit silly but she knew what she had been trying to say. She was also pretty sure that Helen liked her, even though her mother would no doubt deride such an idea.

Helen was asking Laura to tell her more about her memories of her dad. Helen wasn't like other people. Other people liked you to talk *less*. They asked you how you were doing but then looked uncomfortable if you said anything other than 'fine'. And they avoided the subject of her dad even though she was often desperate to talk about him. 'Let's talk about something more cheerful,' they'd say. Or, 'Silly me, upsetting you.'

Helen wasn't like that. You didn't have to pretend to be happy around her. Once, during a session, Laura had been crying and talking – she couldn't remember about exactly what now – and Helen had said simply that whatever it was must have been hard for her. And Laura had felt in that moment that she wished Helen was her mother. She felt very guilty about that, of course, and didn't mention it to anyone, Helen included.

Laura had even grown to like the hot, stuffy little room, the tiny high window cranked open just enough to hear the thrub thrub of the traffic outside. Sometimes she imagined a grown-up version of herself in the room, except in that scenario she would be the therapist and she would be the one doing the helping. She'd mentioned the idea to her mum, thinking she'd be pleased, but Evie had made a big tsking sound and said that Laura would make a 'rubbish' therapist because she was so 'over-emotional'. *Anyway,* she'd said, *you had to be really clever to be a therapist.*

Helen was saying something about their hour being up and Laura stood, smoothing out her school skirt and thinking how weird it was that she did so much crying in this room and still she looked forward to coming here every week.

'I just want to have a quick word with your mum,' Helen said, patting down one of the wispy strings of her hair and smiling.

Laura's mum was sitting in the waiting room reading a magazine and looked surprised to be invited into Helen's room.

'I was wondering if family therapy might be something to consider,' Helen said.

Laura's mum's face scrunched. '*Family* therapy?'

'Yes,' Helen said. 'Laura and I have been doing lots of good work but I just wondered if a few sessions with you here as well might prove beneficial. And, if you felt it was appropriate, maybe even your other daughter too?'

'Jess and I are doing fine, thank you.' Laura's mother's hand was already on the door handle.

'It was just a thought,' Helen said.

The next day, Laura's mum told her that she wouldn't be seeing Helen again and that she was better now. Laura wanted to protest, to say she really wanted to keep going and, at the very least, she wanted to be able to go back to say goodbye. But there was something about her mother's tone that made it clear the decision was final.

Chapter Twenty-Three

Laura didn't know whether to be irritated or relieved to see Jess at the door a full hour before Billy's party was due to start, so she settled for a little of both.

She was glad to have another pair of hands. Even though she'd got up at 6.30 that morning, with tidying the flat, coping with Billy's stratospheric levels of excitement and fielding calls from a mother talking about her daughter's gluten intolerance, she wasn't exactly where she wanted to be in terms of preparation. She still hadn't made the sandwiches or filled the party bags and the 'Happy Birthday' banner was looking decidedly wonky. Oh, and she was still in her pyjamas.

'Come in,' she said to Jess, Hannah and Lola. All three of them looked utterly immaculate and were colour-coordinated in a way Laura didn't imagine could be accidental. No doubt StyleMaven would be blogging about the day later. My nephew's fifth birthday party! #PerfectAuntie

'I thought you could probably use a hand,' Jess said.

Laura heard her mother's voice suddenly: *Why can't you be more organized, Laura? It wouldn't hurt to think ahead. It's a child's birthday party, for goodness' sake. How hard can it be?* But Laura knew she was being over sensitive. Jess was just trying to be nice. Also, she *could* do with a hand. Jon had done *nothing* this morning. He hadn't got out of bed until about half an hour ago and he kept saying he'd do it later when she asked him to empty the (overflowing) bin. She couldn't say anything to him though. She knew he thought she was making way too much fuss about this party.

Jess was wearing the necklace again and Laura felt a stab of irritation. It wasn't so much that she wanted it but the fact that it would have been nice to have been asked.

Billy burst into the room. 'It's my paaaaaaaarty!'

Jess laughed and Lola and Hannah surveyed him condescendingly before agreeing, with a slightly pained air, to go and meet his guinea pig.

'Guinea pig?' Jess said to Laura.

Laura just nodded. She didn't want to get into all that now. Didn't want to give Jess any more reason to hate Jon. Laura heard her mother again: *Jess and I both think you're an idiot when it comes to that man*.

'Right,' Jess said, 'give me a job.'

'Umm, you could make the sandwiches? Or fill the party bags?'

'The party bags?' Jess said.

Laura could read the subtext: *You haven't filled the party bags yet? I do mine days in advance*. She bristled. It wasn't her fault that the rainbow slime hadn't arrived until yesterday evening. Well, it was her fault because she was the one who had accidentally ordered flowers in the shape of a mobile phone instead of the slime in the first place, and then only remembered to order the actual slime when she was on her way to the hospice yesterday morning (thank God for same day delivery). But she'd had a lot to do. One of the other mums from school had said she thought Laura was very brave having a birthday party three days after her mother's funeral. Laura had instantly felt bad. Was it terribly bad form? Was she a failure at grief? A poor excuse for an orphan?

'I'll get the girls to fill the party bags while I make the sandwiches,' Jess said. 'Do you want to get yourself ready?'

Laura looked down at her tea-stained pyjamas. Her mother had always nagged her about her lack of attention to her appearance. *I do wish you'd make a bit of an effort. It takes five minutes to put on some make-up in the morning. A good haircut can work wonders for a round face.*

Jess was rooting around in the fridge. 'What's going in the sandwiches?'

'Half cheese and half ham.'

'Ham?' Jess said, almost as if Laura had said 'poo'.

'Yes, what's wrong with ham?'

'Nothing,' Jess said. 'Just, you know, processed meat.'

As Laura stood in the shower, she replayed the words in her head: *Just, you know, processed meat.* Jess was so bloody annoying.

Laura squeezed out the shower gel, suddenly realizing that her heart was pounding, and guiltily registering that that she hadn't got around to making herself a doctor's appointment since that incident at the wake. She was pretty sure the doctor would tell her it was nothing to worry about and that she'd just had a funny five minutes and wasn't actually dying. She ought to check though – her parents were living (or rather not living) proof that not everyone made their four score years and ten.

When Laura went back into the kitchen, Hannah and Lola had a party-bag production line going, Jess had made the sandwiches and was cutting up carrot batons and the bin had magically been emptied (not, Laura imagined, by Jon, who was sitting on the sofa sipping a coffee and looking at his phone). Even Billy was calm, colouring in a huge 'It's my birthday!' badge that she assumed Jess must have given him.

Laura took a quick swig of Gaviscon and then went over to adjust the wonky 'Happy Birthday' banner, but it was a two-person job, really. She glanced hopefully at Jon but he was engrossed in whatever he was reading on his phone.

'Need a hand?' Jess said, putting down the carrot she was cutting and taking the other side of the banner.

Laura heard her mother's voice again: *Your sister is always there when you need her.* Subtitle (though not subtle-title): *Unlike you.*

'We really need to pin down a date to clear Mum's flat,' Jess said.

Laura had to stifle the urge to scream. Jess had mentioned this at least once a day since their mother had died. 'Can you just let me get one stressful event out of the way at a time?' Her words came out sounding so curt that Jon even glanced up from his phone. 'We'll do it soon,' Laura said, trying to be conciliatory. Jess was helping her right now, after all. 'I wonder what secrets we'll discover?' she said, attempting to lighten the mood.

Jess stared at her.

'I'm only joking,' Laura said. 'I don't think we're going to discover that Mum had a secret penchant for S&M . . . or needlepoint. Well, she certainly wasn't a needlepoint-type of woman. Everyone has some secrets though, don't they? Well, except you. No secrets in the world of Mrs "I'm very honest in my blog".'

Jess was standing completely still with a strange look on her face.

'Err, I'm just joking around with you,' Laura said.

'Haha,' Jess said mirthlessly, turning her back on Laura and returning to the carrots.

Laura looked at her sister's rigid shoulders. What had rattled her cage?

Laura's mobile rang. A mother who wanted to know if it was okay to pick up her daughter about twenty minutes late? It was just she was planning to go into town. No, Laura felt like screaming. 'Sure.'

'Someone cancelling?' Jess said when Laura hung up.

Laura shook her head. 'Just a mum who might be a few minutes late for pick-up.' No point telling Jess the woman was talking 'twenty minutes or so'. Her sister was bound to take a very dim view of that.

'How many kids are coming?' Jess said.

'Seventeen or so.'

'People are terrible at RSVP-ing, aren't they?'

Was that a dig? You should have chased them? No, she was being over sensitive. 'You've got yourself in such a state about this party,' Jon had said to her last night when she burst into tears because she'd ruined a batch of rice-krispies cakes. 'I'm not in a state,' she'd responded hotly. Someone had to care about it though, didn't they?

Her mind flashed back to one of her birthday parties when she was little. She must have been about six or seven; her dad doing magic tricks. Kids wouldn't accept that now. Professional entertainers were de rigueur. 'How much are you paying for Calvin the Clown?' Jon had said. 'Crazy!'

'Shall Hannah and I get Billy ready?' Lola said to her mum.

Laura had to stifle a giggle. True, it would be a good idea to get the party child out of his rather grubby Spider-Man pyjamas, but she wasn't sure he needed an entourage. She half-expected Lola to produce a professional hair and make-up kit.

'What time does it start?' Jon asked.

'Eleven o'clock,' Laura said tightly. She'd told him this several times.

He glanced at his watch and said that was less than twenty minutes away. The realization didn't make him turn his attentions away from the football blog he was reading though.

The bell rang and Laura opened the door to Calvin the Clown, who managed to look lined and tired under his thick layer of white face paint. 'I'm Calvin,' he said, proffering a hand.

Yeah, Laura thought. The multi-coloured costume, face paint and big red nose told me you weren't the DPD delivery guy. She ushered him in and introduced him to everyone, trying not to notice that none of the kids in the room looked especially charmed.

Calvin started to set up, explaining that he'd start with some limbo to break the ice and then there would be party games and magic before finishing up with balloon animals. How many kids were we expecting?

'Seventeen or so,' Laura said, feeling a huge stab of hostess anxiety. What if none of them turned up?

'What can I do?' Jon said.

Finally!

'I think we're all good,' Jess said.

Laura bristled. She was going to say exactly the same thing herself but she would still have liked to have been the one who said it.

Angus Murray was the first to arrive. Of course he was. You don't get invited to many parties when you routinely thump your classmates. His mother asked if Laura wanted mums to stay or drop off but then disappeared before waiting for an answer.

More kids started to arrive and Laura let out the breath she didn't know she'd been holding.

Calvin started his 'wacky' party games. If there was a more soul-destroying word in the English language than wacky, Laura didn't know of it.

A dad arrived with a child with a 'severe nut allergy'. He handed Laura an epi-pen.

'You're not staying?'

'No, no,' the man said, 'wouldn't want to get in your hair.'

Laura felt like saying she'd much rather he 'got in her hair' than left her to deal with anaphylactic shock.

'Zack will be fine,' the dad said, reading her horrified

expression. 'And, if the worst comes to the worst, the epi-pen is easy to use. Just stab it in his thigh.'

And then he was gone.

'Don't worry, I know how to use an epi-pen,' said the mother of the gluten-intolerant child.

'Me too,' Jess added.

How did Jess know how to use an epi-pen?

Calvin was managing to hold the attention of most of the crowd, although there was one little boy who was so scared of him, he had to be taken out of the room by Hannah and Lola.

'It seems a shame for them to miss the show,' Laura said to Jess.

Jess shrugged, said they wouldn't mind. They really were ridiculously well-behaved. Laura wanted to stuff them both full of sugar just to see if she could make at least one of them put a foot wrong.

'What can I do?' Jon asked again.

'If you could be responsible for the sausage rolls?' Laura suggested.

Jon looked at her quizzically.

'They need heating up.'

'They're fine cold, aren't they?'

'They're nicer hot,' Laura snapped, bustling past him.

'All right, all right,' Jon said, wrestling the baking sheet out of her hands. 'Keep your knickers on.'

A little girl appeared at Laura's side in floods of tears. 'Angus hit me!'

'Oh, sweetheart,' Laura said, stooping down to comfort her. 'What do I do about Angus?' she hissed to Jess.

'Leave it to me,' Jess said.

The doorbell rang and Laura went to open it, trailing the still sniffling little girl in her wake. It was Amy with Josh on her hip. Josh was also crying.

'Sorry we're late,' Amy said. 'Are there lots of Dulwich mums?' Laura and Amy liked to laugh at 'proper' Dulwich mums. Amy swore blind she'd once met a woman with play-date business cards.

'I had one woman on the phone about her daughter's gluten intolerance at 7 a.m.' Laura whispered.

Amy grinned. 'I think Joshy must be teething because he's miserable today. I haven't been able to get a thing done all morning. In fact, if you don't mind, I might just leave him with you for half an hour while I nip to Sainsbury's. Do you need anything?'

'Umm . . . err.'

'I do think it's a bit cheeky leaving her little one with you when you've got a party going on,' Jess said as they were setting out the party food.

'It's no trouble,' Laura said. Even though it was a fair bit of trouble, especially as Josh cried every time she tried to put him down. Right now she was attempting to open a packet of Iced Gems one-handed. 'Anyway, Amy's a single mum – it can't be easy.' Jess made a sceptical face. 'Listen, Amy keeps me sane at work. I'm more than happy to help her out from time to time. And she'd do the same for me.'

'What's that smell?' Jess said. 'I think there's something burning.'

Laura glanced towards the oven and looked in search of Jon, who was nowhere to be seen.

Jess opened the oven and pulled out a tray of burnt sausage rolls. 'Some of them are still okay.'

Laura shook her head. 'Chuck 'em.'

Jess nodded. 'Kids never eat at parties anyway.'

Laura tried to smile even though she felt more like crying. There had already been enough blubbing this morning though, what with Adam crying because he was frightened of the clown, Molly crying because Angus had hit her, and Josh crying because his mouth was sore.

Jon reappeared and Laura told him that the sausage rolls had burnt. He received this information totally impassively as if it wasn't the *one* job he'd been given.

A group of kids had got bored with watching Calvin and were running around hitting each other with balloons.

'I'll deal with it,' Jess said.

She really was useful. Laura hated to admit it, even to herself, but she'd be stuffed without her sister.

The party meal was mayhem. One kid needed more squash, another an URGENT poo. A boy who had a thick glob of snot on his upper lip didn't like Hula Hoops or crisps. Laura tried to be patient as she said maybe he could just have the sandwiches and the cakes, but she was ashamed to admit she just didn't warm to the child – you may only be five, sweetheart, but somehow I just don't like the cut of your jib.

She glanced across at peanut allergy Zack and noted, gratefully, that he seemed to be keeping to food from his own Tupperware.

Josh was getting heavy! Where was Amy? It had been one long half-hour.

Calvin was making balloon animals. Angus Murray wasn't happy with his. It didn't look like a lion.

You should be grateful, Laura thought uncharitably.

Then the guinea pig got loose. 'I was just showing him to Jake,' Billy said, his lower lip wobbling.

Jess managed to catch him (of course she did).

'Thank goodness!' Laura said. She glanced at her watch. Only twenty more minutes to go.

Chapter Twenty-Four

Laura was sponging chocolate off the carpet. At least, she hoped it was chocolate. She felt overwhelmingly exhausted and slightly tearful. 'I'm just going to meet Jimmy for a quick one,' Jon had said. 'We'll clear up when I get back, yeah?' Laura nodded, but inside she'd felt sad. Was she being silly? Jon had said they'd clear up when he got back, hadn't he? And wasn't Laura supposed to be his 'little hippy chick'; the very embodiment of laid-back? What had happened to *that* person?

Jess was scraping half-eaten sandwiches and cakes into the food waste bin. Laura had tried not to notice the look on her face when Jon said he was going to the pub. Fuck her and her perfect life though. What did she know about anything?

Laura rubbed at the carpet, the brown mark seeming to get bigger rather than disappear. The party had gone well. Billy had had a good time, Angus Murray had only hit one person and peanut-allergy Zack hadn't gone into anaphylactic shock. Laura *should* be happy. Well, no, she shouldn't, because she was bereaved – happy about the party though.

Jess started washing up.

'You don't have to do that,' Laura said.

'It's fine. I don't want to leave you to do it on your own.' *And there it was!* 'Don't snipe at Jon.'

'I wasn't sniping at Jon.'

Laura rubbed harder at the carpet. 'Yes, you were.'

Jess sighed. 'I mean, I do think it would have been nice if he could have forsaken the pub for a day.'

'It's none of your business,' Laura said.

Billy ran into the room, clutching his red and yellow balloon monkey and announcing that he and his 'coz-ins' were hungry.

'There are lots of carrot sticks left over,' Jess said.

Billy looked at her like she was insane, grabbed a plate of cakes and darted out of the room before she had a chance to protest.

'I know what you think of Jon,' Laura said.

Jess sighed. 'I don't want to argue with you, Laura.'

Laura stared at the 'Happy Birthday' banner. It still looked wonky. The air was thick with tension. How could her sister possibly begin to understand that when Laura had met Jon, she'd felt totally adrift and that he had saved her? That, yes, the initial attraction had been that they were both a couple of free-spirited hedonists, but it was so much more than that. Jon *saw* her. 'You know nothing about my relationship with Jon,' she said quietly.

Jess sighed heavily. A sigh that signalled she found Laura unbearably tedious.

'Mum told me, you know,' Laura said. 'That the two of you both agreed I was an *idiot* when it comes to Jon.'

Jess looked shocked. 'No. *She* said you were an idiot when it came to Jon and I said aren't we all idiots when it came to love? I was defending you.'

'Well, sort of.'

'Oh, for Christ's sake, Laura, believe what you want to believe.'

Laura scratched at a patch of eczema on her arm. She'd been carrying around this lump of anger for months now, and it was hard to just suddenly let it go, even if what Jess was saying did put a rather different complexion on things. Mind you, that was if her sister was telling the truth. 'It seems a kind of funny thing for you to say. I'm mean it's not as if you're an idiot when it comes to love. Mr and Mrs Perfect live happily ever after.'

'Oh, shut up, Laura. You know nothing about my life.'

Chapter Twenty-Five

Jess was putting her coat on when Laura suddenly blurted, 'I want half of everything.'

'I'm sorry?' Jess said, knotting the belt on her trench coat.

Laura shifted from foot to foot. She hadn't meant to just come out with it like that. It had sounded much better when she'd rehearsed with Billy's teddy bear. It was just, she was already so wound up by the row about Jon. Not to mention having eighteen five-year-olds in her house. 'Mum's will. I know she'll have left everything to you and it's not fair. I want half.'

Jess took a step backwards, almost stumbling on the huge jumble of assorted footwear behind her. The palpable look of hurt on her face made Laura feel a flash of guilt but she pushed the feeling away. As Jon kept reminding her, she was only asking for what was rightfully hers.

Jess spoke very quietly. 'Firstly, we haven't even looked at Mum's will yet. Secondly, *if* she has done anything that isn't scrupulously fair, then I'm pretty hurt you would just assume I'd be fine with that.'

'What? You're saying you'd turn the money down?'

Billy burst into the hallway announcing that his guinea pig had done a wee on Lola's hand. He was almost hopping up and down with the excitement. He ran back to the scene of the crime, still squealing.

Jess looked at Laura and shook her head. 'I would absolutely turn the money down. But thanks for thinking so highly of me.'

Laura's head spun. Jess had this way of making her feel guilty all the time. 'I was just saying—'

Jess cut her off. 'I know exactly what you were saying.' She picked up her designer handbag from where it was sitting next to the radiator, and Laura noted with a slight rush of embarrassment that she'd forgotten to remove the underwear that had been drying on there. All those mums and dads who had walked past and looked at her undies. And they weren't even her good pants; they were the chewing-gum-coloured period pants with the knackered elastic.

'Lola, Hannah,' Jess called out, 'it's time to go.'

The girls appeared in the hallway immediately with Billy trailing behind them. 'Buzz did a wee on you!' he trilled. 'Buzz did a wee on you!'

The girls started putting their shoes on. They really did not behave like normal children. When Laura told Billy it was time to leave anywhere, there was an immediate and full-on tantrum. At the last playdate he went to, he'd hidden upstairs under the bed and Laura had had to drag him out while he kicked her repeatedly in the shins.

'Right,' Jess said. 'Well, bye then.'

She was using her 'deeply wounded' tone that made Laura feel like screaming. 'Thanks for all the help with the party and the clearing up.'

Jess gave her a chilly smile. 'That's what sisters do.'

Chapter Twenty-Six

Laura had only meant MsRealityCheck to ever have one outing. In fact, in the cold and sober light of day after posting her comment about Jess' cashmere article, she'd felt deeply ashamed of herself. Whenever she'd done any online journalism, she'd been shocked by just how vicious people could be below the line, and she'd certainly never imagined becoming 'one of them'. Also, Jess was her sister and, while you don't have to be bessie mates with your sibling, you don't post anonymous comments on their site.

But now Laura was sitting here reading an article that Jess had written on transforming your home on a shoestring budget, and she was just itching to take to the keyboard.

You don't need a lot of money to have a stylish home, Jess wrote.

How would you know?

It's easy to find great homeware on the high street.

But easier still to buy it in designer shops.

I found some of my very favourite pieces in skips!

You've found one 'piece' in a skip ever. And it was a skip in Chelsea! Skips in Chelsea don't count.

Laura's fingers hovered over the keypad. Was she just doing this because Jess had wound her up earlier by being so judgy about Jon? Because even if her sister had been telling the truth about the 'idiot' conversation, it was clear she had a pretty low opinion of Jon (and consequently of Laura, for being with him). She'd made Laura furious by acting all mock-hurt about the will too.

If Laura didn't leave a comment on this article, someone else was bound to. And they probably wouldn't say it nearly so politely as Laura would.

Your home is actually filled with very expensive things, she typed.

No, that was no good; she was supposed to be a stranger. *Judging by the photographs on your site, you've got lots of expensive things in your home. Maybe you should come clean and admit it's a lot easier to have a stylish home when you have money?*

She read it back to herself. Nothing wrong with that. It wasn't unkind in any way. And it would be good for Jess to be a bit more self-aware about how she came across. By helping her to do that, Laura was actually doing a good deed.

Even if she did have to admit to taking a bit of pleasure from how much it would annoy Jess.

Chapter Twenty-Seven

Laura hadn't expected MsRealityCheck to get a reply from Jess and she certainly hadn't expected it less than five minutes later. Typical Jess to be so efficient in responding to her audience (not that she'd replied to the cashmere comment, come to think of it).

Thanks for getting in touch. I am lucky enough to have some more expensive things in my home, but lots of it was bought on a budget. Always lovely to get feedback though. x

Laura almost hurled her phone at the wall. True, the things in Jess' home were bought on a budget – but it was a big budget! And the whole tone of her message was just so passive aggressive, especially the kiss at the end.

Aaargh! Jess was annoying even when Laura was being someone else.

Chapter Twenty-Eight

It wasn't like in the movies. You didn't all trek to a dark-panelled solicitors office and sit around while a man with salt-and-pepper hair looked over the top of his half-moon glasses and slowly read out the will. *To my beloved daughter, I leave my emerald earrings and the sum of . . .*

Instead, Laura and Jess were sitting in Jess' immaculate white kitchen with its huge floor-to-ceiling glass doors to the garden. Laura would have preferred to have been in a dark-panelled office; it would have been more comforting. And she would have liked to have a salt-and-pepper-haired man there to shout and rage at. Someone who could be made to look at the figures again because no way – no way – could your 'inheritance' be £212.42.

'Fuck!' Laura said. As she'd walked up Jess' chichi Clapham road this morning – a road where there were never less than three loft conversions being undertaken at any given time – Laura had repeated a mantra to herself about making sure she got half her mother's assets. Indeed, she'd spent days telling herself exactly that. Jess had acted all outraged at the idea that she'd accept everything, so now would be the time to see if she'd literally put her money where her mouth was. What Laura had never even stopped to consider was that there would be bugger all to leave.

The plumber who had been upstairs fixing Jess' boiler

appeared in the kitchen doorway. 'Do you have a bucket, love?'

Jess opened one of the glossy white cupboards and asked him if he knew yet what was wrong with the boiler.

'No idea!' he said, grinning widely.

Jess pulled out a bucket that looked as if it had never been used before. Laura stared at it. What kind of person owns a pristine bucket?

The plumber took it from her and disappeared up the stairs, whistling tunelessly.

'Are you sure we've worked everything out right?' Laura said.

Jess rubbed her temples and nodded. 'I've checked and double-checked. I've triple-checked. I just had no idea how much interest Mum had clocked up with that equity release scheme. I don't think she realized either, to be honest.' She picked up a J-Cloth and started wiping a practically non-existent smear on the stainless steel fridge. She was *always* cleaning; it drove Laura potty.

The plumber reappeared. Did Jess have a screwdriver? Jess pulled one from a drawer and off he went with it, the whistling fading out like the end of a record.

'It was a bit stupid of Mum,' Laura said.

Jess shrugged. 'It's easy to get talked into these sort of things by some sharp-suited advisor. I guess she started off just needing a bit of cash and she didn't realize what she was getting into. Then, of course, she got sick.'

It was typical of Jess to defend Mum and, of course, it made Laura feel instantly grubby and guilty. She pulled at the skin around her nails. She hated herself for being as disappointed as she was. All her life she'd prided herself on not being greedy or materialistic. Also, what kind of person worries about money when they've just lost their mother? 'I guess we won't be buying that holiday home in the Maldives, then!'

Jess laughed. She didn't look as gutted as Laura felt. But

then it was easy for her not to be gutted. She lived in this house, she drove a shiny red Mini, she always had new clothes (not that she bought most of those – she was constantly being sent freebies. Like she needed more stuff). Laura thought about Jon and how he was always sneering at Jess and Ben behind their backs; saying they were so spoilt and how they had no idea how 'real' people lived. Laura knew what he meant, of course she did, but a part of her wanted to defend them a bit too. Because while she and Jon had spent most of their twenties out of their heads dancing in dark clubs, Jess and Ben had been working their proverbial backsides off. So, yes, sometimes Laura felt like the literal poor relation, but she couldn't in all honesty say it was completely unfair.

There was a sound of whistling getting closer and closer again and the plumber reappeared, asking for an old towel. Good luck with that, Laura thought, they're probably still sitting fluffily in their White Company packaging.

Jess disappeared in search of the towel and Laura was left alone sitting at the island unit, her feet dangling in a way that always made her feel faintly ridiculous. She took a sip of the disgusting green tea that Jess had made her. She knew it was supposed to be very good for you, but frankly if swallowing it was the price of a few more years on this earth, she just wasn't sure it was worth it. She realized she'd completely forgotten to make an appointment with the GP, damn it. Still, the incident at the wake was a while ago, so surely if she was going to drop dead it would have happened by now? No need to suddenly start panicking about her own mortality. She washed the green tea down with a big swig of Gaviscon.

£212.42? She had never thought her mother's death was going to make her a rich woman – although her family might share the Kardashians' ability to be embarrassing, their bank balances were wildly different – but she had thought she was going to get enough to buy a new washing machine.

She couldn't even begin to imagine what Jon was going to say. He'd already spent most of the money in his head. Last night he was saying he might get a new laptop so he could write his novel anywhere. (Laura had resisted the urge to say that Jon would still have to be disciplined enough to sit at his computer, whether that was at the kitchen table or in a coffee shop.)

Jess came back rolling her eyes and muttering about how you'd think a plumber might come a bit better prepared and they were paying him enough for goodness' sake. Still, she supposed she ought to be grateful she'd managed to get anyone out; February was peak season for plumbers. Her neighbours were having a hell of a job trying to find someone to install their new wet room.

'I'd better go,' Laura said. Today was the last day of her paid compassionate leave from work (compassion, like everything else, had a time limit, especially when there were 'Shock Confessions' to be extracted from people) and, although she had planned to have the rest of this week off unpaid, the unveiling of her 'inheritance' had made her think that wasn't such a good idea. She decided she'd call her editor and ask her if she could start back tomorrow – she was pretty sure Dani would be keen as her messages of 'sympathy' had still managed to make it clear they were swamped.

Laura stood up and put on her coat. It would do her good to get back to work. And what had she really been planning to do with the rest of this week anyway? She may have talked about things like getting the flat straight and going to art galleries but she'd probably have ended up just sitting about feeling sorry for herself. Well, that and watching back to back episodes of *Queer Eye*. She couldn't imagine Jess ever watching TV in the daytime. And, even when she did watch TV, it was probably things like *Newsnight* and *Question Time*.

Yes, it would be good to get back to work – weird, but good.

Chapter Twenty-Nine

Laura would have loved to have had an invisibility cloak to get to her desk unnoticed. It wasn't so much being back at work she'd been dreading but other people's reactions to her – the orphan – being there. How was the normal office small talk going to go when 'how are you' and 'what have you been up to' felt like desperately loaded questions?

She stood waiting for the lift and trying to breathe. It would be fine. She would soon be talking about story leads and cutting copy. It would be good to get back to normal (whatever the hell normal was).

There were only twelve people on the *Natter* team but they shared the floor with several other titles and as Laura walked in, it felt like all eyes were on her. She tried to keep her gaze focussed on Amy, who was giving her an encouraging smile from the sidelines.

Karen the deputy editor and Natasha the beauty editor came and hugged her. Several others said they were so sorry for her loss. Greta, one of the designers, teared up as she offered to make Laura a coffee. She was going to put oat milk in it because the *last* thing Laura needed right now was dairy.

Laura sat at her desk, her legs trembling.

'Laura,' Dani, her editor, said, sitting down on her desk and tilting her head to the side. 'I'm so sorry about your mum.

106

Are you okay? We don't want you to feel you need to come back before you have to.'

Laura told her she was fine and was looking forward to getting back into a routine.

'Good, good,' Dani said. She'd see her in the editorial meeting in half an hour.

Laura's stomach plummeted. Was she really up to the editorial meeting? To pitching ideas for stories only to have Dani shrug them away. She'd have to be. Anyway, she had some good ideas. She'd spent her commute frantically searching news sites and socials and she was confident Dani was going to love the botched plastic surgery idea.

She decided she needed a glass of water and headed towards the kitchen. Oli from Design was approaching from the other direction, but he suddenly turned and doubled back towards the break-out area. Maybe he'd forgotten something.

Back at her desk Laura couldn't help noticing the atmosphere was very subdued. There was almost always music playing in the design department but there was nothing today. Also, there was no banter flying around about what people had been up to the night before. She hoped the maudlin mood wasn't because of her. *Come on guys*, she wanted to shout. *I can hear 'Dancing in the Moonlight' without bursting into tears (well, at least not because of grief). A few jokes about how bad your hangovers are won't tip me over the edge.*

A stream of people came to talk to Laura and she had variations of the same conversation with them all. *Yes, cancer. Yes, it always does come as a shock even if you're expecting it. Yes, it did feel a bit weird to be back at work but it would probably do her good* (she also very much needed the money; a small detail the likes of which her sister and some of the other mums from school seemed to overlook when they told her it was 'too soon').

After a while, although Laura very much appreciated people

making the effort, she was finding it all pretty exhausting and starting to wish everyone would just ignore her. *Good Grief* had warned her that going back to work could be very tiring and said she might struggle to complete simple tasks, but she was sure even a fairly tricky journalistic endeavour would be more straightforward than navigating the choppy waters of trying to make her co-workers feel okay about her loss. When Gareth had told James he'd seen his mum last night, he'd glanced over at Laura looking utterly mortified, as if the shocking revelation that other people still had mothers would be too much for her to bear.

Amy appeared at Laura's desk and said it was time for editorial. They headed towards the Bunch of Grapes (all the meeting rooms had been named after local pubs, something Laura had always found extremely strange).

As they were walking towards the meeting room, they went past a clump of people who were laughing, but the second they saw Laura they stopped. *It's okay to laugh around me*, Laura wanted to shout. Hell, she wouldn't have even have minded someone making her laugh.

Oli was walking towards them, but when he saw Laura and Amy, he immediately turned and went off in the other direction. Which is when it suddenly dawned on Laura that he hadn't forgotten something earlier when he was on his way to the kitchen, he was just trying to avoid her. Not that she could blame him exactly – given the choice, she'd want to avoid her too.

In the meeting room, Chloe the fashion editor adopted her caring face and said that although she was Laura's colleague, she was also her friend and she was there for her. Laura mumbled her thanks. 'I lost my grandmother a few years ago,' Chloe said. 'So I know just how you're feeling.'

Laura loathed people telling her they knew just how she was feeling – she didn't even really know how she was bloody feeling – and she also bristled a bit about the loss of Chloe's grandmother being likened to the loss of her mum. Which was a bit shitty of her if she was honest because firstly, she and her mum had had what one might generously describe as a complicated relationship, and secondly, grief one-upmanship was a huge bore.

'Right, folks,' Dani said as she sat, 'what have you got for me today? Laura, shall we start with you?'

'I've got a "When plastic surgery goes horribly wrong" story,' Laura said.

Dani leaned forward in her chair and put her mobile down. 'Go on.'

'This woman had lip fillers but it was a botched job—'

Dani interrupted her. 'What? A trout pout? Nah.'

'No,' Laura said. 'Not just a trout pout. This woman had no pulse in her top lip. She almost lost it altogether.'

Dani shrugged. It's pretty difficult for your heart to bleed when you don't have a heart in the first place. 'What else have you got?'

Amy gave Laura a sympathetic look across the table.

'Umm,' Laura though her mind going blank. 'A woman who ended up in a wheelchair after getting bitten by a tic.'

'Great!' Dani said. 'Love it, love it, love it!' She turned to Amy. 'Now what fabulous home and garden ideas have you got for me, Amy?' Amy was just about to start speaking when Dani cut in. 'Oh wait, Laura, I forgot to say, when you were away Lisa had a nice idea for a box-out on the agony page. A sort of issue-of-the-week-type affair.'

So, during the three weeks Laura had been away, Lisa had come up with an idea for *Laura's* page and managed to get the go ahead on it. Was she after her job? 'I'm not too sure about a box-out – it would take up quite a lot of space on the page. I'd only have room to answer two problems or two problems and a problem-ette.'

'I'm sure you'll make it work,' Dani said, closing down the conversation. 'Lisa will write the box-out copy.'

She was definitely after Laura's job.

'But I need your eye on it,' Dani said.

Laura had a sudden image of a disembodied eye tapping away at a computer. 'Great.'

'Oh, and could you help that annoying intern girl with the piece she's supposed to be pulling together on incontinence. Marketing are all over me because they've sold lots of pages to some range of incontinence pads.'

'Yup,' Laura said, wondering what on earth had happened to HR's promise to ease her back in.

Chapter Thirty

On Friday evening, Laura met Jon and Billy in town after she'd finished work. The two of them had been in the Lego store spending the birthday money that Jon's parents had sent Billy and they were both very eager to tell Laura all about it.

'We got the Green Ninja Dragon, Mummy,' Billy said, jumping up and down on the spot. 'And he is so cool!'

'Snapping jaws *and* a swishing tail,' Jon said. He looked almost as excited as Billy did and Laura's heart swelled. Jon may not have planned to become a dad but he adored Billy utterly and completely.

Suddenly a man in a bright orange shirt flicked on a boom box, Bruno Mars' 'Marry Me' started and he and several other people from the 'crowd' broke into a dance routine.

Billy, who'd already been pretty excited to have spent the afternoon in the Lego store and be in the middle of the bright lights of Piccadilly Circus when it was nearing his bedtime, was wide-eyed. 'Look!' he exclaimed as yet another 'onlooker' joined in.

Even though Laura had only been back at *Natter* for three days, it felt like much longer and she was weary to her bones. Despite this, it was Jon and not her who seemed to be very keen to drag Billy away from watching the ever-increasing troupe of dancers. 'C'mon,' he said, 'if we jump on the tube now, we'll have time to build the dragon and read a story before bed.'

Billy stayed rooted to the spot.

'Let him watch,' Laura said, yawning.

Jon rolled his eyes.

At that moment, a man wearing a suit dropped to one knee in front of his girlfriend and produced a small box from his pocket. The crowd erupted.

'Oh, God!' Jon said.

'What's happening?' Billy asked.

Laura couldn't take her eyes off the woman who had tears running down her cheeks and didn't seem to be able to speak but was nodding so hard it looked as if her head might fall off.

More cheering from the crowd.

One of the dancers handed the couple two glasses of champagne.

'They're having a drink, Mummy!'

Laura nodded, blinking back the tears that had appeared in her own eyes. She didn't want to have to explain those tears to Billy (she didn't want to explain them to Jon, either). She told herself she was just tired from work.

'Bloody ridiculous!' Jon said. 'What if she'd wanted to say no?'

Laura swallowed a surge of irritation. 'She didn't want to say no.'

'Yeah, but what if she had? She'd have felt like a right cow when he'd gone to all that fuss. Horrible. A proposal should be a private thing.'

Or a non-existent thing. Wait, why was she thinking like this? She'd had a huge row with her mother once when Evie had suggested that Laura had only really become anti-marriage when she'd found out Jon was.

The dancers had now gone into a new routine to 'She Said Yes'.

'I hope he had a back-up in case she said no,' Jon said.

Laura scowled at him.

'Oh, by the way,' he said, scratching the back of his head. 'I quit the restaurant.'

Laura must have misheard. It was very loud what with all the music and the whooping. 'What?'

'I QUIT THE RESTAURANT.'

She hadn't misheard. She shook her head. 'You walked out on your job?'

'Can I do dancing with them, Mummy?'

'Umm, not really, sweetheart.'

Billy's small brow furrowed. 'Everyone else is.'

'Maybe just have a little dance right here.' Laura turned back to Jon. 'So?'

'What's the big deal? You know I've been fed up there for ages and that Greg is the world's worst boss. We had a row and I told him to stick his job. It felt good.'

The newly engaged couple were locked in an embrace in the middle of the dance troupe. They were swaying gently from side to side as they gazed into each other's eyes.

Laura's brain was struggling to process. *It felt good.* Being able to pay the rent felt good. Having money to buy food felt good. 'You didn't think to ask me first?'

Jon looked genuinely confused. 'No. I knew you'd be supportive. Why would you want me to stay there and be treated like shit?'

Laura thought about Jess telling her she let Jon get away with murder.

'Plus, now I can really concentrate on my novel.'

Yeah, great! Maybe you'll get to four whole pages.

The couple kissed and the crowd started clapping and cheering.

'Everyone is very happy, Mummy!'

Laura tried to smile.

Chapter Thirty-One

Then

Laura hadn't really liked any of her mum's boyfriends, but Mickey was definitely the worst. Come back creepy bank manager or bad-breathed maths teacher, all is forgiven. Mickey just made himself so at home when he was over and he thought nothing of telling Laura what to do. Plus, there were all his jokes that weren't really jokes. Laura was a 'lazy little madam' for not washing up her mug straight away. Was that a skirt or a pelmet? And then tonight as Laura was clearing the plates away after supper: Wasn't it a shame she hadn't inherited her mother's looks?

Laura stared at him, sitting there in her dad's chair at the table, a horrible grin pasted to his face and she felt a flash of pure hatred.

'Oh, come on,' Mickey said. 'It was only a joke. Don't have a sense of humour failure on me.'

Laura said nothing and took the plates into the kitchen. It hadn't been a joke. Well, it certainly hadn't been funny. She could feel tears pricking the back of her eyes. She had thought she was looking a bit better recently. She'd lost a bit of weight (for all her mother's apparent diplomacy with her 'fat ladies' at work, she was very quick to point out if Laura put on so much as a pound), she'd had a better haircut. At Auntie Jen's wedding lots of people had complimented her and she'd thought her mum would be pleased. After all, she was the one who had spent years telling Laura to stop eating so much, do something with that hair and make an effort. But Mum was in a funny mood that day. She kept looking as if she'd just eaten something bitter. And she'd really snapped at Mickey when he said she should stop being a 'lazy daisy and come and dance'. Of course, Mickey responded with a snipe at Laura. Something about closing her mouth before she caught flies.

Evie came into the kitchen. 'Don't be so over sensitive all the time, Laura. Mickey was only teasing.'

'Teasing?' Laura said incredulously. 'He's horrible to me.' What she wanted more than anything was her mum to take her side. But, of course, Mickey was charm itself to Evie. Constantly telling her she was beautiful, turning up with armfuls of flowers, chocolate, perfume, promises of trips to far-flung places. And if there was one thing Laura had learned since her dad had died, it was that her mother could not survive without male attention. It would be like asking a flower to grow in the dark.

'It was a joke,' her mother said, rolling her eyes. 'J-O-K-E.'

'It wasn't a joke,' Laura said, her voice going up an octave.

Evie shut the kitchen door and told Laura to keep her voice down, that Mickey would hear her.

'I don't care if he hears me!' Laura was shocked at herself, actually. She never spoke to her mother like this. She was so jealous of Jess being away at university. Roll on next year when she could get away too (well, if she got the grades, which as her mum constantly reminded her was anything but a given).

Evie's eyes narrowed. 'You know what I think? I reckon you're jealous and you're just trying to ruin this for me.'

Laura scraped congealed scraps of roast beef and potato into the bin, feeling faintly nauseous. It seemed like a long time ago since she'd been cooking this dinner, and she didn't know how to get back to the safe waters of her mother's good books. 'I'm not trying to ruin anything.'

The sound of chirrupy sitcom music came from the living room. Mickey had put on the TV and Laura could picture him in her dad's big, dark green armchair, a glass of wine in his hand and not a care in the world.

Evie had started to cry now. 'I just feel like you don't want me to be happy.'

Laura felt hot with shame. She went over and put her arms around her mother. 'Oh, Mum, you know that's not true.'

'Do I?'

Laura hugged her mother's rigid body tighter. 'I'm sorry. I'm sorry.'

Chapter Thirty-Two

As they walked through the heavy wooden doors to the day spa, Laura and Jess were bickering about when they should sort through their mother's things.

'Next weekend doesn't suit me,' Laura said. She hated the way Jess always expected to just snap her fingers and watch everyone else fall into line. And she was wearing the necklace again.

'Good morning and welcome to the Sabai Day Spa,' the receptionist said, smiling. 'An oasis of calm and tranquillity far from the stresses of everyday life.'

Today had been Jess' idea. In fact, it was her treat. She'd just got a big new paid partnership apparently. Laura had resisted at first, said she couldn't possibly accept, but Jess had kept on about it, saying that they'd both had a rough few weeks and that they could do with some pampering. Anyway, she said, when was the last time they'd done something together, just the two of them?

Now Laura was remembering why they didn't see each other more often.

The relaxation area was stunning. All dark wood, orchids and low lighting. And whoever had been responsible for the sound-proofing ought to get a medal – it was impossible to believe you were seconds away from the hubbub of Oxford Street (and less than ten minutes from where she, Billy and Jon had watched the flash mob last night).

Jess picked up a glossy magazine (no copies of *Natter* here) and started flicking through it. 'So when would suit you to go through Mum's stuff?'

Laura lay back on the recliner with her eyes closed. 'I don't know. Soon.' She knew it would annoy Jess to not be given a definite date but too bad. But then she opened her eyes, looked around her and felt a sudden stab of guilt – it was nice of Jess to do this. 'I'll look at my diary when I get home.'

Jess nodded. 'By the way, I'm reading this book on grief that I'm finding really helpful.'

Laura knew it was going to be *Good Grief*. That the box-ticking approach that irritated her would hold great appeal for her sister.

'It's called *Good Grief*.'

Laura willed herself not to say that she was also reading the book but often had to fight the urge to send it twirling across the room.

'I'd really recommend it,' Jess said.

A softly spoken woman approached and asked them if she could fetch them some ginger tea.

Enjoy the day, Laura told herself. Make an effort with Jess.

The two of them sipped their tea and chatted. Laura asked Jess more about the paid partnership, tried to push away any negative feelings. It was crazy to feel jealous of your big sister when you were thirty-seven. And anyway, maybe she and Jess would be like the tortoise and the hare – although with a hare like Jess, you'd have to be one hell of a tortoise.

They decided to have a swim. As Jess shrugged off the big, fluffy white robe, the necklace glinted at Laura.

'Didn't Dad give Mum that necklace?'

'I think so. Pretty, isn't it?'

Too pretty for me, Laura thought bitterly. Stop it, she told herself. She watched Jess lower herself into the pool. Her body was lithe and gym-toned and Laura suddenly didn't want to take off her robe.

'Come on,' Jess said from the pool. 'The water's lovely.'

Laura got into the pool as quickly as she could. She felt like a big, wobbly elephant. Sometimes it was hard to believe that she and Jess were sisters.

Jess was doing a front crawl, her strokes long and effortless. After their swim they went to the steam room.

'I still miss Dad,' Laura said.

'Me too.'

'Hmm.'

Jess' head swivelled around. 'What does "hmm" mean?'

'It's just I was such a daddy's girl.' Laura knew she shouldn't really say this. But she had been a daddy's girl. And Jess couldn't have Mum *and* Dad; it wasn't fair.

'I did quite like Dad too, you know.'

Laura felt cheap and nasty suddenly. 'I know.'

Back in the relaxation area, Laura flicked through a copy of *Inlustris*. She wondered vaguely if the heath and wellbeing editor role had been filled yet. Almost certainly. In fact, it had probably already been promised to an internal candidate before they put out the job ad. (Don't worry, darling, the job is *yours*. We've just got to be seen to be doing the right thing.)

Laura closed her eyes and rubbed the bridge of her nose. Whatever was the matter with her today? She did things like come to a spa once in a blue moon – she should be making the most of it. And she should be nicer to Jess. Even if that necklace did keep glinting at her. 'That woman on that lounger over there hasn't moved the whole time we've been in here. Do you think she's dead?'

'Probably,' Jess said, giggling. 'How's being back at work?'

'Exhausting – and it's only been three days. I'm already kind of swamped, work-wise. Also, other people can be so wearing. They keep treating me like I'm made of glass. And there's this one guy who just avoids me completely. Yesterday I saw him on the tube platform and I thought he might actually throw himself under the train just to get away from me!'

Jess smiled. 'I know what you mean. There's this mum with a daughter in Hannah's class who noticed me behind her in the queue in Sainsbury's and just left the shop. Goodness knows what they had for supper that night!'

'Weird,' Laura said. She gestured towards the immobile woman on the lounger. 'Seriously, she is *very* still.'

Jess laughed. 'How's Jon?'

'Fine. Good. He's given up his job at the restaurant, actually.' Why oh why had she volunteered this? She knew all too well what Jess thought of Jon, so it was crazy to feed her more ammunition.

'Oh. And how do you feel about that?'

'I mean now I'm an heiress . . .' Perhaps she could joke her way out of this?

Jess didn't laugh. 'It puts even more pressure on you.'

Laura shrugged. 'When he's a best-selling novelist, I'll be a kept woman.' She wished she believed either part of that statement.

'You could tell him it's not okay,' Jess said. 'That he has to get another job.'

'You sound like Mum.'

Jess puffed out her cheeks. 'She wasn't wrong about everything, Laura.'

'She hated Jon.' She waited for Jess to say: well, I don't. But Jess said nothing.

'Look, not everyone wants a husband like yours,' Laura continued.

'A husband like mine?' Jess snapped. 'What, a man who doesn't ride a sodding scooter around London? A man with a job?' Her voice had risen over the sound of the panpipe music and women from surrounding loungers were peeking over the top of their magazines or opening one eye. Even Dead Lady stirred.

120

'I like that Jon rides a scooter.' She couldn't say she liked him not having a job.

Jess sighed and snapped her magazine shut. 'I'm getting in the jacuzzi.'

Laura lay back on the bed, seething. She was fed up to the back teeth with being judged all the time. Wasn't the whole point of family that they were supposed to love you unconditionally?

She got up and stomped over to the jacuzzi. 'Jon is a good dad.'

Jess snorted.

'What does that mean?'

'Nothing.'

'No, go on,' Laura said, climbing into the water. 'If you've got something to say, spit it out.'

Jess stayed maddeningly quiet and closed her eyes as if to shut Laura out.

'Jon adores Billy,' Laura said.

Jess opened her eyes, sighing. 'I'm sure he does. But it's not enough.'

'What do you mean, "not enough"? It's everything. Just because we don't have an Instagram-perfect home like StyleMaven—'

'You don't need to snipe at me.'

Was Laura sniping? She supposed she was. Well, too bad. If Jess could dish it out she could bloody well take it too.

'Anyway, it's not about having a perfect home. It's about Jon changing now he's a parent.'

'Maybe I don't want him to change?'

'What, you don't want him to stop getting pissed every night? You don't want him to bring in some money?'

'Money isn't everything,' Laura spat. 'I've told you before, you know nothing about my relationship with Jon.'

A tiny, barefooted member of staff came over and asked

them if they would mind keeping their voices down. This was a relaxation area, she said, smiling.

'I'm so embarrassed!' Jess hissed at Laura as the woman walked away.

'Course you are,' Laura said. 'You're all about what other people think.' It was a cheap shot, particularly since she was also embarrassed that the pair of them had been told off like two naughty schoolgirls.

They fell into a tense silence. Laura was too hot and would have liked to have got out of the jacuzzi but she didn't want to give Jess a close up of her cellulite so she stayed in the bubbling water, feeling sweaty and cross.

By lunchtime, they were talking to each other again but only in a 'isn't this miso-salmon delicious' sense. And Laura couldn't stop looking at the necklace.

'I wasn't trying to upset you earlier,' Jess suddenly said. 'About Jon.'

Laura took a sip of cucumber water. Jess had this way of apologizing without really apologizing. She'd been the same when they were kids. Sorry *if* it upset you that I got you into trouble with Mum. Sorry *if* you didn't like me borrowing your new shoes without asking. Sorry *if* it's annoying that every single teacher asks you if you're Jess' little sister. 'Let's not talk about it.'

'I just want the best for you.'

Laura smiled tightly. Jon was what was best for her. And Billy. Okay, Jon wasn't perfect, but who was? (Jess – perfect bloody Jess.)

When Jess went off to her massage, Laura lay back on the recliner and tried to relax.

The Sunday before the funeral, she had got up early to go to buy suits for Jon and Billy. Both of them had been asleep when she left. When she got home, Billy's thumb was bandaged. When she had asked Billy what had happened, he said he'd been trying to get himself some breakfast because Daddy was still sleeping, but he'd cut his finger trying to slice the bread. And Laura hadn't said anything to Jon but inside she'd been furious. Because she knew Jon loved his son in a 'I'd stand in front of a moving train' type of way, but she just wished he loved him in a 'get up before 10 a.m.' sort of way.

A soft-voiced woman approached and asked if she'd like more ginger tea. She shook her head. She was sick of bloody ginger tea.

Perhaps Jess was right about Jon?

Laura shook her head and sighed. No, of course Jess wasn't right.

By the time Laura went for her massage, her mind was doing somersaults. In all fairness to Jon, it was her that had changed. He was just how he'd been when she met him ten years ago. Back then, she'd loved that he was such a free spirit. She still loved that. Didn't she?

'There's a lot of tension in your neck and shoulders,' the masseuse said.

Laura sighed. Tried to calm her mind. She really should be enjoying today. A place like this might be a normal part of Jess' life but it certainly wasn't a normal part of hers.

The masseuse had asked her which oil she preferred and she'd chosen rose but now the cloying sickliness was making her feel faintly nauseous.

As Laura and Jess got changed back into their clothes, Laura thanked Jess for bringing her and said it had been a very relaxing day. And then, before she could stop herself, she asked Jess when Mum had given her the necklace.

Jess' hands fluttered to her throat. 'When she was in the hospice. Why?'

'Nothing.'

'Why?'

123

'I just wondered.'

'Wondered what, Laura? Were you just checking I didn't take it off Mum's dead body before you got to the hospice?'

The woman who was putting her make-up on a few feet away looked as if her eyes were about to pop out of her head.

'Don't be ridiculous!' Laura hissed.

Jess brushed her hair in the mirror. 'Mum gave it to me.'

'Well, of course she did.'

Jess sighed, took off the necklace and threw it at Laura. 'Here, take the bloody thing.'

'You're being a baby!'

'I'M BEING A BABY?' Jess yelled. *'I'M* BEING A BABY?'

The whole changing room was openly staring at the pair of them now. Hair straighteners and mascara wands had been put down and heads had swivelled to watch the show. But Laura couldn't have cared less. She was suddenly boiling with rage. This was just what she hated about her sister: the total, utter conviction that she was right all the time. The insufferable smugness! 'DIDN'T YOU THINK IT MIGHT HAVE BEEN NICE TO AT LEAST ASK ME IF I'D HAVE LIKED IT?'

Jess pointed at the floor. 'I'VE GIVEN YOU THE BLOODY NECKLACE, HAVEN'T I? WHAT MORE DO YOU WANT?'

'I'LL TELL Y—' But Laura was interrupted by the arrival of a grave-faced woman in uniform.

'Ladies,' she said in a voice so soft you almost had to lean forward to hear her. 'The Sabai Spa is a place for rest and relaxation. It's a place of calm and tranquillity—'

'Tell *her* that,' Laura said, gesturing towards Jess.

'You started this,' Jess said.

The soft-voiced lady looked them up and down. 'I think I'm going to have to ask you both to leave.'

Chapter Thirty-Three

Laura had absolutely, definitely vowed to never bring out MsRealityCheck again. But that was before her sister humiliated her in front of all those people and got them chucked out of the Sabai Day Spa. All Laura had done was ask her when Mum had given her the necklace. Jess absolutely did NOT have to make a huge scene over it. And in front of all those people too.

Laura sat on the bus, fizzing with irritation. Jess was so bloody sure she was right all the time and God help anyone who questioned her. Once, when they were kids, she'd thrown a giant hissy fit because Mum had accused her of eating all the nice chocolates from the Milk Tray box and Jess had flipped out. And, okay, that time it *had* been Laura who had devoured the hazelnut clusters and praline crisps, but did Jess have to get in such a fit about just being asked? Like she was so used to being Mum's treasured favourite that she couldn't bear that anyone might think she'd done something wrong.

Laura typed 'StyleMaven' into her phone. MsRealityCheck was going to leave a comment on one of Jess' articles that would really get to her. It didn't matter what article it was.

She scrolled through the posts. *The Rules of Shopping the Sales.*

The rules? For goodness' sake!

Hats Off: How to Rock a Beanie. How To Fall In Love With Yourself This February.

The other thing that had really tipped Laura over the edge this evening (as if being screamed at in public when you were just wearing your bra and pants wasn't bad enough) was Jess' remark outside the spa. 'Well, that was money well spent!'

How dare she try to make Laura feel guilty? First of all, Laura had repeatedly turned down the offer to go but Jess had talked her into it, and secondly it was her who went for the jugular just because Laura had asked her a perfectly polite question about the necklace (which was the reaction of someone who felt guilty, now Laura came to think of it).

She heard Jess' voice in her head: *Well, that was money well spent!*

Well, right back atcha with the snide little comments, Laura thought, immediately starting to type as MsRealityCheck.

But then, midway through a sentence, she suddenly stopped. *Was this who she was now?*

She deleted what she'd written. She may be furious with her sister but that did not mean that trolling her was okay.

Chapter Thirty-Four

Laura was wrestling to get the bag out of the bin; far too much rubbish had been wedged into it, flattened down by lazy palms. Jon's lazy palms. He never emptied the bin. She didn't ask much, for Christ's sake. The least he could do was take out the rubbish.

She finally pulled the bin bag loose but the force made it split all the way down the side and ooze its contents all over the kitchen floor. She felt tears of frustration spring to her eyes.

She'd been feeling snappy and irritable all day. When a man on the train that morning had said a loud 'ah-tishoo' every time he sneezed, she'd wanted to punch him.

Then she'd got to work and found that Dani needed her to magic up a couple of extra pages out of thin air because the sales team hadn't sold all their pages. Oh, and she 'wasn't really feeling' the pics for the 'Cancer gave me the love of my life' story. Also, could Laura look after the socials that week? It had been her turn when she'd been on compassionate leave but of course she'd missed it. And there were so many things that Laura wanted to say, like how could she possibly fit in ONE MORE BLOODY THING, and why call it 'compassionate' leave and then make someone feel bad about it. But of course she just said yes.

Laura picked the remnants of fish fingers and baked beans off the kitchen floor. She'd told Jon a million times that they were supposed to use the food waste bin for food. Just like she'd told him to empty the bin, not overfill it.

Gareth from Sales had been loudly exuberant when she'd bumped into him in the canteen. 'Guess what,' he said. 'We're pregnant!'

Laura had pinned a smile to her face. Resisted the urge to say *he* wasn't pregnant. Unless he was a seahorse.

On her way home, she had just missed the train and then, when she finally got on the next one, had to stand the whole way back. She just had to hope the stagey sneezer didn't get on the train because, if he did, she wasn't sure she could be responsible for her actions.

She got a new bin bag out of the cupboard and started stuffing what was left of the old bag into it.

When she got home, she had barely taken off her coat when Jon had said he and Jimmy were going to have a quick pint. As if Billy was a baton in a relay race and it was her turn now. Then Amy messaged and asked if there was any way Laura could have Josh for an hour. Laura wanted to say, 'Again?' but of course she'd said yes instead, because it must be hard being a single mum. Amy was gone for nearly two hours which meant that Laura was late getting Billy ready for bed and he had a meltdown about brushing his teeth.

She scooped an escaped wodge of dirty kitchen roll off the floor. It occurred to her vaguely that it was Valentine's Day tomorrow. Or as Jon described it the 'saddest night of the year, where couples who don't like each other pay a small fortune to ignore each other in restaurants and eat overpriced heart-shaped food.'

Her phone rang and Laura saw it was Jess. Her finger hovered over the green button. It had been nearly a week since their row at the day spa. Goodness, the pair of them had behaved badly. Laura was hot with shame just thinking about the look on the woman's face when she'd asked them to leave. Laura had gone to pick up the phone to call Jess several times to apologize but then not actually done it. She couldn't cope with her sister tonight though.

'Hey,' Jon said, appearing in the kitchen doorway. He was swaying slightly and she could smell the beer coming off him from where she was crouched over the escaped rubbish.

'You didn't empty the bin.'

His face scrunched. 'What? Oh, soz.'

He didn't sound terribly 'soz'. And what kind of a grown man says 'soz' anyway?

'I'm going to go and watch the footie.'

'Can you take this rubbish out first please?' She didn't like her voice, which had gone all prissy and schoolmarmish.

'I'll do it later.'

'No! You always say you'll do it later and you never do.'

Jon was staring at her as if she was nuts.

'We need to talk, Jon.'

Chapter Thirty-Five

Laura wasn't sure how they'd got from arguing about the bin to splitting up in what seemed like about three and half seconds, but somehow, they'd managed it.

They were shut away in the bedroom screaming at each other (thank goodness Billy was a deep sleeper) and now Jon was stuffing things into a suitcase.

Laura knew she should probably say 'Don't go' but somehow the words stayed buried in her chest.

Jon swore as he tried in vain to shut the case.

She should never have tried to talk to him when he was so pissed. Then again, he was nearly always pissed, so when else was she supposed to talk to him?

He was pulling things out of the case now, hurling underpants and socks and T shirts aside. He stomped off into the kitchen and retuned with a couple of black bin bags. They were becoming something of a leitmotif for the evening.

All Laura had intended to say was that it would be a good idea if he got a job, but somehow that had spiralled into an altogether different conversation: *Was she saying he was a bad father? Why didn't she support his writing? Had her bloody sister been putting ideas into her head?*

Low blows had been slung: *Was she behaving this way because of her mother dying? Was she even that sad about her mother dying?*

She responded in kind, or to be more accurate, unkind: *He*

was never going to finish his novel. The idea sounded shit anyway.

Jon stuffed things into the bin bags, which were clearly to be used as his overflow suitcase. He reached for the faded blue T shirt he'd worn when Laura was in labour and she almost threw her arms around him and told him to stay. He'd been fantastic when she was having Billy. Well, not at first when he was in the pub with Jimmy and he missed the sound of his mobile ringing (even though he knew she was over her due date and should have been keeping an eye on it), but when he had finally turned up at the hospital. He'd made her laugh within a few minutes of getting through the door, even though she was cross with him and even though she didn't much feel like laughing at the time. And then, when Jon was handed this bright purple bundle covered in what looked like a layer of goose fat, his face had just shone with this intense and palpable love.

'Where are you going to go?' she said.

'Not that it's any of your fucking business, but I'll probably go to Jimmy's. At least *he*'s not fucking insane.'

'It's not insane to want your partner to earn a living, Jon.'

He shook his head. His face was a mask of confusion and, in many ways, Laura couldn't blame him. It wasn't like he could have seen this coming. Hell, *she* hadn't seen it coming – she'd had no plans to dump him, and yet here she was somehow doing exactly that. What was it they said in *Good Grief* about not making any big changes when you were recently bereaved? Hey ho, it wasn't the first time in her life Laura had ignored a perfectly sensible piece of advice.

Jon picked up his suitcase and his bulging bin bags. 'The woman I fell in love with was a crazy, bohemian creative.'

Laura couldn't help but feel a bit sorry for him, really. Because she *had* changed. When they first met, all those years ago, Laura didn't give a damn about money or mess. If they had an argument then, it was because she wanted to stay out all night dancing again. Once, someone had given them tickets to Glasto at the last minute and Laura had been in their battered old Renault 5 in a matter of minutes, without so much as a change of pants.

He was looking at her with a mixture of confusion and disgust: a man mis-sold a pension. 'What the hell happened to you?'

'I grew up.'

Chapter Thirty-Six

Not only did Laura have to cope with waking up newly single on Valentine's Day, but Billy, to whom she hadn't said a word to about what had happened, was for some reason acting properly furious with her.

At breakfast he wouldn't eat his Cheerios or drink his milk. Laura gave him a signed form to put in his book bag for his teacher and he just scratched his head and scowled at her.

Laura swigged Gaviscon and examined his small, angry face. Jon was rarely up before Billy went to school and it wasn't unprecedented for him to crash at Jimmy's (usually because he was pissed), so Billy should have readily accepted her explanation about why there was no warm lump on Jon's side of the bed: *Daddy stayed at Uncle Jimmy's last night.*

At the school gates, Billy allowed her to kiss him goodbye.

'It'll be me picking you up today.' She hadn't talked to Jon about this last night – well, you don't discuss childcare arrangements in the middle of a row, do you? – so safest to assume she'd pick Billy up, although goodness knows how she'd explain having to leave work early.

Billy's lower lip wobbled. 'I want Daddy!'

The words rang in Laura's head all day long. When she was supposed to be chasing leads, all she could think about was having to sit Billy down and have the proper conversation at some point. (Was she going to have to? Did she mean this? Did Jon?) *Mummy and Daddy are going to live in different houses. We both still love you very much.*

When Greta was asking her if she could cut her copy, Laura was telling herself that lots of kids have divorced parents and grow up fine.

She'd had a row with her mother about Jon once. 'You and Jon aren't going to grow old together, Laura.' *You were right, Mum.*

Billy looked happy enough as his class was led into the playground but as soon as he saw Laura, the smile disappeared from his face. She'd picked up a doughnut for him, a shameless bribe if ever there was one. He ate it in big, greedy mouthfuls, giving himself a sugar beard in the process.

'Can we go to the playground?'

Laura hesitated. She'd told Dani she'd finish up the 'Shock Confessions' at home.

'Daddy always lets me.' He scratched his head.

'Okay, not for too long though. Mummy has got some work to finish up.'

'You're always working.'

Someone has to.

There were some other kids from Billy's school at the playground and he fell in happily with a little gang that had taken control of the climbing frame.

Amy phoned and asked if Laura could possibly have Josh that evening. Don't worry, she said, she hadn't suddenly got a hot Valentine's Day date, it's was just an old uni mate was up in London. Josh would be fast asleep so no trouble. Laura wanted to say no. She had to finish 'Shock Confessions' tonight and last time she'd had Josh when he was supposed to have been fast asleep, he'd actually been very much awake. But then she realized that she might be a single mum herself now. She was tempted to tell Amy that Jon had moved out. She knew that if she did, Amy would bring wine and ice cream and they would talk about men with the same kind of scorn as they did annoying PRs or the Dulwich mums who talked loudly in cafés about how hard it was looking after two homes. But Laura wasn't ready to tell anyone about her and Jon yet. So she just said she was fine to have Josh and then hung up the phone, feeling wretched.

'Hey,' said a woman who Laura thought was called Annie. 'I heard about your mum. I'm so sorry.'

Laura felt tears bubble up in her throat and the woman immediately put her hand over hers. Laura felt like such a fraud. *I'm crying over my failed relationship, not my mum,* she felt like saying. Or was she crying over both? It was difficult to know.

'I lost my dad last year,' the woman said. 'Heart attack. None of us saw it coming. It was awful; brutal.' She started to cry. 'Oh God, I'm so sorry. The last thing you need is me blubbing.'

Laura squeezed her arm, told her it was fine and that she was sorry about her dad.

'When's Daddy home?' Billy said at teatime.

Laura felt her breath catch in her throat. 'You'll see Daddy soon.'

Billy ate his sausages but not his mash because it had touched his carrots.

'I thought you liked carrots.'

'Not these carrots.' He scratched his head.

'Is your head itchy?'

'Yes.'

Oh God, not today!

She got up from the table to scrutinize Billy's blond curls for the creatures she didn't want to find there. He wriggled away from her.

'I have to see Buzz.'

'Can Mummy just check your hair first?'

'I don't have nits!'

'Let's just have a quick check.'

'No.'

Laura's phone rang and she saw it was Jon. She took a deep breath. 'Hello.'

'I called to speak to Billy.'

'Oh.'

There was a long pause.

'I told him you were staying at Jimmy's.'

'I am staying at Jimmy's.'

Laura felt a wave of nausea. This time yesterday, they were still a family. 'Will you be able to pick Billy up from school the rest of this week?'

'Yup.'

'And look after him until I get home from work?'

'Yup.'

'We'll have to discuss plans long-term . . .'

Jon made a kind of snorting sound. 'Can I just speak to my son?'

Was this how they were going to be now? She walked into Billy's bedroom and handed him the phone, saying it was Daddy. As she walked away, she stepped on a Lego brick.

She stood outside the room rubbing her foot and listening to Billy's side of the conversation. She wondered what Jon would say to him. She knew he wouldn't say anything to upset Billy but she wished she had a better idea of exactly how he would explain a second night staying at Jimmy's because, while one night crashing there wasn't unusual, two was, and any more than that, well, Laura didn't know what they'd say about that. Her head spun.

'Bye, Daddy. I love you.'

Laura walked back into the room. Billy was crouched down next to the guinea pig's cage.

'How's Buzz?'

'He misses Daddy.'

She blinked away the tears. 'Right, let's check your head.'

'No!' Billy said, squirming away. 'I haven't got nits!'

'Billy,' she said. She guided him into a sitting position on the floor and started searching through his curls.

Maybe that was just a speck of fluff or something?

No, he had nits.

'Billy—'

Billy wriggled away from her. 'I DON'T HAVE NITS!'

'Come on, let's get rid of them. It won't take long.' The second part of this was a blatant lie and they both knew it. The wet-combing took ages. This was the third time in a year Billy's small head had played host. Laura had gone through oceans of tea tree oil but nothing seemed to keep them away. The trouble was, there was always one kid in the class whose parents didn't seem to think delousing was a priority.

Billy sat between Laura's legs as she pulled the nit comb through each section of heavily conditioned hair and then rubbed the black-spotted white gunk on bits of loo roll.

'Ouch,' Billy said, wriggling. 'Ouch!'

'Not much longer now.'

'Daddy said he's staying at Uncle Jimmy's for a little while.'

Laura's heart stopped in her chest.

'But he's still going to see me all the time.'

Laura swallowed a sob. 'Daddy will always see you.'

'Can I watch *Trolls* after this?'

'Yes,' she said, nodding at the back of her son's head.

'With some milk and biscuits?'

He was pushing his luck but she said yes anyway.

Laura carried on combing. As ever, she was amazed by the sheer number of creatures that had taken up residence on Billy's small head.

She'd have to check her own hair after this, she hadn't

137

made a start on her work yet and Amy was dropping off Josh any minute. Given that she'd barely slept the night before, it was no wonder she felt exhausted.

'Grandma's dead forever!'

Still the sing-songy tone. 'Yes.'

'That's why she didn't buy me a present for my birthday.'

'Err . . . yes.'

'Grandma was your mummy.'

'Yes.'

'I'd be sad if you were dead forever.'

A lump formed in Laura's throat. It was the nicest thing anyone had said to her in a while.

Chapter Thirty-Seven

Laura was sitting at her desk trying not to listen to people around her talking about how they'd spent Valentine's night. Lisa's girlfriend had proposed, Chloe's husband had surprised her with tickets to go to Paris. Even Elaine — the world's grumpiest sub-editor — had received a big bunch of flowers from a mystery admirer (Laura just hoped whoever it was punctuated their message perfectly).

'You're very quiet, Laura,' Chloe said. 'Did you and Jon do anything special?'

Yup, we broke up! 'Umm, not really.' Laura reached for her noise-cancelling headphones. 'Sorry, bit swamped.' Well, that much was true at least. She'd bought three syndicated stories, all of which needed a complete rewrite, she had to edit Lisa's box-out copy on post-natal depression and she had to choose her problems for next week's *Dear Laura*.

She decided she would start with the latter, simply because it was the task she was least dreading. She knew that thrusting, successful types got the things they were *most* dreading out of the way first, but she wasn't a thrusting, successful type.

She sighed and opened a letter that was written in small, neat handwriting. *Dear Laura, Thirty years ago, I was forced to give up my child for adoption. Since then not a day has gone past that I haven't thought about him and now I'm desperate to contact him . . .*

Laura had developed a triage system for deciding which problems would make the page: whiney; sad but okay; desperate.

She put the letter in her desperate pile and was hit by the sudden and unpleasant notion that she would put most of her own problems on the same pile right now. *Dear Laura, My mother died and I'm failing at grief. Dear Laura, I've split up with my partner and the father of my child. Dear Laura, My five-year-old is in pieces and it's my fault.* Even her 'sad but okay' problems like falling out with her sister or being fed-up with her job didn't feel that okay. (Still, she was lucky to have a job. The empty pod that had, until a couple of months ago, belonged to the team on *Beautiful Brides* was a striking visual reminder that the print magazine world wasn't exactly flourishing.)

She opened another letter, which was from a young mother who said she was 'hating' being a mum and couldn't stop crying. Laura put it straight on the desperate pile and made a guilty mental note that it would sit very well against the box-out on post-natal depression. Sometimes it was hard to shake the notion that she made a living off other people's misery, although hopefully she could provide some sort of help to the woman in her reply, especially as this was one where she'd be seeking the advice of a therapist (AKA someone who actually knew what they were talking about).

Amy messaged her: *Emergency meeting?*

Laura smiled and headed for the toilets which was the location for such events.

'Oh, my God, I am having the worst day,' Amy said as soon as Laura walked in. 'First of all I've got some idiot PR who is desperate for me to include their ugly-ass coffee table in next week's issue and yet seems to be unable to produce a single high-res image of it, then Elaine has put her fucking red pen all over my feature on "Kitchen makeovers for less" and now Dani "isn't feeling" my story on "Making your own table runner". The story that she said yes to and I've shot step-by-step images for!'

Laura laughed. 'I don't know what you're moaning about. I still can't get the woman for the "Incontinence ruined my life" article to agree to an interview, I've bought three syndicated articles that could have been written better by Billy, and now Karen has told me I have to look after Georgie next week.'

'Who's Georgie?' Amy said.

'That super-keen intern.'

Amy made a face. 'Oh, God, *her*. Okay, you win.'

Karen came into the bathroom and, because she was such a workhorse of a deputy editor, Laura and Amy started to showily wash their hands in an of course we're not just in here gossiping manner.

Back at her desk, Laura opened an email from a woman whose mother was always making mean comments about her. *She says I'm not strict enough with my kids. She says I ought to make my husband do more chores.* Mean comments? Laura thought. Christ, that would have been her mother being nice. She mentally filed the letter in the 'whiney' category, meaning it was destined to never grace the pages of *Natter.*

Laura sifted through several more emails, all of which fell into the 'sad but okay' camp. One of them might make this week's page and, if not, she'd keep them in case there was a slow week anytime soon.

Then she came to a letter from a woman who'd been 'knocked sideways' by the death of her mother.

As she read, Laura's breath caught in her throat. The woman sounded completely devastated. Here was someone who was grieving properly – how could Laura possibly help her? Laura, who couldn't even keep her own life on track.

Chapter Thirty-Eight

It was weird to be standing in her mum's kitchen. Laura knew Evie hadn't been in the flat for months but she felt sure she could still detect a faint waft of Shalimar. She half-expected her mum to walk in too, telling her that top *did nothing for her* and *did she really need another biscuit?*

Jess was sitting at the kitchen table looking through a pile of paperwork and sorting it into various piles. Ruthlessly efficient as ever. And Laura – well, Laura was eating custard creams.

Jess had messaged her the evening of nit-gate. *Tried to call you. Sorry if I upset you at the spa. x*

Sorry *if*. She'd messaged though, which was more than Laura had done. Laura had written a message back: *Sorry if I upset you. x* She deleted it. Typed: *I'm sorry too. x*

Her hand hovered over the 'send' button. Should she mention her and Jon? What could she say though? *Oh, by the way, I've split up with the father of my child. No biggie.* She'd decided it was better to just not mention it.

'I wish I'd sorted through some of this when Mum was still alive,' Jess said.

Laura sighed. 'You can't always get ahead.'

'S'pose not.'

Laura opened one of the kitchen cupboards and there, right at the front, was the battered frying pan Dad had used for his steak nights. Laura could picture him – an inverately neat cook – lining up everything he needed like surgical instruments. There would be the steaks, butter, Worcester sauce, cream, salt and pepper, finely-chopped mushrooms. Laura took the pan out of the cupboard and clutched it to her chest. 'Do you mind if I take this?'

Jess glanced up. 'Sure.'

'It really reminds me of Dad.'

Jess looked at her and nodded. She had a slightly odd expression and she looked as if she was about to say something. Laura hoped she wasn't suddenly going to make an impassioned plea for the pan.

But then Jess went back to sorting through the piles of paperwork. Laura studied her, noting that she looked a little tired today. She had big, bruise-like shadows under her eyes. That said, even though it was Sunday and she had nothing more exciting to do than sort through her mother's stuff, she looked impossibly glamorous in a leopard-print shirt and perfectly-fitting jeans. Laura glanced down at her own scruffy leggings and sweatshirt – sometimes it really was impossible to imagine the two of them had come from the same womb. When she'd been looking at Jess' Instagram the other day, Laura had felt more like she was looking at pictures of a celebrity than her real-life sister.

'Do you want to start in the bedroom?' Jess said.

'No, I'll start in the living room.' She didn't feel like being bossed around today.

In the living room, Laura picked up a framed photo of her mum and dad. It had been taken on holiday in Greece, the last holiday the four of them would ever go on together as a family. Her parents looked so happy and relaxed caught against the sunset; as if nothing could ever go wrong. Laura traced her dad's profile with her fingertip. Sometimes, even twenty-five years later, it was hard to believe he was gone.

She wished he could have met Billy – he'd have adored him, especially when he was being impish and cheeky. He'd lie on his back and 'fly' Billy on his feet, just as he used to do with her and Jess.

She started counting how many photos there were of her and Billy versus how many there were of Jess and the girls. She wasn't surprised to see that Jess won by a ratio of 3:1. There were four separate photographs just of her wedding.

'Is Billy with Jon?' Jess had asked her.

'Yes.' It wasn't a lie.

There was a packet of her mother's painkillers on the side. Evie had been incredibly brave about the pain. Laura didn't think she'd have been that stoic, not if her experience of childbirth was anything to go by; she'd been asking for the epidural as soon as she arrived at the hospital. Four hours later, they were still telling her the anaesthetist was busy. Things changed as soon as Jon arrived and told them to *Get. Someone. Here. Now.*

Laura opened a cupboard and was amazed at how tidy everything was. At her flat, things fell out of cupboards whenever you tried to open them. Who kept the inside of their cupboards tidy? Her mother. And Jess, of course.

She piled DVDs into cardboard boxes. She didn't know what they would do with them. Take them to a charity shop, she imagined, although she didn't know if anyone still wanted DVDs nowadays. There was a tape with a heart shaped label that read 'Jess and Ben's wedding'. Like four framed photos weren't enough.

'How are you getting on?' Jess said.

Was that code for 'get a move on'? Probably not. Laura must stop thinking the worst all the time.

Jess had picked up one of the framed photos of her and Ben on their wedding day and was staring at it. Laura imagined her sister was thinking what a cute couple she and Ben made. She couldn't help but feel a bit jealous. She knew judging other people's relationships was the ultimate modern sin. You only have to look at social media to see that 'policing' is frowned upon (although apparently it's okay to police policing). How dare someone have an opinion on someone else's decision not to have children, to live in an open relationship, or to marry someone much older/younger? But the truth is, we all judge other people's relationships and use them as a barometer to measure ours against.

Laura had done this with Jess and Ben over the years and concluded that their relationship was predictably perfect. Yes, she knew you couldn't really know what anyone else's marriage was like from the outside – that you only saw the best bits – but they always seemed to just 'fit'. Also, let's be honest, it would be just like her sister to have a great marriage.

Jess put the picture back on the shelf. 'I'll do this cupboard,' she said, sinking to her hands and knees.

The two of them worked side by side. *Oh, by the way, Jon and I have split up*, Laura kept repeating in her mind. Part of her was desperate to say something. It had now been four days since Jon had moved out and Laura hadn't told a soul. But she couldn't stomach seeing the I-told-you-so look on Jess' face.

Besides, Laura didn't know if the split from Jon was permanent. Although the two of them *had* talked yesterday about when and how they were going to have The Talk with Billy. That felt pretty final.

Laura could feel herself starting to cry and was torn between desperately wanting Jess to notice and desperately wanting her not to. She quickly decided on the latter and buried her head deep in the cupboard until she'd recovered herself.

She reached into her handbag, pulled out a bottle of Gaviscon and took a swig.

'You seem to get heartburn quite a lot,' Jess said.

Heartburn is the least of my problems, Laura thought. She shrugged and went back to sorting through the cupboard. The traffic throbbed in the distance and the smell of a roast dinner started to waft through the floorboards. Laura's stomach rumbled. She hoped Jon was giving Billy a proper lunch, that he hadn't just taken him to McDonalds again.

'Do you remember when I was pregnant with Lola and Mum told me that she couldn't believe there was only one baby in there?' Jess said, giggling. 'She really was the absolute master of the drive-by insult!'

'What about the first time she met Jon?' Laura said. 'We were all having dinner and Mum suddenly said to me, "Do you remember that time you had thrush, darling? You were nearly driven mad by the itching."'

Jess clamped her hand to her mouth. 'Oh God, she did, didn't she? And what about that time she told Auntie Ann she thought it was very brave of her to have another child considering how naughty the first two were.'

There were plenty more where that came from and the pair of them traded memories back and forth as they packed things into boxes.

It felt weird to be laughing like this. But it also felt good.

Chapter Thirty-Nine

It's not good when you want to slap the person you're interviewing.

Laura came across all sorts of people in the course of her work and generally managed to maintain a modicum of journalistic impartiality. But today she was struggling.

Tamsin had faked having terminal cancer to try to get a charity to pay for her wedding.

What kind of person does that? Laura thought, sitting opposite from her answer.

They'd met in the dingy bar of a budget hotel that smelled of artificial pine masking the faint, but unmistakeable, whiff of vomit. The only other customer in the bar was a dead-eyed middle-aged man in a sagging grey suit who was staring at a laptop screen as he knocked back whisky with grim determination.

'I'm assuming your fiancé was in on the scam?' Laura said.

Tamsin shook her mass of sleek blue-black curls. 'No. I told Kevin I was ill.'

Laura had no idea how anyone could lie like that. She felt guilty not mentioning the break-up with Jon to anyone, and even though she knew it was her right to wait until it felt a little less raw before she talked about it, it still made her feel deceitful, especially when the likes of Jess or Amy mentioned him. She reckoned Jess would be particularly unimpressed by Laura withholding the news.

'Kevin would have blown it if I'd told him,' Tamsin said. 'He can't keep his big mouth shut, especially when he's had a bevvy or two.'

Laura studied Tamsin. Her mum had been fond of saying that at twenty you got the face God gave you but by thirty you got the face you deserved. Laura had always thought it nonsense but, looking at the twenty-eight-year-old opposite her, it actually made sense. On paper Tamsin had model good looks, but there was an underlying hardness that was starting to calcify.

'I told everyone I was ill,' Tamsin said. 'Kevin, my friends, my mum, my kids.'

'Your kids?' Laura said weakly. 'That must have been hard?'

Tamsin shrugged. 'Sometimes. When they cried and stuff. But I knew they'd be extra-happy when I told them I was going to pull through after all. That it would seem like a miracle. And I was going to take them on the honeymoon to the Caribbean with us. So, y'know, they'd have done well out of it.'

Laura tried to force a smile. She'd probably be dealing better with Tamsin if she'd had a nicer week. On Monday, she'd woken up to find she had no heating or hot water, on Tuesday she'd come down with a streaming cold, and on Wednesday she'd broken a filling. Thursday and Friday had been without specific incident but of course there was the mood music: her mother's death, breaking up with Jon, Billy acting like he needed a course in anger management, the very real fear of losing her job if all the rumours about *Natter* going under proved to be true. Not to mention the fact that it was cold, grey February – the only saving grace of the winter month was that it had the decency to be short.

'You said on the phone you did quite a lot of research?' Laura said.

148

'Yeah,' Tamsin said, before launching into a tale about how she'd read loads and loads of stuff about ovarian cancer so she could get all the details just right. 'I even said my GP first thought it was IBS,' she said with palpable pride. 'The symptoms mean the two things often get mistaken for each other, you see.'

Laura blew her nose and tried not to scream that her mother had died just a month earlier from *real* cancer. 'Tell me a little about how you got found out.'

Tamsin shrugged. 'Can I get another coffee?'

Laura beckoned to the man uninterestedly polishing glasses behind the bar.

'Some old bag at the charity called the hospital,' Tamsin said.

'Uh huh,' Laura said. Although she'd already researched the details, she wanted to hear it all from Tamsin directly. The charity had asked Tamsin for documentation so Tamsin then faked a letter from an NHS consultant. The letter, however, seemed a 'bit off' to Esther at the charity, so she'd called the hospital, only to find out that they knew nothing of Tamsin's supposed condition.

'So the police came and arrested me for fraud.'

Laura nodded. In the judge's statement, she'd commented that Tamsin showed little or no remorse. 'And did you feel bad about what you did?'

Tamsin's eyes narrowed. 'A bit. But you see all these pictures of celebrities having these dream weddings and you think well, why shouldn't I have that too?' She squared her shoulders.

The barman came over with Tamsin's coffee and Laura rubbed her pounding forehead. She thought about people in the office wishing each other a 'Happy Friday' this morning. This was *not* a happy Friday. In fact, Laura suddenly didn't know if she could sit here with this dreadful woman in this depressing place for a second longer. Or whether or not she could bring herself to write up Tamsin's 'story' without eviscerating her.

But then, what were Laura's choices? She was a single mother now.

She was lucky to have her job and this was where she had to be. Sipping vile coffee with a woman who thought it was perfectly okay to tell her kids that Mummy was dying.

This was Laura's lane.

Chapter Forty

Laura was lying alone and sobbing in the middle of Billy's semi-collapsed den.

Billy was spending his first ever night away from her.

Jon and Laura were over.

Her mother was dead.

Her father was *still* dead.

Earlier she'd been okay. Well . . . not okay, but not like this. She'd watched Billy pick up his little backpack, then checked he had his grubby monkey he couldn't sleep without, and promised to feed the guinea pig and tell him a bedtime story.

Jon had noticed her getting a bit watery-eyed. 'It's just he's never been away from me for a night,' she'd explained.

'What? Even when he was in hospital?'

She shook her head. 'I stayed with him.' She was surprised Jon didn't remember. Every detail was etched on her mind. The doctors telling them Billy needed an operation but not to worry (NOT TO WORRY? DID THEY HAVE CHILDREN?), the smell of the recovery room, the child in the other bed who was never going to get better.

When Jon and Billy left, she didn't lose it completely. She told herself that, after her horrible week, it would be nice to have a Saturday evening to herself; she could get things done and then get an early night to see off this cold. She started half-heartedly trying to tidy up the flat and was doing quite well until she was poleaxed by the sight of one small and two large plastic dinosaurs that Billy had grouped together as a family.

She pulled Billy's duvet tighter around her, trying desperately to get the smell of him. That was why she'd come in here – to get a bit of Billy. And, yes, she knew it was faintly ridiculous to be in a child's den without a child, but needs must.

Tamsin, the woman who'd faked cancer, had a daughter the same age as Billy, as well as a three-year-old. How she'd thought it was okay to tell them she was dying was beyond Laura.

Laura lay on her back, the tears rolling down into her hair. She and Billy had used almost every sheet and blanket in the house to make the den. Laura had even strung up some fairy lights. Was she overcompensating? You bet she was. *I may have ruined your life, kiddo, but look at this den we've built.*

She felt desperately, desperately alone. ORPHAN, ORPHAN, ORPHAN, screamed a voice in her head. She wanted her mum here to give her a hug, despite the fact her mum hadn't exactly been the most sympathetic person. If you were recruiting for people to take calls for the Samaritans, Evie would not be first choice (ironic, given the grave reservations she'd had about Laura wanting to do just that). If you wanted someone to make you laugh or to have fun with, she could well be a good bet. But as a purveyor of TLC? Not so much. When Laura had been dumped by her first ever boyfriend, Evie had said he was a 'dreadful boy anyway'. When Laura had failed to get the grades she needed for uni, Evie had said she should have worked harder, like her sister. When Laura was in hospital after a traumatic twenty-three-hour labour, Evie had whirled in, pushed the IV cables aside, sat on the bed and talked about what a day *she'd* had.

So maybe Laura wasn't wishing for her mother, exactly; she was wishing for *a* mother.

She should have gone out tonight, made the most of not having to get up and play Power Rangers at 6 a.m. The thought made her cry harder.

The air was still filled with the acrid smell of burning. Before the den building, she and Billy had made cupcakes. If there was a parenting activity that so richly illustrated the gap between expectation and reality as much as cooking with a small child, Laura was hard-pressed to think of it. The expectation was all about cosy togetherness with a delicious end-product to boot. Eat your heart out, Nigella! The reality, however, usually found Laura screeching, 'No, not in that bowl' and, 'Careful, don't get shell in it!' within the space of about thirty-four seconds. And, oh God, the mess! How could one batch of (frankly disgusting) cupcakes make so much mess?

She wiped her nose on her sleeve and tried to take a breath. She wished Billy was still in the den with her, his warm little body curled up against hers.

Yesterday, she and Jon had talked to Billy and it had gone better than she could possibly have hoped for. Everyone had been calm. Billy had listened to what they had to say and then asked if he could go and play.

It had been almost too easy.

Later that evening, she'd told Billy he had to clear up some of the Lego all over his bedroom floor. She was tired of treading on it all the time.

'You're being horrible!' Billy screamed. 'That's why Daddy went away!'

Laura steeled herself, told herself that this was to be expected and she mustn't be hurt. But she was hurt. Later, when Jess called, asking about when they were next going over to their mum's flat (Laura was amazed Jess had managed to go nearly a week without pestering), Laura had been on the verge of telling her everything. She desperately wanted Jess to say that

Billy didn't mean what he said, of course he didn't, and that he was going to be fine and so was Laura. That it wasn't crazy to throw out a man you still loved because you'd realized he was never going to be the things you needed him to be. But Jess didn't get an opportunity to say any of these things because Laura found herself keeping quiet until suddenly she realized that Jess had started talking about where they should scatter their mum's ashes. Laura sighed heavily, saying that Evie had only been dead a month – what was the rush, for goodness' sake?

Billy's pillow was damp with Laura's tears. *Good Grief* had a whole chapter about 'sad not being bad' but Laura couldn't see how working herself up into this sort of state was helpful to anyone. She needed to pull herself together. Get out of this den, go to her grown-up-sized bed and sleep. Wasn't she always saying she'd like a lie-in? Now she could have one.

She wondered if Billy was asleep. She knew Jon wouldn't have put him to bed on time but surely by 11.30 p.m. he'd be in bed? He was only five. 'Is there a spare bed at Jimmy's?' she'd asked. Jon had looked at her as if she was crazy. 'Oh yeah, it's in the bedroom in the east wing. The one with the ensuite bathroom and walk-in dressing room.' Laura had resisted the urge to slap Jon and packed Billy a sleeping bag.

Perhaps she should call Amy? Emergency: woman unravelling. It was kind of late though.

She rolled over and one of the heavier blankets that made up the roof of the den landed smack in her face.

It felt like her world was collapsing in on her.

Chapter Forty-One

Laura was going to die.

She'd started to get pains in her chest some time ago but she'd dismissed it. She must have pulled a muscle. It was hardly surprising given she'd slept in a child's den.

As time went on she started to feel worse but still, she didn't panic. She had a cold, she was stressed and tired. Also, despite the distinct February chill, she and Billy had spent the whole afternoon in the park. It was no wonder she felt rubbish.

But then, as she watched Billy hurling bits of bread at uninterested ducks, Laura's heart started racing and she found herself struggling to breathe.

She was having a heart attack!

She lowered herself onto a bench and tried to stay calm.

'Have we got any more bread, Mummy?' Billy had the tentative half-smile that reminded Laura so much of her dad.

Laura shook her head. She was too busy trying to stay alive to worry about bread.

What should she do?

She didn't want to alarm Billy by phoning an ambulance.

But she didn't want to leave him to grow up without a mother, either. A sudden image of him at her funeral sprang to mind; tiny in the suit she'd bought him for her mum's funeral, and trying not to cry. He would be the child that other people's mothers hugged a little too hard. Laura wouldn't be there when someone broke his heart, she wouldn't attend his graduation or hold her grandchild.

A wave of nausea threatened to overwhelm her. She was covered in sweat and shaking violently. Surely she couldn't be having a heart attack? That didn't happen to a thirty-seven-year-old woman, did it? But then, most thirty-seven-year-old women took better care of themselves than she did. And they hadn't taken lots of crazy drugs when they were young.

The chest pain was getting worse. She *was* having a heart attack.

She had to get help. But not in a way that sent Billy into a panic.

She tried to call Jon but it went to voicemail. She tried Amy but she didn't pick up either.

'Billy,' she said, trying to keep her voice bright and casual. 'We need to go.'

'The ducks are still hungry!'

Laura gripped the edge of the bench, her knuckles turning white. 'They'll be fine. We need to go.'

'Five more minutes.'

'No!'

She looked around her trying to work out who would help them if she collapsed. The jogger stretching over by that tree? The old woman on the bench with the sad face? The teenagers on skateboards?

As they walked out of the park, a taxi with its yellow light on was speeding towards them. Laura flagged it down.

'What are you doing?' Billy said.

'Mummy's not feeling too well,' she said, trying to smile. 'We're going to go see the doctors.'

'Aww, I thought we were going somewhere fun,' Billy said, his lower lip wobbling. Laura knew he was tired and on the edge (goodness knows what time Jon had got him to bed last night). She sat back in her seat and mopped her sweaty brow. It wouldn't take very long to get to King's from here. She wouldn't die as long as she got to the hospital.

Chapter Forty-Two

Laura was lying in the crisp, cool sheets of Jess' spare bedroom. 'I don't need to come back to your place,' she'd told her at the hospital. 'It was just a panic attack.' But Jess was adamant.

Laura still felt faintly ridiculous about having taken herself to A&E, even if everyone at the hospital had been very nice to her. 'A panic attack and a heart attack can present in a remarkably similar way,' the doctor had said. 'And we'd always prefer you to get checked out.'

Jess came in with a cup of tea. 'How are you feeling?'

'Stupid.'

Jess rolled her eyes. 'Don't be daft.'

As soon as Laura had known she wasn't, in fact, dying, she was keen to just slink out of the hospital and get home. But the nurse was very insistent it would be a good idea to get someone to pick them up and Laura simply didn't have the energy to argue.

Jon's phone was still going to voicemail so Laura called Jess, who was apparently in the middle of a Mandarin class but said she would come straightaway. (Mandarin? Laura thought. It seemed her sister was constantly striving to improve upon perfection.)

Jess handed her the tea.

'I really did think I was having a heart attack. That I might just drop dead right there in the middle of Dulwich Park.'

Jess squeezed her knee through the duvet.

'I keep thinking about dying. Y'know, since Mum. I should take better care of myself. For Billy's sake.'

'You're only thirty-seven.'

'I know but I'm fat and I don't do any exercise and I drink too much. Mind you, Dad was tee-total and he played tennis every day and then he goes and dies in a car accident. Mum ate her own bodyweight in broccoli and spinach and she got cancer.'

'There are no guarantees in life.'

'I should at least take some exercise though.'

'You could come running with me?'

'I'd hate that!'

Jess laughed. 'You didn't tell me about you and Jon.'

'How—'

'Billy told me "Daddy doesn't live with us anymore".'

Laura picked at a thread on the duvet. 'Sorry. I was going to tell you. Are you annoyed?'

Jess shook her head. 'Of course I'm not annoyed. I expect you were worried I'd be all "I told you so"?'

'No,' Laura lied.

Jess squeezed her knee through the duvet again. 'It must have been awful for you. I could have helped.'

Tears welled up in Laura's eyes and Jess took the mug of tea out of her hands and put it on the bedside table. 'Budge up,' she said, sitting down next to Laura and putting her arms around her.

And that was it – the floodgates were opened. It was as if Jess being kind had released some sort of stopper to a previously untapped container of misery. Sobbing, she leant in to the hug, suddenly remembering how she used to climb into Jess' bed almost every night when they were little. The two of them shared a room; by day it was a battleground – Laura's mess was encroaching on Jess' side of the room (marked by an invisible but immutable line), Jess' lame posters were an affront to Laura's sensibilities – but at night, when Laura was afraid of the dark, she'd creep across the rug and Jess would wordlessly move over a little and lift up the duvet. And they'd go to sleep curled up like two little kittens in a basket. The next morning things would be back to normal, the two of them bitter rivals in the battle for their mother, which Laura knew she could never win.

Jess stroked her hair and Laura thought about how Evie had always told a story about Jess' disappointment when Laura was brought home from the hospital and wasn't the fun plaything Jess had been promised. Evie thought the story very funny.

'Sorry about your jumper,' Laura said, when she eventually stopped crying. 'Perhaps you can blog about it? How to get snot and tears out of Cashmere?'

Jess laughed.

'Is Billy okay?'

'He's eating popcorn and making the girls watch back to back episodes of *Trolls*. He said he gets to pick the TV show because it's his mummy who is poorly.'

'Sorry!'

'Don't be. The boy will go far.'

Laura took a sip of her tea. 'Mum would be pleased. She never liked Jon. She used to refer to him as the "giant man-baby".'

'I don't think she'd be pleased, exactly, but I know what you mean. Want to tell me what happened?'

'Not really.' Laura looked at her watch. 'I should get going.'

'Why don't you and Billy have dinner with us and stay the night?'

Laura was tempted. Jess' house was so clean and tidy (really, her sister could teach Marie Kondo a thing or two about tidiness) and this bed was ridiculously comfy. Maybe she could stay here forever? She could steal all Jess' clothes, just like she used to when they were teenagers (apart from the fact she wouldn't get Jess' jeans past her knees). 'I ought to go – we've got school and work in the morning. Plus, I bet Ben would rather his mopey sister-in-law didn't take up any more of Sunday.'

'Don't be daft,' Jess said. 'Ben would love you to stay.'

Laura wondered if this could really be true. She knew he and Jess had a Sunday-night movie ritual. Surely he wouldn't want her sitting in the middle of them, stretching the definition of what film constituted a 'weepie' (right now, *Bridesmaids* would probably make her cry). That said, Ben did seem to be almost ridiculously easy-going. Jess had once let slip that the pair of them hardly ever argued. 'I really should go. Apart from anything else, I need to feed the guinea pig.'

'Are you sure? At least let me pack you some dinner.'

'You don't have to do that.' Laura's voice lacked conviction. To be honest, the thought of not having to worry about sorting out food was an appealing one. She was happy to be mothered for once.

'It's no trouble. Remind me, is there anything Billy doesn't like?'

'Anything with any nutritional benefit whatsoever.'

'Got it.'

Jess was about to go out of the room when Laura said, 'Thank you.'

'Don't be silly.'

'Also, you know how before you went off to university I kept telling you how I couldn't wait for you to go and I was desperate to have the bigger bedroom?'

'Err, yeah.'

'I actually kind of missed you.'

Chapter Forty-Three

Then

Laura would have preferred it if her mother had screamed and shouted. Instead her rage menaced just beneath the surface. It was all the more scary for not being out in the open – like an assassin lurking in the shadows.

It had all started with a stupid remark of Laura's. (How Laura wished she could rewind time and spool the words back into her mouth.) Evie had been regaling Laura and Jess with a story about one of her 'fat lady' customers at the department store. Apparently, the woman had said she 'could not believe' Evie had daughters of eighteen and twenty. She didn't look old enough to have children at secondary school, let alone one at university.

'She was probably just buttering you up, hoping you'd give her a discount,' Laura said. It was meant to be a joke but her mother didn't laugh. (She may have a great sense of humour, but only she got to decide what was and wasn't funny.)

Evie's face changed immediately and Laura glanced across the dinner table at Jess to find she was looking stricken.

'Well, now,' her mother said icily, 'it seems someone is in a bitchy mood this evening.'

'I was just kidding Mu—'

Evie cut her off. 'Yes.'

The rest of dinner passed in a blur, Laura's stomach turning sour and knotty. Was she imagining it, or was her mother talking exclusively to Jess? Did she fail to meet Laura's eye when Laura asked if she wanted more spinach? When she kept going on about how Jess was so kind and thoughtful that was just normal, right?

The next morning, her mother gave Laura the briefest of grunts when she went downstairs, barely looking up from the newspaper. When Laura tried to talk about the night before, Evie waved the conversation away with a swipe of her hand, saying there was nothing to talk about.

Laura's stomach clenched. She knew from previous experience this did not mean everything was okay. For the next few days, her mother was polite – almost *too* polite – but frosty. If she was chatting and laughing with Jess and Laura tried to join in, her mother acted as if she was some stranger who had wandered into their home and sat at the dinner table.

Laura was used to being hyper-attuned to her mother's moods but, at times like this, worrying about them utterly consumed her. She tried harder and harder to please and was occasionally rewarded by a scrap. Her mother would accept her offer of a cup of tea. Her mother's smile wouldn't vanish as soon as they weren't behind closed doors (however annoyed Mum was, she never showed it in public). But then Laura would be back in Siberia.

Jess tried to help out. She pulled Laura into conversations, pointed out how much effort she had gone to with the supper. One time Jess even made a direct appeal for clemency, but Evie just said she had no idea what she was talking about and that she was 'fine' with Laura.

And then suddenly, one day, everything was back to normal. Laura could relax.

Until the next time.

Chapter Forty-Four

Laura wanted to hug her sister one minute, strangle her the next.

When Laura was stuck at work on press day and the school called to say that Billy was running a temperature and they couldn't get hold of Jon, it was Jess who went to collect Billy. 'Are you sure that's okay?' Laura said to her on the phone. Jess said it was fine, that she was working on an Instagram story but she could go back to it later.

Laura got home to find a waft of something delicious coming from the oven, and Billy tucked under a blanket on the sofa, flanked by Hannah and Lola. There was a jigsaw puzzle on a tray on Billy's knees which the three kids were patiently piecing together. Her sister made a much better 'wife' than Jon did.

That said, Laura couldn't help but be irritated when Jess picked up one of Josh's tiny sweatshirts that was lying forgotten under a cushion and said it seemed to her that Laura was *always* looking after Josh.

'Not really,' Laura snapped. 'Anyway, Amy is funny and sharp and great company.'

Jess shrugged infuriatingly. *And?* she seemed to imply.

They argued repeatedly about Jon too. 'He should be paying you proper child support.'

'Give him a chance. We only split up forty-eight seconds ago.'

'He's always late when he comes to pick up Billy.'

Laura made a mental note that she'd been a fool to confide in her sister the other day. She'd just been so upset about everything. Even now, she could still vividly picture Billy, dressed in his coat and wellies, standing with his pale, anxious little face pressed up against the window. 'Jon's not *always* late. Besides, it's not like Billy was left standing outside waiting in the rain.'

Jess had tidied up the flat. Laura felt a mixture of gratitude and irritation. On the one hand, everything did look much nicer; on the other, it was hard not to feel a bit judged. And Jess shouldn't have thrown out the pasta picture that Billy had made at nursery without asking her first, even if it had long since disintegrated into a lone piece of penne on the dog-eared page.

Another simmering source of disagreement was when they would sort through the rest of their mother's stuff. It's March already, Jess had said, (yup, Laura thought, I have a calendar) and she was keen to get it done as quickly as possible (of course she was). Laura said she knew it had to be done but she had enough on her plate right now (a bit mean as Jess was always taking stuff off her plate, but still). Jess said the mortgage company had told her someone could make an offer on the flat at any minute, Laura said screw the mortgage company, they were the ones who sold Evie that terrible reverse equity deal. If they got a buyer, that buyer would have to wait.

Jess got on Laura's nerves when she nagged her about her health too. *Was she really taking Gaviscon again? She must get through litres of the stuff. Had she had any more panic attacks?*

Laura lied and said she hadn't. Well, it was only one and there was no point getting Jess agitated. As it was though, she went on and on and on. *Had Laura thought about yoga?*

Yoga? Laura hated bloody yoga at the best of times. All

those disgusting feet. Not a single laugh when someone let out a fanny fart.

What about meditation or counselling?

Shut up, Laura thought, or I'll have a panic attack right now.

She couldn't deny her sister was a huge help though. When there was an issue about who would pick up Billy next Tuesday because Jon was going to a gig, Jess quickly offered to step in. Laura was hesitant to accept. She felt like Jess was doing her too many favours at the moment, that there was no such thing as a free lunch. Also, the two of them were seeing each other more than they had in years.

When they were kids, although they were bitter rivals, they were together all the time. However much your straight-A, captain-of-the-netball-team, didn't-even-have-spots sister got on your nerves, she was just there. And, however much you claimed she annoyed you, you didn't *always* want to get away from her when you had the chance. Especially if she had friends or a boyfriend over – then you stuck to her like glue.

But as soon as Jess went to uni, a chasm opened up between them as their lives went in different directions. While Jess got herself a job in management consultancy, working twelve-hour days, Laura became a wild party girl. And while Jess was settling down with her uni sweetheart, Ben, Laura was going through a string of more and more unsuitable boyfriends.

The two of them rarely saw each other and barely spoke, their news of each other coming via their mother, who managed, Laura noted, to always fan the flames of competition from afar. Every update about Jess carried the unspoken addendum: *Why can't you be more like her?*

Once Laura had had Billy, they saw each other a bit more, but still not that much. By the time they'd exhausted the subject of Arsenal's back four, Jon and Ben had little to say to each other and Jon was always going on about how bourgeois Jess and Ben were (Laura, to her shame, rarely putting up a word of defence).

Now Laura and Jess suddenly seemed to be seeing each other all the time and it made Laura nervous because everyone knew what familiarity breeds.

The Tuesday Jon was at the gig, Laura arrived at her sister's to find Jess had just de-loused Billy. 'I noticed he was scratching his head all the time so I thought it was best to get onto it quickly,' Jess said.

Laura nodded. 'Thanks. Did you wet comb?'

Jess shook her head. 'No, I always find that so faffy and time-consuming. I used a head lice treatment.'

Laura had always tried to avoid using the chemical treatments. Ironically, she had almost resorted to them recently so she probably would have said yes if Jess had asked her first. *If*.

'Auntie Jess is much gentler and quicker than you are,' Billy said.

'Come on, Billy,' Lola said. 'It's time to play Hungry Hippos now.'

Lola was super-bossy. The apple didn't fall far from the tree.

'Want a drink?' Jess said. 'A soft drink?'

Laura felt a stab of irritation. Why was she specifically being offered a soft drink?

'A glass of wine would be nice.'

'Oh.'

'What?'

'Nothing.'

'*What?*'

'It's just – you did tell me you wanted to cut down on your drinking. And when I tidied the flat the other week, there were quite a few wine bottles in the recycling.'

Dear God! Was Laura really being judged on the contents of her recycling bin? And why did her sister persist in treating her like she was still some dumb-ass sixteen-year-old?

'Careful, Jess. When you open your mouth, sometimes Mum comes out.'

Jess looked stung and Laura immediately felt guilty. Jess had helped her out so many times recently. And she meant well.

When she was a kid, Laura had read *Little Women* and felt unbearably sad that she didn't love her sister with the same fierce and unequivocal devotion that Jo did Beth. What was wrong with her?

Decades later she was still asking herself the same question.

Chapter Forty-Five

Laura was sitting at her desk daydreaming about the job at *Inlustris*. Maybe she should apply for it? Sure, it was a long-shot, but what did she have to lose, really?

She looked across the desk at Lisa. Like almost everyone else around here, Lisa was almost comically young. Looking at them all set off a voice inside Laura's head: *You're too old now. You're no longer exciting or important. You don't matter. You never really did.*

Laura tried to block out the voice but it laughed at her: *Think you could get that job at Inlustris? Are you crazy?*

Laura had once considered herself creative – a good writer, passionate, curious. Now she seemed to be perpetually exhausted. She could barely remember to buy loo roll let alone contemplate humanity or be inspired by Sylvia Plath. People who were showily creative with their art or poetry or whatever just got on her nerves now because they filled her not just with jealousy, but with confusion about how she'd landed this far away from herself.

The voice was right though. Laura just had to concentrate on the job she did have (and hope that all the office gossip about the magazine shutting down was rubbish). She went back to writing the week's horoscopes and frantically started Googling where mercury was in Capricorn.

When Dani had first 'asked' her if she could start writing

the horoscopes Laura had spluttered in protest, 'I'm not an astrologer.'

Dani had raised one eyebrow. 'Oh my God, Laura. Guess what – Santa doesn't make your presents at Christmas, and there's no such thing as the Tooth Fairy.'

Right, six star signs done, six to go. What the hell was she going to come up with for Aries this week? *The time for action is now.* No, that was too similar to the one she'd done for Pisces. *You have a choice to make.* Yes, that was good. Everyone always had some kind of choice to make. Like: do I apply for a job I have no chance of getting?

You have a choice to make so think carefully and consider all the pros and cons. This was such bullshit. Still, anyone who really believed their horoscope had only themselves to blame.

As soon as Laura had finished this she was going to write *Dear Laura*. She was feeling guilty about not having replied to the woman who was struggling with grief. The woman sounded so utterly miserable. The trouble was Laura just had no idea what to say to her, other than 'You put me to shame', which didn't seem entirely helpful. Who was she to be giving advice to anyone, quite frankly? Sometimes she thought she ought to rewrite her bio at the top of the page: *Laura Fraser has royally fucked-up almost every aspect of her own life. Want her to fuck-up yours too? Here's the address . . .*

Anyway, right now she had to finish the horoscopes. Sagittarius: Jess' star sign. *You tend to be a bit on the bossy side,* Laura wrote, *but sometimes it's good to let others have more say.*

Laura's mind drifted again to the job at *Inlustris*. You could argue that, even though she was unlikely to get it, there was no harm in trying. Except there was harm in trying. She'd just get her hopes up and be left feeling silly and sad. She suddenly remembered her mother being irritated by her when she was a teenager and she went through a stage of entering

170

writing competitions. 'I just don't know why you'd open yourself up to all that disappointment,' she'd said.

Dani appeared at Laura's desk. 'Have you got a minute?' Before Laura had a chance to answer, Dani carried on. 'I'm worried the *Dear Laura* page is getting a little gloomy.' She made a cartoonish sad face.

'It's a problem page . . .' Laura responded.

Dani nodded. 'I know. But I think we need a few "fun" problems – you know, like "I want to spice it up in the bedroom".'

'Oh,' Laura said. Dani gave her a tight little smile and stalked off in the direction of the lifts. Laura was left feeling oddly deflated. She knew it really ought not to matter if she answered fewer of her 'desperate' letters. She was all too aware that her advice probably didn't do much good. At least it made people feel heard though.

She went back to the horoscopes. Gemini was her star sign. *If there's a new opportunity in the offing* (like a job at *Inlustris*), she wrote, *then now is an excellent time to go for it.*

Then she deleted what she'd written.

Chapter Forty-Six

It was a weekend of packing up belongings; a weekend steeped in sadness. Yesterday, Jon had been at the flat packing more of his things, Billy having been dispatched to spend the day with Jess and her family so he wouldn't get upset.

'It's not like he doesn't know,' Jon said when Laura told him.

'Doesn't mean he has to watch it happen.'

Now Laura was on her way to her mother's flat so she and Jess could sort through more of her stuff. Laura willed the bus to go quicker. She sent Jess a text: *Running a bit late. See you soon. x*

She didn't mention she had been delayed because Jon was late to pick up Billy. No point giving her sister ammunition. Jon had been late yesterday as well. Laura had been on her own in the flat for over an hour after Jess picked up Billy. She was in a strange kind of limbo state. What did you do when your ex was coming over to pick up the rest of his things? Was it weirdly casual to be doing the ironing? Should she get on with some work? Go out (but then that seemed like an act of hostility)? In the end she settled for pacing restlessly.

Jess was on her mobile when Laura arrived. 'I've got to go,' she said. 'Bye.'

'You seemed in a bit of hurry to finish that call,' Laura said. 'Were you bitching about me?'

'Don't be stupid.'

'Err, I was joking,' Laura said, taking off her jacket and wondering if her sister actually had been bitching about her.

'Do you want to start on Mum's clothes?' Jess said.

Laura thought about saying she'd do a different job but decided that sometimes resistance was futile. She started pulling dresses and tops off hangers. It had been over seven weeks since her mother had died, but it still felt invasive to be going through her cupboards. It was just something that felt 'wrong' – like deleting her mum's number from her phone, which she still hadn't been able to bring herself to do.

Evie's clothes were all brightly coloured and there was an abundance of sparkle and fur. She had been a very glamorous dresser, like Jess. And, now Laura came to think of it, Dad had been a pretty sharp dresser too. She was the odd one out, a scruffy rogue dropped into their midst from another family.

When she was about four, someone at nursery had told her that sometimes in the hospital where babies were born, the babies got mixed up and went home with the wrong family. And Laura had got very excited about this idea and thought maybe Jess had been sent home with the wrong family and she'd get a new sister; a good one who wasn't bossy. But then she'd started to panic because what if it was *her* that had been sent home to the wrong family and one day there might be a knock at the door and someone said that she had to go and live somewhere else? It might be a family where you had to eat kippers.

She pulled a top out of the wardrobe and saw that it still had its tags. Tears filled her eyes. How sad to die before you'd even had a chance to wear your new top.

She carried on folding and sorting. Yesterday, seeing Jon's clothes spread out all over the bed, she'd been struck by how scruffy and dirty most of them looked. It was all she could do not to start stuffing things into the washing machine. But Jon's washing didn't go in the machine with hers and Billy's anymore.

Jess walked into the bedroom with a huge empty box. She had a faint sheen of sweat on her forehead. She'd obviously been going at it full tilt. She still looked perfect, of course – even the sweaty Jess just looked glowy. And her hair, to quote those old adverts, always looked like she'd just stepped out of a salon. Laura had once seen a photo of her sister on a camping holiday with perfect hair. How was that even possible?

'I reckon with one more day after this, we'll be done,' Jess said.

One *more* day? Laura was fed up with packing up. 'Oh, look,' she said, reaching to the back of one of the shelves. 'I bought Mum this dish for her birthday when I was about nine. I didn't know she still had it.'

Jess took the small porcelain dish from her hands. 'It's pretty.'

Laura nodded. 'I think it's supposed to sit on a dressing table and hold jewellery or knick knacks.'

'You should keep it.'

Laura put the dish by her handbag in the hall. She walked back into the bedroom where Jess had just uncovered a huge black hat.

'Is this the one Mum wore to Dad's funeral?'

'I think so. She really was a big-hat kind of person, wasn't she? Even when she wasn't wearing a hat.'

Jess laughed.

'Is it time for lunch yet?' She sounded like Billy.

'Let's do another half an hour.' Jess sounded like her.

'Oh my goodness, so many lotions and potions.'

'Put all the unopened ones in one pile and the opened ones in another.'

'I *know*.'

174

'It's just I'm taking all the unopened ones to a women's refuge,' Jess said.

'Of course you are, Little Miss Perfect.' Laura had meant this as a joke but it just came out sounding snarky.

'I do wish you wouldn't call me that,' Jess said, looking cross.

'I'll never say it again,' Laura said.

'I don't believe you.'

'Me neither,' Laura said, and they both laughed.

They carried on clearing and sorting until eventually Jess conceded that they could eat. Yesterday, Jon had been over at lunchtime and Laura had offered to make him a sandwich but he just looked at her like it was the weirdest suggestion ever. And Laura had suddenly been hit by a tidal wave of sadness because here were two people who had once loved each other, who had a child together, and now Jon looked at her as if her slapping a piece of ham between two slices of bread was an act too intimate.

'I made us a superfood salad,' Jess said, reaching into the fridge and pulling out a Tupperware container.

Laura tried not to notice that ever since she'd told Jess she wanted to lose weight, Jess kept giving her diet food. She ploughed her fork into a mound of quinoa and edamame and tried to imagine it was cake.

'Billy seemed to enjoy the Science Museum yesterday.'

'Yes. Thanks for taking him.'

'How was it with Jon?'

Laura shrugged. 'It was never going to be a fun day, was it?' She didn't mention that she and Jon had bickered over a cheap kitchen knife they'd bought in Ikea, argued about a throw that neither of them liked and then really come to blows about a vase Jon's mother had bought Laura. When she'd seen Jon stuffing it into his bag, she'd protested saying it was a present given to her. *Yes*, he'd said, *from my mother.*

In the end he'd told her she could have the bloody thing. Laura had stared at it sitting on the kitchen counter thinking how ugly it was and how she didn't really want it at all – much like Mum's necklace she'd wrestled from Jess that day at the spa.

'We ought to get back to it,' Jess said as soon as she finished her last mouthful. The whirling dervish didn't stay still for long.

Laura felt a wave of exhaustion as she started to go through the linen closet. All this misery was wearing her down. She piled towels into a box marked 'charity'.

Jess walked past and took them straight out again. 'They're fabric bank not charity.'

Laura sighed. It was going to be a long afternoon.

Eventually though, the hands of the clock did hit four and Jess agreed they could call it a day (although probably only because Laura had to get back in time for Jon to drop off Billy).

Laura picked up the porcelain dish she'd left in the hall. She could remember the day she bought it for her Mum. She'd been with her dad in John Lewis. 'Do you think Mum would like this?'

'I think she'd love it.'

And he'd been right because Evie had looked genuinely pleased when she unwrapped it and, what's more, she'd kept it all these years. Okay, it might have been at the back of a cupboard and not out on a dressing table, but she'd kept it.

'Jess,' she shouted. 'You don't have a plastic bag, do you?'

And then suddenly, before she knew it the dish was out of her hands, falling through the air and hitting the wooden floor, shattering into what seemed like a million pieces.

Laura felt the tears spring to her eyes. She knew it was pathetic to cry over a dish but she couldn't help herself.

Chapter Forty-Seven

It was such an irony: Laura would do anything – anything – to protect Billy from getting hurt and yet she was the one who'd ripped his heart to shreds.

He was sobbing bitterly because he hadn't been invited to Caitlyn's party and, although Laura knew he was upset about Caitlyn's party (and was planning to punch both Caitlyn and her mother later), she also knew that he wouldn't normally be this upset.

'Everybody's going!' Billy wailed.

Laura bent down to his level and put her arms around him. 'I'm sure that's not true.'

Billy sobbed louder. 'It is true! Harry, Freddie, Jake . . .'

'It probably won't even be a very good party.' Stupid thing to say – stupid, stupid, stupid!

'It's at Laser Quest!' Billy was practically hiccupping now.

'I'll take you to Laser Quest.'

'I don't want to go with *you*!'

Eventually he'd stopped crying, and started half-heartedly building a Lego spaceship.

Laura watched him intently, her heart feeling as if it might cleave in two. She had been so determined that she and Jon would give Billy the perfect home. Not in the Jess sense (although, to be fair, Jess' girls had a perfect home at a deeper level too) but in the way that really mattered.

Billy had wet the bed three times in the last week. The first time, he'd shaken Laura awake in the middle of the night and she'd had to stumble around in the half-light dealing with sodden sheets, feeling as if she was dreaming. It had been so long since she'd done this – years.

At least she could change sheets though. Not everything was so straightforward. A lot of the time Billy was angry and aggressive, particularly just after he came back from being with Jon. He'd shout and scream, telling her 'no' when she asked him to brush his teeth or get his shoes on. He called her names too, only things like 'stupid' and 'doofus' because those were the worst words he knew. He may as well have been swearing at her though, judging by the look on his face when he said them and the venom with which they were spat.

'Whee,' Billy said, flying his spaceship through the air.

She found the anger difficult to manage. She desperately wanted to be the perfect mother but that was hard at the best of times, and nigh on impossible when you were feeling overwhelmed, angry and sad yourself; when your patience felt like it was in short supply.

She settled for being completely inconsistent, which she knew was parenting sin number one. One day she was Strict Authoritarian Mummy: *Don't you dare speak to me like that! GO TO YOUR ROOM!* The next she was Let it Slide Mummy, dishing out cuddles and ice cream.

'Daddy left because I was naughty, didn't he?'

Laura felt as if the air had been knocked out of her lungs. She knelt down beside Billy, put her hands on his face and turned him to look at her. 'None of this is because of you, Billy. None of it. Mummy and Daddy were having some arguments and we're going to live in different houses.' She thought about how Jon was still crashing at Jimmy's. It wasn't really the sort of environment you'd pick for your child, but she supposed she didn't get a say in that now. 'You have done absolutely nothing wrong, and Mummy and Daddy love you very, very much.'

Billy started pulling his spaceship apart. Laura instinctively wanted to stop him.

'Do you love Daddy?'

Christ! Laura knew you were meant to be honest with your kids but how do you answer a question when you don't even know the answer yourself? 'I love Daddy in a different way.'

Billy's face scrunched. 'Stupid!'

'It's not nice to call people names.' Her voice lacked conviction. This was another mummy she pulled out of her arsenal sometimes: Toothless Mummy.

'Caitlyn's daddy died.'

Oh. *Oh*. That rather changed things. Perhaps Laura wouldn't punch her or her mother.

'Miss Newman said her daddy was sick. I saw him once in the playground. He was bald. Not like Mikey's dad is bald but bald with little bits of hair. Miss Newman said we must all be very kind to Caitlyn.'

'Yes,' Laura said, choking back the tears.

So. Much. Sadness. In. The. World.

She hadn't told many people at work about splitting up from Jon. They were all still handling her like an unexploded bomb because of her mother dying, so she feared they might get her sectioned if they found out about the latest drama. She'd told Amy now and she'd also confided in Karen. Karen had two daughters and had gone through a divorce a few years ago. 'How the hell did you help your girls through it?' Laura said to her.

Karen had shaken her head sadly. 'It gets easier.'

'How long does it take?'

Karen laughed mirthlessly. 'You don't want to know.'

Billy jumped up from the floor, saying he was bored with Lego. Laura knew she ought to make him clear it up but she couldn't face being told Daddy didn't make him tidy up. So she said nothing and instead started picking up the multi-coloured sea of plastic bricks and scooping them into the box. He had so much Lego and yet she'd still bought him a new set last weekend (Bribing Mummy). He'd been overcome with gratitude for what had seemed like about thirty seconds but then started to talk about how he really wanted a Nintendo Switch. *Everybody* had them. Lola and Hannah had one *each*!

Sometimes Billy seemed fine, as if nothing had happened. But there was always another tantrum or outburst just around the corner. The other day he'd hit Lola. Jess had tried to make light of it, said it was nothing. But Laura had been horrified. He'd never done anything like that before.

She raked her hands through yet another pile of Lego.

Worst of all was when Billy said things that made Laura realize that he was hoping that she and Jon were going to get back together. Sometimes she knew he even thought he could help this along. He told her proudly that Daddy hadn't let him have a McDonalds for lunch and wouldn't let him stay up past his bedtime – things he thought would impress her.

And, although she knew it was vitally important that she and Jon were always civil to each other in front of Billy and didn't slag each other off, it broke her heart when Billy misinterpreted this. She could see the hope in his face when Jon had said something that made her laugh recently. She could see his eyes shine when she said something was nice of Daddy.

She picked up the box of Lego, put it away in the cupboard and had a swig of Gaviscon.

She would be a better mummy from now on.

Chapter Forty-Eight

It was an innocent comment of Billy's that got Laura thinking: *Josh is always here.*

She stopped hunting for Billy's reading record, which she knew must be buried somewhere under one of the piles of condolence letters and bills that were littered all over the place.

Always.

It was exactly what Jess had said.

Laura looked at Billy and Josh, who were sitting on the floor with a huge stack of toy cars between them. Billy was showing Josh his favourite red Ferrari, explaining earnestly that it went super-fast. They looked really sweet together and Billy often seemed happier when Josh was around. God knows, Laura needed things that made Billy happy right now. So she shouldn't get hung up on the 'always'.

She started going through the papers again. It was just that Amy had left Josh with her a lot recently. She'd had him on Sunday night even though she was exhausted after the day clearing out her mother's flat, she'd had him on Tuesday evening because Amy's brother was in London, she'd had him when Amy had to pop out to get a few bits from the super-market (apparently Josh was a nightmare in the supermarket).

'And this car is a Mini,' Billy said.

It was fine though. She loved Josh, Billy loved Josh. And

she knew Amy would look after Billy if Laura ever asked her to.

Laura carried on working her way through the pile of papers. She certainly didn't want to become the sort of person who cared about everything being scrupulously equal. Like those ghastly people who start saying they didn't have a starter when you're splitting a bill in a restaurant.

'NO!' Billy said, as Josh took the red Ferrari and started to chew it appreciatively. 'MUMMY! MUMMY! JOSH IS EATING MY FERRARI!'

Laura wrestled the toy car from Josh's surprisingly firm grip, at which point he promptly burst into tears.

'Eww,' Billy said, taking the car out of her hand. 'It's all spitty.'

'Just give it a little wipe,' Laura said, picking Josh up and jiggling him up and down. 'Do you have a toy car you don't mind Josh playing with?'

'Playing with or eating?'

Josh's yells were getting ever-more furious.

'Either,' Laura said. Wait, were toy cars even safe for a toddler to chew on? Probably not. 'Don't worry,' she said to Billy, taking Josh into the kitchen and getting him a biscuit. The crying stopped instantly as he took it from her and jammed it into his mouth.

'Can I have a biscuit too?' Billy said.

Laura didn't really want Billy to have a biscuit because he was going to have his dinner soon, but what could she say?

'They're Joshy's favourite biscuits,' Billy said. 'The ones with the cows on.'

Laura nodded. She'd popped a packet in her supermarket trolley the other day without even thinking about it. Because Josh really was here a lot now.

She put him back down on the floor next to Billy and went back to looking for the reading record.

'I'm going to play with the marble run now,' Billy said.

'Good id—' Laura hesitated. 'Actually, I'm not sure you should. If Josh puts a marble in his mouth, he could choke.'

'Ohh,' Billy said, his lower lip trembling.

Laura felt torn. Billy had been so fragile since Jon had moved out and, although it was her responsibility to keep Josh safe, she didn't really want to burden a five-year-old with that. 'You can play with the marble run in your bedroom if you like?'

'Yay!' Billy said, running off.

The sudden disappearance of his playmate made Josh start to whinge. Laura sat on the floor and did peekaboo with him. She tried not to think about the fact that she was exhausted from a long day at work and she still had to find the reading record and cook Billy's dinner. And she absolutely wouldn't think about the fact that if Amy said she'd be gone for an hour it was pretty much always closer to two hours. Or that Amy had been a tad too dismissive when Laura had mentioned her panic attacks ('my brother has those all the time') and had barely mentioned Evie's death since the day of the funeral (Laura might not deem herself deserving of sympathy but Amy had no way of knowing that).

Josh had plonked himself on her lap. He was a gorgeous little boy. Laura kissed the top of his head. It was her pleasure to look after him. Of course it was.

Chapter Forty-Nine

Laura's phone pinged with a message from Jess: *Ben is working late and I have enough chicken to feed the 5000. Wondered if you and Billy wanted to join us for an early supper?*

Laura had had an exhausting day at work magicking up four pages out of nowhere because the sales team hadn't sold all their pages (again). The thought of going home to rustle up supper for an angry five-year-old wasn't that appealing – especially since she didn't have anything in and would have to stop at the supermarket. She messaged back saying *Yes please.*

Jon and Billy were lining up cars on the sitting-room floor. 'Hey,' she said.

'Hey,' they both chorused, not looking up from the game.

Laura tried not to think about the fact that normally when she got home from work Billy hurled himself into her arms shouting 'Mummyyyyyyyy!' Not the last couple of weeks though.

Jon stood up, ruffling Billy's hair. 'I've got to get going, mate.'

Yup, Laura thought, those pints don't sink themselves.

'Aww!' Billy said, lower lip trembling.

'We're going to see Auntie Jess and Lola and Hannah,' Laura said.

Billy's face split into a grin. 'Yay!'

'You seem to be seeing quite a lot of your sister,' Jon said as he was about to leave.

Laura shrugged. She knew Jon wanted her to roll her eyes and say, 'Yeah, too much,' but somehow she just couldn't bring herself to. 'Not really. Anyway, see you tomorrow.' She shut the door and was amazed to see Billy behind her with his shoes and coat on. He really did like seeing his cousins.

On the bus, she tried to ask him about his day at school but got monosyllabic answers. 'Did you do your reading with Daddy?'

Billy shook his head. 'We was playing.'

'We *were* playing,' Laura said. She fought a prickle of irritation about the reading. She had specifically reminded Jon about doing it with Billy. Now she'd have to get Billy to read when they got home from Jess' and he would be tired and even less keen than usual.

Weirdly, Jess looked almost as knackered as Laura felt. Still immaculate in a natty little jumpsuit, but pale, with dark circles under her eyes. And she seemed slightly on edge too. When Laura had casually picked up a bottle of perfume that was sitting on the kitchen table, Jess had launched into an impassioned diatribe about how she didn't know why a PR company had sent it to her or, more importantly, why anyone would call a perfume Secrets. What a *terrible* name! She hated the bullshit idea that secrets were fun and exciting when in truth they were normally grubby and sad. Secrets ate you up from the inside like a cancer.

'I take it you're not mad about the name then?' Laura said.

Jess smiled tightly.

'You okay?' Laura said.

'Yeah, just a bit tired. And I've just been replying to some of the less than lovely comments on my site. People can be so mean.'

Laura thought about MsRealityCheck and felt a knife-twist of guilt.

'Mummy,' Lola said, bursting into the kitchen. 'I can't find my Nintendo Switch.'

'That's weird,' Jess said. 'Have you looked in the cupboard in the sitting room?'

Lola nodded. 'I've looked everywhere. And I had it. Just before Auntie Laura and Billy got here. I asked Billy if he knew where it was and he said he had no idea.'

Laura stared at her niece. Was she saying what Laura thought she was saying? No, she couldn't be.

Jess said she'd have a look and disappeared upstairs, leaving Laura sitting at the island unit with her heart thudding. She was being ridiculous. Lola hadn't accused Billy of anything.

'Well, that's a mystery,' Jess said, coming back downstairs. 'It's nowhere to be found.'

'Excuse me a minute,' Laura said. She raced upstairs and told Billy she needed a quick word with him. She took him into the bathroom and closed the door. 'Lola has lost her Switch,' she said. 'I don't suppose you know where it is?'

'I didn't take it!' Billy said hotly.

'No. Of course you didn't,' Laura replied, stroking his arm. She went back downstairs. 'Does Lola think Billy took her Switch?' she blurted.

Jess stared at her. 'No, of course not. What a thing to say!'

Laura felt instantly ashamed. She was struggling to breathe normally too. She was going to have a panic attack at this rate. 'I was just asking.'

Jess rolled her eyes.

Laura wished she hadn't come over here tonight. Suddenly traipsing around the aisles of Tesco Express and cooking a bit of pasta didn't seem like such hard work after all.

Chapter Fifty

'Maybe you should put Billy to bed a little earlier?' Jess said.

Laura gripped the water jug she was carrying a bit harder. 'What does that mean?'

'It doesn't *mean* anything,' Jess said, putting a glass in the dishwasher. 'Just that he seems tired tonight.'

Laura's heart thudded against the wall of her chest. She knew exactly what 'tired' meant. At dinner, there had still been a bit of a hangover from the Switch incident. To exacerbate matters further, Billy wasn't exactly at his best. He'd pushed his chicken around his plate, saying it tasted 'funny', and refused to eat his broccoli. 'You like trees,' she'd told him. 'I don't call them trees anymore. I'm not a baby!' Then Hannah said broccoli was her favourite food and he called her a stupid doofus – said her new haircut made her look like a baby, too.

Jess was stacking the plates in serried ranks. Perhaps when you were StyleMaven, it wasn't enough for your kitchen to look like a show home kitchen on the outside and everything had to be perfect behind closed doors too?

Laura knew she shouldn't get into a row with Jess. That it would be better to just let the comment go, just as she had when Jess had said Billy couldn't have any ice cream because he hadn't eaten his dinner (like she – *his mother* – wasn't sitting right there). She couldn't help herself though. 'He is only five.'

Jess stopped what she was doing, stared at her. 'You're over-reacting.'

Overreacting? That was what her mother always used to accuse her of. *You're upset I embarrassed you in front of all your school friends? You're overreacting. You're hurt because I told you that graduating in Media and Journalism wasn't a 'proper' graduation? You're overreacting. You don't like the fact I phoned you while my grandson was in hospital and all I talked about was a row I'd had with my new boyfriend. You're overreacting.*

'You were having a go at Billy's behaviour tonight. At least have the guts to admit that.'

Jess rolled her eyes. 'For God's sake, Laura. I can't talk to you when you're like this.'

That was another of her mother's classics! 'Fine. We'll just go.' Laura picked up her handbag from the sofa and stepped towards the door.

'What? No!'

Laura stared at the big American-style stainless-steel fridge freezer that was covered with various certificates the girls had earned: Grade 3 Oboe, Winner of the Mental Maths competition, Karate, 7th Dan . . .

She was well aware that her sister had helped her out a lot recently, from constantly looking after Billy, to lending her money when she was a bit short on her rent, to picking her up from hospital that day she had the panic attack. But the trouble was, Jess' favours always came with strings attached.

When they were teenagers, Laura had been desperate for Jess to take her to James Dunlop's party with her, and after endless nagging Jess finally gave in. Though in the days leading up to the party, she'd acted like Laura was her slave: *Make me a cup of tea, would you? Grab my folder from upstairs. Could you do the drying as well as the washing tonight? It's just I've got so much homework.*

More recently, Laura knew that Jess had done all the heavy lifting with their mother's care. She was the one who drove Evie to the oncologist, held her hand when she was having chemo. She was the one who found the hospice. But all this came at a price because Jess and Evie then made it quite clear to Laura that she didn't get much say over any decisions. She was the understudy child.

So Laura was damned if she was going to let Jess criticize Billy just because she'd been good to them recently. 'I'm well aware that Billy wasn't at his best tonight, but as I said, he's only five.'

Jess sighed. 'I just said he seemed tired.'

'He has been through a lot recently. His whole world has imploded.'

'I know.'

'So maybe you could cut him just a little slack?'

'What's wrong with you? I just said he *seemed* tired . . .'

Laura shook her head. 'What's wrong is that you were calling my five-year-old son out on his bratty behaviour at dinner.' She could take her sister constantly taking a pop at Jon: *You've got to start getting him to give you child support. It's about time he took his responsibilities a bit more seriously.* She could stomach her sister sniping at her: *If you want to lose weight, then why do you keep eating biscuits. It's easy to kid ourselves about portion sizes.* But Billy was NOT fair game. 'Not every child can be unnaturally perfect,' she continued.

Jess' face changed. 'And what's that supposed to mean?'

Laura knew she had steered them into choppy waters and she should row back as fast as she could. Their dad had always warned that words were dangerous and they should be used carefully (ironic, considering he'd married a woman with a tongue that could cut you to shreds). So Laura knew she shouldn't say anything more but somehow she was just too angry to stop herself. 'Don't you sometimes worry that Lola and Hannah are almost too well-behaved? That they don't behave like actual children?'

Jess was staring at her. 'That's ridiculous.'

'Is it? Or are they just your little mini-mes, frightened to be anything but perfect?'

Jess turned away from her as she said, 'We're not doing this,' but that only stoked Laura's fury. Everything was always on Jess' terms.

'It's weird for a child to say broccoli is her favourite food,' Laura spat.

Jess spun back round. A vein was pulsing in her forehead. 'Stop it! Please.'

'And, as for Lola, well, she definitely was accusing Billy of stealing her stupid Switch—'

'No, she wasn't.'

Laura waved Jess' comments away. 'Yes, she was. Which is just typical of her. She acts like she's forty-five, not ten. All spookily adult and controlling. She's going to end up with an eating disorder or something.'

Jess blanched and Laura knew she'd gone too far. 'I'm sorry.'

'I think you should go.'

Chapter Fifty-One

Laura sat on the sofa with her laptop balanced on her knees. The child who lived next door had started his nightly violin practice and – although Laura very much wanted to be supportive of a young person playing an instrument – goodness, it was difficult when the sound was *that* bad. Especially since it seemed like there was nearly always some child in her neighbourhood hammering away at some poor instrument – the perils, she supposed, of living in Dulwich.

Laura stared at her laptop screen. She had no idea why she'd found herself on Jess' site. God knows she'd had quite enough of her sister for one evening. And yet when she'd seen an Instagram post about *The Homewear Brand You Need to Check Out Now* she'd somehow found herself clicking. Yup, that was how shallow Laura was: She wanted nothing to do with Jess . . . unless Jess was talking about cushions.

Now Laura found herself moving on from soft furnishings and mindlessly skimming articles: *Lady in Red: How to Wear the Colour of the Season; Seven Smart Storage Solutions; The Versatile Dress Edit . . .*

And then Laura came across Jess' article about losing a parent. She knew Jess had written it but she had avoided reading it up until now.

Recently I lost my mum, Jess started. *And, although it's painful for me, I wanted to talk about it here because death is such a taboo.*

Back in Victorian times, no one talked about sex in polite company but people were quite open about death. Now the opposite is true. And yet death is one of life's certainties . . .

Laura read on and, while she couldn't exactly disagree with anything Jess said – it all being so bloody obvious there was nothing to disagree with – the tone of it really got up her nose. Jess just made everything sound so easy, as if bereavement was simply another item that could be effortlessly ticked off her to-do list.

You have to work through bereavement, Jess trilled.

Or maybe it works through you, Laura thought, digging her nails into her palms.

Laura read on as Jess advised people to continue to talk to their lost loved ones *as if they were sitting right next to you in a chair.*

Oh, please, Laura thought. What if you knew your lost loved one would be sitting there telling you looked like you'd put on a few pounds? She kept reading, the anger fizzing in her belly as the article became increasingly full of gluey sentimentality and schmaltz.

How dare Jess talk about grief in such a reductive way? Where was the truth? The mention of rage, relief, confusion and other unacceptable feelings.

MsRealityCheck reared her ugly head in Laura's consciousness. The last time Laura had been tempted to post as the keyboard warrior, she had been stopped in her tracks by a wave of self-disgust. What had come over her when she decided to create the fake account and why had she thought it was okay to send her sister those messages? One thing was for sure, whatever guff she'd come up with about helping Jess to be more self-aware was nonsense. The truth was Laura would be very ashamed if anyone found out what she was doing. Even Jon, who was not exactly her sister's biggest fan. Laura had resolved that she would put her previous posts down to her being all over the place about her mother's death (hmm) and NEVER post as MsRealityCheck again.

So why were her fingers hovering over the keyboard right now? And why were all kinds of snarky comments racing through her mind?

Laura started typing as MsRealityCheck. Then she stopped. Was this just about her earlier row with Jess? She didn't like to think of herself as (quite) that small.

But Laura's desire to leave a comment now wasn't about their row. Jess' grief article had provoked a visceral reaction in Laura. *Someone* needed to tell Jess not to trivialize grief or make it sound easy, because there would be people out there who were totally unmoored. People who didn't need to be made to feel *even* worse. Laura had written plenty of anodyne articles in her time – she wrote for *Natter* for goodness' sake – but she liked to think she would have tackled something as important as this with a little more honesty. Death stinks.

Laura started typing as MsRealityCheck. *Death might well be a taboo but do you really think your site is the place to tackle it? For me, it makes an unhappy bedfellow with articles about how to wear red and homeware brands.*

And then Laura posted the comment before she could change her mind.

Chapter Fifty-Two

Laura *thought* a lot about apologizing to Jess. She couldn't make amends for her latest outing as MsRealityCheck, of course, even if she did feel horrible about it (the arguments she'd used to justify it to herself at the time seeming less and less valid by the minute). But Laura could say sorry for how she'd behaved in person.

She stood under the shower squeezing her eyes shut, trying to ignore the voice in her head telling her to phone Jess. Or message her – something.

She watched *Queer Eye* without really watching it, ate meals without tasting them and read the same paragraph over and over in *Good Grief.* (To be fair, when she did finally take the paragraph in, it just annoyed her. It was about a woman who'd had to hide her grief because the person who died was her married lover. Laura didn't feel a great deal of sympathy – having had the misfortune to have had not one but two serious boyfriends who'd cheated on her, she could still remember the stomach-churning feeling of betrayal.)

Apologize to Jess, apologize to Jess, apologize to Jess.

At work she found herself having to get people to repeat things when they asked her a question. Sitting in meetings but not actually being there. Could she get an interview with the twins who'd given birth on the same day? Dani wanted to know.

Laura's mind was on the *terrible* things she'd said to Jess.

She pulled herself back to the present as Dani continued. The twins weren't unkind to look at so it would make for some decent photos.

She found herself looking at Jess' Instagram. She wanted to see if she was okay or if their row was making her unhappy too. But it was hard to tell that from a piece called *Style Steals for Spring*. Laura found herself clicking on a link to some sandals. She was an awful person to be thinking of sandals right now. But they would go with everything.

When she'd picked Billy up from school and taken him to the playground, she'd watched him clamber up the monkey ropes. A woman a few feet away kept admonishing her own little boy: *Be nice to your sister.*

Be nice to your sister.

In the supermarket later that afternoon, Billy had whined at her to get him the superhero yoghurts. 'Daddy would let me.' Laura stared at the shelf, the labels changing before her eyes so they read: *Call her!*

She bought the yoghurts but Billy was still not happy. Why was it such a long wait for the bus? He was bored. He tugged at Laura's arm as he bounced up and down. 'Can we go and see Lola and Hannah and Auntie Jess? Can we? Can we?' Laura's chest hurt. She'd told Jess her little girl was going to end up with an eating disorder. *Who* says things like that?

She pulled the nit comb through Billy's hair that evening, unable to believe he had nits again. Last time, Jess had dealt with them for her.

On Saturday, Jon came to pick up Billy.

'New denim jacket, mate?'

Billy nodded. 'Auntie Jess gave it to me. It used to be Hannah's but now she is too big.'

'StyleMaven approved,' Jon said to Laura, smirking.

Normally she would have laughed but today she just shrugged. The least she owed Jess was a bit of loyalty.

Sometimes she got as far as picking up her phone, scrolling to Jess' number. With Dad and Mum both gone, Jess was the only family she had left.

People always said blood was thicker than water, but when push comes to shove do you owe more to people who are only part of your life by the accident of birth? Jess was the person Laura had fought with in the backseat of the car, the person she had endured endless camping trips in the rain with and the person who she was thrown together with for weddings, funerals and Christmas. But did that mean the two of them were bound together forever and whatever – two little orphans clinging to what they had left.

Karen at work casually dropped it into conversation that she hadn't spoken to her brother for over ten years. *What happened?* Natasha asked. Karen shrugged. *A row over toothpaste.* Everyone laughed, including Karen, and Laura stared at her. Was she traumatized on the inside; did she feel as if she was missing a limb? She was certainly hiding it very well if she did.

'Ooh, I don't think I could do that,' Greta said. 'My sister eats meat, drives a four-by-four around Fulham and spouts the worst kind of politics imaginable but I don't think I could just stop speaking to her altogether. What if one of us got run over by a bus?' She turned to Laura, her cheeks colouring. 'Sorry.'

Lots of people acted this way around Laura now. As if she'd forgotten her mother had died two and a half months earlier but the mention of death would remind her. She swore Chloe had looked embarrassed the other day when she'd said her phone had died.

That night Laura couldn't sleep. The light from the lamp-posts leached under the blinds and she stared at a crack in the ceiling. Jess had started it.

Christ, what was she, twelve?

She would call Jess in the morning. It wasn't difficult.

Eventually she drifted off to sleep, but she woke up sweaty and breathless after a dream that Greta was telling her that it was actually her sister that had been run over by a bus. Wasn't that something! Jon was there too. Asking if she'd get a discount at the funeral directors since she'd used them so recently.

In the morning, Billy wanted to play with the guinea pig even though they were already running late.

'You'll miss registration,' she told him. 'Mummy will be late for work.'

Billy was reaching into the cage, pulling out the small ginger and white bundle. 'Buzz will be sad if I don't play with him.'

That was highly questionable. Everything pointed to the fact that the guinea pig endured, rather than enjoyed, Billy's small and clumsy hands wrenching him from his warm straw so that he could be shown a new Lego creation or drawing. But Laura said nothing because her head was elsewhere. She couldn't call Jess now; she'd be getting the girls ready for school. Laura pictured her, immaculate and tiny in something leopard print, doing Hannah's plaits meticulously, reaching out for the occasional sip of matcha tea.

On the tube, she clung to the strap and typed out a message. *I'm sorry if* . . . She stopped, that was what she always accused Jess of doing. Not that Jess had done that this time. She didn't seem to be in any hurry to get in touch. And she *had* been having a go at Billy when she said he seemed tired. Everyone knows that mums speak in code. When a parent comes to pick up their child after a playdate and asks you how they've been, the minimum response is 'fine'. Even when said child has flooded your sink, said the spaghetti bolognese was disgusting and repeatedly called your son a 'poo poo head'.

So Jess didn't really have the moral high ground.

Except she hadn't talked about Billy developing an eating disorder.

Sorry I said those terrible things. x

See, it wasn't hard.

She emerged from the tube, but couldn't quite bring herself to press send.

Chapter Fifty-Three

Then

Laura lay on the hospital gurney with tears rolling down her cheeks.

'I'm sure your mum will be here soon, love,' Adam's mum said, squeezing Laura's hand. 'The nurse has gone to try to phone her again now.'

Laura thought back to the moment a few weeks earlier when she'd told her mother she was pregnant. Evie's disgust had crackled around the room. 'How?' Laura had made a face. 'I mean how could you have been so stupid?' Evie snapped.

'We weren't stupid,' Laura had said. 'We used a condom. It's just—'

'Spare me the details,' Evie'd said, her lip curling.

'There, there, my love,' Adam's mum said now, stroking Laura's hair.

Evie had just assumed that Laura would get an abortion and was horrified when Laura said she was going to keep the baby. 'You're nineteen, for goodness' sake. What about going to university?'

Laura had shrugged and tried to display a confidence she didn't actually feel. She could go to university once the baby was born, she'd said.

Her mother had looked at her like she was insane. 'And what about *him*?'

Him. Adam was Laura's first proper boyfriend and Laura had been desperate for her mother to like him, or even to dislike him; just *something*. But, as it was, her mother was far too preoccupied with her own rather complicated love life (a sea of admirers, all of whom seemed to be kept slightly at bay). Whatever scraps of interest in such matters Evie had left got thrown in Jess' direction. That boy, Ben, Jess had met at uni seemed nice, and weren't the two of them similar – peas in a pod, they were.

When Laura had started bleeding she was at Adam's house. He didn't know what to do and neither did she.

When the bleeding started to be accompanied by cramping, Adam had panicked and gone to get his mum. She had handled the situation as calmly as she had the news of the pregnancy weeks earlier. She had them all at the hospital in less than twenty minutes, held Laura's hand and told her it was going to be okay.

Everyone at the hospital had been nice too. One of the nurses told Laura that this was a bereavement, and not to let anyone make her feel otherwise, that it didn't matter that Laura wasn't that far gone, she had still lost her baby.

Laura looked at Adam's mum. If any part of her thought it was a good thing her nineteen-year-old son's girlfriend was miscarrying their unplanned baby, she was much too kind to say so. She seemed to understand that, even if no one – Laura included – thought this baby was a good idea, that didn't mean that Laura didn't still want it desperately. She had already bonded with the little bean that was growing inside of her, whispered to it that she was going to love it more than anything else in the world. Love it ferociously and unconditionally.

'He won't stay with you, you know,' Evie had said a few days ago, 'that Adam. He'll stick around for a bit trying to do the decent thing, but once that baby arrives and screams all night long, you won't see him for dust.'

Laura lay on the gurney wondering if her mother would

have been proved right. Adam's mum had dispatched him to the café to get Laura a cup of tea and he seemed to have been gone ages, certainly much longer than it took to go the café and back. Laura could suddenly picture him sitting somewhere weeping with relief.

Meanwhile, not a single one of Laura's tears were of relief, even if her rational brain (and her mother's voice inside her head) told her they should be.

Laura wasn't relieved, she was desolate. She could hardly believe she had lost her baby, that she was never going to get to meet and hold him or her. Maybe the doctors had got it wrong and she was still pregnant? They got these things wrong sometimes; everyone knew that.

'You poor love,' Adam's mum said. Laura was grateful to her for not trying to say more. She didn't want to hear that maybe this was for the best or that she was very young.

Adam's mum gently dabbed at Laura's cheeks with a tissue. Laura had decided that, if the baby was a boy, she was going to call it George after her dad, and she had even bought some little baby-sized trainers the other day. The image of them hidden away in her underwear drawer made Laura wonder suddenly if buying them had been tempting fate. Also, she hadn't stopped drinking until she had discovered she was pregnant, and she'd taken paracetamol for a headache more than once. A surge of guilt washed over her.

'Miscarriages happen,' Adam's mum said, as if she could read Laura's mind. 'It's nothing you did or didn't do.'

Laura had hoped her mother's initial anger would dissipate and she would gradually warm to the idea of this new little life, but Evie's rage had just seemed to calcify. She repeated the same mantras daily: *Laura was mad to keep this baby. It was going to ruin her life. And if she thought Evie was going to give up her time to help look after it, well, then she had another thing coming. She was too young to play grandma, way too young.*

Laura started to cry again.

'Sssh,' Adam's mum said. 'Sometimes you just want your mum, don't you?'

Laura felt a tightness in her chest as she looked at the kind woman she barely knew who was stroking her hair so tenderly – a more motherly mother you couldn't hope to find. This was a woman who was always trying to press food on anyone who walked through her door, a woman whose mere presence soothed and calmed.

Laura thought about her own mother, who would no doubt arrive in a puff of Shalimar and try to brush this all away as if it was *nothing*. She would tell Laura that she was relieved, and that this was for the best. Laura could take up her place at uni now, she wouldn't find herself marrying a man who was only at the altar because it was the decent thing to do. And everything that Laura's mother said would be true. But Laura did not want to hear it. She just wanted someone who stroked her hair and squeezed her hand and told her they were so very sorry.

Right now, disloyal though it was, Laura wished Adam's mum was her own.

Chapter Fifty-Four

As Laura stood on the packed tube she wondered if there was any chance that today might be an easy day. It was a faint hope – normally the day the magazine went to print was manic, but there was always a chance. She certainly hoped so as she had quite enough on her mind, what with worrying about whether she'd ruined Billy's life and whether she would ever speak to her sister again.

As she emerged from the tube station her mobile rang.

'Hello,' said an unfamiliar voice at the other end. 'It's Jan Towler.'

The woman who slept with the best man the night before her wedding. Laura's stomach clenched. *Don't say it, don't say it.*

'I don't want you to print that story. I've been chatting with my mate Jackie about it and she reckons I'm gonna get all kinds of grief over it. People thinking I'm a slag. And I'm not a slag.'

Laura stood motionless at the mouth of the tube station while people shoved past her. She stared out at the overcast sky. She was used to stories dropping out, of course, even on the day the magazine was going to print, but she just didn't have the energy to deal with it today. 'I'm sure no one will think you're a slag, Jan. We've told the story very sympathetic-ally. Shown that Mitch had a history of cheating on you.'

Silence buzzed down the line. 'Yeah, but—'

'How about you have a little think and I'll call you back?' Laura said. She'd learned over the years that if you weren't too pushy with people when they got nervy, they often let you run the story after all. Plus, a delay would give her a chance to talk to Dani. The thought of telling Dani made her groan out loud and a man walking past gave her a very strange look.

Laura trudged towards the office feeling gloomy. Last night she'd impulsively looked for the *Inlustris* job ad only to discover that, of course, it wasn't there anymore. Laura had kicked herself for not even trying. She had vowed that next time something came up that sounded good, she was going to go for it. But situations like this reminded Laura exactly what had stopped her applying to *Inlustris*. She wasn't really a *proper* journalist. Proper journalists took things like stories dropping out in their stride. Laura, by contrast, was highly tempted to turn around, go back home and take to her bed with a large block of cheese.

As soon as she got into the office she headed straight for Dani.

'Ahh, Laura,' Dani said, 'I wanted to talk to you.'

Perfect, Laura thought, adopting a mental brace position.

'Did you see that report that has come out today showing that people between thirty-five and forty-nine spend the most time on social media?'

'I did,' Laura lied.

'What do you think about doing an "Is it okay to be a social media addict" story?' Before Laura could mistake this for a question, Dani continued. 'A simple "yes" or "no" debate. You can do the no and then get an influencer to do the yes. Maybe ChiaraPicks or StyleMaven?'

'I'm sorry?' Laura said, not able to quite believe what she'd just heard because surely – surely – Dani had not just mentioned Jess?

'ChiaraPicks or StyleMaven.'

Would now be a good time to mention that StyleMaven was actually her sister and that they weren't really on speaking terms right now? 'Umm, I'm not sure we should get an influencer to do the yes. I mean they would say that, wouldn't they?'

Dani looked at her quizzically. 'That's rather the point.'

'Right,' Laura said. ChiaraPicks better be on board. She turned to go back to her desk.

'Was there something you wanted to talk to me about?' Dani said.

Laura couldn't believe she'd forgotten about Jan Towler for a moment. 'Yes,' she said. 'My bride who slept with the best man has got cold feet about us running the story.'

Dani's face scrunched. 'Can't you talk her round?'

'I can try,' Laura said. The truth was she felt slightly uncomfortable about this. Jan's friend was probably right that Jan would get all kinds of abuse. Also, Laura couldn't shake the feeling that she'd manipulated Jan a bit at the interview stage, especially as Jan wasn't someone who was ever going to trouble Mensa. And, yes, she could say that Jan had got her two-hundred-quid fee and loved being centre of attention at the photo shoot, but Laura knew she'd acted as if she was Jan's friend and that made her feel more than a bit shabby.

'Yes, please do,' Dani said, standing up to indicate that the conversation was over.

As Laura walked back to her desk, she saw Oli Greaves waiting for her, the designer who had gone out of his way (sometimes spectacularly so) to avoid her since she'd come back to work. Just when today couldn't get any better.

'What can I do for you, Oli?' she said.

Oli was behaving as if an invisible piece of string was tethering each eyeball to the floor. 'Shall we nip into the Lamb & Flag?' he mumbled.

'Perfect,' Laura said. 'I could murder a glass of wine.'

'I meant the meeting room,' Oli said.

'Err, I was joking.'

'Oh,' Oli said, not laughing.

Laura followed him, wondering if the woman who had run out of Sainsbury's to avoid Jess was still keeping away from her. And if Laura would ever speak to Jess again to find out.

In the meeting room Oli sat, the invisible strings still keeping his eyes firmly on the ground. 'So,' he blurted, showing her some printouts of a layout for her article about a woman whose husband had dropped dead on a family walk. 'I was just wondering if you'd be able to cut this copy.'

Laura stared at the massive photograph in the middle of the page. Oli could quite easily make it a tiny bit smaller and have room for all the copy. But Laura couldn't face arguing with him and was keen to get back on the phone to Jan Towler as soon as possible. She also had to make a decision about her sister. Even if you set aside their current row, she wouldn't be mad keen on commissioning Jess to write a piece for *Natter* – that wasn't so much inviting Jess to tread on her toes as getting her to stamp heavily all over them. She looked at Oli. 'I can cut the copy. But could you do one thing for me? Could you stop avoiding me?'

The strings broke and Oli looked up, his face puce. 'I haven't . . . I'm not . . .'

Laura wished she hadn't said anything. 'I just wanted to say that I'm fine.' (Highly questionable use of the word 'fine'.) 'You can treat me normally.'

Oli looked as if he might cry and Laura felt awful. She got up to leave the room.

'Laura,' Oli called after her. She turned around. 'I'm sorry about your mum.'

'Thanks.' Why oh why had she said something? Her inter-actions with Oli were bound to be way more excruciating than their non-interactions.

Back at her desk, Laura dialled Jan's number, wishing as she did that the sales team weren't always so noisy. This was a hard enough call as it was.

Jan picked up on the third ring.

'Jan,' Laura said, hating herself for the exaggerated friend-liness in her voice. Would she have had to manipulate her interviewees if she'd got the job at *Inlustris*? Not that it mattered because she'd blown her chance of even being in the running for a job there. 'So, I've just been looking at the article again and I think it paints a really sympathetic picture of you—'

'I don't wanna do it,' Jan said.

Two of the guys in sales had started playing desk table tennis. Laura covered the phone so that Jan wouldn't hear the jeering. 'Look, I can absolutely see why you'd get nervous but I really think people will understand why you were driven to do what you did.' She really hated herself right now. The truth was Laura was the last person who was understanding about such matters. Having been cheated on herself, she knew exactly how much damage it could do, and she took a very firm line on people who had affairs. Of course they would always make excuses, but that's exactly what they were: excuses.

'I don't wanna do it,' Jan repeated.

The table-tennis ball landed with a smack right in the middle of Laura's desk. It was like working in a bloody creche. 'The thing is, Jan, we did pay you for the article.' Another piece of integrity out of the window, but if Laura didn't say it now, Dani would just make her call back.

Silence came down the line.

Please, Laura thought, *please*.

'I'll give the money back.'

Laura stared at the phone. 'Is there anything I can say to persuade you to change your mind?'

'Nah.'

Laura said goodbye and let her head fall into her hands.

'Having a good day so far?' Amy said, appearing at Laura's desk.

'The best.' She got up. 'I've got to talk to Dani.'

Dani looked displeased before Laura even started speaking.

'I'm afraid I couldn't change Jan Towler's mind,' Laura said.

Dani did a whole body sigh. 'Let's run the story anyway.'

'Really?' Laura said.

'Yup. She agreed to it, let us do an interview and a photo shoot, accepted a fee—'

'She says she'll give that back.'

Dani swatted the air. 'We're running the story.'

Laura walked back to her desk wondering how on earth it could possibly still only be 9.40 a.m.

Chapter Fifty-Five

Laura was standing at Jess' front door, unable to believe there was no answer to her insistent ringing of the bell. It shouldn't have come as a surprise, of course, no one knew she was coming, but somehow it just hadn't crossed her mind that there wouldn't be someone at home.

She should have messaged Jess to say she was coming. It was fair to say her sister wasn't exactly Mrs Spontaneous – she and Ben probably diarized sex sessions – but Laura had been worried that if she'd messaged, Jess might have said no, made some excuse about being very busy.

She rang the doorbell again. Maybe they were all at the bottom of the garden?

Laura hadn't planned to come here today. Well, not consciously at least. But in the back of her mind there had been a guilt about their row gnawing away at her, especially when Dani had mentioned StyleMaven and Laura hadn't even said it was her sister. That had felt like a new low, especially when, later that day, Laura had compounded matters by commissioning ChiaraPicks to write the yes part of the 'Is it okay to be a social media addict' story.

But it wasn't just guilt that drove Laura. There was also this pervading feeling that she had already lost Dad, Mum and Jon (a different kind of loss, but a loss nonetheless) and she couldn't lose Jess too. Her sister might be annoying, but she was the only person left who shared the tapestry of their childhood. Laura might feel ridiculous classifying herself as an orphan but she was fully aware that becoming one placed additional weight on the relationship with her sister.

Jon had Billy for the day and Laura had lots of ideas about how she was going to spend her Saturday being busy and productive. She was going to spring clean the flat. Was the 30th of March a bit late to start on such a thing? Probably. If you were a Jess-type person you would be done and (literally) dusted weeks ago. But Laura wasn't a Jess-type person. After sorting the flat, Laura was planning to go to the supermarket and buy lots of healthy food so she could meal prep for the week ahead – she was determined she was going to change into a meal-prepping sort of mother. She also had the very weird sensation of noting that she'd better pick up a Mother's Day card for tomorrow before realizing that she didn't actually need one.

However, as she shut the door to Jon and Billy, Laura hadn't been thinking about cards or plans because she had an overwhelming urge to see her sister. It was a weird feeling, and she had rarely been troubled by such a thing in the past.

And now she was standing in Jess' front garden trying to decide if it was a good idea to wait for a bit. She wondered where they might all be. Perhaps they were out to lunch? A perfect Clapham family sitting in a sunny café on Northcote Road. Laura could picture them; it wouldn't be like when she and Jon took Billy out to eat, instead they would all be chatting and laughing while they ate food off their own plates, no one frightening the other diners. Or perhaps Jess and Ben were ferrying the girls to one of their many improving activities like karate, or Kumon maths or Tiger Sharks? She and Jon had made a conscious decision to avoid all that kind of stuff with Billy. The things he described as 'bourgeois crap'.

Laura glanced at her watch and saw it was just after one.

She'd wait for a bit. It was a nice day and, if she left now, she might lose her nerve about apologizing. She might remember that, actually, although she shouldn't have said what she said, it was Jess who started it all with that bullshit about Billy being tired, not to mention Lola basically calling Billy a thief.

But she didn't want to think about that now, just like she didn't want to think about the fact that after the story about Jan Towler had run, Jan had been absolutely ripped to shreds on social media. Laura had been tempted not to take her call when her phone number had flashed up, but then decided that was the least she could do. Her reward was a sobbing Jan calling her 'the scum of the earth' and saying she didn't know how Laura could sleep at night.

Laura's stomach rumbled loudly and she realized she'd been so busy trying to coax Billy to eat his cereal this morning that she hadn't actually eaten any breakfast herself. She scrabbled in her bag and found a half-eaten packet of biscuits nestling at the bottom next to a lone sticky cough sweet and a tampon that had broken free of its wrapper. The top biscuit was caked in tampon fluff so she threw that in the wheelie bin and ate the next two.

A sleek blonde in head-to-toe lycra looked quizzically at Laura as she passed, and Laura wasn't sure if it was because the woman thought she didn't look smart enough for the house and so could be a burglar, or simply because she was appalled by the sight of someone munching a chocolate HobNob in plain sight.

Laura heard her mother's voice in her head: *You'd look nice if you lost a bit of weight.* She stuffed another biscuit in her mouth and chewed it in big, joyless, sandy mouthfuls.

Laura stared at Jess' glossy front door (painted in the must-have dark grey of the moment from Farrow & Ball) which was flanked by two immaculate bay trees. It all looked so perfect, like it had just been styled for a shoot. She wished

Jess was a little less perfect. But that was never going to happen.

This was crazy. They could be out for the whole day. She'd give it another twenty minutes or so and then go. Maybe she'd leave Jess a note. But, of course, she didn't have a pen and paper on her, and anyway, they needed to have this conversation in person.

If I'm going to wait, I may as well do something useful, Laura thought, but then she found herself opening Facebook and twenty minutes later she'd done nothing more productive than wish someone she'd worked with over ten years ago and hadn't seen since a happy birthday, seen that Sarah Goth had updated her profile picture and watched a GIF of kittens in hats (quite life-enhancing, to be fair).

It was nearly two o'clock. Time to go.

Chapter Fifty-Six

Then

Laura and Jon were late to his grandmother's funeral. They shouldn't have stayed out so long last night. One more beer, one more dance . . . until they were among the last to leave the club and it was starting to get light. The bagel place down the road had already opened its doors, unleashing a waft of warmth and yeasty deliciousness.

Jon's mother was tight-lipped when they arrived at the house. 'We've been waiting for you.' She looked at Laura as if she had no doubt where the blame lay, and Laura was suddenly acutely aware of the shortness of her skirt and the skimpiness of the spaghetti straps (it was the only black dress she owned, one of just a few dresses, for that matter). Great. As if it wasn't enough to have her own mother disapprove of her every waking move. Perhaps she could work towards a situation where she had a whole raft of mothers who found her to be a total disappointment.

A big black car was parked outside and Laura suddenly remembered getting into a similar one the day of her dad's funeral. She felt a wave of sudden and powerful nausea.

'There's only room for *family*,' Jon's mother snapped as Laura went to step in.

'Oh, come on, Mum,' Jon said. 'We can squeeze up.'

She shook her head. 'You've already made us late. And there are plenty of people that can give her a lift.'

As it was, there weren't plenty of people who could give Laura a lift and she found herself half walking and half running the two miles to the church, her new shoes rubbing big, puffy blisters on her heels.

She arrived at the church sweaty and agitated and conferred with one of the men directing people to their seats. Was she family? She was Jon's girlfriend. The man nodded and gave her the chilliest of smiles before directing her to a seat right at the back. Several people had to move to let her in and she started to clamber over bags and feet. 'Sorry, sorry, sorry . . .'

She had only met Jon's parents once before today when she had been to their house for Sunday lunch. Even though she and Jon weren't into bourgeois things like marriage, she liked him more than she'd care to admit and she wanted the meeting to go well. Sadly, his parents didn't seem to warm to her. When they asked her what she did for a living and she said she was a journalist, they reacted very much as if she'd said 'street walker'. And when she responded to their enquiries about her parents with the information that her father was dead, they looked at her as if this was the result of some carelessness on her part. Lunch was a stilted affair and, even though Laura's own family drove her mad, she noted that at least they had the good manners to always talk over each other.

Jon gave her an encouraging smile from the front row and she smiled back. Her temples throbbed. She would win his parents over and, in the meantime, she certainly didn't want him to know it worried her. He always called her his 'little hippy chick' and little hippy chicks didn't stress.

The hymn started: 'Morning Has Broken'. The same one as they'd had at her dad's funeral. Suddenly Laura was twelve years old again, standing between her mum and Jess, biting the inside of her cheek and trying so hard to be brave that it made her whole body scream in protest.

Tears started to roll down her cheeks now. She wiped them away self-consciously.

Jon's brother got up to do a reading, but Laura wasn't listening. All she could hear was Jess reading from the Corinthians, her voice calm and clear. Incredible to think her sister had only been fourteen at the time. Jess may get on her nerves but Laura had to admit she was one tough cookie.

Laura had started to cry properly. She scrabbled in her bag for a bit of loo roll but couldn't find anything. And she didn't even have a sleeve. The woman next to her handed her a peach tissue and patted her roughly on the arm.

The small kindness unhinged Laura even more and she started to sob messily and noisily. People glanced in her direction and she steeled herself, trying to get a grip, especially as the front row of close family were all resolutely dry-eyed. Laura couldn't imagine Jon's mother crying. Well, unless her beloved black lab died. Then she would no doubt weep copiously.

Jon's uncle was delivering the eulogy. Talking about Peggy's ninety-two years on this earth, her service during the war, her devotion to her family, thirty years of doing the flowers for the church.

Thinking about her own dad's eulogy, Laura sobbed even harder. She'd been too upset to take much of it in at the time, but she did remember Uncle James saying that he had asked Laura what she'd like said about her dad and she'd told him that he was someone who made the good things even better and the bad things bearable.

Jon glanced over at her. No doubt he was wondering why she was so upset. She tried to give him a wobbly smile.

She hoped he felt the same way about her as she did about him. They didn't talk about the future any more than they talked about mortgages or pensions. They were 'live in the moment, dance all night' people. C-A-S-U-A-L. But she hoped he was into her. She loved it when he said she was his muse for the novel he wanted to write. And when he said he hoped they were still going to raves when they were seventy, she'd savoured the 'they' like the last morsels of a delicious cake.

Perhaps she should just get out of here, stop making such a show of herself? The trouble was she would have to clamber over six people to get out.

She balled her fists and dug them into her eyes willing the tears to stop.

The peach-tissue lady patted her arm again. *Please*, Laura wanted to shout, *don't be kind! I may be able to stop as long as no one is kind.*

The vicar was doing the final address.

And suddenly they were all outside in the searing sunlight, Laura acutely conscious of her red, swollen eyes. Jon was trying to get to her but people kept stopping him to offer their condolences. His mother shot her a look of pure contempt.

'Are you okay now?' peach-tissue lady said.

Laura nodded because she still couldn't quite trust herself to speak.

'Were you and Peggy very close?'

Peggy? Jon's grandmother. The one she'd met all of once. The one whose funeral she'd just been to.

How did Laura tell the kind woman that it wasn't really Peggy she was upset about?

Chapter Fifty-Seven

Laura didn't know how she was supposed to feel today or even how she did actually feel. It was Mother's Day, the first one she had ever had where she no longer had a mother. Last Mother's Day, Evie hadn't even been ill.

Laura was curled up in bed with Billy looking at the card he'd made for her at school. On the front was a painting of a hyacinth, which Billy had remembered was Laura's favourite flower. Each little splodge of purple paint had been lovingly pressed onto the card by a chubby finger and it was just about the most beautiful thing Laura had ever seen.

'Do you like it, Mummy?' Billy said.

'I love it,' she said, kissing the top of his head which, just when he couldn't get any cuter, was sporting an impressive amount of bedhead.

As Laura had seen the shops start to fill up with cards, flowers and gifts in the run-up to today, she'd felt nervous. She'd also guiltily remembered her words to Jon last year. She had complained that she hardly ever got to appreciate Mother's Day as a mother because the day was always 'totally hijacked' by Evie.

Be careful what you wish for.

'Should I bring you breakfast in bed?' Billy said.

He really did look like Laura's dad – even if her mum hadn't been able to see it. 'No thank you, my sweetheart. We'll get up and have it together.'

'That's good,' Billy said. 'Because I don't know how to make tea.'

Laura smiled. She wasn't surprised Billy's template for Mother's Day was bringing her breakfast in bed because that was what he had always done with Jon (another thing that was different today). Last year Billy had dropped the toast just as the two of them had come into the bedroom and Laura had still eaten it even though there were bits of fluff, and possibly much worse, flecked through the butter.

'Shall we have treat cereal?' Billy said.

Laura laughed. 'Treat cereal' was the tooth-achingly sweet multi-coloured shapes that Billy had talked her into at the supermarket and if there was a food that was less of a treat for her, she couldn't think of it. 'Absolutely.'

'Yay!' Billy said. 'And can I go on the PlayStation before breakfast? Just for half an hour?'

Laura smiled at his opportunism. He had been allowed to do this on his birthday and had obviously registered it as a perk to be enjoyed on all high days and holidays. 'Okay, but only half an hour.'

Laura got up and made herself a cup of tea, guiltily registering as she stood in the kitchen that the flat looked messier than ever. Still, she could hardly be expected to spend Mother's Day clearing up. She may not need a spa day (especially after the last one) or a ritzy afternoon tea, but she wasn't going to spend the day in her Marigolds.

She got back into bed with her tea, wondering if she should message Jess to see if she was okay, but then she couldn't really think of a way to word the message that didn't seem trite. It was such a pity Jess hadn't been there when Laura had gone round yesterday. Laura had felt really disappointed when she got back to her own house, and when she noticed all the weeds from the front garden had miraculously disappeared, she'd briefly entertained the idea that Jess had been waiting at her house at the very same time (because it would have been *just* like Jess to busy herself with weeding while she waited). But then Laura had shaken her head and told herself she'd just watched too many movies. One of the neighbours must have done the weeding.

She took a sip of her tea. It really was a shame Jess had been out yesterday. It would have been so much easier to make up face to face. Laura had even planned to come clean about Dani mentioning her in a work context; make a joke of the whole thing by saying that she'd thought the last thing Jess would want was a commission from *Natter.*

Laura would have to pop over to Jess' sometime in the week, although if the last week at work was anything to go by, it was hard to see when she'd get a chance.

It was weird to think that her mother hadn't even been sick last Mother's Day. In fact, Laura remembered her being particularly hale and vital that day, flirting with the young waiter in the pub they'd taken her to for lunch, remonstrating Billy for failing to sit still like his cousins and asking Laura if she really thought yellow was her colour (no, Mum, that's why I'm wearing it).

Laura felt a sharp pang of guilt as she recalled the difficulty she'd had finding a Mother's Day card. She'd stood in the shop for ages browsing the racks but each and every saccharine offering seemed to be for different sorts of mothers. Mothers who were always there, mothers who made their children feel loved and cherished, mothers who always put their children first. Laura had felt a desperate, empty longing (well, just wait until next year).

Billy came bursting into the room and told her he'd completed level two.

'Excellent,' Laura said, sipping her tea. In the back of her mind, there had always been the possibility on the horizon of her and her mother having a big moment of emotional

219

connection. Laura had never been sure exactly what this looked like or where and when it would take place, she just knew there would be lots of weeping and hugging. 'My poor, darling girl,' her mother would say. And just like that all the years of hurt, anger and disappointment would have been wiped out.

But now, of course, she knew that moment would never happen.

Greta had taken Laura aside at work on Friday and said that she knew that Sunday was going to be very hard for her and that she'd bought Laura a rose quartz crystal (*very* healing) and some of her special home-brewed kombucha. And, even though the Kombucha looked and smelled like stagnant pond water, Laura had been very touched because most people just avoided the subject of Mother's Day around her as if somehow she might not see the 5482 schmaltzy advertisements telling her to 'Make her mother's day' or the endless tributes on social media.

In reality, of course she absolutely knew it was Mother's Day. But she was okay. Even if she didn't feel entirely okay about that.

Chapter Fifty-Eight

There was something about waiting to see the headmistress that made Laura feel as if she was five years old and had been very, very naughty.

She sat on the hard, plastic chair trying to stop herself shaking. The school secretary had refused to say much on the phone. 'If you could just come in Mrs— Miss Fraser. Perhaps with your partner.'

Jon was late. Of course he was.

Laura had a discreet swig of Gaviscon. She'd already had some on the way here but it didn't seem to have done much good. She was feeling as if she might be sick, actually.

She scrutinized the secretary's face for clues. Would she give her that small half-smile if Billy had done something really bad? Could Billy even do something really bad? After all, it wasn't likely they'd been called in because he was snorting coke or pulling a knife. How bad could a five-year-old be?

She glanced down at her jeans and sweatshirt. Just her luck that she'd get the call today, when she was looking her scruffiest. Not that clothes made any real difference, of course, but she was bound to feel slightly more confident if she had to face the headmistress looking a bit more presentable. Her mother had always admonished her for not making 'a bit of effort.' 'You can't conquer the world if you don't dress the part.'

Not that conquering the world felt like much of an issue

at the moment. Laura's mind flashed back to the excruciating incident at that morning's editorial meeting when Amy had accidentally dropped her in it. Chloe the fashion editor had been talking about a zebra-print midi skirt that everyone was after and said it had all started with StyleMaven putting it on her Instagram.

Amy grinned as she turned to Laura. 'You'll have to tell your sister she's a very influential influencer.'

Dani's head had shot up. 'StyleMaven is your sister?'

Laura tried to look as insouciant as possible for someone who had turned puce. 'Yeah.'

'But you didn't think to mention that when I suggested her as someone who might be able to do the yes part of the "social media addict" piece?' Dani said.

'Didn't seem relevant,' Laura said feebly.

She was brought abruptly back to the present when Jon burst through the swing doors looking sweaty and dishevelled. She could smell the hangover coming off him. Great! Whatever Billy had done, no doubt the headmistress would conclude it was hardly surprising, given his gene pool.

'What's this about?' he said.

A wave of nausea washed over Laura. She shook her head. 'They wouldn't say on the phone.'

Jon nodded. 'Don't look so worried.' He squeezed her hand and she felt pathetically grateful.

The headmistress opened the door to her office. She was wearing a trouser suit and had a sharp bob. 'Mr and Mrs— sorry, Miss Fraser and Mr Howell.'

The office had a view over the playground. Laura looked at the empty play equipment, which looked sad and unloved in the rain. Never mind 'April showers', today had been more 'April monsoons'.

'I'll get straight to the point,' the headmistress said. 'Billy has been hitting another boy in his class.'

Laura heard a gasp escape from what must have been her own mouth.

'Are you sure?' Jon said, quietly.

The headmistress said she was quite sure, that a member of staff had witnessed an incident.

Laura hated it being referred to as an 'incident'. It sounded so serious. Like there was going to be some kind of police report. 'Who?' she said.

The headmistress tucked a stray piece of hair behind her ear. 'I hardly think that matters.'

'WHO?' Laura said, more loudly than she'd intended.

'Angus Murray.'

'HE HITS EVERYONE!' Laura said.

The headmistress nodded and sighed. 'We have had some difficulties with Angus in the past. Indeed, we have had to speak to his parents on a number of occasions. But they have worked with us.' Laura heard the thinly veiled subtext. 'Angus has modified his behaviour considerably.'

'I bet it was just self-defence,' Laura said. 'That Angus hit Billy first.'

'Miss Fraser,' the headmistress said. 'I'm afraid that's just not the case.'

'Billy made me the sweetest Mother's Day card,' Laura said feebly. 'He's a very kind child.'

Jon put his hand over Laura's. 'Mrs Jenkins,' he said. Laura was somewhat surprised he'd even remembered the woman's name. He'd never been the kind of dad to get very involved in school stuff. She was the one who went through Billy's book bag, went to parents' evenings and filled in Billy's reading record. 'I don't know if you're aware of the change in circumstances at home recently . . .'

Laura looked at him. He was talking so calmly and rationally and she could see the headmistress' face changing and softening.

'. . . obviously I'm not making excuses for Billy hurting another child, but I do think it helps to have the full picture . . .'

Laura let Jon talk. She stared out into the playground, focussing on a red-and-white-spotted hairband that had been dropped on the ground and was lying sodden in the rain. No doubt some mother would be remonstrating her little girl about its absence this evening. *I've only just bought you that. Honestly, you'd lose your head if it wasn't screwed on.*

Billy wasn't a violent child; he never had been. He could be cheeky or rude and he was a nightmare when it came to eating fruits and vegetables, but he didn't hurt people. Except Lola the other week. Laura shouldn't have ignored that. If she'd punished him properly, she could have nipped all this in the bud.

'. . . he's obviously wrestling with all kinds of different feelings at the moment . . .'

Laura stared at the spotty headband again. She'd sounded like a loon bringing up the Mother's Day card but Billy was a good kid and he certainly wasn't violent. They'd done this to him: her and Jon. She was hit by a wave of nausea so strong that she thought she might actually vomit. Her heart was racing too. She willed herself not to have a panic attack; not now and not here. Breathe, Laura, breathe.

Jon had finished talking and the headmistress was speaking now. Saying how much it helped to have the full picture and, of course, the school would do everything they could to support Billy at this difficult time. Her whole demeanour had changed; in fact, she seemed almost flirtatious towards Jon.

You've seen the best of the man, Laura felt like shouting. *Try stopping him from getting pissed night after night. Try stopping him from banging on about his stupid novel. Try getting him to earn money to put some food in his child's mouth.*

She had to hand it to Jon though – he had been good in this meeting. Way better than her. She was still wondering if there was any way she could get Angus Murray on his own. *Tell me the truth, you little shit! You started this, didn't you?*

The headmistress got up and shook both their hands and Laura could swear she batted her stubby little eyelashes at Jon. She supposed he was still a good-looking man. Even if he did smell a bit unsavoury this morning.

'Where are the toilets please?' Laura said to the secretary on the way out.

'At the end of that corridor on the right. Not the first toilets you see on your left – they're just for the children.'

The nausea was back with a vengeance and Laura had broken into a sweat. She hurtled down the corridor. Out of the corner of her eye, she could see the first toilets: the ones just for children. They would have to do.

Laura threw herself through the door and into a cubicle just in time to hurl the contents of her stomach into the tiny, child-sized toilet.

Chapter Fifty-Nine

It's the little things that unravel you. Laura had been so worried about how she was going to cope with Mother's Day, but actually grief doesn't check its calendar or care about 'special days'. Laura had been fine on Mother's Day, but on a random Tuesday morning a week or so before, she'd had to walk out of Starbucks because she'd suddenly remembered her mother making her snort with laughter when she expressed her utter derision for anyone whose coffee order was 'more than four words long'.

'Who are these people with their "half-caf, no sugar, extra shot, hold the whip and make it a venti" bullshit?' she'd asked.

What had poleaxed Laura today was the realization that her mum would have been great about the whole Angus Murray thing. Evie was not a woman who was afraid of authority. She would probably have laughed and said Angus was a little sod who had it coming to him. Not very PC, but very Evie.

Laura looked at the crumpled leaflet that had been sitting in the bottom of her handbag for weeks. Lilypad Bereavement Support. Lilypad! It had been given to her by one of the nurses at the hospice. Laura had taken it out of politeness, convinced she'd never need it except, maybe, as an example of typefaces to be avoided at all costs.

But now she was lying on her bed staring at the crack in the ceiling, unable to stop crying. She'd had to call work and say she thought she had a stomach bug (easier than saying: *Do you know it turns out, eleven weeks in, I do miss my mother after all. And, yes, she could be a bloody nightmare but still*).

Lilypad Bereavement Groups are open to everyone.

Hmm. Could she really go to a grief group? She hadn't even finished reading *Good Grief* yet. That's how rubbish she was at all this.

Laura knew the dangers of running away from grief; for years she had tried to stop herself from really feeling the weight of her Dad's absence, lest it crush her completely. But she had learned that you can never outrun grief – that you might think you can for a while, but it will lurk in the shadows and wrap its icy tentacles around your heart when you least expect it. Once, when she was in her twenties, she had been on her way to a rave and, for no apparent reason, she'd just starting sobbing uncontrollably. The people she was with had tried to be nice but they didn't really know what to do with her. Did she want to stop at a garage? Was she still upset about that scumbag Pete cheating on her? She'd feel better when she took an E. (No, yes, no.)

Laura wanted to deal with her grief ('deal with it' – like it was a tax return) and felt guilty she hadn't been 'sad enough' since her mother had died.

She felt queasy when she remembered catching herself looking in the mirror the day of the funeral and smiling, actually smiling, because the skirt she was wearing seemed a bit loose on her. She harboured a fear that it was weird she had spent so much of the last couple of months focussed on how much she missed her dad (you've had twenty-five years to get used to that one, Laura). And she was troubled by how few tears she had shed.

Now she was crying though. Real, ugly crying.

Why, couldn't she just be the *right* amount of sad?

Our groups are of a drop-in nature, which means you can come regularly or just when you feel you need to.

When Laura and Jess were little, their favourite game was dress up. They tottered around in their mum's heels, weighed down by jewellery and silky scarves. Sometimes their mum would put a little make-up on them, curl their hair. Often the three of them would end up laughing so hard they could barely breathe. She had a good laugh, Evie, rich and infectious.

Laura would never hear it again.

Just like she wouldn't hear her mum saying that she was crazy to get so upset over being called into the school, that all kids did stuff like this sometimes and there was absolutely no need to worry. She probably would have said that it sounded like Mrs Jenkins needed to get laid too. And Laura would have laughed despite herself.

Our groups are facilitated by a trained psychologist but they're not formal therapeutic sessions. Instead, they're a chance for you to chat to other people about whatever you'd like to on the day. And there's coffee and biscuits too – we're big fans of biscuits!

Evie wasn't like other people's mothers. She didn't have a secret recipe for chocolate cake. Or endless patience. She wouldn't clean your flat the moment your back was turned.

But she was Laura's mum.

And Laura missed her.

228

Chapter Sixty

It was hard not to notice just how much Billy liked the three of them all being together. Even if he was being told off.

'But I didn't really hurt him, Daddy.'

'Still best not to hit, kiddo.'

'Angus is *always* hitting! He gave me the idea.'

Laura could see Jon trying to suppress a smile. The three of them were in a café just down the road from the school. 'I'm not sure we should have this conversation in a public place,' she'd said when Jon suggested it.

He'd laughed. 'I don't think there will be a scene.'

She was too tired to argue. After throwing up in the world's smallest toilet and then spending the afternoon sobbing, she wasn't exactly at her best.

'Can I have a doughnut now?' Billy said.

Laura thought you probably shouldn't give your kid a doughnut when you were having A Talk, that it sent a bit of a mixed message, but she couldn't face arguing.

When he'd been led into the playground at the end of the school day and seen both his parents waiting there together, Billy's face had broken into a grin so wide it looked as if it might split his face in two. Laura's heart had lurched: *We're only together to tell you off. And don't get too used to it. (Well, not to us being together.)*

When they had left the school that morning, Jon had been

solicitous. Had she eaten something dodgy? She looked ever so pale. He insisted on driving her home. Did she want him to hang around until it was time to pick up Billy? Look after her? She'd shaken her head.

It had been nice to know they were going to talk to Billy together though, especially since Jon seemed so much more sanguine about the whole thing than her.

It was good to have Jon with her in the playground too. People she barely knew kept giving her strange looks and she wasn't sure if she was getting pity stares (*poor thing, she lost her mum recently*) or judgy stares (*that's the mother of the hitter. No, not Angus Murray – there's a new hitter in town*).

A woman wearing a faded apron and too much rouge brought Billy's doughnut and clucked over him, taking a greedy pinch of his cheeks. I know he looks cute, Laura thought, but he's actually in disgrace right now.

Billy took a huge mouthful of his doughnut.

'Hitting is serious, Billy,' she said. 'You can't hit people.'

'Even if they're horrible?'

'Yes, even if they're horrible.'

Billy considered this before taking another big mouthful of doughnut. 'What if they hit you first?'

'If they hit you, you tell Mummy or Daddy.'

Billy nodded and stuck his finger up his nose. 'What if they call you names?'

'You tell Mummy or Daddy. And don't pick your nose.'

'Daddy says that everyone picks their nose.'

Laura shot Jon a look and he shrugged. 'I also said to do it in private.'

'What if someone hurts your guinea pig?' Billy said. 'Can you hit someone if they hurt your guinea pig?'

'Did Angus hurt your guinea pig?'

'No.'

It was hard not to think that Billy was just trying to look

for excuses to hit someone. Laura felt overwhelmed by exhaustion. She thought of a line from the Lilypad leaflet: *We can help you with all kinds of loss.*

How about loss of the plot?

'Let's just say no hitting,' Jon said, taking a sip of his coffee.

Laura thought back to Mrs Jenkins getting all coquettish around him earlier. He looked better now, the hangover must have worn off and he had showered and changed.

Maybe she, Jon and Billy could just stay together in this slightly too hot little café forever? With its steamed-up windows and constant supply of caffeine and sugar, it felt cosy and safe. Café-world could be an alternate universe where she and Jon never argued; where it didn't matter that he didn't have a job and never emptied the bin.

She wrestled with the sudden and unexpected urge to tell Jon she wanted him back. Whatever else he was and he wasn't, he was the last decade of her life and there had just been so much change recently. It was enough to make her feel as if she was constantly battling a kind of low-level motion sickness.

The door opened and a woman walked in with two little girls from Billy's class.

'Caitlyn! Dorothy!' Billy said running over and greeting them as if he'd last seen them a lifetime ago and not minutes beforehand.

Laura couldn't help noticing that the girls looked less excited to see Billy. And, of course, Caitlyn was the one whose dad had died. Laura looked at her. How awful it must be to lose a parent when you were old enough to miss them but not old enough to have any understanding of what had happened. Laura felt a rush of sympathy that was almost big enough to make her forget that Caitlyn had left Billy off her birthday party list. Almost.

'So how's it going sorting through your mum's stuff?' Jon said. 'I bet Jess is whipping you into shape.'

'Actually she's been fine.' There was no way she was telling him she and Jess had fallen out.

Jon made a face. 'Really? Not bossing you to within an inch of your life?'

Laura shrugged. Billy was still hanging around the girls like an unrequited lover. *Please talk to him.*

'She had a go at me the last time I saw her, you know,' Jon said. 'When she was at the flat and I picked up Billy. Went on at me about being late. Like Billy was there checking his watch.'

'Billy *was* checking his watch.'

'Billy doesn't have a watch.'

'It's an expression.'

Jon put his mug down on the table. 'Still. It's not for bossy-boots to wade in though, is it? It's not her business.'

Laura sighed. 'You shouldn't have been late. Billy hates it.'

Jon scowled at her.

It seemed you *could* fall out in café-world.

Chapter Sixty-One

Then

When Laura arrived at the restaurant, Evie was locked in conversation with the waiter, who was laughing uproariously at something she was saying. He disappeared in a reluctant manner when she sat down, as if Laura's arrival was a rather unwelcome interruption.

'I've got some news,' Laura burst out before she'd even taken her coat off. 'I'm pregnant.'

'Oh,' Evie said. 'Well, my goodness.'

Laura waited for her to add 'how wonderful' but it wasn't forthcoming. Her mother was beckoning to her friend the waiter to let him know she would like to order a drink. She was probably getting them champagne. Laura prepared herself to say that it was a lovely thought but she wasn't going to have any alcohol. She knew her mother would protest and say everyone had carried on drinking in her day and the babies had all been fine because that's exactly what she'd said repeatedly to Jess throughout both her pregnancies.

'I'll have a G&T please, Antonio,' Evie said.

No champagne then.

'How far gone are you?' Evie said.

'Only eight weeks,' Laura said, instinctively patting her stomach.

'Was it planned?'

'Not exactly.' It hadn't been remotely planned. She and Jon weren't that type of couple. Not like her sister and her husband. Laura was willing to bet they'd tracked her cycle religiously and then shagged to order. They probably worked out when was a good time for a baby to be born in terms of the school year. *Not tonight, darling, that would mean an August baby.*

'Well, at least you're not nineteen this time.'

Laura dug her nails into her palms. She was sure her mother didn't mean anything by the remark.

'Congratulations,' Evie said, smiling tightly.

Laura couldn't help noticing her mother didn't seem exactly overwhelmed with joy. Her friend Clare had told her that her mother hadn't been able to stop crying for about an hour after she'd told her she was having a baby. But Evie looked decidedly dry-eyed. No matter, she was just a contained sort of person.

'You should look at the menu,' Evie said. 'I've already chosen.'

'Yes, sorry I was late. The tubes were all buggered up.'

Her mother's perfectly groomed eyebrows lifted. 'That seems to happen to you a lot.'

Were they really going to do this? When she'd just broken such momentous news? Well, Laura wasn't rising to it. She studied the menu carefully. She must steer clear of any rare meat or unpasteurized cheeses.

'I did think you were looking bigger when you walked in,' her mother said, taking a sip of her drink.

'Really? I don't think I'm showing yet.'

'Hmm. Is Jon pleased?'

'Ecstatic,' Laura said. Which was true if by ecstatic you meant reconciled to the fact the condom had split and Laura wanted no talk of an abortion. But Laura didn't think many men were ready to become fathers before they actually had kids. And Jon would be brilliant with a baby. Well, as long as it could be taught not to wake him before midday. 'It'll really change our lives,' he'd said. *Well, yes.*

'Is he still working as a waiter?'

'Restaurant manager,' Laura said, fiddling with her napkin. 'But he wants to write a novel.'

Evie raised her eyebrows.

'What does that look mean?'

Her mother sighed. 'It means that kids are expensive things. They need food, clothes, a roof over their heads.'

'I'm doing okay,' Laura said. And she was. Not okay, okay like her sister, but not everyone wanted to be a management consultant. Laura had recently been promoted to Deputy Real Life Features Editor and, granted, there were people a lot younger than her doing a similar job but, unlike Laura, they hadn't spent nearly all of their twenties off their face in some field. 'We'll be fine. Anyway, novelists earn money.'

'Published ones do.'

Laura had total confidence in Jon. If he wrote how he talked, then people would definitely want to read him. 'He'll be snapped up.'

Antonio brought over a basket laden with soft, warm rolls and Laura's stomach rumbled. She took one and buttered it generously before helping herself to another.

'Go easy,' her mother said.

'I'm eating for two.'

'Two what? Elephants?'

'Ha-bloody-ha. Look, can you be nice?' *For once.*

Evie took a sip of her drink and started to tell a story about a guy she'd met at the local library who kept giving her unsolicited book recommendations. 'I wish he'd just come clean and admit he wants to get in my knickers.'

'Eww,' Laura said, laughing. 'Gross, Mum!'

Antonio came over with two Insalata Tricolore.

'His name is Barry,' Evie said, slicing into a tomato and continuing with her story.

Laura pushed away the feeling that other mothers would be besieging her with questions now. Was she feeling sick at all? Did she have a date for the scan yet? What was the maternity leave like where she worked? But Evie was talking about Evie (as Jon put it, she was always the star of the show). She was telling Laura how Barry had pressed *Bleak House* in her hands and said he found it very erotic, and how could anyone — anyone — find *Bleak House* erotic?

'I haven't told Jess yet,' Laura said when Evie's story finally reached its climax. Her mother looked confused for a second. 'About being pregnant.' Surely she hadn't forgotten? Jess would be pleased. She liked it when Laura did things that were conventional in nature. She would be delighted to be able to bombard Laura with advice too, and would no doubt consider herself something of an expert because she already had two kids. Laura felt a little stab of guilt that she hadn't been much of an auntie to Lola and Hannah. She'd probably only seen them a handful of times in their whole lives. Still, all that would change now she was having a baby of her own. 'How is Jess?'

'She's great. A bit tired what with working full-time and having a three- and a five-year-old, but you know your sister, she's not one to complain.'

Laura pushed down the feeling that her mother was suggesting that she was one to complain. Evie wasn't always making a comparison.

Evie placed her knife and fork together. 'She looks fantastic. She's had a new haircut.' She reached out and picked up a small handful of Laura's hair. 'Perhaps you ought to get the number of the hairdresser?'

Okay, now she definitely was making a comparison. But Laura wasn't going to rise to it; not today. 'I wish Dad was still around to meet his grandchild.'

'Me too.' Evie took a sip of her drink. 'Has Jess told you about her blog?'

And they were back to Jess. 'No.'

'She's starting up this fashion and lifestyle blog called StyleMaven. Honestly, I don't know how she's going to fit it in, what with having a full-time job and two kids under five. Luckily those girls are so well-behaved. Are you going to find out whether it's a boy or girl?'

Laura shook her head, thrilled her mother was finally showing interest in the baby. 'I know Jess was desperate to know, but I think I'd like to be surprised. I want that movie moment: it's a girl! Or, it's a boy! I honestly don't mind, as long as he or she is healthy.'

'Oh, I agree,' her mother said. 'I find it very distasteful when people express a strong preference for having one or the other. As you say, healthy is all that matters. Well, and not unkind on the eye.'

Laura hoped her mother was joking about the last part.

'You were a nightmare baby!' Evie said. 'I swear you spent the first year of your life screaming. It's a wonder we've a single photo of you when you're *not* crying. It was such a shock because Jessica had been such an easy baby.'

Well, *of course,* she had.

'You weren't much better as a toddler either. So strong-willed.' She did a mock-shudder. 'Honestly, I hope your baby is just like you so you get a taste of what I had to go through.'

'Mum!' Laura said.

Evie rolled her eyes and patted Laura's arm. 'I'm only teasing you, darling. Don't get all over sensitive on me.'

Chapter Sixty-Two

If Laura hadn't been sitting on the wrong side of the room, she'd have made a run for it. But she couldn't exactly cut straight through the circle, picking her way over bags and coats.

The Lilypad Grief Support Group met on Tuesday evenings in St Barnabas' church hall. Laura used to bring Billy to toddler group here, back in the day. It was difficult to imagine that it was the same room; that behind those closed cupboard doors there were boxes and boxes of brightly coloured toys. There had been a little ambulance, fire truck and police car here that Billy had particularly loved. The wahh wahhs.

'My name's Rob,' a heavily tattooed man with a thick neck said. 'I lost my wife to cancer last year.' His eyes filled with tears and he kneaded his hands together as if he was washing them. 'Lynn. She was called Lynn.' He said he had two teenagers to look after and mostly he got it wrong, especially with his daughter.

Jenni, the facilitator, nodded encouragingly. She had the pouchy look of a bloodhound. *I will sniff out your misery.*

'I still can't sleep on her side of the bed,' Rob said. 'Or empty her wardrobe. Stupid, innit?'

Jenni nodded – presumably just by way of encouragement rather than to affirm that, yes, he was indeed stupid.

'I'm Emma,' said a teenage girl with a pale, wary face. She picked at her cuticles. 'My mum topped herself.'

238

'Umm hmm,' Jenni said, nodding vigorously.

'It wasn't because of me! She was an alcho.'

Jenni nodded.

The faint strains of *Amazing Grace* leached through the walls. It sounded slightly off-key.

Why the hell was Laura here? She was an agony aunt, for goodness' sake – someone who dealt with other people's problems. She ought to be on top of this. And anyway, there was so much to be said for denial. Why not just stay locked in denial forever? Especially when there was so much else to contend with, from Billy turning into Mike Tyson, to falling out with Jess, to the break-up with Jon.

'Preena,' said the next woman in the circle. 'My sister was killed three years ago in a hit and run.'

Laura felt a stab of guilt. She should call her sister.

Preena rummaged fruitlessly in her sleeve and the man next to her handed her a box of tissues. 'I used to talk to her every single day. When the phone rings I still think it's going to be her. But now I can't tell her when my husband is being a dick.' There was a ripple of laughter. 'Sorry. Or when something nice happens . . .'

Emma kept picking at her cuticles and it was all Laura could do not to jump up and stop her.

She felt the sweat starting to bead under her arms. She couldn't do this. For a start, there was just too much misery in this cold, ugly room. Also, what was she going to say: *I'm an imposter. I'm not sad like the rest of you. Well, I am sad but not unequivocally sad.*

She wondered what Billy and Jon were doing now. Jon had actually been on time to pick him up, which she considered something of a miracle. If he managed to feed Billy a proper dinner on top of that, he'd practically have walked on water.

'My husband died of cancer six months ago,' said a woman called Mary. 'I was at home having a shower, and feeding the dog.' She looked up at the ceiling, blinking back tears. 'I hadn't left the hospital for seventy-two hours before that.'

Preena reached over and patted her hand.

It was Laura's turn. Her mouth felt dry. 'I'm Laura and I lost my mum twelve weeks ago.'

Jenni nodded. She was like one of those toy dogs people put on the back shelf of cars.

'And my dad twenty-five years ago.' Well, that sounded weird.

She looked towards the older man next to her, willing him to take the spotlight off her. 'I'm Alan. My wife had a massive stroke three years ago.' He pushed his glasses further up his nose, smoothed his bald head. 'One minute she was there, the next minute she was gone. It still doesn't seem real.'

'Hmm,' Jenni said, nodding. 'Hmm.'

Laura wondered if the nurse had also given Jess a leaflet for the Lilypad Grief Support Group. Or perhaps Jess hadn't looked like she needed one? Perhaps the nurse thought Jess might just be better at grief?

A tiny skeletal woman with eyes that almost looked bruised was talking now. She was so quiet people had to lean forward in their chairs. Her name was Ann. She'd lost her daughter. Leukaemia.

Laura felt a sob rise in her throat. To lose a child. If something happened to Billy . . . it just didn't bear thinking about.

Jenni was doing her wrap up. They could come every week or just when they felt they needed to. There wasn't a set structure to the sessions. It was up to them to talk about anything they wanted to talk about.

What did Laura want to talk about? How good the last season of *Catastrophe* had been? How exciting the prospect of a Spice Girls reunion tour was?

Anything but grief, really.

Chapter Sixty-Three

Then

Laura was at her mum's flat with Billy one Saturday. The plan had been to let him have a run about on Clapham Common but then it had started to pour with rain. Billy had been unable to settle. He'd spent a couple of minutes reluctantly drawing before screwing the paper up and deciding it was rubbish. He wanted to play football. Laura remembered chatting to a woman at a party when she'd been pregnant and the woman asking her if she was having a boy or a girl. When Laura had said she didn't know, the woman had said that she had four boys and the best advice she could give Laura if she was to have one was to think of him exactly like a puppy. 'They need food and they need to run around outside,' she said, laughing. Laura had been quietly appalled to hear her unborn child being likened to a dog, but as soon as Billy was a toddler, Laura suddenly understood exactly what the woman had been saying.

'I expect we'll be able to go to the park a little later,' Laura said, getting Billy's dinosaurs out of his backpack and then breathing a sigh of relief as he started to line them up on the sofa. But soon Billy was bored with his brontosaurus and fed up with his fukuiraptor. He interrupted Laura's conversation with her mum. WHEN COULD HE PLAY FOOTBALL? WHEN?

'He's not like Hannah and Lola,' Evie said. 'They can keep themselves entertained for hours.'

Laura bristled. 'They are considerably older.'

Evie shrugged, took a sip of tea.

Laura knew she should leave it but she could feel the heat rising up her chest. When it came to her mother's approval, she felt like a hamster on its wheel, running faster and faster but getting nowhere. 'I just don't know why you'd say a thing like that.'

Evie snorted. 'Oh, for goodness' sake! You're overreacting.'

Was she? She swallowed hard. But her mother was comparing Billy to Jess' girls just like she had compared Laura and Jess all these years. And it wasn't right.

Her mother was talking about the new butchers that had opened on the high street. On a Saturday, there was a queue snaking all the way down the road. Ridiculous, people queueing for a few chops – like it was wartime!

Laura was still trying to squash down the rage that was fizzing inside her. Move on, she told herself. It was nothing.

She looked at Billy, his tiny head bent over his diplodocus, whispering to it. She loved him with a ferocity that was all-consuming. Did her mother love her like that? Or even Jess? Laura didn't think she did. With Evie, love was something transactional, earned. It could be given but it could just as quickly be taken away.

Laura's heart pounded and her fists clenched.

She jumped up and starting stuffing dinosaurs into Billy's backpack, ignoring his protests. It was time to go, she said.

'We've only just got here,' Billy said.

'You're being ridiculous,' Evie said.

Laura looked at her mother. She didn't know if she was being ridiculous or not.

But she did know she was leaving.

Chapter Sixty-Four

Dear Laura,
I've seen an ad for a job that sounds absolutely
perfect for me. It's a much more interesting role than
my current one, the salary is better and there is more
chance of promotion. Realistically though, I reckon
I've got zero chance of getting it. Which is why I
haven't applied for it. The trouble is, I made the
mistake of mentioning the job to my mum and she
keeps nagging me saying it's at least worth a try. To
be honest, I'm almost tempted to pretend I've applied
just to shut her up! Please tell me what I should do.

Laura sat back in her chair. This was the weirdest timing ever because only last night she had seen that the job at *Inlustris* had been re-posted. She had been hit by a tidal wave of optimism – *this is fate! The job was waiting for me!* – and filled in the application form immediately. But then that optimism had started to seep away like a deflating balloon. Just because the job was being re-advertised didn't mean to say she'd get it.

'Every time I come over here, you're working on *Dear Laura*,' Elaine said, appearing noiselessly beside Laura.

Laura minimized her email. She loathed people reading over her shoulder and she wasn't mad keen on being told how much time she should and shouldn't spend on her various pages. 'What can I do for you?'

Elaine sighed heavily as she presented Laura with her piece on someone who was about to get married for the seventh time, which was covered in red pen. 'There are a lot of mistakes in this. Also, would you like me to explain the difference between "t-h-e-y-apostrophe-r-e" and "t-h-e-i-r"?'

Laura could feel herself starting to flush. The office, which was normally noisy, suddenly seemed quiet. Greta had stopped telling Oli that takeaway coffee cups actually weren't recyclable, Charlotte and Lisa suddenly didn't seem quite so interested in 'Celebrity Style Fails' and even the sales team were unusually subdued. 'I do know the difference.'

Laura wanted to say that not only was her personal life something of a car crash, but also she'd been working under a ridiculous amount of pressure, and she wasn't surprised she was making mistakes – frankly, anything less than dropping dead at her keyboard should be considered a triumph. But she thought she might come across as just a tad defensive. She took the heavily marked-up article back from Elaine and smiled sweetly. 'I'll sort it out.'

As Elaine walked away, Laura got a DM from Amy. *Someone needs to buy her a ten-inch dildo.*

Laura laughed, sent Amy a wink emoji and turned her attention back to replying to Faye from Colchester.

I hope you won't mind but I'm going to agree with your mum here! The thing is, while you might not have a great chance of getting this new job, you've got everything to gain and nothing to lose. . .

Laura hesitated thinking about her unsent application form for the job at *Inlustris*. Her advice to Faye could just as easily be levelled at her. Except *Inlustris* were re-posting the same job, which was surely a bit dodgy? Without thinking too much about it she typed out a quick message to Ruth her old friend from uni who now worked in HR asking her if it was weird for the same job to be re-advertised. Ruth replied immediately. *No, it happens all the time. Either they didn't think the applicant pool was strong enough the first time around or they offered it to someone and then it all fell through. x*

Laura's heart was thumping. Was this her second chance? Could she possibly get this job?

She pushed the thought to the back of her mind. Right now her actual job was replying to Faye from Colchester. Elaine was probably right that she spent too long on *Dear Laura* (not that it was her place to say so) and Laura knew Dani would be appalled and bemused if she knew the trouble Laura took over it, but she liked to think that, in some small way, she was helping people. Often, the problems were more complex than Faye's, which meant Laura might not be able to completely solve them but she could at least offer some kind words, signpost some organizations where experts actually did know what they're talking about, and make people feel heard. Her mind flashed back to when, at the age of twelve, she'd wanted to be a counsellor. This wasn't as good as that, of course, but it was something.

> *. . . Plus, did you know that women tend to under-value themselves and not apply for new roles that they're actually very well-qualified for?*

As Laura's hands were flying across the keyboard, she suddenly stopped short, picturing her own unsent application form again. Shouldn't she be taking her own advice now?

She thought about her words to Faye: *you've got everything to gain and nothing to lose.*

But then, maybe this was a classic case of do what I say, not what I do.

Chapter Sixty-Five

Laura stared at the small blue-and-red console.

She had been trying to find Billy's Spider-Man pyjamas, wading through the overstuffed drawers in his bedroom when her hand alighted on it, hidden amongst a tangle of small clothing.

Laura took a step back, her bare foot landing on a Lego brick. This room was a mess! Her life was a mess!

'Billy,' she called out. 'Can you come here please?'

'I'm watching *Trolls*.'

'Come. Here. Now.'

'What?' Billy said, appearing in the doorway, looking grumpy. Then he looked down and saw the console and his face fell.

'You took Lola's Switch,' Laura said.

Billy stared at his feet.

The music from the TV chirruped away in the background.

'Mummy asked you if you took it and you said no.'

Billy lifted his head. 'They've got two!' His voice was defiant but his eyes had filled with tears.

'Excuse me?'

'Lola and Hannah have got two Nintendo Switches and I haven't got one. It's not fair!'

Laura's head spun. First she had found out that Billy was hitting someone and now that he was stealing. Her mother's voice barged unbidden into her head: *That child is out of control!*

Sod off! Laura said to her mother in her head. She looked at Billy. 'It's not right to take things that aren't yours. You know that.'

He nodded, his whole body suddenly seeming to sag. 'I'm sorry,' he said, bursting into tears.

Laura pulled him into her arms. 'Why did you lie to Mummy? We've talked so much about how important it is to own up to things.'

'But owning up is hard,' Billy said, his voice cracking.

Laura hugged him tighter. She ought to make him take the Switch back to Lola immediately, but it was late and Lola and Hannah were probably already tucked up in bed. Jess and Ben would be curled up together in front of a movie, their Sunday-night ritual. Laura pictured the idyllic scene – a perfect family in their perfect home – and tried to squash down her feelings of inadequacy.

She would take the Switch back tomorrow. She would make Billy say sorry to Lola. And she would apologize to Jess.

It was about time.

Chapter Sixty-Six

As soon as Laura saw Jess she knew something was terribly wrong. She'd been talking to Georgie the super-keen and super-annoying intern, when she got the message. *Have you got ten minutes? I'm downstairs.*

She got into the lift. Why was Jess here? And right at the beginning of the working day. It was like she had some kind of sixth sense about the bloody Nintendo Switch and had arrived to demand Laura's grovelling apology (jeez, Laura thought, give me a chance. I was planning on coming over after work).

And then she saw Jess. Pacing around reception. Ashen faced.

'What's up?'

'Not here.'

Laura steered Jess towards the nearest café, pressed her gently into a chair.

'I've found a lump in my breast.'

Laura reeled. She didn't know what she'd been expecting but it wasn't this. Voices shouted over one another in her head. *I should have apologized after our row. Preena at grief group had a sister who died. I'm going to lose my sister just like I lost Dad and Mum.*

Her biggest worries this morning had been Billy having taken Lola's Switch, whether Jon would be on time to pick up Billy, and if she'd manage to get an interview with the sex-addict. Now none of those things seemed important.

'What can I get you?' said a hard-faced waitress with frizzy hair who had appeared at their table.

Laura wanted to scream at her to go away but she mumbled something about two coffees. Jess didn't even drink coffee but in the moment Laura completely forgot. Normally, Jess would have jumped in, said she couldn't stand coffee, that it stained your teeth and gave you breath that smelled like dog poo. But today she didn't say a word.

Laura reached over and took her sister's hand. 'Most breast lumps aren't anything to worry about.'

Jess' eyes filled with tears. 'But . . . Mum.'

'I know.' Laura squeezed her hand. The café smelled of stale oil and cheap air freshener. 'Have you booked a doctor's appointment?'

'I haven't done anything. I found the lump and came here.'

'Were you in the shower?'

Jess shook her head. 'Just doing a routine breast examination.'

She actually did routine breast examinations? Well, of course she did, she was Jess. 'That's good. It means the lump can't have been there that long.'

'Maybe. I think I forgot to do it last month. Anyway, things can happen very fast. As we know.'

The waitress slapped two mugs of coffee down on the table and their surfaces quivered.

'Does Ben know?'

Jess shook her head. 'He left for a business trip to the States this morning. He's gone for ten days.' She'd started to cry now. 'He's going to be away for Easter.'

Laura stroked her arm. 'Listen, you're going to be absolutely fine. Now give me your GP's telephone number and we'll make an appointment.'

Jess sat there, motionless. Laura could almost see the thoughts that were swirling round in her head: *This lump wasn't innocent.* It was going to be like their mum's. She wasn't going to see her daughters grow up.

'The GP's number . . .' Laura said gently.

Jess moved her arms as if they were made of lead. She picked up her phone and found the number. 'Will you talk to them?' she said, handing Laura the phone.

Naturally the receptionist was one of the Rottweiler types. There were no appointments today. Try again tomorrow.

Laura lowered her voice, told the woman on the other end that her sister had discovered a lump in her breast and that she needed to see someone today.

Silence buzzed down the line.

'Our mother died twelve and a half weeks ago. Of breast cancer.'

'Could your sister come at two o'clock?'

Laura said she could. 'Okay,' she said to Jess, after hanging up. 'I've got you an appointment.'

Jess nodded.

'It's. Going. To. Be. Fine.' She wished she felt half as bullish as she was trying to sound.

Chapter Sixty-Seven

Laura and Jess had swapped roles. Jess was all over the place, forgetting a shoot that had been arranged at her house that lunchtime. Laura spoke to Jacob the irate photographer, soothed and calmed and rescheduled for another day. She arranged for the girls to be picked up from school by a friend's mum (just in case she and Jess got delayed at the doctor's) and made Jess eat some lunch despite her protestations that she wasn't hungry.

Now they were sitting in the GP's waiting room, a modern, airy space that was all self-check-in and blonde wood; cool, corporate.

'I feel bad about you taking the day off work,' Jess said for about the thousandth time. 'I could have come on my own.'

'Don't be silly. It's fine.' She'd decided to just tell Dani the truth and Dani had told her to go immediately. 'Don't worry about work.' Laura knew 'don't worry' meant 'do it tonight instead', but she was still inordinately grateful.

Laura stared at her sister's leopard print skirt until the pattern started to blur before her eyes. She glanced at her watch and was surprised to see it was only ten past two. She felt like they'd been sitting in this waiting room for hours. And that it had been a lifetime since she'd discovered that Billy had actually taken Lola's game console, and an eternity since Jess saying Billy looked tired felt like a big deal.

'It's probably nothing,' Jess said. 'A cyst or something.'

'Yeah, drama queen!'

Jess tried to smile but it didn't quite reach her eyes.

A GP called Jess' name.

'Come in with me?' Jess said to Laura.

The two of them sat side by side on plastic chairs. Laura sized up the GP; decided she was kind-looking (good), rushed (bad) and quite old (good).

Jess explained she had found a lump.

'Most breast lumps are nothing to worry about,' said the GP. They went through a few questions; size and location of the lump, family history. Laura tried not to scrutinize the doctor's expression when Jess told her their mum had died of breast cancer.

A baby was crying in the distance.

'Okay, let's take a look.' The GP ushered Jess behind the curtains and told her to strip to the waist. Tapped away on her computer while Laura stared at her, willing her to say everything was okay. Like that was her decision.

'Ready,' Jess said from behind the curtain.

Laura sat the other side, listening to the doctor talking about how her hands might be a bit cold. She kept thinking about Preena from grief group. But Preena's mum and dad were still alive. Laura couldn't lose Jess as well as her parents. That just wouldn't be fair.

Besides, Jess couldn't get cancer. She ran five times a week, ate organic food, drank two glasses of wine on a big night out.

The baby was screaming now. Laura supposed he or she must be getting an injection. At least she hoped that was all it was.

Jess and the doctor emerged from behind the curtain, Jess buttoning her shirt.

'I don't think there's anything to worry about,' the GP said.

Think.

'But I'm going to make an urgent referral to the breast clinic just to be on the safe side.'

Urgent referral.

Jess made a tiny, almost imperceptible gasp.

The doctor smoothed a stray piece of hair away from her forehead. 'I really don't want you to worry.'

Was there anything more worrying than being told not to worry?

Chapter Sixty-Eight

Then

Jess wasn't in the habit of turning up at Laura's flat unannounced, so Laura was surprised to see her at the door. She was also a bit embarrassed about how messy the flat was and couldn't help picturing Jess' oh-so-perfect home. But not everyone has the time to arrange their cookbooks in alphabetical order or make sure all their tins of baked beans are facing in the right direction. A couple of years ago, Jess had given up her job as a management consultant to concentrate on her StyleMaven blog, and nobody could convince Laura that that was a full-time job.

The pair of them picked their way across the elaborate train track that Jon and Billy had built a week or so ago, a car alarm starting in the distance.

'It's Mum,' Jess said, as soon as they got into the kitchen.

Laura steeled herself to be tough. She'd recently interviewed a woman who had 'divorced' her parents and, while Laura had known that she didn't have it in her to be quite that ruthless, she'd also known how much happier and lighter she'd felt over the last three months. She deserved a holiday from her mother, at the very least. 'Look, Jess,' she said, 'I appreciate you trying to help, but as I've told you countless times, I really don't want to speak to Mum right now—'

'Laura,' Jess cut in.

Laura held up her hand. She knew exactly what her sister was going to say: *Mum is happy to put everything that's happened behind her,* aka, all is forgiven. Laura's younger self would have been meek and grateful, but as she'd got older she found it all a bit more complicated (*but do I forgive her?*). She would find herself stiffening when her mother doled out a hug. 'Oh, you're a cold one,' Evie would say.

Laura kneaded her temples. 'I know everyone thinks what Mum said about Billy that day was nothing, and it was nothing. It wasn't about what she said per se, it was about her pitting Billy against Lola and Hannah just like she has you and me all these years. Why couldn't I have got A level results like yours? Why don't you have my creative flair? You must see it yourse—'

Jess put her hand on Laura's arm. 'She's sick, Laura.'

'What?'

'She's got cancer.'

Chapter Sixty-Nine

It was the longest eight days Laura could ever remember.

On the Tuesday she took Jess to the hospital, and looked away as the nurse inserted a large needle into Jess' left breast. She had already had an ultrasound and a mammogram and she looked grey and strained.

'All done,' Edith the nurse said, applying a dressing. She was a big, solid-looking woman with an easy laugh and a toothy smile. The sort of person you couldn't imagine giving you bad news. Except you knew that was ridiculous because she must give people bad news day in and day out.

'Your breast will probably feel a little sore and you'll probably get a bit of bruising.'

Jess nodded and Laura squeezed her hand. She couldn't remember ever seeing her sister like she had been the last couple of days. Jess was a classic doer, and normally when something went wrong, she threw her considerable energies into trying to fix it. Now she was just quiet and compliant. She hadn't so much as mentioned getting back to their mum's to sort through more of her stuff, and when Laura had said she had phoned the mortgage company and checked that they still hadn't found a buyer, Jess looked impassive. It was like she wasn't really there.

'The biopsy results come through in about a week,' Edith said. 'I know,' she continued, seeing their faces. 'It feels like a very long time. But try to remember that most breast lumps are nothing to worry about. And don't Google!'

The days that followed saw Laura split herself into several different people. When she was with Jess, she was upbeat and positive. She cooked meals, made sure the girls did their homework and cancelled Jess' work commitments and social plans. 'Are you sure you don't want to tell Ben?'

'Absolutely not,' Jess snapped.

She was so adamant that, even though Laura thought it was the wrong call – that Jess could do with her husband's support right now and that Ben would want to know – she didn't push. She was grateful to leave at least one area where her sister was still in charge.

When Laura was away from Jess, she was so busy trying to keep on top of her work and make sure Billy was okay and not thumping any of his classmates, she barely had time to think. A couple of times she'd felt a panic attack coming on but she forced herself to breathe until she was okay. She didn't have time for panic attacks.

But at night when she went to bed, and she didn't have the distraction of being busy or the need to be strong and positive for Jess, her mind spiralled into panic.

She would be wide awake and sobbing at 2 a.m. She was haunted by memories of their row. Why had she let them fall out over something so trivial? And she couldn't stop thinking about her dream and whether it meant something. Well, of course it didn't. Dreams were horseshit, everyone knew that. Jess would be okay.

But what if Jess wasn't okay?

The next morning, she would be back to the various other Lauras. *Eat your Cheerios, Billy. I'll get that copy to you by end of play tomorrow, Karen. Let's run through your spellings, Hannah. Jess, eat some of your pasta.*

'Is it really only Thursday?' Jess said suddenly as Laura stacked plates into the dishwasher.

'Yes. But it's nearly the end of Thursday.' She tried not to think about the fact that Jess wasn't even trying to rearrange the things she was stacking, or telling her she was doing it all wrong.

It was the Easter weekend and, while Laura would normally have been delighted to have four days off work, all it seemed to do was make the clock tick even slower. To add insult to injury, the weather was absolutely glorious. What good was bright sunshine and blue skies when you were carrying a dark cloud around in your heart?

On Good Friday, at Laura's insistence, they all trekked to Battersea Park, but Billy wanted to play football and the girls said football was boring. Laura and Jess trailed behind the bickering kids, Laura talking and talking, her tone way too bright. 'Do you remember when Mum was at the station buying a sandwich and the guy behind the counter asked her if she wanted to go for a drink and she said no thank you, she had a boyfriend. And the poor guy said, "No, I was talking about the meal deal. When you buy a sandwich, you get a drink free."' Jess managed a flicker of a smile.

Then they went to the cinema and no one liked the film. 'How about sausages and mash for tea?' Laura chirruped.

On Saturday, Laura suggested that Jess and the girls came to hers 'for a change of scene', which meant she found herself making everyone lunch in a kitchen that was roughly the size of Jess' island unit. Jess sat on the sofa, her feet curled beneath her and Laura suddenly realized how weird it was to see her so still. 'Ben's not working this weekend,' she suddenly volunteered, apropos of nothing. 'But it would have been crazy for him to come home when he's got another meeting in New York next week.'

After lunch they all headed out down Turney Road. 'Aren't

all the blossoms gorgeous?' Laura said, but Jess didn't seem to be listening. In Dulwich Park, they rented banana bikes for the kids. 'It's going to be fine,' Laura said. Jess' eyes filled with tears.

They walked back home through Dulwich Village. 'Did you know most of these are the original eighteenth- and nineteenth-century buildings?' Laura said. Christ, what was she, a tour guide? They stopped to have tea and overpriced cakes in a crowded café that Laura normally couldn't stand but was prepared to put up with today on the basis that her flat was just too small for five people and all the unhappiness they were carrying around with them.

On Easter Sunday, they were back at Jess' and Laura hid small, brightly coloured Easter eggs all over the garden, while simultaneously cooking roast lamb that no one would really want to eat. By the time the kids got around to hunting for the eggs, most of them had melted in the sun.

Laura was almost grateful when Tuesday morning rolled around. Later that afternoon they would get the results. Which would have been great if later hadn't actually been 348 hours away.

The editorial meeting crawled. Laura shuffled in her seat and tried to look interested as Harriet talked about next week's 'Celeb News'. The next few hours were similarly slow with Laura trying to force herself to concentrate on her work and squash down irritation as the people around her wittered on about how they may or may not try going gluten free, what they'd watched on telly the night before and goodness knows what else. *Don't you know my sister might be dying?*

At two o'clock she rushed over to Jess' house.

'I've been Googling,' Jess said to her in the kitchen.

'Edith told you not to.'

Jess shrugged. 'If something happens to me, will you help

Ben take care of the girls? He's great but he's a bloke and sometimes girls need their mum. A mum.'

'Stop talking like that.'

'It's good to be prepared.'

'You're going to feel like a right neurotic Nancy when you get the all-clear. Now, get your coat on.'

Back at the breast health clinic, Laura sat in the pale green waiting room feeling sick. Jess was sitting beside her, staring into the middle distance.

'It's going to be fine,' Laura whispered to her. She took a swig of Gaviscon and looked around the waiting room, which was filled with anxious faces. A man was cracking loud and unfunny jokes to his wife. A woman with pink hair was crying noiselessly. Laura weighed up the idea that if five of the people in this room were waiting for results, it was likely that at least one of them would get bad news. She was filled with a fierce hope that it was anyone but Jess. Because it may be a commonly peddled idea that suffering makes you a nicer person, but suffering can actually make you pretty damn selfish, and right now, Laura didn't give a damn about any of those other women as long as her sister was okay.

Chapter Seventy

Then

If Evie had been a nightmare before she got sick, she was even worse afterwards. Now, no one could challenge her. She was dying, for goodness' sake.

During the few months Laura and her mum hadn't been speaking, Laura had kept thinking about how, when Billy had been born, it was as if some kind of switch had been flipped inside her. She was enraptured by this tiny human. She gazed endlessly at his beautiful face (beautiful to her, at least. When she looked back at photos now, she could see he looked a lot like a potato in the beginning). His slightest cry pulled at her heartstrings and she couldn't stop touching his podgy feet. She could have been a mother in a nappy ad.

Laura knew with certainty that her mother had never felt that way about her. (Maybe she was just unlovable?)

Now Laura pushed all those thoughts to the back of her mind. Every time she visited Evie, she steeled herself. Whatever her mother said or did, she would be the epitome of the perfect daughter. After all, motherhood had humbled her; taught her that there is no such thing as the perfect mother. Hadn't Evie just been doing her best all these years?

Laura resolved that she would exclusively focus on her mother's good points. She would marvel at how brave and uncomplaining Evie was about everything from the nausea to the pain. Be proud that she was still cracking jokes and caring about putting her lipstick on.

If she and her mother talked about the past, Laura would make sure she described an *idyllic* childhood and a *perfect* mother. She'd run into trouble so many times before when her memories didn't match Evie's, who had always stubbornly refused to acknowledge there had ever been so much as a cross word. Now Laura vowed to only serve up the airbrushed tales her mother preferred.

And it wasn't just the past Laura planned to cede control over. She wouldn't react when Evie told her she was putting on weight. She would smile sweetly when her mum said it was a shame she didn't have a nice house like Jess' and *imagine* renting when you were pushing forty. Laura would not say a word when Evie said she wished Billy was doing as well at school as the girls were.

But there was always at least one remark that just chafed too much. One thing that made Laura snappy and irritable. And, of course, that would be the moment that some nurse came in to check her mother's canula or to see if she needed more pain meds.

They all loved Evie, thought she was a hoot and a trooper. And they would look at Laura like she was the most horrible daughter in the whole wide world.

And she would think: if only you knew.

Chapter Seventy-One

The wait seemed interminable and Laura felt a prickle of irritation. She knew the NHS was overstretched but it was cruel to keep people waiting in this sort of situation.

The woman with pink hair had started reading a book, although Laura couldn't help noticing she hadn't turned a page once in the last ten minutes.

She glanced at Jess, who looked grey and tired. 'How's work?' she said, simply for something to say.

Jess looked at her strangely (as well she might because Laura *never* asked about her work). 'It's okay. I've been a bit distracted recently. What with this . . . and everything.'

'Everything?'

Jess pulled at the sleeve of her jumper, staring down. 'It's just—' She stopped herself.

'What?' Laura said.

'Nothing, nothing.'

Laura looked at her sister, knowing that she was holding back. 'What?'

Jess met her eye briefly and then stared at her shoes. 'You know, sometimes life gets a bit . . . complicated.' She pulled at her sleeve again. 'Is it me or is it very cold in here?'

'Don't change the subject.'

Jess gave her a small unhappy smile. 'Oh, and I've got a troll.'

Laura felt her heart start to thump and her throat constrict. MsRealityCheck was coming back to bite her. 'What sort of troll?' she said, her voice sounding slightly strangulated.

'A horrible one.' Jess sighed and leant back in her chair. 'I wish they would call us in.'

'What has the troll said?' Laura said, trying to sound casual.

'That I deserve to be raped and then killed.'

Laura breathed an inward sigh of relief that Jess wasn't talking about MsRealityCheck before realizing she was breathing a sigh of relief when someone was threatening to rape and kill her sister (her sister who could be dying of cancer). She was a bad, bad person. 'That's terrible. When you first mentioned a troll I thought you just meant run-of-the-mill sniping.'

'Oh, I get lots of them too. But this guy is different.'

The woman with the joke-cracking husband walked back out into the waiting room after her appointment. She had obviously been crying and neither of them looked much in the mood for a gag anymore.

'Poor thing,' Jess whispered.

'Awful,' Laura agreed. 'What are you going to do about the troll?'

Jess shrugged. 'Not much I can do. Ben was all for tracking down his IP address but I don't think it's that simple.'

Laura was wrestling with a complex and contradictory mass of emotions as Jess' name was finally called. The two of them stood up.

It wasn't Edith, and Laura suddenly felt panicky. Where was Edith? It *had* to be Edith.

'Take a seat please,' not-Edith said.

Laura swallowed down a feeling of panic. She had been willing away the hours, desperate for this moment to arrive, and yet now it had, she suddenly couldn't bear it. When she'd told Billy that it was time to apologize to Lola about the

Switch, he'd protested, saying he 'wasn't ready'. Laura felt the same now. *NOT READY, NOT READY, NOT READY*, she wanted to scream.

She reached over and took Jess' hand.

And then not-Edith told them that the lump in Jess' breast wasn't cancer, it was a fibroadenoma and harmless. It didn't even need treatment, Jess should just keep an eye on it.

And Laura sat back in her seat, clutching her sister's small, cold hand and trying to take everything in.

Jess was going to be okay.

Chapter Seventy-Two

Fibroadenoma. Laura was still turning the word over in her mind as she sat at grief group. It sounded like something serious but it wasn't. Jess was going to be okay. She looked at Preena guiltily: I get to keep my sister.

Laura hadn't planned to come tonight. After the first Lilypad session, she had been sure she would never return, that she'd eaten her first and last Bourbon there (a slightly soggy Bourbon, if truth be told – even the biscuits were sad at grief group). But Billy was with Jon this evening and somehow Laura had found herself reaching for her jacket and shoes and walking down Turney Road almost as if she was on autopilot.

'Sometimes I call her mobile just to hear her voice,' Preena said, dabbing at her eyes with a balled up tissue.

Laura felt even more guilty. If Jess had died, would Laura have called her mobile just to hear her voice? She'd certainly never even thought to call her mother's phone. And her mother had such a nice voice; soft and mellifluous.

The harsh fluorescent lighting was too cruel for the faces beneath it. Everyone looked weighed down by sadness; defeated. Even Emma, who couldn't be more than sixteen, looked old. Like she'd seen things that couldn't be unseen and inside her smooth skin was a wizened little old lady.

Laura suddenly thought back to her mum's reaction when, as a teenager, she had announced she wanted to be a therapist: 'You'd be rubbish, darling. You're so over-emotional.' Laura

266

had (naturally) been discouraged but occasionally as an adult, the idea had popped back into her head and she'd flirted with the possibility of retraining. But really she knew she was being silly. She *would* be rubbish as a therapist – she could barely deal with her own pain let alone other people's. Besides which, she didn't even have the guts to apply for the job at *Inlustris*, so a radical career change would definitely be beyond her.

Rob didn't know what he was supposed to do when his daughter had 'women's problems'; Lynn had always dealt with stuff like that.

'You mean period pains?' Emma snapped.

Rob nodded, scratched the tattoo on his neck.

'Just give her some painkillers and a hot water bottle.' Emma's voice dripped disdain. Just what Rob needed, Laura thought, to come out to have other people's teenagers make him feel as inadequate as his own did.

Jenni was nodding so hard it was a wonder her head didn't fall off. 'Sometimes it's difficult to take on parenting roles previously filled by our partner.'

Laura thought about the parenting roles she and Jon fulfilled, how they had taken shape without discussion but now seemed immutable. Sometimes it made her furious that she didn't get to be Fun Parent and she would have given anything for Jon to care if Billy ate his broccoli. Jon was good at calming her down when she was worrying about Billy though. He'd been brilliant about both the hitting and the Switch stealing. 'I wouldn't put him down for a place in a youth offender programme just yet!'

Mary was talking about how little time there had been between her husband's diagnosis and his death. He had been dead by February and yet in December, everything had been normal. She'd rushed around like a crazy person while he sat in his armchair saying you could eat chocolate all day long because it was Christmas. You could even have a tipple before midday!

When he'd asked her what she wanted from him, she had got cross and told him it would be nice if he surprised her occasionally; if buying her own gift wasn't yet another thing on her already too long list of things to do. She was ashamed of that now.

Laura thought about the things she was ashamed of with her mum. Not going to see her enough, going to see her but not being nice enough, getting irritable when she asked for the blanket one minute and complained she was hot the next. The list was endless.

Ann was talking now, her voice barely audible over the clatter of the choir arriving for rehearsal. Rosie hadn't been a planned baby.

'Mmm hmm,' Jenni said, nodding.

Billy hadn't been planned either. Well, of course he hadn't. If she and Jon had had to decide they were ready to be parents, it never would have happened. How could two people who couldn't keep a houseplant alive have a baby? Jon had looked horrified when Laura had first told him she'd done a test and it was positive, and she had known if she'd suggested a termination, he'd have leapt at the idea. But the second he had held Billy, he'd fallen instantly and deeply in love with him. In one of the many rows Laura had had with her mother about Jon, Evie had accused him of not taking his role as a father seriously enough.

'He's a great dad,' Laura had said.

Evie had rolled her eyes. 'He's a great big man-baby!'

'She had colic,' Ann whispered. 'I paced the floor with her screaming night after night. I felt very sorry for myself.'

Laura had to look away from Ann (Laura would definitely make a rubbish therapist). She knew the thinking behind groups like these. That other people's experiences would help you make sense of your own. But sometimes it felt like you were just soaking up even more pain.

Chapter Seventy-Three

As Laura turned into her road, her head still full of the conversations at grief group, she saw her sister in her front garden. Bizarrely, it looked as if Jess was pulling up weeds.

'Just popped round for a spot of night-time gardening, have you?' Laura said.

'Haha. I was waiting for you and I thought I might as well make myself useful.'

Laura raised her eyebrows. 'Yes, that's very normal. Who wouldn't be weeding someone else's garden at nine o'clock at night?' She suddenly remembered the day when she'd come home to discover a miraculously tended front garden. 'I know this seems like a totally mad question, but have you done this before? The Saturday before Mother's Day?'

Jess laughed. 'Yes, as a matter of fact. We weren't speaking at the time and I'd popped round to try to make amends. Again, I thought I may as well do something productive with the time.'

'That's so weird,' Laura said. 'I mean a) because it is weird and b) because I was waiting outside your house at exactly the same time.'

'You're kidding me?' Jess said.

Laura shook her head. 'Like a rom com, right?'

'Just,' Jess said. 'Apart from the fact we're, y'know, sisters. Anyway, can we go inside?'

'We can,' Laura said. 'If you're sure you don't want to paint the fence or pressure-wash the path?'

'Next time,' Jess said, smiling.

They walked up the stairs.

'So,' Laura said, opening the door to her flat. 'What are you actually doing here? Apart from the weeding.'

'You've been amazing with everything recently.'

Laura felt a knife-twist of guilt. It would be easier to bask in her sister's praise if she didn't know she'd trolled her. And, okay it was in the past – and she'd never do such a thing now – but still.

Jess was fiddling with the button on her coat. 'There's something I want to tell you.'

'That sounds ominous.' Laura waited for her sister to laugh but she looked deadly serious. 'Do you want a drink?'

Jess shook her head. 'I had an affair,' she blurted. 'Well, a kind of half-affair. I've ended it now.'

Laura felt as if all the air had been knocked out of her lungs. 'You?'

Jess gave a small mirthless laugh. 'Yes, me. Do you think I'm too boring or too nice?'

Laura's brain was struggling to process the news. Her perfect sister had cheated on her perfect husband. Her sister who did everything by the book and was still guilt-ridden about the single litter duty she had picked up in secondary school. 'An affair?'

Jess nodded.

Laura rubbed her temples. Now she understood why Jess had been so snappy that time she thought Laura was reading the message on her phone. And why she'd once suddenly come out with that impassioned speech defending adulterers.

'Say something,' Jess said.

Laura looked at Jess. She knew exactly what her sister wanted from her right now. She wanted her to trot out the sort of softly, softly response she'd give someone who'd written in to *Dear Laura*: *You made a mistake but you're owning up to that mistake and that's important . . .* And in some ways, shouldn't it be easier to be nice to Jess now Laura knew she wasn't so annoyingly perfect?

The trouble was, Laura had visceral memories of being cheated on. The desperate ache in her stomach. The trembling hands and racing heart. The sorrow that had been so murky and all-consuming she'd felt it must be as visible to the outside world as a gaping wound. When Laura had felt like that, she had decided that anyone who cheated had crossed an uncrossable line.

They stood there not saying anything in the half-light, Jess twisting her button and Laura's mind turning cartwheels.

The silence stretched between them.

'Who is he?' Laura said eventually.

Jess sighed. 'A guy called Aaron. He's a photographer I met through work.'

Laura nodded, 'And what do you mean a half-affair?'

Jess reddened. 'We didn't actually have sex. Mum said it was all very teenage.'

'You told Mum?'

Jess nodded. 'Goodness knows why I decided to confide in her. Let's face it, she wasn't exactly a "love you unconditionally" type of mum. More of a "you'll have to earn my love over and over" mum.'

'That's for sure,' Laura said. 'And what about Ben?'

Jess shook her head. 'He doesn't know, but I'm going to tell him.'

'Are you mad?' Laura said.

'I owe him the truth.'

'The truth will do nothing but hurt him—'

'But—'

'But nothing. You said it was over, right?' Jess nodded.

271

'Then there's absolutely no reason to tell Ben. Wait, is this why you didn't want to tell Ben about the lump? Because you didn't think you deserved for him to be worrying about you?'

'Yes,' Jess said, starting to cry.

'Hey,' Laura said, stroking her arm. 'You've just been told you're not actually going to peg it, remember?'

Jess laughed tearfully. 'You know the stupidest thing of all? I'm not even sure I was that crazy about Aaron. I mean, I thought I was for a second or two, but the truth is I hardly knew him. I don't know how he votes or whether he's one of those terrible people who likes to get to the airport in the nick of time.' Laura made a face. 'The point I'm making is he wasn't worth risking my marriage for. I love Ben, I love my life.'

'Then why—'

Jess shook her head. 'I don't know. It's a question I've asked myself a thousand times and, honestly, I think it was about not being the person everyone expects me to be; not being the person *I* expect me to be. I needed to go "off script", to surprise myself. Jesus, I sound like some pathetic middle-aged-man who buys a Porsche.'

Laura puffed out her cheeks. 'It's a pretty radical way to change your brand.'

'I know,' Jess said, wiping away a tear with her sleeve. 'I'm an idiot.'

Laura squeezed her hand. 'You really are.'

'And so greedy and selfish.'

'Couldn't have put it better myself,' Laura said, squeezing Jess' hand harder.

Jess gave her a watery smile.

'Why did you suddenly decide to tell me?' Laura said. 'Today of all days?'

Jess shrugged. 'Because if you're finally going to start liking me after all these years, I want you to like the real me.'

Chapter Seventy-Four

Laura was sitting at her desk reading an email to her and Amy.

> *Hi both, I can hardly believe it's May next week! Which means Harriet is going off on mat leave any minute and I was thinking it would make a lot of sense if you two were to split the Celebrity section between you. It'll mean your job titles look oh-so-impressive and I'm sure, between you, the extra pages won't be a problem. I may even be able to keep the intern on a bit longer to provide additional support. Dani x*

The blood rushed to Laura's head and she had to breathe deeply to make sure she didn't start to have a panic attack. There was absolutely no way she could take on half of another section on top of her current workload. She was already overwhelmed. She perpetually felt as if she was behind – short on answers, barely keeping up.

She'd have to tell Dani she couldn't do this. Then again, the magazine had been understanding about her taking time off, not just when her mum died, but more recently when she'd had to go to appointments with Jess (although Laura had always made sure she got any outstanding work done in the evenings).

She sat at her desk feeling utterly wretched. As it was, she scraped through each day feeling like she was just about keeping her head above water. *Good Grief* was always talking about how important it was to make time for yourself, as was Jenni from grief group, but between work and trying – and mostly failing – to keep Billy on track, Laura had no time left. The other day she had managed not only to get to the chemist to buy a thrush pessary but also to find a moment to whack it in too, and it had felt as close to a self-care moment as she was ever going to get.

She reached into her handbag and took out a bottle of Gaviscon. What made things even worse was that Amy was out at a press show right now so Laura couldn't suggest an emergency meeting in the toilets. Amy was a no-bullshit kind of person who might well tell Dani she simply couldn't foist this on them.

Laura took a swig of the Gaviscon and wrote a reply to Amy.

Can you believe that Dani has dumped this on you and me when we're easily the most overworked editors in the building? I am so sick of all Dani's faux sympathy about my recent bereavement. How about she puts her money where her mouth is and stops burying me under a ridiculous pile of work? L x
P.S. I am taking some comfort from laughing inwardly about the trousers Dani is wearing today, which look much like a giant nappy!

Chapter Seventy-Five

Of course Laura had hit reply all.

She was sitting in the Lamb & Flag with Dani, her face a similar shade of beetroot to Oli's the day she'd asked him why he was avoiding her.

'I don't understand why you didn't come and talk to me,' Dani said. 'My door is always open.'

Since they worked in an open-plan office, Dani had no door to leave open or otherwise – and Laura had always hated that expression. Still, she had to admit Dani was right that she should have talked to her. It certainly would have been a more grown-up way of tackling the problem than bitching about her over email. Her mother always said she acted before engaging her brain. 'I'm sorry,' she said. 'I should have talked to you.'

Dani nodded. 'The thing about Dani is that she values honesty and openness.'

Jesus, had she just referred to herself in the third person?

'I'm not just a boss, Laura, I'm a friend.'

Well . . .

'And if any of my team are having issues, I want them to tell Dani.'

'Right,' Laura said. 'Yes, I absolutely should have talked to you.'

'I know you've had a lot to deal with recently and I've gone out of my way to make things easier for you.'

'Yes, and I'm very grateful.'

Dani nodded approvingly. 'Anyway, I hear you about your workload, but this is a fantastic opportunity for you. You get to be Real Life Features Editor and Celebrity Editor. That's great for your CV.'

Laura nodded. Deep down, she harboured the secret fear that she was lazy. (Was there anything more shameful than being lazy in this age of busy, busy, busy? Of just wanting to watch *Queer Eye* while shovelling pizza into your mouth?) Everyone around her seemed to have so much energy and Laura felt sluggish and stupid by comparison. Yes, her workload was heavy but so was everyone else's. Why was she the one who couldn't keep up or make the grade? The one who was Not Enough?

Dani stood up and Laura followed suit, grateful to get out of this room and away from this conversation as quickly as possible.

'Oh, and by the way,' Dani said, giving her a chilly smile, 'these trousers are Prada.'

Chapter Seventy-Six

'I think I'm going to have to get a job,' Jon said, sighing heavily.

You're a thirty-nine-year-old man, Laura thought. It wouldn't be that weird to have a job.

They were in Dulwich Park with Billy. The last time Laura had been here, she had been with Jess and the kids that awful weekend before Jess got the all-clear. Thinking back to all the tortuous waiting made Laura shiver even though it was a warm day, and all around them coats and jumpers had been shucked off.

She and Jon had agreed to come here together because today was the day they were going to teach Billy to ride a bike without stabilisers and neither of them wanted to miss that. *Besides,* Laura had said, *it's nice for him to see that we can still do things together.*

Jon was looking troubled. 'I don't know what I'm going to do. I guess I could get another job in a restaurant? Or maybe be a band roadie for a bit? Jimmy's brother said they're always looking for new people.'

It was hard to shake off the feeling that you were talking to a teenager about a summer job.

'You're lucky that you do something you enjoy,' Jon said.

He always talked like this and it made Laura furious. Excruciating reply-all emails aside, she did like her job, but that didn't mean that most of the reason she did it wasn't because she bloody well had to. She wasn't living the dream when she raced to squash herself into a packed tube every morning. She wasn't satisfying a creative itch when she tussled with how to make incontinence a fascinating story. And if she won the lottery tomorrow, well, her life *would* change. A lot.

Billy raced across the wobbly bridge, brandishing an imaginary lightsaber at a little boy he'd hooked up with at the see-saw. He had insisted they have a quick trip to the playground before they started with the bike lesson. Laura couldn't help but notice he didn't seem all that excited about it. She'd been desperate to get her stabilisers taken off her bike as a kid. The second Jess' came off, she'd nagged Dad to do hers too. 'But you're a bit smaller, Scout' (that was what he used to call her; she couldn't even remember why now). Laura insisted and when she bloodied her knees she bit the inside of her cheeks to stop herself crying and jumped straight back on the bike.

'He hasn't hit anyone since we had that chat with him?' Jon said.

Laura shook her head. 'Nope.'

'We're model parents.'

'Well, apart from the fact our child was hitting anyone in the first place.'

'Yeah, but only Angus Murray.'

They both laughed. Laura had finally plucked up the courage to speak to Angus' mum about it. She'd been incredibly gracious. Put her hand on Laura's arm and told her not to worry.

'Billy does quite often say he doesn't want to go to school in the mornings though,' Laura said.

'Really?'

'Yeah. And there's often a convenient "tummy ache".' She pressed her fingertips into her temples. 'You don't think he's unhappy at school, do you?'

Jon shook his head. 'Most five-year-old boys would rather play with their toys than sit in lessons all day. Besides, I don't think when he started school last September, he realized he'd have to go there *every* day.'

Laura smiled.

A woman on a bench a few feet away was trying to breast-feed a baby while applying suncream to a furious and squirmy toddler at the same time. Every now and again the woman would be forced to move enough to unlatch the baby who would squeal in angry protest. Laura had sometimes wondered what it would have been like to have another child and she supposed there was her answer. Well, not her whole answer; she was sure there would be wonderful moments too. She was happy though. Billy was enough. No, he was more than enough; he was *everything*. She suddenly thought about the woman at the grief group whose daughter had died of leukaemia, the haunted look in her eyes.

'Maja's moved in with Jimmy.' Jon volunteered.

Laura had only met Maja a couple of times. She wore a lot of pink and sweatshirts with pictures of cats on them. 'Is it still okay for you to stay there?'

'Oh yeah. You know Jimmy. And Maja's quite chill. A truly terrible cook but quite chill. She's a big one for clubbing. Always trying to get us all to go out.'

Laura couldn't remember the last time she had been to a club. She used to love them. Losing yourself to the thump of the music, a sweaty amorphous mass of bodies who cared about nothing but that moment.

Billy rushed over and took a quick glug of water. 'My new friend is called Kyle!' Having delivered this newsflash, he shot off again.

'Someone's having a nice time!' Jon said.

Laura nodded and smiled. She watched a little girl being pushed on the swing by her dad and had a sudden visceral memory of her dad doing exactly the same with her. The sensation of gripping the chain, swishing through the air, begging to go higher and higher. Her dad laughing. 'Don't kick the clouds!'

'Got any food?' Jon said. 'I'm starving.'

Laura shook her head.

Billy's new friend was summoned from the wobbly bridge by his dad and told they had to get home. The dad glanced apologetically at Laura and Jon.

Billy came over, his lower lip dangerously wobbly. 'We were having the best game.'

Jon scooped him up and blew a raspberry on his bare tummy. 'Then we're just going to have to do something even more fun, aren't we?'

They retrieved Billy's bike and Jon's scooter from the railings and Laura's mind flashed back to Jess' comment: *A grown man who rides a scooter!*

Billy was still looking mutinous. 'I don't want to do bike-riding.'

'Oh no?' Jon said, raising his eyebrows.

'No.'

'Okay, how about being a bat?'

Billy's nose crinkled. 'A bat?'

Jon tipped him upside down so he was hanging from his feet. 'Yes, a bat. An upside-down bat.'

Despite himself Billy started giggling. 'You're silly, Daddy.'

Laura smiled. Whatever else Jon was or wasn't, he was great with kids. Perhaps because it wasn't too hard for him to get into their heads.

Chapter Seventy-Seven

Laura retched over the toilet bowl, her body not seeming to have got the message that there was nothing more left in her stomach.

Finally she sat back, leaning, sweaty and shaky, against the bathroom wall.

Jess was on the verge of finding out about MsRealityCheck. Finding out that Laura was such a mean-spirited, jealous little person that she felt compelled to create an anonymous account and leave nasty, spiteful comments for her own sister.

Jess had phoned Laura sounding tearful. For a second, Laura wondered if Jess had ignored her advice and confessed to Ben about the affair. Or worse still, there had been some mix up at the hospital and Jess' breast lump actually was cancer after all.

'The troll sent a picture of my house on Google Street View,' Jess said. 'He said he knows where I live and aren't I stupid.'

Laura gasped. 'What are you going to do?'

'Ben's found this company called Unmask,' Jess said. 'I wasn't even going to tell him at first because . . . well, you know why.'

'Jess,' Laura said. 'Stop with the hair-shirt thing. It's not helpful.'

'And then I realized I had to tell him because what if this

guy turns up at the house . . .' She started sobbing down the phone. '. . . The girls! What if he hurts the girls? Anyway, I told Ben and he was adamant we have to do something and we have to do it now. We've reported it to the police but Ben says that's not enough. That he wants to find this guy and stop him hiding behind the safety of his computer. That's what Unmask do.'

'They find people's IP addresses?'

'Not just that. They use a combination of high-tech stuff and good-old fashioned detective work. They find out who this person's online friends are, look at their most frequented sites: basically, they follow all their digital footprints.'

Laura's hands had gone clammy and her stomach started turning cartwheels. 'Will Unmask just look into this specific guy?'

'No. Apparently trolls often have several fake accounts and they start off posting milder stuff first. So Unmask will look at all the comments on my site.'

Laura felt the floor start to disappear from beneath her and the nausea rise. She thought about Billy in the park the day before when his stabilisers had first been taken off. 'I can't do this,' he'd wailed. 'It's too hard!'

She told Jess that sounded like a good idea, to try not to worry too much in the meantime, and that she had to go but would call her later.

Now she sat on the bathroom floor feeling utterly wretched. Jess would probably never speak to her again. Word would get around and Laura would have to face people in the full knowledge that they knew what she really was.

Billy would ask her why they didn't see Auntie Jess and his cousins anymore. Oh God, how on earth would she explain things to Billy?

Chapter Seventy-Eight

Turns out Laura didn't find owning up any easier than Billy had about the Switch. She knew that was what she had to do and that, however angry Jess might be if she told her the truth about MsRealityCheck, she would be a whole lot more furious if she had to find out from Unmask, but that still didn't make Laura do it.

'I don't want to go to school,' Billy said, pushing his Cheerios around his bowl. 'My tummy hurts.'

'You have to go to school,' Laura said. 'Just like Mummy has to go to work.'

'But my tummy huuuuuuurts!'

'Would a cuddle make it better?'

Billy shook his blonde curls.

'A few Smarties?' That was who she was now: a mother who bribed her child with Smarties for breakfast. Once you'd trolled your own sister the only way was down, really.

'Maybe.'

Laura handed him three Smarties.

'My tummy needs five. Orange ones.'

On another day this might have made Laura laugh. Sometimes when she ran through the conversation with Jess in her head, she thought it would be okay. None of her comments had been that bad (well, apart from that last one). On the other hand, what she had actually said was almost beside the point; it was the mere fact she'd created a fake account that was weird. And it was weird, however you looked at it. Laura kept hearing her mother's voice in her head: *Oh, Laura! How could you?*

'Go and clean your teeth and put your shoes on,' she said to Billy.

'I don't want to go,' he mumbled. But at least he was heading in the direction of the bathroom.

Laura stood at the sink, regretting not having done last night's dishes and wishing her head wasn't so fuzzy from lack of sleep and her eyes didn't feel as if she'd got grit in them. She had to speak to Jess as soon as possible.

Before she was unmasked.

Chapter Seventy-Nine

Laura hadn't been able to think about anything else all day long. She'd been distracted at work ('Earth to Laura,' Dani had said more than once), missed her stop on the tube and not listened while Billy did his reading.

She kept going over and over the same thing in her mind. Was there any good way to broach this with Jess? Finally, she decided the answer was no but that she still had to try.

The trouble was it was nine o'clock at night and Billy was fast asleep in bed.

She called Jon's mobile but it just rang and rang. Laura pictured it vibrating away on some sticky pub table. Jon never picked up his phone when you needed him. He was the reason she hadn't got to her mum when she was dying.

Laura heard her mother's voice in her head: *man-baby*.

Still, she didn't have time to get cross with Jon now. She had to get to Jess and tell her the truth about MsRealityCheck before Unmask did.

Maybe she should phone Jess? No, this was a conversation that had to happen face to face. Even then it wasn't going to be easy.

Laura paced around the living room. She would have to wait until tomorrow to speak to her sister. She just hoped she'd still have the courage by then. And that it wouldn't be too late.

She started washing up. Billy had been in a febrile mood this evening. He didn't want fish fingers and he didn't want to play with his toy cars. Laura thought about Josh chewing his red Ferrari that time and was hit by a sudden flash of inspiration. Amy's mum was down from Manchester for the week, which meant that she would be able to babysit for Josh if Laura got Amy to come here.

She pulled off her rubber gloves and picked up her phone. Was it too cheeky to ask Amy? She and her mum were probably midway through a bottle of wine and a catch up by now. On the other hand, Amy was always saying that as single mothers they had to stick together and, even though it had been a bit of a one-way street up until now, Laura was sure that was because she had never asked Amy to have Billy.

Also, the thought of not talking to Jess before Unmask did was worse than the thought of begging a favour. Laura started typing out a message at which point another problem occurred to her. She could hardly tell Amy the truth about why she suddenly had to leave the house. 'I just have to confess to my sister that I'm her online troll' wasn't likely to cut it on the sympathy front. Laura had to think of an excuse that sounded sufficiently urgent though. You can't just ask someone to babysit late at night because you fancy a stroll. She would tell Amy she had to go to Jess because Jess was sick. Given recent events, it was a lie she wasn't one bit comfortable with, but really what were her choices?

Hi, she typed, *Any chance you could do me the biggest favour and babysit for Billy for an hour or so? My sister has got this horrendous stomach bug and I need to pop over there and help/play nurse. Xx*

Amy was typing.

What about her husband? Xx

Laura tsked. Bloody journalists and their need to question everything. *He's away xx* She started to put her trainers on, mentally psyching herself up for the conversation with Jess.

Would love to help, Amy's reply read, *but Mum and I are mid-movie. Xx*

Laura stared at her phone, shaking her head. And then she realized that this was completely her fault – she'd made the request seem casual. She messaged again: *Any chance I could change your mind? I'm really quite worried about my sister. Xx*

This time the reply took ages even though Laura could see the two blue ticks that told her the message had been read. Laura's jaw clenched as she thought about all the times she'd had Josh. She really didn't want to be *that* person, but was one favour in return too much to ask?

Finally Amy's message appeared: *Have you asked Jon? Xx*

Laura gripped the phone, her heart thudding against the wall of her chest. Amy hadn't exactly said no, but she definitely hadn't gone out of her way to say yes.

Chapter Eighty

Laura was standing in the school playground thinking about the night before. She was glad Amy had been out of the office at a press show today otherwise she wasn't sure she'd have been able to hold her tongue. She had always been so sure that Amy would help her out if she ever asked. Not that there was much point in Laura losing her cool, especially since she ought to be preserving all her energy for owning up to Jess.

Billy's class was led out and Laura pushed her worries to the back of her mind and pinned a smile to her face.

'Mrs— sorry, Miss Fraser, please may I have a word?' Billy's class teacher said.

Laura's heart sunk. Just when things couldn't get any worse. Billy had obviously been hitting again. What on earth was she going to say to this ridiculously young teacher? *No, it seems we can't get our five-year-old under control. Good luck to us dealing with the teenage years, eh?*

She wasn't even supposed to pick Billy up today. She was meant to still be at work rewriting the latest terrible batch of syndicated articles (it was bad when you thought about *that* wistfully). But, improbably, Jon had a work interview so here she was, sweating as she squeezed herself into a ridiculously tiny plastic chair.

There was a board on the wall. Today is: Tuesday 30th April. The weather is: Sunny. We are feeling: Miserable. (The last one was only there in Laura's mind.)

Miss Newman sat in another tiny chair (with considerably less difficulty) and began to umm and ahh. She had big starey brown eyes that reminded Laura of a frightened deer and there was a splodge of blue paint on her neck. 'So, this is a bit difficult . . .'

Laura hoped it was Angus Murray that Billy was hitting. His mum had been so nice about the whole thing last time. As long as it wasn't one of the really tiny fragile-looking girls. Or, God forbid, Caitlyn! Imagine the shame if he was thumping the girl who had the dead father!

'I think one of the other children might not be . . . umm . . . not be being that kind to Billy.'

'Sorry? What?'

'We've observed that one of the children isn't behaving nicely towards Billy.'

Laura stared at the paintings of birds on the wall. Billy's was like a giant yellow football with a beak and two stick legs. 'Someone has been hitting Billy?' That little sod, Angus Murray! She'd kill him!

Miss Newman shook her head. 'Not hitting. It's just she . . . this particular child leaves Billy out of things; excludes him. And the thing is, this particular child often influences other children so that they leave out Billy too.'

That was why Billy kept saying he didn't want to go to school in the mornings, why he kept insisting he had tummy aches. Her poor baby. She should have listened to him.

'I've spoken to the parent of the child concerned but I thought I ought to speak to you too.'

Something clunked into place in Laura's brain. The party Billy hadn't been invited to. The way Miss Newman had said parent not parents. 'It's Caitlyn, isn't it?'

Miss Newman went scarlet and scratched frantically at her neck. 'I really think— '

Laura cut her off. 'It's Caitlyn?'

She nodded.

Laura looked outside the window where Billy had been left with the teaching assistant. He was playing in the sand, making a pattern in it with a stick. His tongue was poking out with the concentration. She felt a wave of shame: I should have listened to you. It's my job to look out for you.

'I'm sure you're aware of the circumstances? Of everything that's happened to Caitlyn's family recently?'

Laura nodded.

'Obviously we want to tread extremely gently. That said, we don't want Billy to be unhappy either—'

'No! Especially since Billy hasn't exactly had a great time of it either. My mother died three and a half months ago, you know.' Laura had no idea why she'd said that. Her mother and Billy hadn't exactly been close. 'You know children bore me before the age of five, darling!' And if Billy was wrestling with any deep-seated grief, then he was hiding it very well. He'd only recently stopped his upbeat proclamations of 'Grandma's dead!'

These tiny chairs were really so uncomfortable. 'Also, Billy's father and I split up.'

Miss Newman coloured. This was probably her first job out of teacher training college. 'I heard. I'm sorry.'

Laura sighed. 'What sort of things have been happening?'

'Oh you know, kid stuff. Leaving Billy out of things. Not picking him when it's time to find partners for an activity.'

The list of phonics on the wall swum before Laura's eyes. She could hear her mother's voice in her head: *You're always so emotional, Laura.* She dug her nails into her palms and swallowed hard.

'Anyway, I spoke to Caitlyn's mother yesterday.'

'And?'

Miss Newman hesitated, pulling at the neck of her sweater. 'And I'm sure she'll talk to Caitlyn.'

There was a poster on the wall entitled 'Find the Right Mum' (the *right* mum? Laura had never known you got to choose). You had to match the chick to the chicken, the lamb to the sheep.

Laura looked at the woman on the other side of the teeny plastic table. 'What are you not telling me?'

'Nothing. I . . . I . . .'

Laura shifted as much as she possibly could in the tiny plastic chair. 'What?'

'Sometimes parents find it difficult to accept that their child has been behaving in a certain way.'

'She didn't believe you?'

'I wouldn't say she didn't believe me.'

Laura stared at her.

'She found it hard to imagine that Caitlyn would be deliberately unkind. She wondered if Billy might be being a little over sensitive.'

'Over sensitive?' Laura felt a wave of annoyance. Her mother had always levelled that one at her and now the same label was being used against Billy. Laura could see why Caitlyn's mother would struggle to reconcile her daughter's behaviour against the image of her 'perfect' little girl, but it still felt very unfair. 'She thinks Billy is making it up?'

'Err. She thinks Billy might be seeing things that aren't there.'

'But you've seen Caitlyn's behaviour with your own eyes?'

'Yes, as has Mrs Harris, our TA.'

Laura tried to get up but found the little plastic chair started to move with her. She pulled it from her bottom with as much dignity as she could muster. 'Thank you for telling me.'

Miss Newman stood. 'Of course. May I ask for your discretion though? I'm sure you understand this is a very difficult situation for all involved.'

Yes, Laura thought. Particularly Billy.

Chapter Eighty-One

Laura sat across from her sister in Leon, desperately wanting to put off the moment when she told Jess about the trolling. *Lunch would be lovely,* Jess had said when Laura messaged her earlier asking if she wanted to meet.

Don't bet on it.

While Jess poked half-heartedly at a superfood salad, Laura shovelled down a halloumi wrap and fries. She wished being miserable put her off her food but it always seemed to have rather the opposite effect. She was already eyeing up the lemon and ginger crunch.

Laura took a deep breath. 'So now I know all your secrets—'

Jess gave her a strange look. 'You don't know all my secrets.'

Laura was thrown for a second. What did *that* mean? But she was probably reading too much into Jess' words. It was the type of remark people made flippantly. And anyway, she couldn't afford to let anything steer her off course right now. 'Well, I need to tell you something.'

'Oh?' Jess said, putting down her spear of broccoli.

For a second the resolve drained out of Laura and she considered lying. She could tell Jess about the problems Billy was having at school, pretend that had been what she wanted to talk to her about. Her heart pounded against the wall of her chest. 'How's the Unmask investigation going?'

Jess' face scrunched at the apparent change in topic. 'Slowly. But they think they're making good progress.'

Laura took a deep breath. 'Look, there's no easy way to say what I want to say, so I'm just going to come straight out with it. But before I do, I want you to know that I'm so, so sorry and I don't expect you to forgive me because I don't forgive myself.'

Jess was staring at her. 'It can't be that bad. And you know Dad always used to say if you really loved someone there was nothing they could do to change that.'

'I posted some horrible comments on your site.' Jess blanched. 'I'm not the person who threatened to rape and kill you and told you they know where you live . . . I mean, obviously.' Laura looked down at her hands. She had to get through this and she couldn't look at Jess when she did. 'But I did post some nasty comments. I created a fake account.'

Jess was silent for the longest time and Laura sat there thinking this is how it ends, the new-found peace between her and her sister. Their mother had always said she didn't know how Jess 'put up with Laura's petty jealousy'. Well done, Mum, you called it.

'Why?' Jess squeaked eventually.

Laura shook her head. 'Because I'm a bitch. Because I'm jealous of you. Because you are always so fucking perfect.'

'I think you can drop the 'perfect' label now you know the truth about me,' Jess said.

'Well, at least you're not a troll.'

'Yes,' Jess said sadly. 'Listen I've got to go.'

Laura watched her sister walk out of the door and then she burst into tears.

Chapter Eighty-Two

Laura was done with loss.

A tear rolled down her cheek. She could see a woman at the next table glancing across at her. In other circumstances she might have felt embarrassed about sitting blubbing in Leon but right now she was too miserable to care.

She thought about Jon; how one minute the two of them had been arguing about the bin and the next he was gone. And it wasn't just Jon Laura had lost when he walked out of that door. In an instant, the childhood she desperately wanted for Billy seemed to disappear. Laura had been so determined that Billy would grow up in a home that was a place of stability and certainty. She hadn't had that growing up; not just because of her dad's death, seismic as that was, but also because her mother's moods were as unpredictable as a British summer. Laura could still remember that, as a teenager, every time she put her key in the front door, she would hover for a second, offering up a silent prayer that all was good on the other side. Laura had promised herself that Billy would have a home that always felt safe, where he was never worried about walking through the front door.

Laura pulled her paper napkin into shreds. She thought about her dad and how the last time she'd ever seen him alive, she'd had absolutely no idea it was the last time. The day had seemed just like any other day. Laura hadn't paid her dad any particular attention at breakfast. She'd been more caught up with Jess and Mum, wondering if the former was ever going to stop banging on about her stupid piano exam (like she'd get anything but a distinction) and whether the latter was being a bit frosty (Laura couldn't think of anything in particular she'd done wrong but with Mum it was hard to know). Dad was just there reading his paper and eating his toast and marmalade.

If Laura had realized, she would have drunk in every detail of her dad, she would have stared at him until she had committed every single angle of his face to memory as if she was about to paint him. She would have hugged him with all her strength and told him again and again how much she loved him

'Bye,' Dad said, kissing them all and going out to work. Laura couldn't even remember if she'd looked up from her Weetabix.

A guy was clearing tables. He took one look at Laura and backed away. Better not take her empty packaging.

Laura hadn't known it was the last time she'd see her mother either. Even though everyone knew Evie was gravely ill, the doctors were reluctant to say exactly how long she had left. So when Laura had trekked to the hospice she was more consumed with why there was such a long wait for the bus and how crappy the weather was instead of thinking: this is it. She had even been – to her subsequent shame – resentful about having to give up her Saturday afternoon. The exchanges between her and her mum had been limited and tetchy. Laura wanted Evie to take her haloperidol, the older woman was focussed on Laura's hair. (How many people in real life got movie deathbed scenes?)

Laura looked at the empty space across the table where her sister had been sitting.

She did not want to lose Jess.

Chapter Eighty-Three

Less than five minutes after she'd walked out, Jess came back in through the door. She sat opposite Laura, reached across the table and took her hand. 'Listen,' she said. 'You're a troll but you're my troll. Literally my troll, actually.'

Laura managed to laugh through the tears.

'Also,' Jess said. 'It suddenly occurred to me that I'm in no position to take the moral high ground. You know, what with me being a cheat and all that. Which you've been very kind and non-judgmental about, by the way. Now, do you want a cup of tea?'

'Will you poison it?'

'Probably.'

Laura gave her a watery smile. 'A cup of tea would be lovely.' She wiped away a tear from the side of her nose. 'And a lemon and ginger crunch.'

Chapter Eighty-Four

Laura stood in the school playground. After yesterday, she'd had quite enough difficult conversations, so why she was planning another, she really couldn't have said. Especially since she kept hearing her mother's voice screaming inside her head: *Don't do what you always do and go in two feet first.*

She crossed the tarmac to talk to Caitlyn's mother, all the time wondering why she was doing this. Later she would look back and think that there was something about the way Tanya Webb had looked at her when she'd walked past; the haughtiness with which she raised her chin and swished her blonde hair. The way she pointedly stood as far away from Laura as possible as if it was Laura who ought to feel bad.

Laura got closer and closer. Tanya was surrounded by a cluster of women. She'd always been one of the popular mums and she was even more of a magnet recently. Everyone wanted to be seen to be supporting the widow although no one was talking bereavement today and, instead, there was an earnest conversation going on about the box blight that was hitting Dulwich. If you had box plants anywhere in your garden – and why wouldn't you – this was a serious problem. Heaven help those who had box balls flanking their steps.

'Hi,' Laura said, interrupting. 'I'm Billy's mum.'

'I know who you are,' Tanya said.

'I wonder if I could have a quick word with you? Privately.'

Tanya exchanged glances with the women around her. Elinor, who was head of the PTA, and had never forgiven Laura for forgetting her shift at that one cake sale, looked at her with naked hostility. Tanya stepped about a foot away from them.

'So,' Laura said. 'It seems that Caitlyn and Billy have had a few problems recently.' She waited for Tanya to say she was so sorry that Caitlyn had been upsetting Billy and she was going to make sure it didn't happen again. But Tanya just stared at her coolly. 'I understand that this must be a very difficult time for Caitlyn.'

Nothing.

'But this has all been affecting Billy very badly. He has been saying he doesn't want to come to school in the mornings. He has been getting tummy aches.'

Finally the other woman spoke. 'It sounds like he's quite over-emotional.'

Laura took a deep breath. PTA Elinor was looking over. Oh, keep your beak out, you tragic cow who does PowerPoint presentations about the secondhand uniform sale! We all know you were a high-flyer in the City before giving up work to concentrate on your poor children. 'He's not over-emotional. He's just upset because he's constantly being left out of things. Ostracized.'

'So he says.'

Laura could feel the anger rising inside her. 'No, not so he says. So Miss Newman says and Mrs Harris.'

'Miss Newman is very young.'

'So? Also, Mrs Harris isn't very young. She has been a teaching assistant for years.'

Tanya shrugged.

'You have to believe them.'

'I don't *have* to do anything.'

Laura blew out her cheeks. 'Listen, I'm trying to talk to

298

you nicely about this; mum to mum. But if you won't at least try to sort things out, then I'm going to have to take action. Your daughter is bullying Billy and it's simply not acceptable.'

'Bullying is a strong word. Caitlyn doesn't have to like Billy.'

'No, of course she doesn't.' Laura couldn't imagine why anyone wouldn't like Billy; her sweet little baby. 'But that doesn't mean she's allowed to turn other kids in the class against him. Or tell him she hopes his guinea pig dies.'

'Who told you she said that?'

'Billy.'

'And no one else heard it?'

'What difference does that make?'

'What difference it makes is that it sounds to me as if Billy is just making it up. Just like he made up everything else. It sounds to me like he's an unhappy little boy who doesn't have many friends and he's just trying to get attention.'

Laura stared at her in disbelief.

Tanya turned on her heel.

'That's it? You're just walking away?'

'Well, what do you want me to say?'

'I want you to say that you're sorry that your little cow of a daughter has been upsetting my son.'

'Oh, we're calling five-year-olds names now, are we? That's very mature.'

Laura felt about two feet tall, especially as she was sure she could hear tutting from the nearby coven. 'I'm sorry. It's just that this is all very upsetting.'

'Yes, I can see you're upset. No wonder Billy is such an emotional child. But, you know what, I watched my husband die of cancer recently. So *this* I can cope with.'

Really? She was playing that card? 'I'm sorry about your husband. I also had a bereavement recently. My mother.'

Tanya stared at her, her face clearly showing she knew she had aced the game of Grief Trumps.

'If you could just try to talk to Caitlyn?'

'If you want.'

'If I want? Yes, I want. You need to explain to your daughter that her behaviour is not okay. That it's important to include people. Oh, and by the way, I don't think it was particularly kind of you to allow her to invite everyone but Billy to her birthday party.'

'She can invite who she wants to her party.'

'There are twenty-six kids in the class and you invited twenty-five. It's just not the done thing. We had a party for Billy and we invited everyone, even Angus Murray. Do you think we wanted Angus Murray there? Of course we didn't!' Laura was shouting now and, out of the corner of her eye, she could see Angus' mum staring at her. Christ!

'I can't have this conversation with you anymore,' Tanya said. 'It's less than two months since Simon died.' Her eyes filled with tears, and even though Laura was almost sure they were fake, they immediately got the sympathy of the crowd, with PTA Elinor rushing over to lead Tanya back to the safety of their gaggle and shooting Laura a hostile look before leaving her standing completely alone.

The playground bully.

Chapter Eighty-Five

Laura opened the door to see Jon in a white rhinestone-encrusted suit clutching a suitcase and two bulging black bin bags.

'Can I crash here? Jimmy has booted me out. Well, Maja really. Jimmy said the words but they were coming from her.'

Laura's brain was struggling to process. It was eleven o'clock at night. She had been replaying her earlier conversation with Tanya Webb and wondering if there was a single person in that playground who had been on her side (not judging by their faces). She was just about to clean her teeth and fall into bed. But now she was standing here in the doorway with her strangely attired ex asking if he could stay over. 'Why are you dressed like that?'

'Oh, I'm Elvis. A woman in the supermarket said I looked just like him. That she ran a lookalike agency and I could make good money just for turning up at parties and store openings.'

Laura guessed he did look a bit like Elvis. He'd certainly looked very much like the young Elvis when she'd first met him, and she supposed there was still a look there now if you squinted. Elvis in the later years – after all those deep-fried peanut-butter-and-banana sandwiches.

'What happened with Jimmy?'

'Can I come in?'

'I suppose so. I don't think you can stay though. It'll be too confusing for Billy when he wakes up in the morning.'

'He'd love it.'

'That's not really the point.'

Jon sighed heavily. 'Fine. I'll just stay on the sofa tonight and then tomorrow I'll go to my parents. I just know they're going to drive me nuts though.'

Laura felt like saying that she was pretty sure his parents didn't dream about having their thirty-nine-year-old son and his black bin bags move back in with them either. And that even if your parents did drive you nuts, you should remember that one day you suddenly wouldn't have them. That it would feel weird using the term 'orphan' because you felt too old for it, but that was what you were, and anyway, not having any parents did make you feel like a little kid.

She stepped aside to let him in. Had he dyed his hair darker for this 'role'? She was pretty sure he had. 'You could rent a flat.'

He looked at her like she had suggested he run the North Pole Marathon. Naked.

He set the suitcase and bin bags down in the hall. 'How does it feel to be the pariah of the playground?'

Laura groaned. 'Marvellous.'

Jon grinned. 'I could do with a beer.'

'There are some in the fridge.'

He helped himself to a beer, settled down on the sofa and rested his feet on the coffee table.

'If you do stay tonight, you'll have to leave before Billy wakes up.'

A look of irritation passed over his face. 'But he gets up at half six.'

'Jon.'

'Fine.'

She sat on the sofa next to him, fiddling with her mother's locket. She'd taken to wearing it recently, not so much because she liked it but more because it seemed like the right thing to do after making so much fuss about having it. 'What happened with Jimmy?'

He took a swig of his beer. 'Like I said, it wasn't really Jimmy, it was Maja. She got all arsey because she said I never helped around the flat. Said she was always cooking us delicious dinners – they were actually rank – and then I couldn't even be bothered to do the washing up.'

'Mmm hmm.'

Jon looked at her and rolled his eyes. 'She's a cow. And Jimmy's pussy-whipped. I never thought he would be, but he is.'

'That's not a particularly charming expression, Jon.'

He shrugged. 'Billy okay?'

Laura had told him all about the Caitlyn situation on the phone earlier. 'I guess. I hate to think of that little madam being mean to him.'

'I know,' Jon said, sipping his beer. 'Poor little man. I'm sorry I told you everything was fine when you first said you were worried. We should have listened to your instincts. Although maybe not unleashed you in the playground!'

She gave him a mock punch in the ribs and then gestured towards the outfit. 'So I assume you were doing lookalike work tonight?'

'Nah, I'm just method.'

She laughed.

'I did a meet-and-greet in Catford.'

'And were they suitably delighted to have Elvis in the building?'

'I hope so. It's only the second gig I've done.'

'I've always thought it must be so weird to be a lookalike. No offence.'

He grinned. 'It is weird. But it's easy work and it pays good money. I really like the woman who runs the agency too. She's this little five-foot firecracker who knocks everyone into shape. You should have heard her on the phone to "Victoria" about how she has to stop falling out with "David" all the time. "No one wants Victoria without David," she told her.'

'Haha! Well, Elvis, I'm going to bid you goodnight. You know where the spare duvet is.'

'I was going to be Jesus,' Jon said, as she was about to leave the room. 'But Shirley said there's not much call for Jesus nowadays.'

Laura felt as if she might be in a dream.

Chapter Eighty-Six

Despite the fact Jess had been ridiculously forgiving about the whole trolling thing, and the two of them were getting on so much better recently, Laura couldn't help but feel a ripple of irritation when she got a message from Jess saying she needed to talk to Laura about something.

People didn't say they needed to talk to you about something when it was just a casual chat. You didn't 'need to talk to someone' to say you'd made a banging fish pie the night before or caught a great new programme on Netflix.

Jess must want to tell Laura off about something (Laura couldn't think of any recent transgressions, but who knew). Either that or she wanted to issue a fresh set of bossy instructions.

Either way Laura hated the portentousness of it all. If you've got something to say, then bloody well spit it out. Don't trail it in advance.

Chapter Eighty-Seven

Laura and Jess were at the funfair with the kids but nobody was having much fun.

Jess had called Laura at 6.45 that morning. 'Ben knows,' she said, her voice breaking.

Laura gasped. 'Oh, God. When you said you had something you wanted to talk to me about I never imagined it would be that.' She felt guilty now about being irritated.

'What?' Jess said, sounding confused. 'Oh, that was . . . something else. Ben didn't find out until last night.'

'Oh,' Laura said. Part of her wanted to press for information – so what the bloody hell *were* you trailing before? – but given what a state her sister was in, it seemed a little insensitive.

Laura and Jess stood at the bottom of the luridly-coloured helter-skelter. It was a gloriously sunny May day; the weather not having got the memo about the mood. 'So, tell me what happened,' Laura said.

Jess sighed. 'A parcel arrived for me and I didn't think anything of it. I get sent loads of freebies because of work. But, as soon as I saw the Creme Eggs, I had a sickening memory of Aaron once offering me some expensive-looking truffles and me saying that I hated posh chocolate and to give me a Creme Egg any day. I didn't even need to look at the card, I just knew they were from him. I was shaking. Ben asked me who they were from and I said a photographer had sent them. And he said, "He must know you very well." And I tried to pass it off, said something like, "Oh, you know me. I'm always banging on about Creme Eggs."' Tears had started rolling down Jess' cheeks. 'But Ben does know me. Really, really well. He just stared at me, a muscle pulsing under his eye, and it was as if the whole world had gone quiet and even the traffic outside had stopped. And then he just said, "What's the deal, Jess?" It was awful—' She broke off into a sob.

Hannah, Lola and Billy whizzed down the helter-skelter, one after the other on their coir mats, and Jess looked at the ground so that they wouldn't see she was crying.

Laura waited until the kids were out of earshot before speaking. 'And what happened after you told him?'

'He didn't shout or rage, he just sat there very quietly at the island unit, his eyes filled with hurt and disappointment. And I kept thinking about a row I once had with Mum when she referred to Ben as "boring Ben" and I went wild and said that being calm was a *good* thing. Mum didn't apologize, of course. She said it was just a joke and not to be so over sensitive.'

Billy whizzed down the slide on his coir mat a second time, all smiles. Lola appeared seconds later, closely followed by Hannah who smacked into the back of her.

'Oww!' Lola said, scowling. 'You're supposed to wait.'

'No,' Hannah said. '*You're* supposed to get off quicker.'

The kids started to climb the stairs again, trailing their mats behind them.

Laura reached out and squeezed her sister's shoulder.

'Since then, he won't talk about it,' Jess said. 'He hasn't walked out on me but it's like he may as well have done. He's there but not there, if you know what I mean. And he just looks so sad all the time. I look at him and look away because

I hate myself so much when I realize that I did this to him.'

Laura stroked her arm.

'I just keep telling him I'm sorry all the time,' Jess said. 'But the words seem so flimsy and inadequate. You say sorry to people when you accidentally step on their foot on the tube or are ten minutes late to meet them, not when you take a blowtorch to your marriage vows and casually destroy nineteen years of trust.'

The kids whizzed down the helter-skelter again. Billy said he wanted to go to the shooting range so he could try to win one of those giant green ducks. Laura said they would in a bit, to have another go on the slide first.

'I can't believe I've been so stupid,' Jess said. 'I, of all people, should know that infidelity destroys lives.'

'What do you mean you "of all people"?' Laura said.

Jess looked at the ground. 'Nothing, nothing.'

Laura puffed out her cheeks. 'You've made a mistake, Jess. People do make mistakes. But there must be a way back from this. You and Ben have been together forever. Also, you're good together.' As she said this she realized how true it was and how the same couldn't be said for her and Jon; that even if she still loved him, they definitely weren't 'right'.

'He's so distant, Laura. When I told him I want us to go back to how we were before he said that's *never* going to happen. *Never*. I feel like there's no hope.'

Jess was not a 'no hope' kind of girl; she did *not* give up. She'd once crawled the last two hundred yards of a marathon. 'What about counselling?'

'I've suggested it,' Jess said.

'There will be a way through this,' Laura said. Because surely that had to be true?

Chapter Eighty-Eight

Laura was hoping to channel her mother in a 'take no pris-
oners' sense but she feared she might actually be channelling
unhinged lunatic.

She was sitting in a pub with her brother-in-law, having
ambushed him as he emerged from the office. 'Laura,' he'd
said, looking taken aback. 'What are you doing here?' Laura
told him they needed to talk and steered him across the road
to the nearest pub before he could argue.

Now the pair of them were sitting opposite each other,
gazing warily across a faux mahogany table and sipping G&Ts
(Ben had tried to order a Diet Coke but Laura had told him
he'd need something stronger).

Laura fought off a wave of awkwardness as she was struck
by the realization that, although she'd known her brother-in-
law for nearly twenty years, she didn't really *know* him at all.
Oh, she knew he supported Arsenal and couldn't bear cauli-
flower, and once, on a camping trip, had accidentally wiped
his penis with a toilet wipe instead of a baby wipe (the latter
disclosed by an uncharacteristically drunk Jess one night) but
that wasn't a huge help right now.

Ben took a sip of his drink. 'I guess you must be worrying
about the trolling thing.'

Laura was wrong-footed because, not only was that not
the thing she had planned to talk to Ben about this evening,

but also she suddenly realized, with a flash of pure embarrassment, that he must know what she'd done. Well, of course he knew – Jess would obviously have mentioned it, however tense things were between the two of them.

Ben put his glass down. 'This company we've got looking into it are fantastic. They'll definitely track the bastard down.'

So, Ben *didn't* know about MsRealityCheck. Jess had spared her that. 'Great,' Laura said. 'Actually, it was you and Jess I wanted to talk to you about. I know about everything that's happened.'

Ben stared at the table. 'O-kay.'

'Heartbreak Hotel' started playing and Laura thought of Jon pretending to be Elvis. It was a strange way to earn a living but at least he was doing something, she supposed. She forced her mind back to the present and looked across the table at Ben. 'Look, it's awful for you, really it is, but you need to talk to her.'

Ben didn't look up. 'It's sweet of you to look out for your sister, Laura, but I'm not going to discuss my marriage with anyone but Jess.'

'But that's the thing,' Laura said, almost knocking her drink over. 'You're not talking to Jess.'

Ben looked at her. 'Laura, firstly, please can you keep your voice down, because there are people from my work in this pub, and secondly, this really isn't your business.'

Channel Mum. She never gave a damn whether something was her business or not. 'Did Jess tell you about what happened when you were in New York? About how she found the lump in her breast?'

'Yes, of course she told me.'

'You could have lost her, Ben. She could have had cancer like Mum. That's how it works. One minute we're all going about our business, worrying about petty nonsense, and the next minute, "poof" – a person we love is just gone. And I

310

really thought it might be Jess. I could picture her going through chemo and losing her hair and wearing ridiculously stylish scarves. I could imagine her being told that nothing had worked and that she didn't have long. And I knew that we'd all go to pieces, but Jess would be amazing. That she would start making us all lists and writing the girls' birthday cards for the next ten years.'

Ben put his head in his hands. 'Stop talking like this – she's okay. The lump is harmless.'

'Yes, but it's a wake-up call, isn't it? Don't lose her if you don't have to.'

Ben stood up. 'Okay, Laura, that's enough. As I said, I think it's good of you to look out for your sister. But I absolutely don't want to have this conversation with you.'

He started to walk away but Laura jumped up to go after him. 'Don't you think that Rob at my grief group wishes his wife was still around? Don't you think that he'd do anything – anything – to be able to have one more conversation with her?'

'Laura, please!' Ben said, heading for the door.

She ran after him. 'She didn't even have a bloody affair, Ben.'

Ben turned round to face her, his face a mask of hurt. 'I said I don't want to have this conversation with you.'

'Then have it with Jess.'

He paused and then shook his head. 'It's not that simple.'

Laura stared at him. He looked so sad and broken standing there in the street that she felt a wave of sympathy. But then she remembered she was adopting the role of her mother. 'It *is* that simple. You cannot lose Jess over this.'

Chapter Eighty-Nine

There was a new person at grief group and he was unmistakably hot. *For goodness' sake!* Laura told herself. *You do not pick people up at grief group. You only just split up from Jon. This guy is way out of your league anyway.*

Misery bloodhound Jenni asked him if he'd like to introduce himself.

'I'm Marcus,' he said.

Jenni nodded enthusiastically. 'And what brings you here today, Marcus?'

He'll be a widower. One who has only recently lost his equally hot wife and is never ever really going to get over her.

'My dad died. Six weeks ago.'

Not a widower. So almost certainly married.

Jenni nodded. 'Welcome to the group, Marcus.'

Like she was the greeting him at the door of some swanky members club rather than a dingy den of misery and sorrow.

'Right,' Jenni said. 'Who would like to start today?'

Emma raised her hand. 'I wanted to ask what to do about people who say stupid things.' She bit furiously at her cuticle. 'There's this teacher at my school who said my mum is probably in a better place now. And I should never forget to cherish the time we had together. She talks like a fucking Hallmark card.'

Mary gasped.

'I think it's best if we try to avoid bad language,' Jenni said.

'Fuck, fuck, fuckety-fuck,' Emma said.

Laura noticed Marcus trying to suppress a smile. He had very nice eyes. Christ, she was like a dog in heat! And, anyway, he was definitely married, even if he wasn't wearing a wedding ring. And definitely out of her league. Also none of that mattered because she was *not* interested.

'It can be difficult for people to know what to say,' Jenni said to Emma.

'Yeah,' Rob chimed in, 'people keep telling me I should be thinking about dating.'

As Laura looked at him, a memory rose up of her confrontation with Ben: *Don't you think that Rob at my grief group wishes his wife was still around?*

'It's like time's up on feeling miserable,' Rob said.

Jenni nodded. 'In today's world, we're used to things happening *fast*. We send an email and expect an answer almost instantly. We pop food in a microwave because we want to eat in minutes. But grief isn't something that can be hurried.'

Preena nodded. 'I get people telling me my sister would want me to be happy. Like it's that simple.'

Marcus gave Preena an encouraging smile. He had a nice mouth too. Oh, for goodness' sake!

'People tell me I'll find a way of making sense of Rosie's death,' Ann said quietly, her eyes shining with unspilt tears. 'But it makes no sense for a beautiful, bright girl with everything to live for to die of a horrible disease. Especially when there are so many vile people left walking around.'

Laura suddenly remembered a phase she'd gone though after her dad had died, where she kept looking at people around his age that were still alive and judging them inferior to him. Like a long life was something you got on merit.

'My dad wasn't that nice,' Marcus said. 'I mean, I loved him because he was my dad, but if you look at it objectively he was a bit of a—' He glanced across at Mary. 'He wasn't the nicest. He was a womaniser, a gambler and a drunk. When me and my ex-wife told him we were having a little girl, he said you couldn't win them all. So you'd think my grief would be easy-peasy, right? But actually it has knocked me for six.'

Laura stared, open-mouthed, at Marcus. Every minute that she'd sat in these groups, she'd wished she had the courage to come out as an imposter. To own up to the fact that her grief was simply not good enough.

And now there was someone who seemed as if they were on exactly the same page.

Chapter Ninety

Jess handed Laura a gift-wrapped parcel. 'It's a little thank-you present for ambushing my husband the other day. I wouldn't say things are suddenly all okay between us but we're talking.'

Laura pulled on the ribbon. 'You didn't need to do this.'

'Least I could do. Ben said he'd do almost anything if I kept you away from him from now on!' She winked.

Laura tore open the wrapping paper to reveal a white porcelain dish that was crisscrossed with gold lines. Laura turned it over in her hands. 'Oh, it's so pretty. Wait, is this is the dish I broke at Mum's?'

Jess nodded.

'What?'

'It's a Japanese thing called Kintsugi. There's a leaflet in the box that explains it.'

Laura took out the leaflet and read aloud. 'Kintsugi is the ancient art of repairing what has been broken. Fragments of dropped ceramics are put back together; mended using lacquer dusted with powdered gold that leaves the repair visible. The revitalized ceramic becomes a symbol of fragility, strength and beauty.' She kissed Jess on the cheek. 'Wow, that's so beautiful. Thank you.'

Jess smiled. 'You're welcome. I read about it ages ago and I've just been waiting to have the right thing to use it for. I love the spirt behind it. The idea that the broken can be beautiful and that we need to forgive ourselves and forgive others – embrace our "cracks".' She laughed. 'She says, sounding unbearably pretentious!'

Laura laughed. 'Glass of wine?'

'I shouldn't really. I'm supposed to be writing a blog post tonight.'

'Just a small one.'

'Oh, go on then,' Jess said. 'To celebrate the fact Unmask have tracked down my online troll.' She winked. 'My *other* online troll.'

'Don't,' Laura said, making a pained face. 'Who is he?'

'A chef from Tottenham.'

'A chef?'

Jess nodded. 'The police went to have a word. Apparently, he looked as if he was going to burst into tears. I don't think he'll be messaging me again any time soon.'

'Christ!' Laura said, opening the wine.

They were sitting in Laura's kitchen. She had given up worrying about what Jess thought about the fact that she always seemed to have a pile of dirty dishes teetering near the sink, and that you were more likely to find a pile of (clean) knickers on the table than a scented candle. To be fair to Jess, she didn't seem to care – although Laura *had* once caught her washing mugs she'd just taken out of the cupboard before using them.

Jess picked up the dish and traced one of the gold lines with her fingertip. She grinned. 'This line here symbolizes me forgiving you for being the world's worst bridesmaid.'

'I was not the world's worst bridesmaid.'

They were both laughing now.

'You were so hungover, you had to stop to be sick in a plant pot just before we went into the church.'

'At least I didn't hurl as we walked up the aisle.'

'You didn't organize a hen night—'

'You didn't want one.'

316

'I didn't want a stripper.' She took a sip of her wine. 'You were late to every dress fitting and you shagged the best man in the toilets just before he had to make his speech. Which did, I have to admit, take the edge off his nerves!'

Laura held up her hands. 'Okay, okay. I wasn't a *great* brides-maid. But you did make me wear green.'

'It matched your face.'

Billy burst into the room, announced that Lola was cheating at Hungry Hippos, grabbed three biscuits without asking, and then ran out again.

Laura picked up the dish and pointed to another gold wiggly line. 'This line here symbolizes me forgiving you for being a smug cow about your A level results.'

Jess gave her a mock punch on the shoulder. 'What do you mean?'

'You got two As and a B and you never stopped complaining about the B.'

Jess laughed. 'I was only a few marks off an A. But fair enough. Right, my turn again.' She pointed to another gold line. 'This one here is for you being so utterly rubbish when Lola was born, barely coming to see me at all in those first few weeks and then expecting me to make you tea when you did finally pitch up.'

'Sorry. I had no idea what it was like. And, anyway, at least I didn't keep telling you to put some make-up on like Mum did.'

Jess laughed. 'Your go.'

'This line says I forgive you for stealing my platform sandals that time BEFORE I'D EVEN WORN THEM.'

Jess winced. 'Not sure you should forgive me for that one!'

They carried on playing and they carried on drinking until they realized they'd finished the bottle. At that point Jess completely abandoned the idea of writing her blog post and they ordered takeaway pizza for everyone.

As Laura burnt the roof of her mouth on a molten string of mozzarella, she looked across the table at Jess and thought about all the 'I forgive yous' they'd avoided.

I forgive you for being Mum's favourite.

I forgive you for always sniping about me being an influencer.

I forgive you for not liking my son's father.

I forgive you for not helping more when Mum was sick.

I forgive you for always being better at everything.

I forgive you for saying my ten-year-old would probably end up with an eating disorder.

She thought about Preena at the grief support group. The raw pain in her voice when she talked about always waiting for her sister to call but realizing that she never would. It made Laura want to call Preena every day: *I know I'm not her and I'll never be as good as her but you can tell me when your husband is being a dick.*

Billy was shovelling pizza into his mouth and arguing with Hannah about whether she was his guinea pig's cousin too. Lola was looking at them both, quiet and watchful, and Laura felt a surge of guilt and protectiveness. *I'm sorry,* she said to Lola in her head. *I will be a better auntie. I will look out for you.*

'Want one more glass of wine?' she said to Jess.

'I really shouldn't. . .'

'Go on, just a small one.'

'Mummy's drunk!' Lola said, looking a little horrified.

'I'm not drunk!'

'I want wine,' Billy said. 'Or beer. I want beer like Daddy.'

'You're five,' Hannah said.

'Five and a quarter.'

Laura looked around, at the Kintsugi-ed dish, more beautiful now than it had ever been before, at everyone's smiling faces around the table. One of the spotlights had blown out a while back and she hadn't got around to buying a new bulb and, even though it had been getting on her nerves and it meant she could barely see when she was trying to cook in the evenings, she had to admit now it was casting a rather pretty glow. Like a lazy man's candlelight.

Jess looked happier and more relaxed than Laura could remember seeing her for what felt like forever, and even though Laura knew that was mostly down to the verdejo, she hoped it was also because she was a little happier.

As soon as the pizzas had been devoured, the kids shot off back to Billy's bedroom.

'One more glass?' Laura said.

'I really shouldn't,' Jess said, holding out her glass to be refilled.

'Hey,' Laura said. 'You know the other day, before all this blew up with Ben, you sent me that message saying you needed to talk to me about something – what was all that about?'

Jess' face froze. 'Oh, I can't remember.'

That struck Laura as highly improbable but she let it go. Jess had almost certainly wanted to tell Laura off about something and now didn't want to spoil a nice evening.

'I really should be writing that blog post,' Jess said.

'Yup,' Laura said, 'and I should be writing next week's horoscopes. Christ, my job is shit at the moment. Ahh, I shouldn't say that. If you believe what you hear, *Natter* could be closed down any minute. That would serve me right. A real case of "be careful what you wish for".'

Jess took a sip of her wine. 'You've been fed up there for a while. Perhaps you should look for something else?'

Normally Laura would bristle at this. Would think Jess was acting just like their mum by being so quick to tell her what she was doing wrong with her life. But, whether it was down to the wine or the mood, she didn't mind the way she normally would. 'I did actually see a great job advertised at *Inlustris*. I filled in the application form and everything. But there's no way in the world I'd get it.'

'Isn't it worth a try?' Jess said.

Laura puffed out her cheeks. Put like that it sounded so simple. 'I'm sure the closing date for applications has long gone.'

'Where did you see the ad?' Jess said

'On a journalist's group on Facebook. But it will be too late.' She grinned. 'Now, drink up your wine and stop bossing me about.'

'It wouldn't hurt to have a quick look,' Jess said.

Laura rolled her eyes and reached for her phone. 'Oh. The closing date is the 12th May – that's tomorrow.'

'See,' Jess said.

'I haven't got a chance of even getting an interview,' Laura said.

Billy came into the kitchen. 'Why won't you get an interval?'

Laura tousled his curls. 'An interview, Big Ears. And never mind.'

Billy shrugged. 'Can I have some ice cream?'

Laura said they didn't have any and Billy sighed heavily before heading back to whatever game he and the girls were playing.

'Did you say you'd already filled in the application form?' Jess said the second Billy had left the room.

'No. Yes. Maybe. I haven't proofread it.'

Jess made a face. 'That will take all of five minutes. Come on, where is it?'

Laura looked at her laptop, which was balanced on a teetering pile of papers on the worktop. She supposed she may as well have a look at the application form. She could barely even remember what she'd written.

The two of them sat side by side reading it. Jess finished first. 'I'd give you the job,' she said.

Laura laughed. 'It's not yours to give. Also, I think you might be biased.'

'Why not send it?' Jess said. 'You've got everything to gain and nothing to lose.'

That was exactly what agony aunt Laura had said to Faye from Colchester. Laura sighed. 'You're not going to let up about this, are you?'

Jess shook her head. 'Nope.'

Laura laughed. 'Okay, okay, I'll send it. But I'm only doing it to shut you up. Oh, and because getting that dish Kintsugi-ed was such a sweet thing to do. I haven't got a chance of getting this job though.'

Chapter Ninety-One

Laura opened the door to see Amy standing there, with Josh on her hip.

'I don't suppose you could do me a small favour and have Josh for a bit, could you?' Amy said. 'I've just realized I haven't got anything to wear for that wedding I'm going to tomorrow.'

'Oh,' Laura said. 'Jon's just picked up Billy for the day.'

Amy looked at her but said nothing. Surely she wasn't expecting Laura to spend her child-free Sunday babysitting so she could go clothes shopping?

'It's just I'm a bit stuck,' Amy said. 'I could order something online and pay for next day delivery but then what if it doesn't fit or I don't like it?'

Laura wasn't quite sure what to say. 'I'd love to help, it's just I have plans.' The truth was she was a little hungover after sinking two bottles of wine with Jess. She had been intending to clean the flat as quickly as possible before lying on her bed and watching back-to-back episodes of *Queer Eye*. A large mug of tea and a chocolate brownie were also on the agenda.

Those weren't the sort of plans that couldn't be changed though.

Amy was still staring at her, a sort of pleading look on her face.

Laura vacillated. Cleaning the flat could wait. The Fab Five could wait. The brownie could still be eaten.

But Laura couldn't help thinking about the night she'd wanted to confess to Jess that she was MsRealityCheck. Her asking Amy if she could look after Billy for an hour when he was asleep. Amy not even hesitating to say no. Shutting the metaphorical door in Laura's face. Laura had always been so sure that Amy would help her out if she ever needed her; so adamant that Jess was wrong when she said the friendship was a one-way street.

Laura looked at Josh, happily spouting gibberish as he chewed on his picture book. He really was a gorgeous little boy. She looked at Amy, whose face was full of expectation.

'I'm sorry not to be able to help,' Laura said.

Amy stared at her in disbelief before offering the brusquest of goodbyes and disappearing back down the stairs.

As Laura shut the door, her heart was beating very fast but for once in her life she didn't feel even the slightest bit guilty.

Chapter Ninety-Two

As Laura was leaving grief group, Marcus fell into step next to her. She felt her palms start to sweat and told herself not to be so stupid. Marcus was *not* interested in some plump frump of nearly forty. And she wasn't interested in him (even if his eyes did crinkle in a very appealing way when he smiled).

'Well, that was a fun and relaxing way to spend an hour,' he said to her, grinning.

She smiled. 'Yeah, every time I go I tell myself I'm never going back.'

Despite the fact it was nearly eight in the evening, Calton Avenue was still warm and there was a strong smell of honeysuckle in the air.

'So what do you do when you're not talking about death and coping strategies?' Marcus said.

'I'm a journalist.' Sort of.

'Oh,' Marcus said. 'My sister used to be a journalist. Now she works for a content company called Bridge. Do you know it? Or is that like an American asking you if you know their cousin Bill when you tell them you live in London?'

Laura smiled. 'I do know Bridge. What do you do?'

'I'm a doctor. I work at King's.'

A doctor. *Get a grip of yourself, Laura; you are not someone who's impressed with stuff like that.* I mean obviously doctors are useful because they save lives and other trivial stuff, but it's not impressive in a dating context. And, anyway, there is no dating context.

'This is me,' Marcus said as they came up to a shabby-looking grey Golf. 'Can I give you a lift anywhere?'

Laura shook her head. 'I only live a short walk away.'

'Okay,' Marcus said, unlocking the car. 'Well, see you next week for the misery fest.'

Laura said she'd see him next week and pushed away the thought that she would definitely go now.

She walked down the wide, leafy street feeling extremely odd. Marcus was way out of her league (she had this sudden memory of being sixteen and confessing to her mum that she had a crush on Harry Fowler, and Evie looking appalled and saying that Harry could have *anyone*), and, anyway, Laura wasn't interested in dating. She'd only just broken up with Jon and she didn't even know if that was a permanent thing.

She crossed Dulwich Village and headed down Turney Road, passing endless red-brick Victorian houses with neatly tended front gardens. Houses that the (many) local estate agents would describe as 'beautifully presented'.

Marcus hadn't been at grief group when Laura had first arrived there this evening and she'd swallowed a feeling of disappointment. Jenni started the session by doing what she called a bit of 'housekeeping'. They were looking for volunteer grief counsellors, she said, full training would be given. Laura briefly considered putting her name on the list for more information – she had, after all, been interested in becoming a therapist all those years ago and she did have plenty of first-hand experience of bereavement – but then she remembered her mother telling her how 'rubbish' she'd be and how 'over-emotional' she got. Jenni moved on to talking about an 'entirely optional' social evening in a few weeks' time, at which point Marcus arrived, apologizing profusely for being late. Anyone who might be interested should give her their mobile number, Jenni had continued, once Marcus was seated. She would start a grief group night out WhatsApp group (an idea Laura found beyond depressing).

Save for the occasional jogger or elderly couple walking their elderly dog, the streets were quiet and Laura surprised herself with the realization that it was pleasing to her that she lived in an area that was so peaceful and yet so accessible to the centre of town (a short hop on the number-three bus). The thought surprised Laura because it was so very Dulwich in its nature. Perhaps she was developing Stockholm Syndrome?

Her mind flashed back to the look of compassion on Marcus' face as Ann talked about how she'd always loved walking because it was a time to really be alone with her thoughts, but, now that her thoughts were so painful, she never went for a walk anymore.

Laura passed the sports ground, where the distant cheering suggested someone had just scored a goal.

Marcus had been really kind to Mary too, offering to go over and fix her kitchen cupboard after she started crying saying the door was hanging off and that was something her husband would normally have seen to. Marcus said he loved doing DIY, almost making it seem as if Mary would be doing him a favour rather than the other way round.

Laura shook her head. She had to stop thinking like this. Marcus was a kind guy but so what? He wasn't interested in her and she wasn't interested in him.

She turned left on to Croxted Road and told herself she would not give Marcus another thought.

Chapter Ninety-Three

Laura's resolution to not give Marcus another thought was made a whole lot easier by Billy, who – in that way that five-year-olds have – demanded every single scrap of her attention from the second she walked in the front door.

'Mummy, Mummy!' he said urgently. 'You have to see my picture I painted at school – it's of an alien spaceship and there is blood all over its wings! Also, you have to see Buzz because Daddy bought him a new toy and it's like this tube and Buzz *loves* it! Also, also, look . . .' He opened his mouth and wobbled his front tooth dramatically. 'It's nearly out!'

Laura and Jon both laughed. 'Sounds like you've got a lot to do,' he said.

'So it seems,' Laura said. 'Thanks for getting him bathed and in his pyjamas though.'

'No worries. We did his reading too.'

'You did?' Laura said, trying to keep the shock out of her voice.

When Jon left, Laura cooed over both the painting and the guinea pig toy and listened to a long, involved story about a game they had played at school in which Billy and Caitlyn were the vowel sounds (Caitlyn, Laura thought to herself, scrutinizing Billy's face to see if the interaction had been a happy one). 'Right, Mister,' she said. 'Let's get you to bed.'

'Awww!' Billy said. 'Can I have a story? A proper one with

you reading and not me? Because I already did my reading with Daddy.'

Laura said he could and she settled herself on Billy's bed while he chose a book.

'Miss Newman is picking people to act in our play,' Billy said with his back to her.

'Are you going to try to get a part?' Laura said.

Billy shook his head. 'I won't get one.'

'What makes you say that?' Laura asked but before Billy could answer she could hear her own voice the other night telling Jess that she wasn't going to apply for the job at *Inlustris* because there was no way she would get it. Billy had overheard her saying it (children are *always* listening – except, of course, when you actually want them to be).

Billy pulled *Hamsters of Havana* off the shelf.

Laura was thinking about how frustrated Billy had got the other day when she'd tried to teach him how to tie his shoelaces, how he'd kicked off his trainers and told her that *everyone* else could already tie their laces. And Laura had heard herself in the words because she too was always comparing herself to others – from her sister, to her colleagues, to people on social media – and finding herself lacking.

Billy climbed up onto the bed next to her and handed her the book. She kissed the top of his slightly damp head and breathed in the smell of baby shampoo.

Laura started to read the story but her mind wasn't on the small, smartly dressed rodents with a talent for solving crime because she was thinking of Billy trotting out one of her classics the other morning when he told her he 'looked a sight, as usual'. At the time she'd laughed, but now it didn't seem quite so funny.

All her life Laura had thought her mum was her harshest critic but actually it was someone even closer to home. Which is not to say her mother hadn't been a worthy contender for the title – credit where credit's due, the woman could make Laura feel four inches tall with one well-aimed 'tsk' – but Laura's inner voice was even meaner.

'He's so clever, isn't he, Mummy?' Billy said as the hamster brought the villains to justice.

Laura smiled and said he was. After her own upbringing, she had been determined that her child would never feel that they weren't good enough. So she made sure she gave Billy lots of praise and held back from criticizing him. She thought she was doing everything possible to make her little boy confident.

But she'd forgotten that children copy what they see.

Chapter Ninety-Four

Laura really hoped no one from work walked past and saw her and Greta. They were on a little patch of green hidden away behind the Southbank, having a ceremony to say goodbye to Laura's inner critic.

They were sitting cross-legged doing a small meditation while all around them workers picnicked and spoke loudly into their mobile phones. *She never . . . what a cow . . . really . . . you're shitting me.*

Laura had no idea how she'd let herself get talked into this. To say it wasn't really her cup of tea was something of an understatement. Despite having been very much a festival chick back in the day, her previous attempts to meditate had been something of a disaster, with either her thoughts refusing to be silenced and shouting over each other, or Laura falling fast asleep and waking up with a jolt to find a string of drool hanging from her mouth.

'Inner critic who we have named Evan,' Greta intoned. 'We are here today to let you go . . .'

Laura tried not to giggle as she opened one eye to the mortifying realization that a man sitting a few feet away had paused with his egg salad sandwich a few inches from his mouth and was openly staring at them.

Also, what had Laura been thinking calling the inner critic Evan? (Greta had insisted it *had* to have a name.) Evan though – it was just a lazily masculine take on Evie.

Laura's back was screaming in protest. Unlike Greta, who'd settled herself on the hard and scrubby grass as if it was a pillowy sofa, Laura was not used to sitting cross-legged.

'We know you believe the words you say are about tough love,' Greta said (Greta didn't do horrible, even when she was silencing inner critics). 'But they are causing Laura pain . . .'

Laura tried not to be distracted by the sound of a dog having a luxuriant wee against a tree a few feet away from her. Why, oh why, had she decided to start talking to Greta in the kitchen? It was the morning after Laura had heard Billy speaking Evan-style (she was embracing the Evan thing now. Frankly, she was already cross-legged and meditating in broad daylight right in the middle of central London, so it was very much time to go with it). Laura had made some silly comment about how she had absolutely no idea why she'd been asked to be a mentor at the Women in Journalism event, and then checked herself saying that she mustn't talk like that, and she was trying to stop being her own worst critic all the time. And, of course, Greta had leapt on that, putting down her vegan no-yo and granola, a fierce light in her pale green eyes. 'That is so wonderful to hear, Laura. I have done a lot of work to silence my inner critic and it is so healing. I even have a little ceremony I did to bid farewell to my inner critic. Would you like me to do one with you?' Laura was desperate to say no, to slink back to her desk and tell Greta to leave her chakras alone, thank you, but of course she said yes, because she hadn't seen Greta this happy since the work canteen had stopped offering single use plastic cutlery.

Greta took Laura's hands in hers. 'Om.'

'Om,' Laura mumbled. She opened her eyes. Greta was beaming at her. Egg-sandwich man was gone, thank goodness, and even though Laura knew that Evan was going to be considerably harder to shift, it didn't feel entirely bad to have acknowledged that she'd like him to go.

Chapter Ninety-Five

Jon was telling Laura why it was so much better to be a dead celebrity's lookalike. 'Otherwise you run the risk of ending up like poor old Martin, who has just had his whole livelihood wiped out. He's a tribute artist for Garry Nunn. Or rather, he was a tribute artist for Garry Nunn.'

Garry Nunn was an ageing rockstar who had been splashed all over the papers for the last few days because he'd allegedly been having sex with underage boys. 'Yes, I can see bookings for a lookalike Garry would rather have plummeted.'

Jon laughed. 'Yeah. And even when it's not that dramatic, you can still never be sure what your celeb is going to do next. Janice hasn't had a single booking since Licia Lucas sent that tasteless tweet. Not so much as a sniff of a Bar Mitzvah or a ribbon cutting.'

Laura laughed. 'Want some more pasta?'

'Yes, please.'

She hadn't planned on cooking Jon dinner tonight. But after bringing Billy back, he'd ended up staying to give him his bath and his story. It had broken Laura's heart a little to see how pleased Billy was when she'd gone in to kiss him goodnight. 'All four of us together.'

'Four?'

'You, me, Daddy and Buzz.'

After Billy had gone to bed, Laura and Jon had started

talking about the whole bullying thing and how things seemed – fingers crossed – to be better. 'Apparently Caitlyn even sat next to him at circle time yesterday.'

They carried on chatting and, after a while, she offered him a drink and then, when she started to get hungry and he was showing no signs of going, she offered to make them both something to eat.

'This is delicious,' he said, tucking into his second helping of spaghetti carbonara.

Could have done with a bit more pepper, Evan said, popping up in Laura's mind. *Oh shut up, Evan.* 'Thanks.'

'So much better than my mum's food,' Jon said. 'It's meat and two veg night after night. Like we're stuck in the nineteen fifties. My goodness, my mum can murder a vegetable too. I think she boils the green beans for about three and half hours.'

Laura laughed. 'How are you finding it living with them again?'

'Tricky. They still treat me like a kid.'

Laura pushed away the desire to say: *well, if the boot fits. . .*

'They expect me to tell them exactly what time I'll be home. Also, you know they're a bit weird about booze. Mum was horrified the other day when I came back from the supermarket with a six-pack of beers. She asked if I was really going to drink alcohol at home. And on my own. I think she's a heartbeat away from signing me up for AA.'

'Did you tell them that rock stars have to drink? That it goes with the territory?'

Jon laughed. 'They don't really understand the lookalike work. I think they think I just put on the Elvis outfit for kicks.'

'I mean, you never seem in a hurry to get out of it!' Laura tried to imagine what it would be like to live with her parents now. She reckoned she and Evie would have lasted about four and half minutes without wanting to batter each other to death with the frying pan. As for her dad, she didn't know really. She'd been a little girl when he died. How would they have got on now she was a (sort of) grown-up? She'd like to think well, but it was easy to idolize people once they were dead. They'd talked about it at grief group. 'Oh yes,' Rob had said. 'I want to laugh in people's faces when they talk about Lynn like she was some kind of saint. It was her wicked side that attracted me to her.'

'That's pretty,' Jon said, gesturing towards the Kintsugi-ed dish.

'Jess got it for me. Well, actually I got it for Mum years ago and then I broke it and Jess got it fixed for me using Kints—' She laughed. 'It's complicated.'

'You seem to be seeing a lot of Jess.'

Her shoulders stiffened. She knew what he wanted from her here. She was supposed to roll her eyes and say 'Yeah, too much' and then he'd go on about just how boring Jess and Ben were. But Laura wasn't playing. 'Want another beer? While your mum isn't looking.'

'Yes, please,' Jon said, laughing.

Laura handed him a beer. 'How is your novel going?' she said, not sure if she really wanted to hear the answer.

'Really well, actually.'

Maybe Laura had been unfair?

'I've finished the first two chapters.'

Nope, she hadn't been unfair.

'I know that's not loads,' Jon said. 'But it's important to get it right, isn't it?'

Laura didn't trust herself to answer. If Jon came out with the 'No one said to Michelangelo. . .' line again, she'd be forced to whack him repeatedly over the head with Billy's lightsaber.

Jon took a sip of his beer. 'No one said to Michelangelo, "Look, mate, you're taking quite a long time on one ceiling."'

Breathe, Laura, breathe.

Jon laughed at his own wit. 'How is work going for you?'

'Same old, same old, really. Dani keeps dumping too much

work on me. Dressing it up as flattery. "If I give a job to you, I know it'll be done right", "You're my best editor, Laura." Shame she doesn't remember that one when it comes round to pay rise time.'

They sat at the rickety table and carried on chatting for ages. And it was nice; familiar and comfortable. They both avoided any conversational landmines like regular child support (now he was working he gave her money, but not a set amount, and not at a set time).

Suddenly it was eleven o'clock and Laura said she'd better get to bed.

'I'll help you clear up.'

'Well, that's a first!'

He laughed and slapped her on the bum. 'Not true.'

Was it weird he'd slapped her on the bum? In their time, they'd explored every inch of each other's bodies, every mole, tickly bit or curve. But now . . .

She washed and he dried. 'Y'know,' she told him. 'So the dishes will actually be clean.'

He was jubilant when she handed him a pasta bowl that still had a tiny bit of pancetta clinging to it. 'Err what were you saying about things actually being clean?'

In the hallway, he put on his blue suede shoes (which he'd bought for work but, apparently, decided could be worn off duty too), thanked her for a nice evening, and leaned in to kiss her. And it was slightly awkward because she thought he was going to kiss her on the mouth and for a nanosecond – just a nanosecond – she wanted him to. The sex between them had always been good, long after other things weren't. And when he wasn't in a white, rhinestone-studded suit, he was still pretty handsome.

'It's going to take ages to get all the way back to Edgware now.'

Laura pretended not to get the hint.

Chapter Ninety-Six

Laura was deeply regretting not letting Jon stay over and not because she wished they'd spent the night having incredible sex (although . . .). Billy had woken up at 4 a.m., having been sick all over his bed, which meant that as Laura was comforting him and cleaning everything up, she was also struggling with every working mum's worst nightmare: what do I do about childcare if my child can't go to school?

Jess was in Liverpool for the day doing some project with another influencer, Jon would be fast asleep in Edgware with his phone switched off, and Amy not only worked full-time herself but was also being really frosty with Laura since she'd said no to having Josh last Sunday. Laura supposed there were a couple of school mums she could ask, but it seemed like a big favour and she didn't feel she was exactly flavour of the month since having a go at 'poor grieving widow' Tanya Webb in the playground.

Laura got back into her own bed, her heart thumping. It was fine; she would just tell Dani she was going to work from home. Dani would be okay with that, even though her only 'babies' were her cats and to say she was a little irritated by having to make allowances for mothers was something of an understatement. Amy had once pretended she had to go to the STD clinic rather than admit Josh was running a temperature again.

Lots of people had mums who could step in at a time like this, of course. Hot tears of self-pity filled Laura's eyes, and she wasn't sure if it was because she didn't have a mum, because her mum wouldn't have been the sort to help out anyway (once, when Billy was a toddler, Evie had told her simply that she 'didn't like vomit'), or both.

Two hours later, Billy marched into her bedroom. When Laura asked him how he felt, he seemed almost surprised. 'Fine,' he said. 'But I'd like some Ribena and some breakfast.'

'Oh,' Laura said, getting out of bed. Would it be really evil to send him to school if he was okay now? She knew you weren't supposed to; that the school had a strict policy of not letting any child back until it had been at least twenty-four hours since they'd vomited. Of course they didn't want people spreading bugs. But Billy probably didn't even have a bug. Jon had let him eat loads of chocolate the night before so it was probably just that.

Could she? Should she?

She made up a glass of weak Ribena and handed it to Billy, who drank it in one greedy gulp.

This wasn't a child with a bug. He could go to school; she could go to work.

Billy's face suddenly paled and he threw up all over the kitchen floor.

'Oh, sweetheart,' Laura said, trying to cuddle him without stepping barefoot in the bright purple vomit.

After Laura got Billy back into bed and the kitchen cleaned up, she stroked his hot little head with one hand while calling Dani with the other. She must not feel nervous, or think about the fact it was still so awkward with Dani since the reply-all email. 'Hi Dani,' she said trying to sound breezy. 'I thought I might work from home today. I've got loads to get through and I could really do with just getting my head down. Plus, I'm interviewing the woman whose false nails saved her from tragedy at 8.30 and I reckon I'll get much more out of her if I don't have those noisy sales boys in the background.'

Dani sounded a bit displeased but said that was fine. As long as Laura's eight pages were ready by print day tomorrow, she didn't care where she was.

Laura hung up the phone feeling relieved. She fetched a sick bucket for Billy and told him she was going to be in the sitting room doing her work and she would keep coming to check on him but, in the meantime, to shout if he needed her. She was going to be on the phone but he could interrupt her if he needed to.

'Even if there's no blood?' Billy said seriously.

Laura nodded. She didn't always love it when she heard her own words coming back at her.

She glanced at her watch and saw it was nearly half past eight already. She'd have liked to have chucked a coffee down her throat before the interview but there wasn't time. In fact, there wasn't even time to clean her teeth and get dressed. Thank God it wasn't a Skype interview. Laura found Sandra's number, put the call on speaker phone and took a deep breath.

'Hi Sandra. It's Laura from *Natter* magazine. How are you this morning?' (If you're not covered in splats of purple vomit, then you're doing better than me.) 'Thanks so much for agreeing to share your wonderful story with us.'

Sandra said that was fine. It was a story people should know. She started to tell Laura about how she *always* has acrylic nails. They make her feel glam and 'finished'. She used to be a nail-biter, would Laura believe? Anyway, she always has her acrylics. The girls in the office call them her 'talons'.

Laura heard Billy get out of bed and her stomach clenched. Please, she thought, don't throw up again for another twenty minutes.

Sandra said she'd been coming home from a night out; a friend's birthday. It was dark when she left and she didn't see the man lurking in the shadows. Before she realized, he had grabbed her.

Billy appeared in front of Laura looking sweaty and agitated. Laura pressed the mute button so Sandra wouldn't hear her or Billy. 'Do you feel sick again?'

Billy shook his head. 'Buzz has escaped.'

Dear God. 'We'll find him as soon as Mummy is off the phone.'

Billy's eyes filled with tears.

'Okay, okay,' Laura said, getting up from the kitchen table, grabbing her dictaphone and following Billy into his bedroom. 'But you have to be quiet.'

Billy put a finger to his lips to indicate he was a man of the world and knew how to handle such situations.

Sandra was still talking. Terrifying, it was. She saw her life flash before her.

Laura unmuted her side of the call. 'Awful,' she said robotically as she got down on all fours and looked under Billy's bed.

'And then,' Sandra said, portentously, 'instinct took over.'

'Right,' Laura said, looking under Billy's chest of drawers and trying not to notice how tearful he looked.

'I just gouged my nails into his eyes,' Sandra said. 'And he was so shocked.'

'Well, yes,' Laura said.

'Mummy,' Billy shouted.

Laura put her finger to her lips. 'Sorry,' she said to Sandra. 'Noisy office.'

She went over to the spot where Billy was hopping up and down and saw that the guinea pig was cowering in a corner underneath the wardrobe. Billy pointed at him theatrically and Laura nodded.

'I just ran and ran,' Sandra said.

'Amazing,' Laura said.

Sandra said it *was* amazing; that she could hardly believe it now she thought back to it. Her 'talons' had saved her from goodness knows what. The police had told her afterwards that her attacker was known to them and he was a nasty piece of work. There was no knowing what he might have done to her.

Billy was practically exploding with the agony of the rescue mission being delayed. Laura tried to get Sandra off the phone but she was too busy telling her what her friends Jane and Linda had said about the whole night. Also, when was the photo shoot going to be? It couldn't be on a Tuesday or a Thursday evening because that's when she went to Zumba. Oh, and Wednesday she had her mammogram. What did Laura think she should wear for the photos? Sandra had thought her favourite red top but her daughter said that made her look a bit 'loose'. Was black okay or would that look too wintery for May?

Eventually, Laura managed to get Sandra off the phone, coax the guinea pig out with a bit of carrot and get Billy back into bed with her iPad.

She sank down into a chair at the kitchen table, utterly exhausted. She didn't need Evan to tell her that hadn't been her best interview. Then she realized she'd forgotten to switch on her dictaphone. She groaned and let her head sink into her hands. It was every journalist's worst nightmare.

But it was okay; she'd be able to remember what Sandra had said. She just had to get it down quickly while it was still fresh in (what was left of) her mind.

This day really had not started well. And she still hadn't cleaned her teeth, had a coffee or checked her emails.

Christ, her emails! She better look at those before writing up the story, just in case there were any from Dani. God help you if you were working from home and then unresponsive.

Laura opened her inbox, skimmed them and was relieved to see there was nothing from Dani. Such was her relief, she decided to treat herself to a quick peek at her personal emails, and could hardly believe her eyes when she came across an email from *Inlustris* inviting her in for an interview.

She was a proper journalist, after all! (Apart from this morning.)

She mustn't get ahead of herself though. She thought about the last interview she'd been to about a year or so before. It was at a magazine called *Put Your Feet Up*. The woman interviewing her, although young, had the weary demeanour of someone who thought life to be a perpetual series of disappointments. She asked questions in a way that suggested she already knew, and thought poorly of, the answers. At the end of the interview she told Laura she wasn't sure she was 'digital enough'. I'm not a fucking computer, Laura had thought.

She wouldn't get this job.

Shut up, Evan!

She reread the email, unable to believe it.

Chapter Ninety-Seven

You imagine a person's ashes would come in a fancy urn, right? But Laura's mother was in an unprepossessing looking box, which was in a hessian bag for life (bag for death?). It was sitting on Jess' kitchen worktop, right next to the Alessi fruit bowl full of lemons.

'I guess she'd want us to scatter them with Dad's ashes?' Laura said.

Jess shook her head. 'I asked her about that and she said she didn't want to end up in the outer Hebrides. She said it was a bloody miserable place where it never stops raining, and to scatter her ashes in a place she liked instead.'

'What? Like that Turkish restaurant on Lavender Hill? Or the beauty department of Selfridges?'

Jess laughed. 'You're evil!' She pushed her hair back off her face. 'It's weird to think that's Mum in there, isn't it?'

Laura nodded. Heard Evie's voice telling her that at least they could have got a proper urn.

'We really do need to sort out the last of her things,' Jess said. 'Clear the flat.'

'We'll do it this Sunday.'

'This Sunday?' Jess looked insanely pleased, like she might be about to break out into a little jig.

'Chill out, or I'll change my mind.'

'Want a glass of wine?'

'As a reward?'

Jess laughed. 'Something like that. Also, to toast you getting an interview at *Inlustris*.'

'It's only an interview.'

Jess rolled her eyes. 'Well, you can't get the job without getting the interview, can you?'

Laura pulled at a hangnail. 'I won't get the job. Anyway, how are you and Ben?'

'Better,' Jess said, taking a bottle of wine out of the fridge. 'I mean, it'll take time to get his trust back, but we're talking. And he has even agreed to go to counselling.'

'That's great news,' Laura said, trying to smooth down a particularly unruly curl. She gestured towards the hessian bag. 'Should we move Mum?'

'Nah, she was always on for wine o'clock.'

Laura grinned.

Jess handed her a glass of rosé.

'To Mum,' Laura said, surprising herself a little as she raised her glass in the direction of the hessian bag.

'To Mum.' Jess took a sip of wine. 'We don't have to scatter the ashes straight away. We can wait a while. Until we think of a good place to do it. And until we feel ready.' She yawned. 'Sorry, I was up really late last night watching about a zillion episodes of *Queer Eye*.'

'You watch *Queer Eye*?' Laura said.

'Yes,' Jess said, laughing. 'Why?'

'I don't know. I just always imagine you watching serious stuff. If you even watch TV at all, that is.'

Jess rolled her eyes and gave Laura a mock punch on the arm. 'I'm not *quite* as dull as you make me out to be.'

Lola burst into the room, saying that Hannah was cheating at Bop It.

'That's a lie,' Hannah said, appearing just behind her. 'Just because you're rubbish at it.'

Billy appeared last. 'They are fighting!' He sounded quite

343

excited about this, as if he was rather thrilled to have a ring-side seat.

'Girls,' Jess said. 'If you can't play nicely with Bop It, I'm going to have to take it away.'

This was met with muttered protests but they trailed away, clearly deciding that they would rather stomach each other than have the game confiscated. Billy followed in their wake, looking rather disappointed.

'I've never seen them fight before,' Laura said to Jess.

'Oh, they have their moments.' She took a sip of wine. 'I know Mum was always harder on you than she was on me.'

Laura shifted in her seat. Where had that come from?

'And I wanted to say I'm sorry if I didn't always stick up for you as much as I should have.'

It sounded as though Jess had planned this conversation; carefully selected the words in advance. Laura thought about one of her sister's recent blog posts about setting aside some time on a Sunday to plan your outfits for the week. 'It's not your fault she preferred you. You were easier to like.'

'Don't say that.'

Laura laughed. 'Yeah, that might be Evan talking.' Jess' brow furrowed. 'My inner critic. Yes, I have named "him" and no, I am not going mad!' She thought back to the ceremony with Greta and couldn't quite believe she'd gone along with it. 'Anyway, I do actually think you were easier to like when we were kids. '

Jess looked towards the hessian bag. 'Mum liked me when I was her good girl. When it was all gold stars and yes, Mummy, no, Mummy, three bags full, Mummy.'

Whoa! Laura didn't know what to say for a second. 'She always liked you best.' She smiled. 'But, no worries, because Dad clearly preferred me.' Laura had meant this last comment to lighten the mood but Jess looked so sad suddenly, she felt an immediate rush of guilt.

'Laura,' Jess said. 'Th—'

She was interrupted by Billy belting into the kitchen looking for his dinosaur.

'Sorry,' Laura said to Jess as soon as Billy and his dinosaur disappeared. 'You were going to tell me that wasn't a very nice thing to say and you're right. It was meant as a joke but it's a rubbish one and I'm going to stop saying it.'

Jess stared at her. 'Actually—'

Laura held up her hand to stop her sister continuing. 'Don't let me off the hook. I'm sorry and that's all there is to it. Top up the wine, will you? That was more of a thimble than a glass.'

For a second Jess seemed frozen, but then she smiled, rolled her eyes and refilled Laura's glass.

'I've been going to this grief group,' Laura said.

'Really?' Jess said.

'It's called the Lilypad Grief Support Group.'

'*Lilypad*?'

They both started giggling.

'Does it help?' Jess said.

'Not really.' Laura took a sip of her wine. 'You should come.'

They both started laughing again and this time they couldn't stop.

Eventually Jess pulled herself together, wiped the tears from her eyes. 'Your evil is rubbing off on me!'

'Yup. Time to shed this "good girl" thing. It's getting boring now!'

Jess rolled her eyes. 'What are the other people like?'

'Sad.' Jess made a face. 'Well, yes. But overwhelmingly sad in a way that makes you feel like they're never going to be happy again.'

'Sounds great.' Jess said. 'Are there any hot guys there?'

'No,' Laura said firmly. Because truthfully what was the point of telling Jess about Marcus?

Chapter Ninety-Eight

Laura opened one of the kitchen cupboards and was hit on the head by a flying bottle of Gaviscon.

She had decided she couldn't put off tidying the flat for a moment longer. It was all very well saying she liked the lived-in look, laughing at the likes of Jess and her mum for being uptight and saying her home may be messy but it was an organized mess, but actually, this had got a bit beyond a joke.

Dirty dishes teetered in and around the sink, clothes lived on the backs of chairs and on the floor and there were so many small, sharp toys underfoot, you took your shoes off at your peril.

The child who lived next door had recently given up violin and there had been a brief and peaceful hiatus before he started learning trumpet. He was practising now and managing to achieve the seemingly impossible by making Laura yearn for the sound of him playing violin.

Laura wiped out the kitchen cupboard. This was good. Although she may need to speed up a bit if she wanted to finish sometime before Christmas.

Billy was at Angus Murray's house. Laura had messaged his mum to apologize after that day in the playground and she had replied almost instantly: *Don't worry about it. Also, Tanya is a total cow! x* Laura had almost wept with gratitude.

Laura started to deal with the huge and messy stack of papers on the kitchen table: letters from the school, bills, pizza menus, there was even a crushed packet of Gaviscon in there. Laura never remembered seeing a huge pile of papers in her mum's place. Or Jess' for that matter. Did the two of them pay every bill they got the second it came in? And how on earth did they ever order a pizza?

Ahh, here was the application form to do the training as a volunteer grief counsellor (so much for the organized mess/I know where everything is theory). Laura had decided she would give it a go, and, yes, she might be 'rubbish' but she might just surprise herself/her mum/Evan.

Laura moved into her bedroom and started scooping clothes off the floor. She came across the red top her mum had bought her and had a sudden image of the two of them giggling in the John Lewis changing room. The memory felt like a punch in the stomach. Jenni who ran the grief group was always telling them that you shouldn't push your feelings away. That sometimes you just needed to sit with them. It wasn't always practical though. You can't turn into a shuddering mass of snotty sobs in the middle of the frozen foods aisle in Asda. Well, you can, but it unnerves everyone around you and you tend to forget the frozen peas.

The bedside table was covered in clutter that was coated in a thick layer of dust. Books she would never read, a Lego spaceship, balled up tissues, hairbands, three bottles of Gaviscon.

She had thought the flat would be tidy with Jon gone. In her mind, he'd always been the messy one. Tricky to argue that now though.

It had been weird between the two of them the other evening. Laura had felt as if she was being pulled by two very strong opposing magnets. He was funny and attractive, not to mention the father of her child. But at the same time, she knew they weren't right, that they'd outgrown one another. No, that wasn't right – Jon hadn't outgrown anything; that was the problem.

She glanced at her watch and saw she had less than an hour before she had to pick up Billy from Angus'. There was no way she could get everything done today. Never mind, Rome wasn't built in a day.

She did have to clean the guinea pig cage out before she left to pick up Billy though. There was only so long you could mask the smell of wee-soaked hay with air freshener. (Jess had bought her an expensive scented candle that was purportedly a gift but also definitely a hint.)

She would just tackle the bathroom and then the guinea pig cage before getting Billy.

The bathroom was bad. There were a ridiculous amount of hair products, from mousses, to serums, to oils – the evidence of spending a lifetime locked in mortal combat with her own hair. By the side of the bath, empty bubble-bath bottles vied for space with bath crayons and foam letters. And, of course, there were the inevitable four bottles of Gaviscon containing varying amounts of viscous pink liquid.

Laura picked one up to move it to the bathroom cabinet. And that's when she realized. She couldn't remember the last time she'd actually taken Gaviscon; the last time she'd needed it.

Maybe she was better?

Chapter Ninety-Nine

It shouldn't have come as a shock, really.

Laura knew circulation figures were down.

She'd heard the sales team constantly bemoaning ad revenue being 'shite'.

She'd seen the all-too-frequent closed-door meetings from which senior people emerged looking grey-faced.

And, of course, there was the stark visual reminder provided by the empty pod where the *Beautiful Brides* team had once sat.

But for all that, to have been sitting at her desk rushing to finish a story about a mum who was addicted to sex – just as you would any other Tuesday morning – and then suddenly find out *Natter* was shutting down still felt like a body blow.

She sat on the tube clutching her carrier bag of belongings. A half-eaten box of bran flakes, a tube of hand cream that smelled far too strongly of rose and some photos that had been taken at the Christmas lunch – a whole lot of nothing, in other words.

The only thing Laura had found on her desk that was actually significant was the letter from the woman who had been 'knocked sideways' by the death of her mother. Laura had gasped when she found the creamy-coloured envelope under a big stack of papers and realized she had never replied. She was a bad, bad person. She grabbed a sheet of paper and started hastily scribbling a reply. It felt weird to be responding in person rather than on the pages of *Natter* but since there was no *Natter* anymore, Laura was left with no real choice. She couldn't remember exactly what she'd written now. *Sorry for your loss . . . have you got a good support network . . . some people find counselling or a grief group helpful.* Oprah, she wasn't, but it was better than ignoring the poor woman.

The girl opposite with the leaky headphones was staring at Laura and she realized she had tears streaming down her cheeks.

The interview at *Inlustris* was tomorrow morning. Perhaps she'd get the job there and then all this wouldn't matter? Not having a notice period to work could even be a good thing.

Except she wasn't going to get the job at *Inlustris*, and that was reality talking, not just Evan.

The train had stopped in the tunnel. An announcement from the driver said they were being held at a red signal and he hoped they'd be on their way shortly.

Laura felt like her life was being held at a red signal.

A few of the others had gone to the pub, but Laura had just wanted to get away. She felt awful for Amy, who had a week off and was up in Manchester with her parents. Dani had asked Laura if she wanted to break it to Amy before she got the official word, and Laura had said she did because, even though things had been a bit strained between them of late, she still thought it would be easier for Amy to hear this from her and not some random HR person who then went on to explain how she was entitled to next to nothing.

A sweaty-looking boy dressed in black asked Laura if she was okay. A small part of her wanted to be honest; to say she was actually very far from okay.

Dear Laura, I've just lost my job . . .

Dear Laura, I've just lost my mother . . .

Dear Laura, I've just lost my partner . . .

The boy had the smallest amount of downy hair across his damp top lip and eyes that seemed to be perpetually mid-blink.

'I'm fine, thank you,' Laura said to him.

Dear Laura, I've just lost my mind.

Chapter One Hundred

As Laura walked into the swanky West End office that was home to *Inlustris* magazine, she took a deep breath and reminded herself, for what seemed like the one hundredth time since she'd woken up this morning, that she had to think positive.

It wasn't beyond the realms of possibility she could get this job. She just had to keep calm and banish Evan from piping up during the interview.

She sat on a stylish but deeply uncomfortable bench waiting to be collected from reception. She felt like her whole body was sweating; even her kneecaps felt damp.

At least she looked vaguely presentable. She'd reluctantly allowed Jess to choose an outfit for her and even though she'd been sceptical about pairing the blue midi skirt with a bright green top, she had to admit it worked. She'd also, out of deference to her mother and ignoring her bank balance, shelled out to have her hair blow-dried.

This job would mean everything to Laura and not just because of the obvious reasons like her now being an unemployed single mother. This job would be validation; surprising proof that she was in fact Good Enough.

As Laura waited, she thought about her conversation with Amy the day before. Amy had been grateful to Laura for telling her about *Natter* before HR did, and had even volunteered a mumbled comment about how she knew she'd taken

Laura for granted a bit recently. It certainly wasn't the most grovelling of apologies, but it was enough for Laura. More than enough really – she had been content just knowing that she had drawn a line.

A wisp of a person who barely looked much older than the girls in Billy's class appeared and said she'd take Laura up to the fourteenth floor.

They got into the lift together and the girl punched away at her phone as if Laura wasn't with her. No matter, it was a good chance for Laura to gather her wits and summon up a few more positive thoughts ahead of the interview. Harriet had interviewed Saskia Fenner for *Natter* a few weeks ago and Saskia had said she attributed the success she'd had recently to *The Secret*. Apparently, all you had to do to achieve anything you wanted in life was to *really* visualize it. Laura tried to imagine herself getting a call later on today. 'You got the job.'

'Fantastic views,' Laura said to the young girl as they emerged from the lift on to the fourteenth floor.

The girl looked at her quizzically and showed her into a meeting room. She told her Liz would be with her shortly.

Liz had been the name of Laura's first ever editor; the one who'd given her a chance as a journalist. It was a good omen, surely?

Visualize success, visualize success.

Yeah, like *that's* going to work.

Shut up, Evan. Or was it her mum? Either way, shut up. There was no room for negativity now.

A smiley and slightly dishevelled woman with a big, lopsided smile came into the room and introduced herself as Liz.

Laura breathed an inward sigh of relief. She'd been expecting her interviewer to be some terrifying glossy creature but Liz looked friendly and normal. She didn't even have great hair.

'We're just waiting for my colleague and then we'll get started,' Liz said.

Laura surreptitiously wiped her sweaty palms across her skirt. She wished there wasn't another interviewer coming and it was just going to be her and friendly Liz. It would be fine though – the other interviewer was going to be nice too. Think positive.

'Did Becca offer you a glass of water or a cup of tea or coffee?'

Becca was too busy WhatsApping. 'I'm fine, thanks.'

Liz raked her hands through her messy hair. 'I've had quite the morning. We had a story drop out last minute and then I had to magic up four pages out of nowhere because the sales team hadn't sold all their pages.'

Laura laughed. This woman was so nice and, having faked positivity all morning, Laura suddenly actually believed that she could get this job.

Then the door opened and in walked Tanya Webb.

Chapter One Hundred and One

Laura looked at the red espadrilles of a woman who had just got on the bus. She wondered vaguely if she should ask her where she got them and then wondered just as quickly if it was odd to be focussing on footwear when she had so many other more important things to be worrying about.

Dear Laura, Is it weird that I feel kind of okay despite the fact that just days ago I failed to get my dream job (which I needed more than ever because I lost my non-dream job).

Suffice to say, Laura hadn't needed to wait for a phone call to say that she wasn't going to be *Inlustris'* new health and wellbeing editor.

Her mind flashed back to the interview room. For what seemed like about a week after Tanya walked in, Laura couldn't say a word and just sat there with her mouth opening and closing like a goldfish (slick).

'Well, this is a coincidence,' Tanya said brightly to Liz. 'Laura's son is in the same class as Caitlyn.'

'Small world!' Liz said. 'Right, shall we get started?'

'No. Yes. Sorry,' Laura blurted (slicker).

Tanya looked at her CV. 'So you worked for *Natter*?' She said *Natter* much as one might say 'a child sex ring'.

Laura rediscovered her ability to talk then. In fact, she gabbled so fast that what she said was pretty much unintelligible, and at one point she even drooled a little on the table (slickest).

355

She shuddered at the memory, which was even more painful than not being offered the role. She would have expected the latter to devastate her, especially since she now desperately needed a job — it wasn't just about self-esteem, pride and validation anymore; it was about putting food on the table — but she wasn't devastated, or if she was, she was a sort of functioning 'devastatee'. There had only been one moment where the grief of it had fully hit and she had sobbed in the shower, turning the pressure up so Billy wouldn't hear.

The espadrilles were a sort of orangey red that Laura thought would go with lots of different outfits.

She really ought to be more upset, especially as there were so many other things going on right now too.

Dear Laura, Also — also! — I recently became an orphan, split up from my partner and went through all manner of issues with my five-year-old. So you'd probably expect me not to be okay; for this not to be the time I've stopped needing Gaviscon?

In fairness to the odd workings of Laura's mind, some things were easier recently: Billy seemed happier at school, she and Jess were getting on better than they had in years and she and Jon weren't at each other's throats. Also, surely she'd get another job somewhere?

Espadrille Lady stood up and Laura felt a surge of panic. The chance to find out where the shoes were from was literally walking away from her.

Focus on the big stuff, Laura told herself. Shoes aren't important right now. You are dealing with grief, unemployment, a broken relationship. And anyway, you don't have the money for unnecessary fripperies (see: unemployed).

'Excuse me,' Laura said to the man next to her wearing headphones. 'EXCUSE ME.' The man languorously moved aside and Laura shoved her way towards the front of the bus just as it was about to stop. 'I love your espadrilles,' Laura said to the woman. 'Where did you buy them?'

Chapter One Hundred and Two

Laura walked towards her mother's flat, enjoying the May sunshine. For all her feelings of being strangely at peace, she knew today wasn't going to be easy. Jess would be in full whip-cracking mode and not just about clearing the flat. She'd grill Laura on her job-hunting plans, nag her about getting Jon to 'do his bit' and ask for the thousandth time if Laura was sure she didn't need to borrow any money.

Today was also probably the last time they would set foot in their mum's flat. The mortgage company had accepted an offer on it. Which meant today was the last time Laura and Jess were likely to stand in a bedroom their mum had slept in or drink a cup of tea in a kitchen where she'd munched a slice of toast while she flicked through the newspaper.

Laura knew it would take her years to reconcile her complicated, messy feelings about her mum. That she would never really get over Evie, just as she hadn't and wouldn't get over her dad. But today she could live alongside it. And today was a start.

She walked into the flat to find Jess cleaning the oven. 'Why on earth are you doing that?' Laura said. 'We don't owe the mortgage company anything.'

'I know. But Mum always kept everything so pristine. I just think she'd want us to leave everything nice.'

'You're a fool.'

'Thanks. Why don't you start on that cupboard with all her paperwork?'

There was a cupboard for paperwork? So *that's* where the teetering piles lived.

Except when Laura opened the cupboard there were no teetering piles, just neatly labelled box folders: Tax, Medical, Utilities . . .

'Do we have to keep old bank statements?' she shouted at Jess.

'Only ones from the last two years.'

How did Jess know stuff like that? Had she been born knowing it?

She appeared beside Laura and took off her apron.

'These storage boxes are good,' Laura said.

'Ikea,' Jess said, reaching for the box file marked 'Tax'.

Laura sighed. 'I need to go there and get some storage stuff.'

'I could come with you?' Jess said, in a tone that suggested she'd be accompanying Laura to a glitzy Hollywood party and not a Croydon superstore.

'Yeah,' Laura said, shrugging.

'Ooh, we could get some shoe racks and some hessian baskets and drawer dividers. Drawer dividers are life-changers. And we should definitely go for modular storage – that way every inch of space gets utilized.' Laura was staring at Jess but she continued unabashed. 'I could help you tidy the flat and put everything away afterwards too.'

'Knock yourself out,' Laura said.

Jess flicked though the pile of papers that had been in the folder. 'What's this bank statement doing in the tax folder?' she said, sounding mortally offended. 'Do you remember Mum's bank manager admirer?'

'Ian?'

'Yeah, that's it.' She smiled. 'Poor bloke – he didn't have a chance.'

358

'Nope. Didn't he come to Christmas lunch that time with two of Mum's other admirers?'

'Yes! Goodness that was quite a weird day, wasn't it? Am I remembering right when I say that Mum wasn't really speaking to either of us?'

'What, even you?' Laura paused for a second, her memory searching for the file. And suddenly she could picture herself and Jess in the kitchen preparing the sprouts, their mother mute and icy as she set the table. 'Actually, I do remember and you're right. What had the pair of us done?'

'Oh, I don't know. Looked at Mum in a funny way, breathed wrong. You know what she could be like.'

'I do. I think it was all okay by the time we had lunch though, wasn't it? Who else was there? You, me, Mum. Auntie Shelia and Uncle James with Joe and Ella. Ian, the bank manager, and then Mum's two other potential suitors who also didn't have a chance in hell. One of them was a teacher, I seem to remember. He kept telling us he could help us out with maths.'

'That's right. And he was very quiet and meek, except when the turkey was taken out of the oven and he came over all macho and insisted on carving, saying he was something of an expert.'

Laura laughed. 'Yes. Mum kept telling him to get a move on. That he might be a mathematician, but she didn't need each slice of turkey to be exactly three millimetres thick. That the roast potatoes would go cold and soggy if they had to sit around much longer. Who was the third guy? Nigel? Norman?'

'Nigel, I think.'

'Big sideburns. He was a car dealer. Kept making lascivious comments about taking mum for a ride.'

'Eww.' Jess pulled out the box folder marked 'Travel'. 'Aww, look, here's mum's passport.'

'She looks proper scary in that photo, doesn't she?'

Jess laughed. 'Do you remember that holiday she took us on to Majorca when we were teenagers?'

'Yeah. The three of us rubbed cola all over our legs because that German lady Mum chatted to on the coach had told her it was the secret to really tanned legs.'

'Did people not think about skin cancer then?' Jess said.

'No, I don't think they did. We attracted swarms of wasps, I seem to remember.'

'Yeah, we had to race into the sea and desperately try to wash the cola off.'

Laura's mind was back on that white sandy beach, the water clear and warm. She remembered looking at Jess' perfect sixteen-year-old body and feeling lumpy and large by comparison. Her mother snapping at her: *Oh, do take your jeans off instead of just rolling them up, Laura! You're sweating away like a pig!* They'd had a lot of fun on that holiday though. Laura could picture the three of them crying with laughter by the buffet one evening, although for the life of her she couldn't remember why.

'Didn't the hotel have a Spanish dancing evening?' Jess said.

'Yeah, and Mum called it "flamingo dancing" and you and I got hysterical.'

Jess laughed. 'She was mistress of the malapropism, wasn't she?'

'Yup. She had a photogenic memory. And talked about how a rolling stone gathers no moths.'

'Yeah. And she was really dismissive if you tried to correct her. As if her way was just better!'

Laura grinned. 'To be fair, I do really love the idea of a flamingo dance.'

At lunchtime Jess let them sit down at the table and didn't fuss about how much there was still left to do. And she didn't even mention Laura's non-existent diet when she pulled out two pieces of lemon drizzle cake.

'Weird, isn't it?' Laura said.

'Very.'

Laura got up from the table, stood behind Jess and put her arms around her.

'What was that for?'

'Dunno. Don't worry, it won't happen again.'

Jess grinned. 'C'mon, we've still got heaps to do.'

'And she's back.'

The two of them went back to working side by side.

'Oh, look at this picture of you and Dad,' Jess said, pulling it out of a folder.

Laura must have been about five or six. She was sitting on her father's shoulders and she looked like the happiest person alive. 'I can't have been much older than Billy there.'

Jess smiled. 'How is Billy?'

'He seems a bit happier, thank goodness.'

'Good. Is Caitlyn the little witch being a bit nicer to him?'

'I don't think we call a bereaved child a little witch.'

Jess shrugged. 'She was horrible to my nephew. Also, we hate her mother for not giving you the job.'

'I thought you tried not to hate anyone,' Laura said, winking.

Jess laughed. 'I did say that, didn't I? God, how sanctimonious. Anyway, even if I was "trying not to hate anyone", I'd make an exception for *her*. Silly cow.'

'Tanya is a silly cow,' Laura said, laughing. 'But it's her loss.' She opened a box. 'Mum has got an insane amount of receipts from the beauty place.'

'Yeah, she was rigorous about keeping up standards. Even when she was in the hospice, she made me get someone go in to wax her upper lip.'

'I reckon you'll also still care about looking your best when you're old.'

'I will not.'

'You so will. I can't imagine a shabby StyleMaven. Not

361

even when she's old and saggy. Not like me. I can't even be arsed about that stuff now. I haven't shaved my legs since Jon moved out.'

'That's nice. Best get you on Tinder as soon as possible.'

'It's a feminist statement.'

'It's because you're a lazy cow.'

'That too.'

Chapter One Hundred and Three

Laura stood in the hallway of her mum's flat staring at her phone. Her heart was thudding and her mouth was dry.

She'd just got off the phone to Nadia, one of the therapists she sometimes consulted for *Dear Laura* and now she couldn't get Nadia's words out of her head.

It was a crazy suggestion.

Except Nadia wasn't crazy; she was one of the smartest people Laura knew.

Then again, she'd probably just been joking. Laura stared at a small crack in the ceiling.

Jess appeared, carrying a big bag of recycling. 'You okay?'

Laura nodded. 'I'm not skiving, by the way.'

Jess laughed. 'Sometimes you make me feel like a monster.'

Laura smiled and raised her eyebrows. She was tempted to tell Jess what Nadia had said, although she wasn't sure to what ends.

'Are you sure you're okay?' Jess said. 'Did someone upset you on the phone?'

Laura shook her head. 'It was a woman called Nadia Romensco. She was one of the therapists I used to go to for advice when I got a problem for *Dear Laura* that I felt was out of my depth. I'd called her about someone whose very religious parents couldn't accept her being gay. Nadia was on holiday at the time and had just picked up my message. She didn't even know *Natter* had closed down.'

'So you're upset because you talked about the magazine folding?'

'No,' Laura said, biting her thumbnail. 'Really, I'm fine. Let's get back to it.'

Jess put her hand on Laura's arm. 'Hold on a minute.'

'Wait, did you just say "hold on a minute" when I said, "let's get back to it"?'

Jess made a face. 'Yes. Now, tell me what's really going on here.'

Laura paused. Her head was seething with ideas and it was very tempting to voice them. On the other hand, she didn't want to sound crazy.

'Tell me,' Jess said more insistently.

Laura sighed. 'When I told Nadia the magazine had closed down, she suggested I retrain as a psychotherapist—'

'Isn't that what you wanted to do when you were twelve?' Jess said.

'Well, yes,' Laura said. 'But to be fair, I also wanted to be a band member in Take That and/or a trapeze artist.'

'Don't wisecrack your way out of this. You also thought about volunteering for the Samaritans when you were at uni, right? And you've told me you really love your *Dear Laura* work. You've even put your name down for the training as a volunteer grief counsellor. There's a theme here.'

Laura chewed her nail. 'Well, yes—'

Jess didn't let her finish. 'I can absolutely see you as a psychotherapist.'

'What?' Laura said, 'because I'm so in control of my own life?'

Jess rolled her eyes. 'I can tell you're excited by the idea. Otherwise, you wouldn't be standing out here mooning over your phone like Eddie Redmayne has just called you.'

Laura puffed out her cheeks. 'Okay, I admit to being slightly excited by the idea. I'm also more than a bit flattered that someone like Nadia thinks I might be capable of being a therapist, despite the fact it proves beyond any reasonable doubt that she's never read *Dear Laura*.'

'Don't tell me Evan is holding you back?' Jess said.

Laura laughed. 'I *really* regret telling you about my weirdly named inner critic. Anyway, yes, he's throwing in his two pennies worth as usual, but it's not just that. Think about it, Jess, there's no way I could become a therapist at this stage of my life. It would take years of training and years without income. I'm a single mum now.'

Jess chewed her bottom lip. 'Okay, but where there's a will there's a way. What about if you did the training while you were still working as a journalist? You were saying you might go freelance anyway?'

'It would be very hard.'

Jess nodded. 'Of course it would. But I'd help you as much as I possibly can – you know, with Billy and stuff.'

Laura's brain swirled. 'All that studying.'

'Yup,' Jess said.

Laura looked at her sister. 'Do you remember what Mum said when I told her I wanted to be a therapist?' Jess shook her head. 'She said I'd be terrible. That I was too over-emotional.'

'Mum wasn't right about everything.'

Chapter One Hundred and Four

Laura reached for the last box folder. She'd banned Jess from talking about her retraining as a therapist but she hadn't managed to ban her own brain from thinking about it, and as she sorted things into piles her mind fizzed with possibilities. It was such a crazy idea. And yet . . .

'This box folder is unlabelled.'

'How very sloppy,' Jess said, grinning.

Laura put it on the floor and started to go through it. She could see why it hadn't been labelled because it was as close as anything of her mum's came to the teetering pile on Laura's kitchen table. Old bills were mixed with insurance documents, a letter from HMRC rubbed shoulders with a receipt for kitchen units.

She worked methodically, putting things into their designated piles.

'Oh my goodness,' she said. 'Here's my birth certificate! Mum could never find it. She said it was a nightmare getting my first passport. And, here it was the whole time.' She looked up at Jess, who was staring at her with kind of a strange look on her face. 'It wasn't like Mum to lose something so important, was it? She was so organized. I'm glad I've found it though. Weird not having a birth certificate; like you're not a "proper" person.'

She stood up and was about to put the certificate into her handbag when she looked at it one more time. *CERTIFIED COPY OF AN ENTRY, Pursuant to the Births and Deaths Registration Act 1953.*

And then her eyes skimmed a little farther down the page and landed on the section marked: *FATHER*. But the name underneath wasn't her dad's, it was Arthur Robert Keele.

Laura's head swum and she felt as if she'd forgotten to breathe. There must be some mistake.

Except when she looked up at Jess, she saw that her sister had abandoned the files she was sorting through and was standing behind Laura, her face ashen, tears rolling down her cheeks.

Which was when Laura realized two things.

There hadn't been a mistake.

And Jess had known all along.

Chapter One Hundred and Five

'How long have you known?' Laura whispered.

Jess shook her head, rubbed away the tears with the heel of her hands. 'I didn't want to keep it from you, Laura, believe me. I had so many rows with Mum over the years when I told her that she had to tell you because you deserved to know the tru—'

'HOW. LONG?'

Jess stared at the floor. 'I found out the night of Dad's funeral.'

Twenty-five years ago. Laura turned her back on Jess.

'Laura!'

The pulse in Laura's ears was deafening. With trembling hands, she wrenched her coat from the hook in the hall and tried to pull it on, unable to find the arm holes.

Jess was behind her, trying to pull her back. 'Mum didn't even tell me. I found out by accident. It was the night of Dad's funeral and I was coming down the stairs because I couldn't sleep and I was thirsty suddenly . . .'

Get to the point, Laura felt like screaming. This is no time to amble around the houses.

'. . . I heard Mum saying something to Auntie Sheila about how it was such an irony that you were so upset about Dad. Do you know how many times I've wished that I never heard

368

that, Laura? Wished that I hadn't decided to go downstairs and get a glass of water just at that moment?'

Jess was crying now, really crying, so it was hard for her to get the words out. But Laura didn't feel sympathy, she felt rage. Stop feeling sorry for you. This is about me. I'm the one who has just had my whole world tipped upside down.

A memory jagged at Laura's consciousness: Her mother's incredulity when she had said Billy looked a bit like her dad. Evie's smile – did she find it *funny*?

Laura's skin was clammy and her whole body was shaking. She headed towards the front door.

'Laura,' Jess wailed. 'Please don't go. Let's talk about this.'

'Bit late for talking, don't you think?'

'When Mum died, I realized that it would have to be me who told you,' Jess said. 'But I just couldn't. I didn't want to do it straightaway because it seemed like too many shocks in one go. Recently, I've psyched myself up to tell you a few times but then I always bottled out. When we weren't getting on, I was terrified you'd think I was telling you out of spite and when we were getting on I was terrified of destroying that.'

Laura's legs felt as if she couldn't trust them to keep her upright. She stared at her sister. She suddenly remembered Jess messaging her that time saying there was something she wanted to tell her. And there were other occasions too, when she could recall Jess seeming as if she was on the verge of saying something and then pulling herself back.

Still, Jess had known the truth for *twenty-five* years.

She couldn't have tried that hard to fill Laura in.

Chapter One Hundred and Six

All Laura wanted to do was run (well, look at that, Jess, you actually did get me running).

Thoughts clamoured for position in her mind, shoving each other out of the way.

Her breath was coming in big, hiccupping gulps and her eyes were blurry with unchecked tears.

How could they all have lied to her for so long?

People were staring at her as she careered along, moving their children out of the path of the crazy lady. Laura didn't care.

She ran across the road and cars screeched their horns in angry protest. A man in a Prius rolled down his window and screamed, 'You're going to get yourself killed, lady!'

Laura pounded along the pavement.

So much made sense now.

Nothing made sense now.

Laura came to a main road, ran straight into the path of the oncoming traffic without stopping.

On her left, a bus was coming towards her.

But Laura didn't see the bus.

Because all Laura could see was her birth certificate.

Chapter One Hundred and Seven

Then

'Who do you prefer, Dad – me or Jess?'

'That's a silly question,' he said, laughing. 'You can't pick between your kids.'

The two of them were in the car. Dad was taking her to a sleepover party at Beth's and, although Laura had been looking forward to it for weeks, right now she just wanted her and her dad to keep driving forever. She loved it when it was just the two of them, and the car was like their own little bubble. 'You said there were no silly questions.'

Dad laughed even harder. 'I *did* say that. But I guess that was the exception to prove the rule.'

'Mum prefers Jess.'

'No she doesn't.'

'She does. So, if you preferred me, that would be fair.'

He grinned and rolled his eyes. 'The thing is, Scout, I couldn't love you or your sister any more than I do. It's "infinity love". So there is no "more".'

'Hmm,' Laura said, not entirely satisfied with that answer. She looked out of the window. It was raining heavily and the pavements were black and shiny. People were scuttling around with their heads down.

The news came on the radio and Dad reached out and turned up the volume. He loved the news, couldn't get enough of it. Laura didn't understand why – it was boring with a capital B. She zoned out and let her mind wander. Sarah Baxter had a boyfriend, Jessie Makin had a bra, and not just some pretend training number but a proper bra like grown-ups wore. Laura was getting left behind.

She tuned back into the present to hear the man on the radio saying that in America someone called OJ Simpson had been arrested for the murder of his wife. 'Dad,' she said. 'You know how you always say that if you really love someone, there's nothing they can do to change that? Well, would you love me if I murdered someone?'

That made him laugh again. 'Why – are you planning on it?'

'No,' Laura said. If she *was* going to murder someone, it would definitely be those boys on the bus who teased her and Beth all the time, but she didn't actually want them dead, just not on the number thirteen.

'Love is All Around' came on the radio and now it was Laura's turn to crank up the volume. 'I love this song.'

'I don't,' Dad said. 'I think it's wet, wet, wet.'

'Your jokes are the worst,' Laura said, groaning.

Dad grinned. 'It's not even an original song, you know. It was first recorded by The Troggs.'

Why did grown-ups tell you stuff like this? Or even care about it? Maybe when you got old you suddenly started being interested in random facts? And the news.

Laura looked out of the window at a couple of little boys who were splashing in a puddle like it was the most exciting thing ever. A memory rose up of her and Jess doing the same thing when they were little. They were in the garden of their old house and the two of them were laughing as if splashing in that puddle was the best thing in the whole world. That had been when the two of them still liked each other. Actually, in truth, sometimes Laura still liked her sister. It was just that

Jess could be so annoying, going around thinking she was 'it' all the time just because she was fourteen and she had periods now. She was such a huge suck-up to Mum all the time too – yes, Mum, no, Mum, three bags full, Mum. Shut up, Jess, Mum already thinks you're perfect.

They drove past a poster advertising the yoghurts that Julie Marshall always had in her lunch box and Laura suddenly thought about how sad Julie must be right now; probably too sad to even eat yoghurt. She hadn't been in school for weeks. 'Julie Marshall's dad died of cancer.'

'That's terrible,' Dad said, turning left. 'Poor people.'

'I couldn't bear it if you died.'

Her dad reached over and squeezed her hand. 'Don't worry, I'm going to live until I'm a hundred and be super grumpy and annoying.'

They stopped at some traffic lights. A woman who was pushing a pram with one hand and holding a toddler's hand with the other crossed the road. The baby was under a rain-proof pram cover and the toddler had a tiny bumble bee umbrella, but the mother's hair was soaked through and slicked to her head. Laura supposed she just didn't have enough arms for an umbrella of her own.

'I can't wait to learn to drive,' Laura said as they got going again.

'And I can't wait to teach you.'

'Yeah, I don't want Mum teaching me. She's a rubbish driver.'

'Laura!' Dad said, but he was smiling. He always defended Mum, but even he couldn't say she was a good driver. A couple of weeks ago she'd crashed into a skip and still claimed it wasn't her fault.

'Sarah Baxter has got a boyfriend,' Laura said.

'Oh,' her dad said. 'Twelve is quite young to have a boyfriend.'

Laura shrugged.

'You're going to have all the boys in the world queueing up to take you out when you're older, Scout. And then, one day when you're much older, you'll choose one of them who will be lucky enough to marry you. And I'll walk you down the aisle and it will be the proudest, happiest day of my whole life.'

'You said proudest, happiest day of your life,' Laura said, bouncing up and down in her seat. 'What about when you walk Jess down the aisle? See, I *am* your favourite!'

Dad laughed and Laura suddenly thought how it was a sound that made her ridiculously happy.

Chapter One Hundred and Eight

Later, Laura wouldn't remember exactly how she got home, although she'd never forget the stricken face of the bus driver and the high-pitched squeal of the brakes as the bus stopped just inches away from her.

Outside her front door, she fought to compose herself so that Billy wouldn't see her like this, but luckily it turned out that Billy was transfixed by whatever he was watching on YouTube.

Jon took one look at her face, led her into the bedroom and shut the door. Laura promptly collapsed into a fresh wave of sobs. 'My father was not my father,' she told him. 'They *all* knew.' (Nearly getting herself killed didn't even make the cut for 'traumatic events of the last hour'.)

Somehow Jon managed to get Billy to accept that Mummy had a bit of a headache and, no, it was best not to go in and say goodnight, that Daddy would say it for him just this once.

Laura and Jon lay on the bed, him holding her tightly while she sobbed. They had long since stopped talking. What was there to say? Her whole life had been a lie and her whole family had been complicit in it: Mum, Jess, Dad – well, the man she'd called 'Dad'.

Jon stroked her hair.

Who the hell was Arthur Robert Keele? Had her mother been in love with him or was he just a shag? Did he know about her or had he been lied to as well? Was he alive? Did he have children? (*Other* children.)

So. Many. Questions.

'Do you want anything?' Jon said. 'Water? Tea? Wine?'

She shook her head. It was unfathomable that Jess knew. Had she and Mum talked about it behind Laura's back? Laughed at her? She had a sudden, sickening memory of always telling Jess that she'd been their dad's favourite. No wonder Jess had never seemed to mind that much. 'Actually, can you pass me the Gaviscon?'

Jon handed her the bottle and she took a greedy swig. As if it might help with heartache and not just heartburn. 'I'm probably not even an orphan,' she said flatly.

Jon nodded. 'Will you try to find him?'

'I don't know.' She guessed she should at some point, if only to find out about his medical history. Those were questions doctors always asked you, weren't they? Have any of your close family ever had cancer, heart disease, diabetes? Wait, do you mean my *actual* family or the people pretending to be my family?

'You don't need to decide now,' Jon said. He rolled over on his back, adjusted her body against his. 'You should eat some dinner.'

'I can't.' It was one of those rare moments when she had absolutely no appetite whatsoever, where the idea of food repelled her. Perhaps she would lose a few pounds? She could market this as a new diet: *Find out your father is not your father and shed that belly fat forever!*

She had this sudden memory of going into her dad's office with him one day and this woman saying that she didn't look anything like him. And he had been uncharacteristically snappy. 'She has just got different colouring, that's all.' Now it all made sense.

Maybe this was why her mother had never seemed to like

her that much? Laura had spent her whole life chasing her mother's approval, feeling as if there must be something very wrong with her – what kind of person isn't liked by their mother – but maybe it was nothing to do with her? Maybe she was just a painful reminder of a mistake that Evie had made? A mistake that could have cost her her marriage and she'd have to live with for the rest of her days. Maybe Evie hated Arthur Robert Keele? Or worse still, maybe she really loved him? Either way, she didn't want him gazing back at her every time she looked at Laura.

She was crying again. She hadn't even realized until Jon handed her a tissue. 'I've lost my dad twice,' she whispered.

Jon wiped a tear from her cheek with his thumb, kissed the top of her head and told her that everything would be okay.

And she reached across and kissed him hard on the mouth.

'No,' he said, pulling away.

'Yes,' Laura said, pulling him back and reaching down to undo his belt.

She could hear her sister's voice admonishing her in her head: *Don't do this. You know you and Jon aren't right. You can't have casual sex with the father of your child.*

Well, fuck you, Jess.

Chapter One Hundred and Nine

Eight months later

'Remind me why you got us here three hours early?' Laura said as they cleared airport security.

Jess shrugged. 'It's just such a treat to have lots of time, don't you think?'

Laura looked around Heathrow Airport's Terminal 3. A group of sweaty-looking teenagers were stretched across a bank of hard plastic chairs trying to sleep, a toddler was having a full-on tantrum in duty-free and a cleaner was uninterestedly mopping at an unpleasant-looking puddle. 'If you say so.'

'I just love getting to the airport early,' Jess said, looking much like a small child on Christmas Eve. 'We can do a bit of shopping, grab a coffee . . .'

'You're insane,' Laura said to Jess' back as her sister headed towards WHSmith.

Laura stood looking at the travel adaptors and neck pillows. *End the nightmare of trying to sleep on an uncomfortable aeroplane,* it said on the packaging for the neck pillow, which Laura thought a tad over-dramatic.

'Oh, don't buy those,' Jess said, patting her rucksack. 'I've already got some.'

A woman with a bright red wheelie case dragged it over Laura's foot just as her phone started vibrating in her pocket. Jon would like to FaceTime.

Laura stepped outside of the newsagent and pressed 'accept' to see Billy and Jon, the latter of whom was in full Elvis gear, appear on her phone screen.

'Are you at the airport already?' Jon said.

'Yup,' Laura said. 'That's what happens when you travel with my sister. Billy, do you think you could turn off your Switch long enough to talk to Mummy?'

Billy reluctantly looked up. Jess had bought him the Switch for Christmas and it seemed to have been permanently welded to his hand for the two weeks ever since. Laura stared at Billy's sulky little face on the screen and felt a wave of maternal love so strong it almost seemed as if it would knock her over. She had been so worried about him at one stage but now she could say – if it wasn't tempting fate – he seemed happier than he had in a long time.

'So Vegas, eh?' Jon said.

Laura grinned. 'Yeah, baby.'

'Just don't lose everything on the roulette table,' Jon said.

'Don't worry,' Laura said. 'I've hardly got anything to lose.'

Jon laughed. 'So what are your plans for your boys' weekend?'

'Well,' Jon said. 'This morning Billy is going to come with me while I get my new headshots taken and then, this afternoon, once I've de-Elvis-ed I'm going to whup this young man's bum at football.'

Billy made squeals of protest and Laura laughed. 'Do you think it's normal to be *quite* so competitive with someone who isn't even six yet?'

'I'm nearly six,' Billy protested.

'It's absolutely normal,' Jon said. 'It's just as much fun to nutmeg a small child as it is a fourteen-stone IT consultant.'

Laura grinned and rolled her eyes.

'Tomorrow we're going to go to the London Aquarium,' Billy said, 'and we're going to see REAL crocodiles and sharks.'

Laura said she looked forward to hearing all about it.

When she went back into the newsagent's, Jess was ensconced in the Richard and Judy Book Club section. 'Which one do you think I should go for?' she asked, holding up a thriller with a dark grey cover and a drip of blood running through the title, and a novel with a purple cover that *The Times* described as 'A big, clever, tender, love story'.

'I'd go for the thriller on account of you having no soul.'

Jess poked her tongue out and joined the queue, the thriller in hand.

As they walked past a boutique, Jess saw a pink dress in the window that she insisted would look amazing on Laura. Laura told her there was no way she was spending that much on a dress she'd hardly ever wear, but Jess said it would show off her new look perfectly and, anyway, why would she hardly wear it?

In the changing room (Laura had tried on the dress just to appease her sister and because how else were they going to fill the nearly three hours until take off) Laura was distressed to admit the dress did in fact look good. She turned this way and that, convinced the store must have installed some fairground mirrors that were offering up an unrealistically flattering reflection. She knew she'd lost a bit of weight recently, but not that much. Hell, in this light she didn't even appear to have a mum tum.

'Can I see?' Jess said, wrenching back the curtain without waiting for an answer. 'Wow! You have to buy that.'

'Is it approved by one of the UK's top ten influencers?' Laura was almost surprised that the last comment came out without so much as a hint of bitterness. In fact, if she hadn't known better, she'd have said she was actually pleased for her sister.

'I can't believe you persuaded me to drop seventy-five quid on a dress,' Laura said as they walked out of the shop.

'It's an investment,' Jess said. 'Plus, there's no point working so hard to get yourself in such great shape and then not buying clothes to show it off.'

Laura knew she wasn't in 'great shape' but she was a whole lot fitter than she'd been six months ago. After her mother had died, she'd been gripped by a fear that she was going to suddenly drop dead herself (she'd had a similar fear about her mum or Jess dying when her dad had been killed. As if the Grim Reaper loved nothing more than a two-for-one deal) but she'd mostly managed to set aside that worry by channelling it into becoming a reluctant jogger.

'The neckline looks really good with your new hairstyle too,' Jess said.

Laura's hand fluttered towards her hair. Jess had talked her into going to some fancy salon in Soho and, even though the hairdresser gave Laura a deal because she was StyleMaven's sister, it was still eye-waveringly expensive. 'Ahh, yes, that's another small fortune you cost me.'

'Stop moaning,' Jess said.

'I'm allowed to,' Laura said, 'what with me being a poor student.'

Jess gave her a mock-punch in the ribs. The truth was, Laura was loving studying to be a psychotherapist. Which wasn't to say it wasn't exhausting, particularly given the fact she was still doing lots of freelance journalism as well, but she found it absolutely fascinating. Jess had been true to her word about helping out wherever she could, and she told everyone and anyone that her sister was training to be a therapist.

'Anyway, the haircut was worth being poor for,' Jess said, darting into duty-free and spritzing herself with perfume. 'I bet even Mum would say it looks great.'

'Don't be ridiculous,' Laura said, and they both started laughing.

Chapter One Hundred and Ten

'Bye, darling. I love you.' Jess ended her call and Laura made a vomiting motion with her fingers. 'Oh, you can talk!' Jess said, laughing.

'Yes,' Laura said, 'but you and Ben have been together for over twenty years. You shouldn't be able to utter his name without spitting venom by now. The mere sight of the man should irritate you. Those are the rules.'

Jess rolled her eyes. 'It's good to get to the gate early, don't you think? That way you can be sure of getting a seat while you wait and you don't have any of that last-minute panic.'

Laura sighed and gestured to the almost empty seating around them. 'I think we can safely say that last-minute panic isn't an issue travelling with you.' She got her book out of her bag and Jess took out her iPad. 'Tell me you're not working,' Laura said, glancing over at Jess' screen.

'Just replying to a few DMs.'

'Of course. Mustn't keep our loyal audience waiting. Any horrible messages?'

'Not today.' Jess winked. 'I guess you can't post when you're sitting right next to me.'

'Not funny,' Laura said. She looked out of the window at their plane. Hard to believe it was taking them to Las Vegas. And hard to believe what they were going to do when they were there.

382

After that terrible day in their mum's flat, she and Jess had gone three months without speaking, although Jess had made several attempts, and not a day went by when Laura didn't question herself about whether the huge lump of anger she was carrying around with her was actually being directed at the wrong person. She kept away from Jess though, even when Billy repeatedly moaned about how much he missed his cousins.

Then one morning Laura opened her front door to a courier who delivered a brightly wrapped rectangular package. Laura opened it up to find a dark green leather photograph album. She turned the first page and saw a picture of the man she had always thought of as her father. He was grey-faced but grinning as he held a tiny newborn bundle in his arms that Laura knew to be her. On the next page was a photograph of her and her dad in which she was about six months old and he was blowing bubbles for her in the bath. Then there was a photo of him holding her by both hands as she took teetering steps, a photo of them on her first day at 'big school', her dad's eyes shining with pride, a photo of the two of them grinning as she held up her third-prize trophy from the one and only running race she had ever been placed in.

The heavily made-up stewardess behind the desk tapped the microphone and started inviting people to the gate.

By the time she'd got to the end of the photo album, Laura's face had been streaming with tears. She took out a small white envelope and opened it.

Being a dad isn't about biology, it's about love, and Dad loved you so very, very much. The proof is right here in this album.

Look at the first picture of Dad holding you in the hospital just after you were born, look at his eyes and the pride and adoration that's shining out of them and tell me that you're not already his.

383

Look at the picture of Dad getting you out of your cot. Do you remember how he always talked, making it sound as if it was a wonderful thing, about how he did all your night feeds and it took you ages to sleep through?

Look at the picture of you, Dad and that toy monkey you used to love so much. Dad once drove seventy miles in the dark and the rain to go back to Auntie Sheila's house and get that monkey because you couldn't sleep without it.

There are photos of Dad teaching you to ride a bike, playing with your doll's house like it's fascinating to him, reading you a story (he will have been doing all the voices).

And don't forget all the everyday moments that might not have made the photo album but do make a dad. The cuddles when you weren't well, the kisses to grazed knees, the testing and retesting on spellings and times tables. Dad earned the right for you to call him that because he was the one who cried as he watched you play Shepherd Number Three in the school nativity play, the person who, patiently and gently, helped you learn long division, the person who made lame jokes to try to make you smile when you were fed up. I read a newspaper article recently where they interviewed some kids in care, and something one little boy said really jumped out at me: 'It's not who borned you that matters but who looks after you.'

Dad was – and is – proud of you and you will always be his little girl. (And, sadly for me, his favourite!)

Laura had called her sister straightaway.

Chapter One Hundred and Eleven

Jess was sleeping but Laura was damned if she was going to miss a second of flying to Vegas. She could still scarcely believe they were actually doing this.

As she sipped her wine, she found herself thinking back to the day she and Jess had hatched the idea of this whole crazy trip. They had been talking about how neither of them had ever been to Vegas and, although Laura had said she was quite happy to never go, as she'd said the words she'd known she was lying to herself. Because tacky though Vegas was, it was also somewhere she felt she needed to see, even if it was just to prove to herself it was awful.

'Mum always said she regretted not going there,' Jess said. 'And that she never got to see the Grand Canyon.'

'Let's take her,' Laura said. Which is how they finally decided what they were going to do with their mother's ashes. Or cremains, as the undertaker insisted on calling them, even though Laura hated the word and thought it sounded like the name of a fancy pastry. Ooh, those cremains are to die for.

'More wine, madam?' the stewardess purred. Madam decided it would be rude not to and held out her glass.

She reclined her seat a little and gazed out of the window, her birth father suddenly popping into her head as if she'd seen his face right there in the clouds. She had found Arthur

Robert Keele on Facebook one evening after one too many glasses of pinot grigio (her, not him, although judging by his profile, Arthur appreciated a glass of wine or seven). Arthur had a big, red, friendly face; he looked kind, although Laura had read enough about people finding birth parents to know it was important not to idolize them.

Laura's head had spun with all the new information. Her father lived in Devon, just a few hours away from her. He loved the beach, especially in winter. His wife – a plump-faced woman with a huge smile – was called Soraya and was a retired art school teacher. Laura had two half-brothers, one of whom looked spookily like her.

Jess adjusted her eye mask but, annoyingly to Laura – who was desperate to have someone to share the excitement with because they were going to Vegas! – stayed asleep. 'I'm just going to have a little doze,' she had announced, as soon as she had doused the tray tables with anti-bac hand wash and wiped them down.

After finding Arthur online, Laura had shut her laptop without messaging him and she had yet to make any form of contact. She wasn't sure she was ready to deal with all his emotions as well as her own just yet. 'Will you ever contact him?' Jon had asked her. Laura had said she probably would, but that she wasn't ready yet.

She looked out at the clouds and, despite herself, felt her eyelids starting to grow heavy.

Chapter One Hundred and Twelve

Of course the airline had lost their suitcases.

'My mother's ashes are in one of those cases,' Jess said.

The woman behind the desk tried to keep the smile pasted on her glossy fuchsia lips. 'Let me see what I can do, honey.' She picked up her desk phone and started hammering at the keypad with the side of her thumb (presumably protecting her talon-like fuchsia nails from impact). 'Hi, it's Jeannie. We've got a bit of a situation here . . .'

Laura stood there feeling wilted and crumpled, regretting the four glasses of wine on the plane.

'I hope they manage to track down Mum,' Jess said.

Laura raised her eyebrows. 'She always was a bit of a liability at airports.'

Jess laughed. 'True. Do you remember when we lost her in Majorca?'

'Yeah, she was being chatted up by the guy in duty-free.' Laura couldn't believe they had gambling machines in McCarran airport. Or that dead-eyed people were sitting feeding coins into them with a look of grim determination when they were just a short cab journey away from some of the world's biggest and best casinos. Welcome to Vegas!

Laura's phone pinged with a message from Marcus. *Landed safely? Love you xx*

Yes, Laura messaged back. She didn't mention the lost bags because, like her sister, he was a bit of a worrywart. *Love you too. xx*

Even though they'd only been seeing each other for four months, her relationship with Marcus felt easier and more established than it had any right to be. Recently, they'd even introduced each other to their respective children (Marcus had a daughter six months younger than Billy). The weird thing was, Laura hadn't even been that keen to go out with Marcus at first. She was fresh from her ill-feted attempt at making a go of things with Jon (who was now dating Beyoncé – although sadly, just the lookalike) and she didn't want to get into another relationship, but Marcus had been quietly and persuasively insistent and made it clear he wasn't going to be shaken off easily. On their third date, he'd told her he loved her and Laura hadn't known whether to be thrilled – because damn, the guy was hot, smart and funny – or horrified by how fast things were moving.

'Is this weird – what we're doing?' Jess said.

Laura laughed. 'No. Everybody flies to Vegas for a weekend with their dead mother and then takes a helicopter ride to the Grand Canyon where they land and scatter her ashes.'

Jess laughed. 'To be fair, I've heard weirder. Some people have their loved ones' ashes shot into the air on a firework or in a helium balloon, some people scatter them on their favourite team's football pitch. And I told you about Hank Jax, didn't I?'

'He snorted some of his dad's ashes?'

Jess made a face. 'That's right. I mean, no thank you. No offence to Mum, of course.'

Laura giggled. 'I think Mum would be fine with us not wanting to snort her.'

'We must remember not to stand upwind,' Jess said. She had watched endless YouTube videos about how to scatter ashes (yes, such things existed) and this was a key piece of advice. Also, to take baby wipes with you so you didn't have to disrespectfully wipe the last of your loved one on your jeans (not that leaving them on a baby wipe seemed much better to Laura).

Jeannie was off the phone and was furnishing them with an update. The suitcases had been tracked down to Seattle. Laura hoped some poor bugger hadn't opened the grey suitcase thinking it was theirs and been greeted by a large bag of human remains.

Jeannie said the airline was so sorry and they would have the suitcases at the hotel by tomorrow morning at the latest. Where were they staying? Oh, The Venetian, they were in for a treat! They were to be sure to take a gondola ride. And they should definitely eat at Tao. T-A-O. The shrimp tempura was just too good. And the crispy pork bao buns – she was getting hungry even thinking about them!

Laura left Jess to talk to Jeannie about making a claim for basic toiletries and underwear (even though Laura knew Jess had packed both in her hand luggage).

They had decided not to make the scattering of the ashes a formal thing. There weren't going to be any readings or music or poems and there would only be Jess and Laura there (the helicopter pilot keeping a pre-arranged discreet distance at this point). Both Jess and Laura would share a favourite memory of their mum. Laura had been somewhat surprised to find that she didn't struggle in the least to find something to say, even though up until fairly recently, and certainly in the immediate aftermath of finding her birth certificate, she'd had very few nice things to say about her mother at all.

Jess and Jeannie said goodbyes to each other that were so warm Laura was half expecting to be invited to Jeannie's for Sunday lunch. 'Are you ready?' Jess said, turning to Laura.

'I'm ready.'

Acknowledgements

My first thank you goes to my extraordinary agent Tanera Simons. Not a day goes by, Tanera, that I don't think how lucky I am to have you in my corner.

The same goes for you Katie Loughnane. Not only do you have the appropriate levels of enthusiasm for leopard-print, but you're a brilliant and insightful editor. You're also a total pleasure to work with – even when you suggest I cut 20,000 words.

My third shout-out goes to the wonderful Sabah Khan, head of publicity. You are unrivalled at what you do, the best champion any author could wish for and a total force of nature.

Thank you to everyone at Darley Anderson, with special mention to Mary Darby, Kristina Egan and Georgia Fuller.

Thank you to the peerless team at Avon. I am grateful to each and every one of you, especially Ellie Pilcher, Sanjana Cunniah, Caroline Bovey, Holly Macdonald, Beth Wickington, Rebecca Fortuin and Phoebe Morgan.

Thank you to all the fantastic book bloggers and book sellers out there. The energy and enthusiasm you bring is humbling. I am especially grateful to Hazel Broadfoot and the team at Village Books in Dulwich.

I am also indebted to Vicky Grut whose writing workshops I attended. People who say you can't teach writing haven't met Vicky.

Gemma Champ, Caroline Garnar and Steve Clinton, thank you for reading *We Are Family* when it was in no fit state to be read. Your encouragement and advice were invaluable. You are brilliant writers and brilliant friends – a combination I rather took advantage of.

Hedy-Anne Freedman, you have been in my life since our school days and not only can you make me cry with laughter, but you are a font of wisdom on everything from grief to trainer socks.

Debra Davies, thank you for being a brilliant mate and for being so incredibly supportive about my writing. God help anyone who knows you and doesn't buy my books!

Honourable mentions also to this lovely lot: Sally Bargman, Brian Davies, Sara Nair, Krish Nair, Phil Lewis, Frani Heyns, John O'Sullivan, Nicky Peters, Sue Arkell, Ruth Mc Carthy, Carol Deacon, Alex Judge, Katia Hadidian and Angeli Milburn.

And so, appropriately enough in a book called *We Are Family*, to my family. Mum, thank you for believing I could do this even when I didn't. I still don't know why literary agents weren't more impressed when I said my mother thought I wrote well. Patrick Crichton-Stuart, thanks for being the best brother anyone could ask for and for reading my books even though they contain scant reference to Alex Ferguson! Sophie Crichton-Stuart, my lovely sister, thanks to listening to me bang on about this *forever*. Big hugs to the rest of the crew too: Kit Crichton-Stuart, Harry Crichton-Stuart, Freddie Crichton-Stuart, Toby Green, Lex Green, Jenny Crichton-Stuart, Jo Dangerfield and Uncle Bill.

To my dad, to whom this book is dedicated. I wish you were around to see this.

To my husband, Stuart, who I fell in love with when I was 'just a baby' and I have grown up with. Thank you for being with me every step of the way. I promise one day I will learn to work track changes on my own.

To my sons, Charlie and Max. I know I don't mention it much but I love you so, so much and I am ridiculously proud of you.

Finally, a huge thank-you to all the readers who buy, review and recommend my books – and especially anyone who takes the time to contact me personally. Those messages bring me a huge amount of joy.

If you enjoyed *We Are Family*, you'll love
The Neighbours…

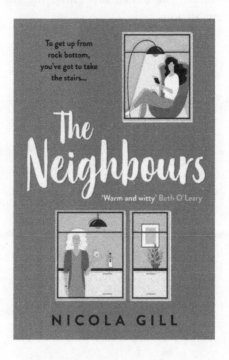

Available now in paperback,
ebook and audiobook.